# just come over

# just come over

escape to new zealand,
book twelve

rosalind james

Cover design by Robin Ludwig Design Inc.,
http://www.gobookcoverdesign.com/

Formatting by Polgarus Studio,
http://www.polgarusstudio.com

*Rhys Fletcher is not in love with his sister-in-law.*

*That would be a very, very bad idea, and he doesn't entertain bad ideas. He also doesn't lie to himself.*

*Both of those things can't be true, so he'll do what he's done since the long-ago night when his brother, Dylan, turned up in an Auckland bar after a brutal rugby match between their two teams, and introduced his new girlfriend—a dark-eyed, impossibly short, much-too-young girl named Zora.*

*He'll lie.*

*Now, his brother's gone, and Rhys is back in New Zealand and settling into his new job as the head coach of the Auckland Blues. Surely, being there for Dylan's widow and their son is the right thing to do. He can control himself. He's had forty years of practice. Until he gets a call from his lawyer, and flies to the States to find that handsome, charming, endlessly irresponsible Dylan has left yet another loose end for his big brother to sort out.*

*This one is six years old. And her birth certificate says she belongs to Rhys.*

*The heart wants what it wants, or else it does not care.*
- Emily Dickinson

# contents

# author's note

The Blues, All Blacks, and other teams mentioned in this story are actual rugby teams. However, this is a work of fiction. Names, characters, places, and incidents are products of the author's imagination or are used fictitiously and are not to be construed as real. Any resemblance to actual events or persons, living or dead, is entirely coincidental.

# the escape to new zealand series: past characters

**Sir Andrew (Drew) Callahan, Hannah Montgomery Callahan.** JUST THIS ONCE. Drew, a former blindside flanker (No. 6) for the Auckland Blues and the All Blacks, and the two-time Rugby World Cup-winning captain of the All Blacks, is coaching rugby in the Bay of Plenty; Hannah is a marketing executive for 2$^{nd}$ Hemisphere knitwear. 3 children.

**Hemi Ranapia, Reka Hawera Ranapia.** JUST FOR YOU. Hemi, a former No. 10 for the Auckland Blues and the All Blacks, coaches with Drew in the Bay of Plenty. 4 children.

**Koti James, Kate Lamonica James.** JUST GOOD FRIENDS. Koti is a centre (No. 13) for the Auckland Blues and the All Blacks; Kate is an accountant for the Blues. 2 children.

**Finn Douglas, Jenna McKnight Douglas.** JUST FOR NOW. Finn, a former No. 8 for the Auckland Blues and the All Blacks, is strength & conditioning coach for the Blues; Jenna is a teacher. 4 children.

**Nic (Nico) Wilkinson, Emma Martens Wilkinson.** JUST FOR FUN. Nic is a fullback (No. 15) for the Auckland Blues and the All Blacks; Emma is a knitwear designer for 2$^{nd}$ Hemisphere. 2 children.

**Liam (Mako) Mahaka, Kristen Montgomery Mahaka.** JUST MY LUCK. Liam is a hooker (No. 2) for the Wellington Hurricanes and the All Blacks; Kristen (Hannah's sister) is a fashion buyer. 1 child.

**Nate (Toro) Torrance, Allison (Ally) Villiers Torrance.** JUST MY LUCK. Nate is a halfback (No. 9) for the Wellington Hurricanes and the All Blacks, and captain of the All Blacks; Ally is a climbing instructor.

**Hugh Latimer, Jocelyn (Josie) Pae Ata.** JUST NOT MINE. Hugh is an openside flanker (No. 7) for the Auckland Blues; Josie is a TV star and model. Raising Hugh's two half-siblings, plus twin boys.

**Will Tawera, Faith Goodwin.** JUST IN TIME. Will is a first-five (No. 10) for the Auckland Blues and the All Blacks; Faith is a novelist.

**Iain McCormick, Sabrina (Nina) Jones.** JUST STOP ME. Iain is a lock (No. 5) for the Auckland Blues and the All Blacks; Nina is an international model.

**Kevin (Kevvie) McNicholl, Chloe Donaldson.** JUST SAY YES. Kevin is a wing (No. 11) for the Auckland Blues and the All Blacks; Chloe is a ballet dancer and teacher. 1 child.

**Marko Sendoa, Nyree Morgan.** JUST SAY (HELL) NO. Marko is a blindside flanker (No. 6) for the Auckland Blues and the All Blacks; Nyree is a painter.

# like a thunderbolt

"I told you it was going to be ninety dollars," Zora Fletcher's son, Isaiah, informed her. "It's ninety-two, actually, so I missed two dollars. We were only supposed to spend eighty. If we put back the pineapple and got the other kind of oil, it would be eighty-three. That's closer. Or else we have to only spend sixty-eight next time."

The cashier, a comfortable lady of middle age, fortunately didn't sigh. She may have had to put back the olive oil herself a time or two in her life, Zora suspected. She told her son, "We'll do ninety-two for now. And next time, I'll believe you when you add up."

He grinned, showing off a couple missing teeth. "Even though I'm eight."

"But *very* good at maths." As she swiped her EFTPOS card, she thought yet again that, whatever her dad had said, she'd been right to sell the house. She didn't need that stress.

The cashier handed her the receipt and said, "Careful out there. We could get a tornado, they say. A cyclone's enough to be going on with. There'll be trees down, that's sure."

"Lucky I made my deliveries earlier today," Zora said. "It was blowing hard enough then. A good night to stay home." They headed to the door, and she told Isaiah, "Zip up," as a shopper ran in with a shopping bag held over his head.

There wasn't an anorak in the world that would protect you from this, but they pulled up their hoods all the same. The wind came at them like a shrieking animal, and the rain

1

slapped against their bodies in waves. She was gasping, and Isaiah was laughing. "It's like being on a tall ship," he shouted. "One that's about to wreck!"

She had to laugh, too. He was right. It was an adventure, a spot of excitement, and they were barely five kilometers from home. February, the height of summer, and only six o'clock in the evening, but the Auckland sky was dark with storm, the carpark of the Mount Albert Pak 'n' Save swirling with sheets of water. "Run!" she shouted, and they headed down the path between the aisles of parked cars. Why were you never parked close when you needed it? She was gasping by the time they turned into their aisle, and their spot was all the way at the end. Isaiah had the trolley now and was out ahead of her. She was shouting, "Slow down!" and reaching for him when a gust of wind swirled into them from behind and sent him and the trolley flying forward, straight at a silver SUV that had just turned the corner.

Everything happened at once. She was leaping after Isaiah, shouting his name, slipping and skidding to one knee on the wet asphalt, feeling the pain of it only dimly. Isaiah was hauling back on the loaded trolley, pulled by its momentum and the wind, and the SUV was stopping with a rocking jolt, faster than she'd have imagined it could. Which was followed by a second jolt, as the front of the trolley smashed into the car's bonnet and Isaiah bounced off the trolley's handle, staggered, and looked back at her.

White face. Open mouth. Round eyes. "Sorry," he said. She saw it more than she heard it, the shape of the word on his lips, his hand clutching at his skinny chest, and she got to her feet and went to him, and tried not to shake. He was all right. He was all *right*.

The rain and wind drowned out everything else, except the man who erupted from the driver's side like a thunderbolt. His anorak was unzipped, his ink-black hair, on the long side, was plastered to his head with rain, and he looked, at that moment, the size of two men, with the strength of three.

Very much, in fact, like Rhys Fletcher.

*Exactly* like Rhys Fletcher.

Who didn't like her in the first place, wasn't meant to be in Auckland in the second place, and whose obviously-latest-and-greatest model of . . . oh, brilliant, it was a BMW—now had a sizable dent in the front, in the third place.

And who was, in the fourth place, her brother-in-law. Or he had been. Once.

♡♡♡

Rhys *wasn't* shaking. He was shouting. Call it his happy place. That had been a bad moment, when he'd slammed his foot practically through the brake pedal and known he wouldn't stop in time.

"Are you all right?" he yelled at the kid, who had scrambled backward to his . . . mother? It was hard to tell under the anorak hood. She wasn't very big. The way she had her arms around him, though, she had to be his mother.

She asked, "Rhys?" He heard that voice, saw the way her hand went up to her hood, like she was about to touch her hair, her habitual gesture, and thought, *What? No,* even before he registered the face. The one he'd seen in too many dreams.

"I'm OK," the kid—his nephew, Isaiah—said. "I'm sorry about your car. I didn't mean to hit it." Behind him, a sedan pulled up with an impatient splash of water and a screech of brakes and hooted.

Oh. They were all standing in the middle of the carpark, and his SUV was blocking the road.

He told both of them, "Go get in your car, out of the wet. I'll come unload you," then ran around and pulled the SUV into an open space to the tune of some more angry hooting from the bloke behind him. If Rhys didn't respond the way he may have wanted to, that was because he'd had forty years of practice in controlling his temper, whatever it looked like.

He should get points for that. He never actually did. Apparently, *looking* fierce was enough to earn you that

3

reputation. And, possibly, raising your voice a bit, when necessary. And tackling like you were pushing a fella's ribs through his spine, but that was just rugby.

Was Zora in the car when he got there? Of course not. That would have been too easy. Also, she would have had to do what he'd suggested. Instead, she and Isaiah were standing in the blowing rain, unloading carrier bags into the back of a pink van. Who had a pink van? Zora, naturally. If Isaiah had been more than bruised, though, surely he wouldn't be unloading bags. That was a relief. Rhys told them, "Get in. I'll do this."

Zora grabbed two more bags, slung them into the back, and said, "Already done. Climb in, though, and we'll talk about your car."

Her voice sounded like she was trying to keep it from trembling. Her hands actually *were* trembling. That had scared her too much. He wanted to give her a cuddle, and he absolutely couldn't. He also had absolutely no desire to talk about his car. Isaiah had hold of the trolley, and Rhys took it from him and said, "I'll put it back. Get in the car and wait."

"OK," Isaiah said, just as Zora said, "You don't—"

Rhys didn't wait to hear what he didn't have to do. He headed across to the trolley collection area and dumped the thing, then ran back to the van. It was raining, yeh, and blowing, too, but he was used to rain. He'd been out with the boys in it half the afternoon, in fact. When you played rugby, you didn't get to choose the conditions on match day. If you didn't know how to hang onto the ball in the wet, your opponent probably did.

Not that anybody had complained, of course. He could think they'd been trying to impress their new coach when they'd jogged on out there, but it was probably more that they'd been coached well by their last one.

Never mind. For right now, he climbed into the van's passenger seat, shut the door, twisted around to look at Isaiah, in the back seat, his hood pushed back, his anorak unzipped, and his dark eyes too big for his face, and said, "You hit the trolley handle pretty hard, mate. How much does it hurt?" In fact, the boy had his hand on his ribs, where he'd slammed into that metal handle.

"I'm OK," Isaiah said. His teeth were chattering, though, and it wasn't cold out here, just wet. Shock, probably, and some pain. He'd got tall, surely, for ... seven? Eight? How old was he now? Tall like his father, Dylan. Built slim like Dylan, too, instead of solid like Rhys. A back, not a forward. If he played.

He should play. His uncle should know whether he played. Rhys hadn't been doing his job, and he always did his job.

No excuse, not for this. He could say he'd been overseas. He could say he'd been busy. He could say heaps of things. He knew the real reason.

He told Zora, "You could put the heat on," and she looked at him out of those sloe eyes that should have belonged to a Slavic princess, then turned the car on and did it.

Check, check, and check. The eyes. The broad cheekbones and wide forehead, and the unexpectedly pointed chin. The perfectly soft, wonderfully pink mouth with its lush bow that made you think about kissing her, no matter how hard you tried to stop yourself. Just now, that mouth was saying something, but he'd lost it in the distraction.

"Pardon?" he asked.

"I'll pay you for the car," she said. "Just tell me how much."

He blinked. "The car?"

Isaiah piped up from the back. "Because I bashed it with the trolley, Mum means."

"Let me know how much," Zora said again. "Let's hope they don't have to replace the entire fender. Why do I think that BMW will require complete replacement?"

"If it's heaps," Isaiah said, "we could do a payment plan like we're going to do for the van, Mum. We have two hundred and forty-five dollars a week extra," he told Rhys, "because we have a better house now, but you can't spend all your extra, because things happen, and Mum needs a new van, too. And then a heat pump and a new roof, but the van matters more, because that's her live . . . live . . ."

"Livelihood," Zora said. She had some pink in her cheeks. "Nah, love. We're all good."

"Maybe we could spend a hundred dollars a week to fix the car," Isaiah said. Clearly, a boy who knew how to keep to the topic. "Then we'd still have a hundred forty-five to save for the van, and for emergencies."

"You don't need to worry about that, mate," Rhys said. "It's just a prang. Adds character. Sometime or other, when somebody bashes me from behind at a stoplight, I'll get it fixed."

The color deepened on Zora's cheeks. Temper, embarrassment, or something else. Outside, the storm had picked up even more. She'd turned on the windscreen wipers, but they could barely keep up with the driving sheets of rain. The sky was an eerie deep purple until it was lit by a sudden flash, the ground nearly shaking with the crash of thunder. The carpark's lights, which had come on hours before schedule, flickered, then revived.

The air in the van, though, smelled sweet. Scented. And Zora's hair was as mink-brown and wavy as ever, and looked as soft and touchable. A little disheveled from having her hood up, like she'd just got out of bed. It was cut shorter now, to above her shoulders, and fell in a fringe across her broad forehead. She said, "You're thinking something. Something unflattering."

"I am?" He tried to think how to answer that, and couldn't.

"Isaiah is interested in money," she said. "And brilliant at maths. He likes to budget. I don't . . ." Her mouth closed on the words.

He filled in the rest of the sentence. "You don't put your worries onto him."

Another crash of thunder. The van nearly shook with it. "It's empowering," she said, still sounding stiff. "To understand your circumstances and help to cope with them. Even for a child."

"Especially for a child," he said, and she gave him another startled look.

Silence for a moment, and he was reaching for the door handle when she said, "I should ask you why you're in Auckland at all, let alone in the Pak 'n' Save carpark. I should ask you to dinner."

"Well, not if you're going to ask like that, you shouldn't." He couldn't help smiling, and after a second, she did, too.

In fact, she laughed. "You're right. I should *graciously* ask you to dinner. Considering that it's raining buckets out here, and you'll be in some hotel and not wanting to go out again. So. Just—come over."

"Actually," he said, "I've shifted up here. Coaching the Blues now, with Aleke Fiso gone off to Wales. Didn't anybody tell you?"

"Ah . . . no. They didn't. You have?" She hesitated, then asked, "Are you . . . on your own, still? Or not?"

"Yeh. I am." His marriage had done its final spectacular bit of falling apart around the same time Dylan had died. The two things could have been connected. When he felt pressure, he tended to throw himself more deeply into his work, or to go out on the water. Alone. Neither of those had been marital benefits for Victoria, he could see now. He'd had time enough to admit his part of the disaster, or maybe it was even simpler than that, and they'd both just married wrong. Whatever the reason, he was still waiting out the separation period to make it final. Two years could feel like a long time, when all you wanted was to move on.

"Oh," Zora said. "I'm not sure I ever said it at the time, but I'm sorry."

"I'm not. Anyway, I was coming in for provisions, as my furnishings arrived today and were unloaded, from what I hear, and this is my day to get out of that hotel. Unless they dumped it all on the driveway, in which case, I'm buggered. But yeh, I'm a resident. And a hungry one." He threw all caution to the winds. He needed to know how she was doing, and Isaiah as well. What was that about her needing to do a payment plan? He needed to find out. Also, his house *would* be shocking. It would also be empty.

That was why he said yes. Surely.

# sparks

Rhys drove his own car to the house, which gave Zora a few minutes to collect herself. Or it would have, if Isaiah hadn't asked, "Why don't you like Uncle Rhys?"

"I like him fine," she said. That was the problem. When he'd climbed up into the van and turned that fierce gaze on her, it was like all the air had been sucked out of the car. She'd had to remind herself to breathe. He might be coaching now instead of playing, but he still looked like all he wanted in the world was to lace up his rugby boots, run out there into the storm, and bring some men to the ground. With emphasis. It might be the black scruff and the too-long hair, it might be six-foot-three of hard muscle that hadn't gone anywhere in the years since he'd finished playing, or it might just be the elemental essence of him. Rhys was twice as much *there* as everybody else. You knew it. You felt it.

She'd felt it the first night she'd met him. When Rhys's Crusaders had played Dylan's Blues in Auckland, and she'd gone out after the game with the two of them, and some of the rest of the Blues, too. Dylan had been the life of the party, as usual, laughing, joking, jumping up to dance between the tables. Rhys had been nearly silent, his forehead and cheekbone bruised red from the game, the lines of his jaw squared off almost aggressively, a day's stubble covering the cleft in his chin. That, and his unexpectedly sensual mouth, were the only things about him that didn't look tough, and she had a feeling that if he could have changed them to match

9

the rest, he would have.

He was Dylan's older brother, though, so she did her best. She wasn't sure if she liked him, she was fairly sure he didn't approve of her, and that flutter in her stomach when he looked at her had to be nerves. It was important that he like *her,* though. However complicated the relationship was between the brothers, there was nobody Dylan looked up to more. So she asked, "Where did the nickname come from? Drago?"

He turned to look at her. He had to turn, because he'd been watching the three young women standing at the high-top next to them in an idle sort of way. Probably because they were flipping their hair back over their shoulders and casting glances over at the two rugby-intensive tables, especially this particular spot. Just before Rhys had turned away, one of them had touched her finger to her lower lip in a move that would have done justice to a schoolgirl. Or, rather, a porn star pretending to be a schoolgirl. It was so hard not to laugh.

When Rhys finally looked at Zora, his expression was amused. Not that he smiled. He just . . . expressed amusement. Around his eyes, maybe. They were a startling hazel-green, not what you'd expect with the swarthy skin, the black hair, or the Maori tattoo that ended just below his elbow. A single half-arm tattoo, instead of Dylan's full sleeve, not to mention the ones on Dylan's calf and his chest. She knew about Rhys's unadorned arms and legs because she'd just seen him in a rugby uniform. She was guessing about the chest. The intricate black tattoo on his upper arm, with its emphatic pattern of chevrons, triangles, and the curve of koru, said, "I'm Maori, yeh, and I'm proud of it. But I don't need to shout about it." Actually, all of him said that.

"Does that work?" she asked him, then inclined her head toward the table of girls in a saucy way she was quite proud of. She got more amusement from him, and she had to smile back.

Dylan slid into the chair opposite her and asked, "What?"

"An invitation from across the way," Rhys said. Even his

voice was almost gravelly. How much testosterone did this man have in his body? He was very nearly frightening. He *should* have been frightening. Instead, he was just... something close.

"Don't let us stop you, mate," Dylan said. "I've got my girl." Which made Zora feel fluttery again, for a different reason. Or the same one, probably. She was excited because Dylan *was* exciting. Because over the past few months, her life had gone from black-and-white to full color, like she'd started taking some powerful drug, and now, she was addicted.

"It was this," she said. She put her index finger on her lower lip, opened her mouth just a little, and widened her eyes at Dylan, who burst out laughing. She laughed herself and asked Rhys, "Did I do it right?"

He wasn't laughing. His face had hardened instead. "Yeh," he said. "That was it." He took another sip of beer. He was still on his second. Dylan was putting away his fourth. But then, Dylan's team had lost. "You asked about my nickname," Rhys said. "Dunno. Got it a long time ago."

"Drago?" Dylan said. "Because that's what Rhys means, in Welsh. Dragon. Our Nan told us that when we were little kiddos. Well, I was a little kiddo. Rhys was all of ten or so, and already shaving."

"Nah, mate," Rhys said. "Eleven."

"So I started calling him 'Drago,'" Dylan said. "Thought it was cool as. Dangerous as. And it got picked up. Of course, I may have been a wee bit jealous of it, too." He raised his pint glass at his brother. "Always, bro. Whatever I did, you were still older, you bugger. Bigger and stronger, too. Then Dad took you to Aussie, and I didn't have to compare anymore. Good times."

That last part had carried an edge. If Rhys was aware of it, he didn't show it. His voice was calm when he asked Zora, "How old are you?"

"Mate," Dylan protested as the player beside him put a palm to his face. "That work for you? You pull in the pub with that often, do you?"

Another slow look from the hazel eyes, and Dylan said, "You probably do. Still—no. Or, rather—yeh, you're right, Zora's the prettiest thing you ever saw. *And* she's doing her degree in architecture. She's not tall, that's all. And then there's that pretty bit, because that's exactly what she is. A pretty bit."

Rhys looked Zora over some more, and she could feel herself flushing. "I'm twenty," she said, with a snap to her voice. "I'm five foot two, I weigh forty-nine kilos, this is as big as I'll ever get, and I'll have my degree in a year and a half. Does that answer your question?"

"Yes," he said. Fifteen minutes later, he stood up to leave, still with only two beers under his belt. Dylan walked out with him, and when he came back, his brown eyes were sparkling more than ever. There was an edge to him when he said to Zora, "Let's go. We're still celebrating, eh."

Another rush at the heat in his eyes, the faint roughness of his voice, and the fact that he'd said it in front of his mates. Something primitive about it. And when they got back to her flat and her roommate was out? They didn't make it past the foyer. And she felt . . . claimed. Overwhelmed. Excited in a way that was almost too much to take, and completely and utterly sexual.

Later, lying in bed, her hand on Dylan's chest, still giddy at the thought that somebody so beautiful and so exciting was hers, she asked, "What did Rhys say to you, earlier?"

"Said to get up faster from the tackle," he said. "Bastard always thinks he's a coach. He's been doing *that* all his life as well, with a notebook and all. Bloody annoying. 'You won't be playing any rugby from the ground.' Like I need to hear it from him."

"How much older is he?" Her heart was beating harder at what Dylan had shared with her tonight, and that he'd wanted her to meet his brother. Whatever she thought of his brother.

"Five years. Thinks it's ten. Twenty-five and thirty isn't much of a gap anymore, but try telling Rhys that. He was born old." Suddenly, he laughed, his mood flipping back to 'sunny' in an instant. Dylan could never stay angry. "He also said you were too young, and it wasn't right, so you can be narky along with me, if you like. I told him you were older than me in every way that counted, and he said, 'Not old enough to make that choice. She's blinded by it. The rugby. What she thinks is the glamour. She doesn't know better yet.' And *I* said, "What do you want me to do about it, then? Tell her she's too good for me and nobly let her go? Fat chance of that, mate. I get hard just looking at her."

Zora sat up in bed. "You did not tell him that."

Dylan laughed, pulled her down again, and kissed her. She was still outraged, and she was still so keyed up, too. Her body switched on again like it was in a perpetual state of need, which was pretty much true, and it was fifteen more gasping minutes before Dylan said, a laugh still in his voice, but tenderness, too, "Nah. I didn't tell him that. I'm not going to talk about you, baby. Not when I'm this crazy in love with you."

"You . . . are?"

"Yeh. I am. And if you feel half as much as I do . . ." His hand went out to brush down her cheek, and her heart melted. It wasn't just that he wanted her. It was that he *needed* her. She was sure of it. "I think you should move in with me," he said. "The flatmates aren't bad blokes, just a couple fellas far from the whanau and missing home, and it would be sweet to have you there with me."

The next day, he'd helped her move, and her life changed again, just like that. The next exhilarating downhill run on the roller coaster, your hands in the air, accepting the challenge and embracing the ride, so much more exciting than you'd imagined your life could ever be. Dylan had been selected for the All Blacks on the Northern Tour the season before. His brother was a perennial fixture. The two of them were New Zealand celebrity, manliness, and glamour personified, and if that excited her—what girl wouldn't feel that way?

That eager, headstrong, heedless girl had left the building a long time ago, though, and they were nearly home. Rhys was following in his unfortunately dented SUV just behind her, and surely, Isaiah had asked her a question. "What did you say, love?" she asked.

"Why you didn't like Uncle Rhys," Isaiah said. "And you said you liked him fine. But then he must not like *us*. Because he never comes to see us, not like Uncle Hayden."

"Uncle Hayden lives here in Auckland. Rhys was coaching in Japan when Dad fell ill, remember? But he came back to see Dad every chance he could."

"I remember a bit. So that means he liked Dad," Isaiah said with all his relentless logic. "But he's only come two times since Dad died, so I think he must not like *us.*"

They were home. She pulled into the driveway, and Rhys pulled in behind her. Boxing her in. The thought made her breath come faster, even though it was the only place to park, and he'd be leaving once dinner was over.

She needed to see some men besides her brother. Preferably ones she could breathe around.

A couple weeks ago, Hayden had asked, after he'd finished mowing the lawns at her house and wiping the sweat off with the hem of his T-shirt, "So when are you going to be getting out there? You've got some fit blokes driving by and taking a peek. Why isn't one of them here mowing the grass instead of me?"

"If they're looking at you," she said, "they're not going to be spending time with me."

He sighed. "Would you kindly trust the gaydar? Who was out here with me, weeding the borders in her cute little skirt?"

"Skort," she said. "And they were not. Looking."

"Oh, yeh," he said. "They were. They *are*. You're still bloody adorable, even as old as you are, and you have to know it."

"I am fourteen months older than you. We're practically twins."

"Except that you're older. But no . . ." He waggled his fingers. "Sparks? No pixie dust settling over the two of you when you meet Sophie or Caleb or Anthony's gorgeous single dad at the school pickup?"

"First," she said, "you're vastly overestimating the number of gorgeous single dads out there. Second—I think my pixie dust left me a good while back." She tried to make it a joke, but it didn't come off. Something about the lump in her throat.

Hayden put an arm around her, and she rested her head on her brother's shoulder and thought about how good that felt, and how completely inadequate. He said quietly, "It's been nearly two years."

"And three since he fell ill."

"Three since you decided to leave him, too," Hayden said with that bluntness that could only come from a brother. "You stayed instead, because he *did* fall ill. You did the right thing, I guess, though I don't think I could have, but what did it do to you? Killed something inside, maybe."

"Nah," she said, and tried to smile. "Stunned it, more like. I notice now, a bit, if somebody's good-looking. Sometimes I even notice if they're being flirty. I just don't want them, is all."

"Not your type."

"I don't think I have a type anymore."

It wasn't true. If she hadn't known then, she'd just been reminded. When Rhys had got into the van, and all the air had left.

The truth? The last time she'd felt sparks? It had been at her husband's tangi, at the marae in Atawhai, outside of Nelson. One more gorgeous day at the serenely beautiful north end of the South Island. A gorgeous day for something other than a funeral, anyway. Dylan's home, and not hers. His family, too, and not hers.

Her mum and dad had come for the last bit only. "A funeral's hard enough," her mum had said. "Why do they drag it out so long? I can't imagine."

At least Hayden had stayed for all of it. "If you have to do it," he'd said, "I have to do it. Case closed." Thank God for Hayden.

Worst of all, the sparks had come at the end of those three

days, after all the songs and speeches and endless hours of sitting beside Dylan's body, taking turns with the aunties and uncles and cousins, because there was no grandma and no mum to sit there anymore. Days when she'd waited until the marae's flag had been lowered at the end of the day to eat, and when the food had turned to chalk in her mouth, her throat closing around her attempts to swallow despite the long fast.

And then, on the third day, the final haka had been performed, the crowd following after the hearse and through the red gates of the marae, sending her husband on his way. When Dylan had been put in the ground and the earth had closed over his casket, she'd dipped her hands in water outside the cemetery, flicked the moisture from her fingers, coached Isaiah to do the same, and walked, her arm around his skinny six-year-old shoulders, toward the car. The whanau had held the feast, the hangi that had been roasting in the ground for hours, there'd been singing and more speeches, and she had eaten barely a bite and felt as old and tired as she ever had in her life. More than all the time in hospital, more even than at the end.

She was twenty-eight. She felt eighty.

She'd been waving away a group of cousins in their cars when she'd become aware of Rhys beside her. He stood there, filling the night with his solidity and his size, and asked quietly, "All right?"

*No,* she'd wanted to say. She'd wanted to scream it. *No, I'm not all right. All I've done for the past year is this, and now I don't even have this to do, and I don't know how I'm going to do all the things that will come next. All the things I can't shut out, because they're there, and there's only me to deal with them. I've spent a year trying to keep my son going and my husband alive. I've been watching the money going out and not coming in, and I haven't been able to do anything about it, and now, I have to. I weigh forty-five Kg's, and my black dress is too big, even though I waited to buy it until three weeks ago, because I didn't want to jinx him, like I'm afraid I already did. I was planning to leave him, and it seems like I'll feel guilty about that for the rest of my life.*

Extremely helpful thoughts to share. "Yeh," she said instead. "I'm good." She was an expert, now, at holding back, even though there would have been no shame in letting go. You were meant to express your emotions at a tangi. Dylan's whanau probably thought she was cold, but she couldn't help it. Maybe it was that she wasn't Maori, or maybe it was just that, if she started, she wouldn't be able to stop.

A sigh from him, felt rather than heard. "I don't reckon you are." He put an arm around her, and that arm felt solid. She turned into him, and his other arm came out to grasp her. Her head was on his chest, and that was a secure place to be, acres wide, fathoms deep, and strong enough for anything. His hand stroked over her hair, and he said, "It'll be better. Sometime."

She hadn't cried all those three days, or during the days before, when Dylan had been slipping away, a pale wraith of the laughing, irresponsible, impossibly handsome rugby player who'd alternated his brilliance with frustrating lapses, on the field and off, and had never understood why. She'd watched him leaving her, and she'd been numb. Stunned into silence even in her mind, pulled into the ghost realm where the almost-dead walked.

Now, if you believed in Maori tradition, Dylan's wairua, the quicksilver brightness that was his soul, free of the suffering and the fear, had winged its way northward to Te Rerenga Wairua, the leaping-off place of the spirits at the northernmost tip of New Zealand. The essence of him, the best of him, had slid down the pohutukawa root and into the sea, and had gone home to Hawaiiki to be with the ancestors. But she was still here. And it was so hard to be here.

The sob ripped from her chest like it was taking a piece of her with it. And then the rest came, and she could no more hold them back than the Tasman could keep its waters from merging with the Pacific. The tears rolled down her cheeks and soaked Rhys's white shirt, and he held her in those strong arms, said nothing, and waited them out like the shelter waited out the storm. And when she'd finished crying at last, she hadn't wanted to go.

Rhys was the first one to step back. Afterwards, she remembered that, and burned with shame. He handed her a wodge of tissues, smiled a bit, and said, "Clean. I brought them in case somebody cried."

"Not . . . you?"

"I don't cry in front of other people."

"I was just thinking that," she said, doing her best to mop up, aware of her swollen face, her streaming nose. "That I'll never be . . ." Her voice wobbled, and the tears threatened again. "Maori. Good at expressing myself. I'm Pakeha all the way."

"Oh, I dunno," he said. "I thought you did all right just then. And it's not that I never cry. I just do it alone. Our secret, eh."

"Our secret," she repeated, and something passed between them and tried to take her with it, strong as a rip that caught you in the sea and pulled you out, away from safety.

His face solidified again. That was the only way to describe it. His features would soften for a moment, then harden once more, as if you'd only imagined the softness. She didn't even know anymore. She was hallucinating from lack of sleep, probably. She was empty, except for that spark of life when he'd pulled her into his arms, and she'd felt . . . held. Protected, for the first time in so much longer than a year.

Wanted.

Female.

He said, "How are you and Isaiah getting back to the house?"

"I should . . . I should stay. Say the goodbyes." The house would be full of aunties and uncles and endless cousins, of more talking and laughter and tears. And she couldn't. She *couldn't.*

He said, "Grab Isaiah, and come on. I'll drive you."

He hadn't taken them to his Auntie Rose's, but to the blessedly anonymous white-and-glass elegance of The Sails in Nelson instead. He went in to register them, then walked them upstairs and through the door of the apartment, done up with the kind of austere simplicity she needed now. Black couches, white linens on the bed, and the sea beyond the green grass of the Domain, everything outside vibrant with life, because the rest of the world went on, no matter how your own world had shattered. Rhys set a plastic carrier bag on the kitchen bench. "Roast," he said. "Meat and kumara and veg left over from the hangi, in case you get hungry again, Isaiah. You could watch some TV, eh. They have DVDs, too." He crouched down by the TV cabinet and asked, "Toy Story? Or Shrek?"

"Shrek," Isaiah said instantly.

Rhys smiled. "Good choice. That would've been mine, too." He put the DVD into the player, found the right button on the remote, and got it queued up. After that, he paused the film, handed the remote to Isaiah, rested his hand on his nephew's dark head, and said, "It's ready when you are. Keep the sound down, though, so your mum can sleep if she needs to, OK?"

Isaiah said, "OK." His face was closed down. He was six years old, and done in. He needed time to be quiet, too. At least, Zora hoped so, because she had to shut down. She had nothing left to give, not even to her son. It was a frightening thought.

She told Rhys, "I'll have to ring up and tell them I've come to stay here for tonight. Not sure how to say it, though. I don't even have a change of clothes, and I don't care."

"I've already told them. They'll know that everybody handles things differently. Or if they don't—" He grinned. "Bugger 'em. There'll be a dressing gown in the closet in there. A tub with jets as well. You should use it." He hesitated. "And I asked them to send up a bottle of wine. You could have a bath. Get a little pissed. Order up some chocolate cake for the two of you. Let it all go for a night. Time enough to pick it up again tomorrow. I'll get your car here for you in the morning, and leave the keys in the office."

"Thank you," she said. "Though I do wonder how you know, about the dressing gown and the spa tub and all." She was nearly rocking in her heels now, she was so tired.

"Stayed here when the All Blacks played a test once." She thought he was going to put his arms around her again. Instead, he said, his voice nearly harsh, "And don't thank me. He was my brother."

She hadn't seen him again for six months.

# adventures in curry

He couldn't really see the house, not through the storm. He could see enough to know it was a move down—way down—the property ladder, though, and it was making him furious.

*Get it under control.* Not something he had to tell himself often. Other than when he saw Zora.

He got out of the car and ran to the front door. No choice. He was committed. The door opened straight into a kitchen. A bit of an . . . odd one. The backsplash was huge red tiles, the attached seating at the breakfast bar was red plastic, the floor was gray lino meant to look like tile, and the cabinets were some kind of glossy black metal.

It smelled fantastic, though, like an Indian restaurant. Whatever that smell was, he wanted it.

He got his shoes off and put them on the rubber tray, then unzipped his anorak and hung it on a hook beside the other two, and everything dripped. Zora stood in the middle of the tiny square of work space, smoothed her hair, and told Isaiah, "Let's see your chest, darling."

Isaiah put his arm across his skinny body and said, "I'm good." He slid his eyes across to Rhys, though, and something in them tugged at Rhys hard.

It was the look Dylan had given him when they were kids. Part apprehensive, part worshipful, and part waiting to hear what to do next. It had exasperated Rhys no end at the time, because so often, he hadn't known what to do next. He'd had to make it up.

This time, he knew. "Let's have a look, mate," he told his nephew. "You did well being brave about it, but injuries need to be looked after. We'll get some ice on it. Sure to be a good bruise."

Isaiah set his teeth into his lower lip, but he let his mum lift his shirt and expose the angry line of red on his upper chest. Rhys said, "Ice, definitely. And a paracetamol tablet as well, if you were one of my players."

Zora got the tablet from a bottle in a cupboard and said, "Go change out of your wet jeans and socks, love. Or better yet—go have your bath and warm up. You're shivering. Dinner's in twenty minutes. We'll strap the ice to you then. If I do it now, you'll turn into an ice block yourself."

She smiled and pushed back his hair with a gentle hand, and he fidgeted under the caress, glanced at Rhys again, said, "OK," and headed off.

Zora told Rhys, "You're in shorts, but I can't do anything about that, except that I'm going to start the fire, February or not." The storm was still raging outside, the raindrops spattering against the kitchen window like they were trying to get in.

Rhys said, "I'll do it," and followed her through an archway and into a tiny dining nook.

Just enough space for a table and four chairs, and a little black cast-iron stove on a brick hearth. Half the wall was brick, and the other half was red. Somebody had *really* liked red. She flipped a rocker switch, yellow flame appeared behind the stove's glass wall, and her eyes were laughing as she told him, "That's it, I'm afraid. No manly skills required. Sorry."

He had to laugh. She'd never seemed scared of him. Always a little saucy, a little challenging. And if that heated his blood, no matter how hard he worked to cool it down . . . that was his problem.

It would have helped if she hadn't been wearing snug jeans and a slim-fitting long-sleeved T-shirt printed with delicate wildflowers on stems, both items clearly showing that, as she'd told him the first night she'd met him, she was five foot two and forty-nine Kg's, and she was never going to get any bigger. If she hadn't been so . . . pocket-sized, like you could carry her around with you, could hold her up with one arm while you kissed her breathless. Up against the wall.

He didn't need the picture that conjured up. It would be there anyway tonight, imprinted on his mind when he closed his eyes. He knew it. He'd had experience.

That first night, after he'd left and gone to meet some of the boys from his own squad for a final beer, he'd wanted to go home with the blonde who'd come over to chat, and stayed to put her hand on his arm, to look at him, then look away, and lean forward just enough to let you look down her shirt. He'd wanted to shut it all out, to sink into the blissful oblivion of her willing body.

He could say he'd gone to bed alone instead because easy sex, the kind that had nothing to do with the person he was and everything to do with the person he appeared to be, didn't hold the appeal it once had, but it wouldn't have been true. That night, it had held every bit of appeal it possibly could.

No, the problem had been knowing that, when his body was heading over the edge into the dark abyss of that orgasm, where he couldn't control anything anymore, it would have been Zora's face underneath him. It would have been her dark eyes he'd watched closing, her soft mouth he'd seen opening. It would have been his beard burn on her neck, her hands clutching his shoulders, her legs wrapped around his waist. It would have been unacceptable.

He needed a night, he'd thought then, and that was all. Some distance, and some discipline. He could find that. He always had. Tomorrow.

Now, he told himself the exact same thing, even as he said, "You didn't tell me you were moving. If you have a pair of Dylan's track pants, I could wear those. He always did wear them too long, and his jeans too short. He dressed like a back, no matter how well I educated him."

She didn't smile. "I don't," she said. "Have any. It's been

23

almost two years. I had to start over."

That sounded defensive. He wanted to tell her that he always needed to remind himself of Dylan around her, but how could he say that? Instead, he said, "I should've known that, I guess, as you aren't wearing your rings anymore. I could have come and helped you sort his things, anyway."

"Never mind," she said. "Hayden did it. And I took the rings off . . ." A sigh. "Oh, nearly a year ago. One day, I took them off to do some gardening, and I didn't put them on again. Not an easy day, whatever you think." Defensive again.

"I reckon it wasn't. I took my own ring off faster than you did, and I'm still married. Technically. I remember the day I did it, too. How is Hayden? He always made me laugh."

"Oh, you know. He's Hayden." A smile of her own, like the sun coming out. Not a blazing sun. A gentle one, like the view over the paddocks to the sea in the evening, the kind that set your heart at rest. "He said the same thing you did, about Dylan's trousers. Still not settled down with somebody nice, but he said one of us jumping too early was enough." Confusion crossed her face, and she stammered, "I—I mean—"

"Never mind," he said. "Tell me what to do here, and I'll do it. Your jeans are wet, and I think you fell, back there in the carpark. Hurt yourself, maybe. You could go take your own bath." *And I won't think about you in it,* he promised himself. *I can't live this close and think about that.*

She hesitated, then shrugged and pulled a bag of something out of the freezer and tossed it onto the bench, got an onion and a red capsicum from the fridge and a knife from a magnetic strip on the wall, and started to cut the veggies into thin slices. "I have to wait for Isaiah to be done. We have one bath. You could look for candles in the closet for me, between the dining room and the lounge. We could have a power cut." Even as she said it, the lights flickered. "I've got a gas cooker, but I'd rather not use it in the dark."

He found the candles, noticed again how small this place was—he kept feeling that he needed to turn sideways to get through a room—then came back and said, "You brought a hungry man home, one who's willing to work for it. Give me directions."

Her mouth opened, then closed, and her color rose again. What? Why? That had been polite. He was her brother-in-law. She didn't say anything, though, just fossicked about amongst the books on the bench top, pulled out a slim paperback, found a page, and said, "Do this, then, to fix the peas, and put the bag of rice into the microwave for a minute, shake it up, and then do a minute more. If the power goes out, cook it in a saucepan on the stove instead." She walked out, and he didn't look at how those jeans fit, at the curve of her waist and the still-bloody-wonderful swell of her backside.

*Get a grip,* he told himself, slicing onion with some savagery, and welcoming the sting in his eyes. *Pull your head in. You're too old for this.*

Pity he didn't feel that way.

Dinner was a relief. Isaiah made a pretty fair chaperone. And when Rhys tasted the first forkful of silken chicken in a luscious brown sauce, nutty basmati rice, and the spiced peas he'd made on the cooktop, his eyes opened wide. "Bloody hell," he said, "that's amazing."

"That's ten minutes at noon, then leaving it to cook all afternoon while I'm gone," Zora said, "on my busy day."

"That's Monday and Friday," Isaiah informed him. "Also Saturday, but I can help then." He had an ice pack wrapped around his chest, secured with a sling fashioned by his mum, amidst a fair bit of laughter, from a couple of tea towels. "Mum does businesses on Monday, and houses on Friday. Our best day is Tuesday. Nobody has a funeral or a wedding or anything on Tuesday. That's when we do walks and fun things."

"What would that be on Mondays and Fridays, exactly? You're not doing cleaning, are you?" Rhys asked Zora, his blood running cold at the thought.

Wait. No. The pink van. It sounded—it *looked*—like massage. Surely she wasn't an outcall massage therapist. She could get herself into too many dodgy situations that way, the size that she was. If that was it—or if it was the cleaning—he didn't care whether it was appropriate, he was speaking up and stepping in.

He hadn't said she shouldn't have sold the house in the hills, had he? That she should have come to him first, because that house had to be appreciating at twenty percent a year? This place couldn't be ninety square meters. It was smaller than his first apartment, the road was too busy, and it didn't even have a heat pump. Yes, this little corner where they were sitting was cozy, with the brick wall and the fire and all, but she'd given up too much, selling that house on one of the best streets in Titirangi—what?—six years after they'd bought? Five? He hadn't said anything about that. He was going to say something about this.

"Of course I'm not doing cleaning," Zora said, and laughed. "Or whatever else you're imagining. The look on your *face,* Rhys." Isaiah was laughing, too, but Rhys was waiting to laugh himself until he heard what it actually was. "I'm doing flowers, of course, same as before."

"Oh." He felt stupid, as well as relieved. "Right. But not in the shop anymore? I thought the flowers were temporary. You got your diploma in architecture."

"And it's not worth much without some other things. Internships that you don't wait years after your diploma to apply for, for one. I've got a gap in my CV so big, you could drive a truck through it. Never mind. I love doing flowers, they fit into my life better than architecture ever would, and I'm on my own now, doing them the way I like. Edgy. Modern. Zora's Florals. Didn't you see the van? Pink, with orange and purple flowers and all the greenery? Came out so well. I need a new van, and I think half the reason I've put it off is because I love the paint job. Plus, this one's got me through heaps. We may have been stuck on the side of the motorway together a time or two, but she's always carried me home, in the end."

"Mum does subscriptions," Isaiah fortunately said, before

Rhys got *himself* stuck explaining how the pink van had definitely *not* looked, no, not at all, like it belonged to a massage therapist, or saying what he thought about her being stuck on the side of the motorway. The boy continued, "It's businesses on Monday, so they have flowers during the week, and houses on Friday. It's brilliant. She read about it in a magazine, and she was the first one to do it. Now, there's more competition, so that's harder, but she's the best one."

"Isaiah and I could be a wee bit prejudiced," Zora put in.

"She gets up at five on Mondays and Fridays, though," Isaiah said. "I have to go to school those days, so I can't help. But at the weekend, I do."

"That's right," Zora said. "That's the other best thing about our new house, is that we have such a good workroom."

"Besides that it's two hundred dollars a week cheaper." Isaiah again, of course. The kid was obsessed with money. "That's why we have two hundred forty-five dollars extra," he told Rhys. "Because the other house was all in . . . in . . ."

"Equity," Zora said. "Worth heaps, but not doing anything for us. So now we're here, cozy as bugs, ten minutes' walk to school and about two to the shop, and around the corner from the Waitakeres, if we want to have a walk and a chat after a hard day, or maybe invite a mate along. But besides that, I've got a shed somebody was using as a darkroom, with a sink and tap and electrics, room for all my gear and a fridge, and with a concrete pad underneath that stays cool. I'm ten steps from the back door and Isaiah, and that's why we say we have a better house now." Her eyes dared Rhys to contradict her. "Exactly the right size."

"And the shed stays extra-cool in summer," Isaiah said, "because we put Pink Batts up above the ceiling."

"Insulation," Rhys said.

"Yeh. I handed them, and Mum shoved them in. And now it's cool enough for flowers. Afterwards, we did it in the whole house, because we'd learnt how. So it's warmer *and* cooler. Depending. Also, I think the gas bill will be less."

"Hayden could've helped with that, surely," Rhys said.

"Hayden," Zora said with another flash from those dark eyes, "has his own life. And Isaiah's right. Insulation's easy as to install. We did it ourselves."

The power cut happened while they were doing the washing-up. Zora had already sent Isaiah to bed with another ice pack, and Rhys had told himself it was only brotherly to do the washing-up with her before he left.

One moment, he was tipping the contents of a slow cooker into a plastic container, and she was loading the dishwasher. The next, a clap of thunder seemed to hit the house at the same moment the sky lit up bright, the two things together like a flash-bang grenade going off, and Zora let out a startled squeak. Rhys set down the pot in the dark, feeling for the edge of the plastic container so he wouldn't tip butter chicken all over the kitchen, and turned, his hands outstretched, to find those candles.

He'd forgotten how small the space was. One step, and he bumped into something soft. When he pulled his hand back, it landed on something that could never, ever have been anything but a woman's breast, and he realized he was behind her, and pressed too close. He couldn't see a thing, but he could identify the parts just fine. A frozen second, and he jumped away, crashed into the benchtop, caught his elbow on something, and felt it sink down into wetness.

A flare of light, then another one. She'd found the candles. She brought one over, her face lit from below like a Byzantine saint on a postcard, then started to laugh.

"You're helpful, mate," she said. "Oh, what a mess. Oh, bugger. There's tomorrow's lunch gone."

He already had a bad feeling. He looked down. Yes. He *had* tipped over the plastic container of butter chicken, rice, and peas, and half of it was on the benchtop and oozing down the cabinet. The other half was on his arm and down his side.

He started to smile, and she laughed harder, until he had no choice but to join in, then start sopping up the mess with a roll of paper towel and chucking it into the bin. "Now," he said, "I owe you two dinners."

"I reckon you do. Especially if I tell Isaiah, and he puts it on his list. You may have noticed that he keeps track of things. Give me two or three of those." She wet them at the sink, then grabbed his wrist and started sponging down his arm.

He froze. He couldn't help it. He wished the light were better when she stepped back, slapped the towels into his hand, and said, sounding a little breathless, "You can finish that up better than I can."

Wonderful. She'd noticed. He said, "Adventures in curry. I should be going before I do any more damage."

"Probably. Especially as you have a new house of your own. You'll need to take some candles, and a box of matches. There are more in the closet."

"Nah. I'll go back to the hotel instead. I'll have a restart tomorrow, when the worst of the storm's passed. I need to do some work tonight to get ready for training in the morning, especially if we're doing it in the wet."

"Because you're coaching," she said. "Here."

"Yeh." He waited a minute, and when she didn't say anything, said, "You could come by on Sunday, if you like. You and Isaiah. To see the place. Give me . . . ideas of what to do with it, and give me a chance to get to know my nephew better."

"Where is it?" She was working on the front of the cabinet now, crouched down with a sponge and a tea towel and wiping curry sauce off everything.

"Here. Titirangi."

She looked up fast. "Here?"

"It's . . . ah . . ." He rubbed his nose, then realized he was still holding the paper toweling. Now he probably had curry on his face, too. No, he definitely did, because his eyes were starting to water, and his nose to run. He needed to leave before the lights came back on. "Where the best house was. The place I like best in Auckland, too. In the trees."

"You feel that as well? But you grew up on the sea. Your family are fishermen. And then you were in Australia, in

Brisbane, Dylan said, playing League. Surely Titirangi is nothing like Brissy. I've only been once, but I don't remember that."

He hoped Dylan hadn't said *much* about Brisbane. Like, for example, any or all of the things Rhys had told his brother when he'd had Dylan over to visit, hoping to impress him like the stupid kid he'd been. That wasn't a good thought at all. "No. It was city life there. Dunno. Maybe I was reincarnated. Some Maori ancestor, up in the bush, living amongst the kauri."

"Sounds romantic," she said. "Probably wasn't. All that fighting over land and women. Not too flash for the women, either."

Something in the way she said it had him heating again. She did call to that ancestor, whoever he was. A story straight out of those days, two brothers who wanted the same woman. Back then, they'd have fought for her, she was right about that. Competed to offer her the most, to prove that he could provide for her best, or just fought. That would have worked for him. He'd have fought hard. Now, she absolutely got to choose, which was nothing but right. He reminded himself of that, and that she'd already chosen.

"Yeh," he said. "I'll text you the address. And if you and Isaiah come by on Sunday, I'll show you the place and take you to breakfast. Get one of those meals I owe you out of the way. He can take a quick look at my portfolio, too, and calculate my return on investment. I've been thinking I need to rebalance."

She laughed. "You joke, but in a few years, I think he'd do it. He's not odd, you know. He's just . . ."

"Very bright," he said. "And concerned about his mum, maybe, because he knows he's got a good one."

Another intake of breath. She'd forgotten about scrubbing, was standing there with the sponge in one hand and the tea towel in another. Looking soft, and touchable, and . . . vulnerable. His voice had softened, he realized belatedly. "Maybe," she said. "Though, like I said—"

"You try not to make him worry," he finished. "Yeh. I know."

He didn't kiss her cheek when he said goodbye. He didn't trust himself to.

He was all the way back at the hotel in the CBD when he realized that he'd never asked her why they'd needed to sell the house. How much insurance had Dylan left her? He and Dylan had talked about it, hadn't they? Why wasn't she covered, then? Why wasn't she secure?

And why hadn't he known?

# not a choice

That was Monday. By Tuesday, Rhys had talked sense into himself again. Of course, he'd have to start all over again on Sunday, because Zora and Isaiah *were* coming by the house then, the day after the final match of the preseason.

That was a thought for Sunday. This wasn't Sunday. If you couldn't compartmentalize, as a rugby player or a coach, you couldn't do the job. Just now, he was talking tackling.

"Anticipation." It was raining again, the tail end of the cyclone, so he raised his voice to compensate. "You can't tackle him straight on if you don't know where he's going. You'll be bouncing off, and he'll be going straight through you. You don't want to be that guy. But if you watch the film enough times, you know what the fella's got up his sleeve, and you can counter it. Let's have it again."

The blast of his whistle, and the ball went from the halfback to the first-five, Will Tawera. A cutout pass over the next man in line, all the way to Kevin McNicholl, who had to reach up for it. He pulled it in, stepped, then stepped again, so lightning-quick that if you'd blinked, you'd have missed it, shifting his line.

He didn't fool Marko Sendoa. The flanker was on him like an avenging angel, but pulled his tackle at the last second. No point bruising your mate's ribs two days before the match.

Rhys blew the whistle. "That's a hospital pass, Will," he told his first-five. "You've left Kevvie hanging out to dry. Watch your leading hand. The moment you lose focus, start

32

thinking about the rain and how you hope this is the last round, the leading hand is off anywhere but where it's meant to go. And Marko—how did you see where Kevvie was heading?"

Marko considered a moment, then said, "He knew I was coming at him. I knew he was going to step. Couldn't step to the right, because Koti was there, so I knew he'd step to the left. I was watching for it."

"Yeh," Rhys said. "Right, then. Same again. Choose a different target, Will." He was about to blow the whistle when he saw one of the younger fellas say something to his neighbor. Tom Koru-Mansworth had been the player on the left when Kevvie had stepped. The player Kevvie had known he could beat. He dropped the hand with the whistle and called out, "Kors. Got something to share?"

The kid looked discomfited, as well he might. "No. Just having a laugh."

Rhys let a bit of the fire show. "And you had a laugh during the time before as well. Just because the drill hasn't started, that doesn't mean you're switched off. If your body's here, your head had better be here with it. You're switched on, and then you're switched higher. Those are the only two choices. Why is Marko doing this drill? He knows how to tackle. Why is Hugh doing it? The skipper knows how to tackle, too. They're here because knowing how isn't enough. They want to do it better. Better's always out there, just out of reach. It's your job to grab it. Start again. This time, focus like there's a point to it. Winners do extra. You'd bloody well better want to be a winner, or why be here at all?"

The corner of Kors's mouth twitched. A laugh, or a grimace. It had better have been a grimace. Rhys breathed the fire back and said, "If you're satisfied with where you are, you may as well hang up your boots and stop wasting everybody's time. Switched on, switched higher, or go home. Same again."

They kept on. Beside Rhys, Finn Douglas, his assistant coach and a legend himself, said, "The talent's there. Nothing really wrong with his work rate, either, not lately."

"You can't coach hunger," Rhys said shortly.

It had surprised him, when he'd first realized it. Shocked him, in fact. Even before high school, the way some kids did exactly what they were told to do, some shirked even that, as if it would happen by magic, and others did more. He'd assumed that everybody would do more. If you loved something, didn't you want to get better? Didn't you want to be the best? What was the point in trying at all, then?

He'd tried to explain that to Dylan, more times than he could count. It had never worked. Now, he gave a player the message once, loud and clear. If they didn't get it the first time? He cut them loose. He could coach passing. He could coach kicking and tackling and scrummaging, too. He couldn't coach drive, and he couldn't coach heart.

Another forty-five minutes, and the squad headed into the sheds, the younger boys moving faster, like horses heading toward the barn, some of the veterans taking a few more minutes. Will having a final few kicks at goal, because his boot had been off today in the wind and the wet. Three others running lines, practicing a tricky play they'd been working out.

Kors had been headed in, pulling his beanie off along the way. Now, he hesitated, then tugged the hat back on and jogged over to the little group, positioned himself along the line, and ran the next one with them.

"Better," Finn said. "Even if all he's doing is showing you."

"Push him harder in the gym tomorrow," Rhys said. "If he's not going to level up, we may as well find out in preseason."

"Righto," Finn said, and they headed in, scooping up rugby balls along the way. In the coach's room, Rhys stripped off his jacket and track pants, both sodden with the soaking rain, and sat behind the desk to make a few notes before he headed out.

He had six voicemails, he saw, none of them from anybody he was particularly keen to talk to. Five of them could wait, but when your lawyer said, "Ring me back today," you probably had to answer that one.

It had better not be about Victoria. It was bound to be about Victoria. Two months to go until their divorce was finalized. He rang the lawyer back.

"Afternoon," Colin said. "You settled in, then? Everything go OK, getting into the house?"

Stalling. This didn't sound like Colin at all. It *was* Victoria, then, and it was bad. The property settlement, or the alimony, which was meant to be done and dusted after this year.

"All good," Rhys said. "What's up?"

Across the room, Finn looked up, his blue eyes sharpening in his rough-hewn face.

Colin said, "Do you have a few minutes to talk?"

"Yeh. Go on." Rhys didn't sigh. The problem, whatever it was, would be there whether he ran from it or walked toward it. Walking toward it got it over sooner.

Colin said, "A woman in Chicago, a Ms. India Hawk, has died and left a child. *Your* child, apparently, as you signed an Acknowledgment of Paternity. I could say that I wish you'd told me, because this could certainly affect your property settlement with Victoria, but that's a matter for another day. Right now, I need to know what you want to do about the child. Who would appear to be your daughter."

♡♡♡

Rhys said, *"What?"* Never the brightest answer. After that, he gathered his resources and said, "I haven't acknowledged anything, because there's nothing *to* acknowledge. Explain why you think there is." Across the room, Finn looked up again, then picked up some papers, stuffed them into a backpack, and headed out the door, closing it behind him, but Rhys barely noticed.

"Your signature's on the document," Colin said. "Recognizably yours. I have a copy in front of me here, which I'll send over to you in a minute. Voluntary Acknowledgment of Paternity, State of Illinois, dated eleven days after the birth. It's your name, and your address at the time. Your phone number and date of birth as well. Signed in front of a witness. Te Rangi Walton, whose address is given as Motueka. In addition, as passed on to me by the Department of Children and Family Services via a friend of India's, you also paid child support for a number of years. That appears to have been an informal arrangement, because there's no paperwork or any order on file. Next time, tell me first. The legalities are there to safeguard you as well as the child."

Rhys was drowning in words. Time to start swimming. He said, "I won't be telling you, because there'll be nothing to tell, exactly the way there isn't now. It's not true. But before you ask—Te Rangi is my cousin. And that, and all the rest, means exactly nothing, because whoever signed that, it wasn't me, and I imagine it wasn't Te Rangi, either. The rest of it, the address and phone number, isn't impossible information to come by, and as for my signature, it's out there on a million rugby balls and T-shirts and game programs. Nice way out for whoever it was, though, putting my name to it." The warmth in the office was suffocating. That was because his blood was boiling. "Wait," he realized. "When am I meant to have done this?" He'd been gone from home half the time while he was playing in New Zealand, and almost all the time after that, first in Japan, playing and coaching, and then in France. You couldn't get a girl pregnant if you weren't there, and he'd been to Chicago exactly twice in his life. That was a relief.

"We're going back almost seven years," Colin said. "Chicago, early November. The first All Blacks test in the States."

"I remember." Not so much of a relief, then.

"India Hawk, as I said. Unusual name." As always, Colin got more deliberate, to the point of sounding sleepy, the more the tension ratcheted up. He'd been an All Black himself, in the amateur age, and understood the particular issues of sportsmen. That was why Rhys liked him. Normally. He wasn't a fan of this particular line of conversation.

"I don't know anybody by that name," he told Colin. "And seven years ago, I was engaged to Victoria."

"I'm your lawyer," Colin said, "not your judge. I can only help you if you tell me the truth."

Rhys was trying not to lose his temper. Unfortunately, his temper was trying to lose him. "You think I'm afraid to tell you? I'm not afraid to tell you. If I had a kid, I'd be looking after it. I'm not, because I don't have one, no matter who puts my name to their problems. It never happened. It isn't true. Fight it. Starting bloody now." That last part came out in a bit of a roar. Usually, that was for effect. This time, it was the dragon.

That should have been the end of it. It wasn't. "I'm sending across a couple photos," Colin said, "and that acknowledgment. I'll wait until you have a look."

Ten long seconds, and the email was in his inbox, and Rhys was clicking on it. And then on the first attachment.

An easy "no." If he'd ever seen this woman before, he didn't remember her. He'd met a lot of girls, and he'd slept with some of them. He hadn't slept with this one, though. He hadn't slept with anybody seven years ago, other than his fiancée.

Why, then, was his heart thumping out of his chest?

The girl, who surely looked younger than she actually was—he hoped so, anyway, because she looked eighteen—was blonde, pretty, and smiling, holding a toddler on her lap. The kid, whose hair was dark, was dressed up in white tights, a frilly blue dress with petticoats, and shiny black shoes, but stared stolidly at the camera as if she wasn't on board with the frilliness or, in fact, any part of the occasion.

It was a photo to make you laugh. Why wasn't he laughing?

"I don't know this girl," he said. "No."

"Did you open the second one?"

Oh. There was another photo. Rhys clicked on it.

He stopped breathing.

It had been taken at school, probably, the kind of thing where the photographer snapped a different kid every minute until he'd herded the whole class through. A girl in a long-sleeved red T-shirt, with some sort of plaid dress over it. Standard issue. Her skin was the color of light honey, and her dark hair was swept straight back off her forehead and pulled up into a high ponytail that revealed her widow's peak, that vee of hairline dipping down in the center of her forehead. She had her elbow propped up and her chin in her hand, which was probably the pose they'd all done, but she wasn't smiling. Instead, she looked at the camera as if she were staring it down. The same way the toddler had.

The same way Rhys did.

Her eyes were a clear hazel-green, like a stream in the Scottish Highlands. Relic of Rhys's great-grandfather on his dad's dad's side, his Nan had told him. Angus Fletcher. The fletchers, the arrow-makers, running down a hill in the Highlands and onto the enemy, their kilts swirling around them, a broadsword in one hand and a bow and quiver strapped to their backs.

Warriors on both sides of the bloodline.

They were Rhys's eyes, and his hairline.

"Right," he said. "She looks like me. But I still didn't sleep with her mum. Absolutely *not.*" His mouth said the words, even as the rest of him was acknowledging the truth.

"I'll give you the gist of the statement from the friend," Colin said. "Elizabeth Hartwell." He was speaking so deliberately now, his words came down like concrete. "India met you in a pizza place—Pizzeria Uno—two days before the All Blacks game, with a few other men who introduced themselves as New Zealand rugby players. As All Blacks. She was a waitress there, and you ended up exchanging numbers. You were persistent. She was excited. After the game, she met you in a sports bar—I don't have the name of that—by previous arrangement. You had drinks, and you talked about flying her over to London for the next stop of the Northern Tour. You went home with her, and left her place before dawn, saying you had to get back to the hotel in order to fly out with the team. You promised to email her, but when you did, you said the London trip wouldn't be possible. She was disappointed. The rest of the email was about . . ." Colin gave a dry little lawyer-cough. "Intimacies. You definitely gave your name to her, though, as Rhys Fletcher, and you definitely told her—multiple times—that you played for the All Blacks. You wouldn't let her take your photo."

"So far," Rhys said, "it's nothing." Except for that school photo, and those eyes.

Colin went on. "When she emailed you a few months later to tell you she was pregnant and was having the baby, you promised to take care of her, but asked her not to contact you again, because you'd got married since the two of you had met. You sent her four hundred dollars a month for three and a half years, deposited directly into her bank account, after which the payments became sporadic, and then stopped altogether. I find that timing significant, given what you've just told me. I'm sure you do, too. Her emails went unanswered, and as the United States and New Zealand don't have a reciprocity agreement for child support, she had no way of collecting. 'She couldn't afford to go to a lawyer for nothing,' were the friend's exact words. 'She knew she was stuck.' If you're certain it wasn't you, we have to ask ourselves why she looks so much like you, and why the actual father gave your name."

What Rhys *wanted* to say was, "It's a sad story, but it wasn't me, too bad. I'm not the only man in the world with hazel eyes. It was some other tattooed fella, feeding a pretty blonde a line to get her between the sheets. 'I'm an All Black' isn't the least-used tactic in the world for a Kiwi abroad, I hear."

He didn't say it, because the All Blacks hadn't been the only team playing that weekend, and because Te Rangi had more than one cousin. The Maori All Blacks had played the night before the marquee event, and Dylan had been selected for the Maori All Blacks that year. Not happy to have been left out of the ABs squad once again, and resenting, as much as happy-go-lucky Dylan had been able to resent anything, his big brother, who *hadn't* been left out. Also as usual. Borrowing

Rhys's name, and his stature, for a night, and looking enough like him for a girl checking out a photo online to be fooled. A too-young, too-credulous girl, maybe, who believed in Cinderella, in flights to London and a whirlwind future. In being swept off your feet. Rhys's hand was fisting at the thought.

Dylan had also been married. Another excellent reason to borrow your brother's identity, if you had a wife and a year-old baby at home. And if that baby had just had surgery for a hole in his heart, and you were a man who thought life hadn't been quite fair to you, and what was the harm in snatching a little harmless fun when you had the chance? What Zora didn't know wouldn't hurt her, and she barely had time for you, anyway.

Which meant that Dylan wasn't getting as much sex as he wanted. Rhys hadn't needed to hear that last bit spelled out. He'd wanted to put his fist through the wall when Dylan had said it, after Rhys had caught him kissing a pretty brunette in the toilet corridor of a Christchurch bar, a couple months before Chicago. Actually, he'd wanted to put his fist through his brother.

He didn't want to ask the next question, but there was no way around it. He had to know. "What is it, exactly, that I'm meant to do now?"

"The mother died, as I mentioned," Colin said. "Suddenly, without being able to make plans for her daughter. Hit by an inattentive driver—an uninsured driver, unfortunately—at a pedestrian crossing, on her way to work. Which leaves the other parent as sole guardian. As things stand—you."

Yeh. A gut punch.

"I'm single," Rhys said. "Not in a position to take care of a kid."

"She could have said the same, of course."

He wished Colin wouldn't be so bloody reasonable. "There must be somebody else," he realized with relief. "Somebody more fit. They're probably frantic now, the grandparents or the auntie or whoever, thinking they've got to let her go to En Zed, to a dad she doesn't even know and who never cared enough to meet her. Who's she with now? That's where she should stay, surely."

He'd pay. He'd have to pay. No getting around it. Those eyes. That hairline. The defiant way she looked at the camera.

Most people ran from fear. Other people made fear do the running. He had a feeling he knew which kind she was.

"Now?" Colin said. "She's in temporary foster care. She's been there for . . . let's see . . . six days. That's how long it took them to track you down and get in contact with me, after finding your name on the birth certificate, the Acknowledgment of Paternity filed with the state, and hearing the details from the friend."

"No grandparents, then," Rhys said. "No aunties." That hollow feeling in his stomach? That was what it felt like to have the lift drop ten stories all at once beneath you.

"No," Colin said. "Just you. If you want the girl, you call them and tell them so, and she stays in foster care until you come to get her, simple as that. That's one option. If you don't want to take her, I tell them, sorry, he denies it absolutely. His signature was forged, and he wasn't the one making the payments. This is the first he's heard of her. At that point, she'd become a ward of the state. As I mentioned, New Zealand has no reciprocal agreement with the United States, much less with the state of Illinois. They can't compel a DNA test, or child support, for that matter, any more than they could six years ago. You can ask for a test, of course. That would probably be simplest, if you're certain it would absolve you. Anything less than ninety-nine percent probability would be as good as a total miss. 'Close' doesn't count."

"I just have one question," Rhys said.

"Go ahead."

"Why the hell would you tell me that, when you know it isn't an option? And when you know bloody well that if it had been me in that hotel room, that apartment, whatever it was, I'd have stepped up six years ago, and kept stepping up, for the same reason I will now, and not with four hundred dollars a month, either? Because it's not a choice." The dragon was loose. No holding him back. "She's my responsibility, and you know it. Where would I have been if my Nan had felt that way, or the aunties? If they'd said, 'Sorry, mate, got no room for you and your little brother. Good luck to him once the two of you are separated, but there's nobody here with time or space in their life to cope with that nuisance.' It's not a bloody *choice*. Why would you tell me it was?"

"Because," Colin said, "it isn't my choice. He wasn't my brother."

# casey moana

It was freezing in Chicago. Literally. When you added the biting wind to the mixture, it was worse. Rhys remembered that from the Chicago trip. It was about all he *did* remember, other than the match itself, and the hockey game some of the boys had gone to see a couple nights before, during which time Dylan had been chatting up a teenaged waitress at the pizza place.

Who'd been barely nineteen, as it turned out, and just out of high school. Rhys had had to stuff down another blast of cold rage when he'd learned that. Dylan had been nearly thirty.

He hadn't even eaten any deep-dish pizza on that trip. Not on his nutrition plan. He hadn't eaten it last night, either, after he'd arrived at the hotel, even though there was a place down the street serving it up, and it smelled amazing. Just because your life was falling apart, though, just because you'd left your team in the care of your assistant coach days before their first Super Rugby match of the season, and you'd been flying out of Auckland when you should have been having a breakfast date with your sister-in-law, that didn't mean you lost your discipline. Comfort eating led to no comfort at all, when you were sweating off the extra Kg's in the gym. Life was all about consequences.

He finished paying the driver and headed across the pavement, accepting the polar blast until he got through the glass doors and into the lobby of the Children and Family

Services building, a drab thing made of concrete that matched the steel-gray sky overhead, heavy with the frozen promise of snow. Up in the lift, down the corridor, giving his name to a receptionist, then sitting in the last available seat, in an arrangement of chairs like a doctor's waiting room, only less cozy.

There was a reason it was the last seat. To his right, a woman was holding a toddler. Barely. The kid—a boy—was thrashing, crying, his eyes and nose streaming in his dark face. "Want to go *home*," he moaned. "AJ all done. All done. Want to go home." Rhys knew how he felt.

He had to look at the kid, because to his left, a woman was nursing a baby, and he wasn't looking over there. It wasn't that he thought she shouldn't be doing it. He just didn't think he should be watching. He was also too big for this chair, he was having to hold his elbows close to his sides to keep from banging into somebody, and he was the only man in the place.

The toddler had stopped crying, at least. Instead, he was staring at Rhys, his brown eyes big as saucers.

Rhys tried a smile. "Hi," he said.

The kid started crying again. Brilliant.

After what felt like an hour, but was probably fifteen minutes—during which time somebody *else* started feeding her baby, and Rhys seriously considered just closing his eyes until it was over—a woman appeared at the doorway and called out, "Rice Fletcher?" Exactly like a doctor's office, mangled name and all.

He got up with a silent prayer of thanksgiving. "Rhys," he said, pronouncing it the way you were meant to. *Reece.* "I'm here."

"Jada Franklin," she said, shaking his hand. "We spoke on the phone." And yet she'd forgotten how to pronounce his name. "Come on back."

He followed her, not into an office, but into a cubicle, where he wedged himself into another chair in not enough space.

"So," he said.

"So," she said. "Casey Moana Hawk. Your daughter. She's ready to go."

Nine words, dropping into the restrained hubbub around them like nine nails being driven into his coffin. He said, "It can't be that simple, surely. You aren't just going to hand her over without knowing more about me than that. I had some of it done for you, though. Background check." He reached into the inner pocket of his jacket, pulled out a sheaf of printed papers, and handed them to her together with the passport he'd picked up at the consulate that morning, which would allow the girl to travel to New Zealand with him. Colin had pulled major strings to get it this fast, but the kid had been in foster care for two weeks now, and Rhys needed to get her out. Anyway, if you had to do something, you didn't moan about it. You just went ahead and *did* it.

Jada's brown eyes held a career's worth of shattered illusions, and she didn't even look at the papers, just handed them back. "You've acknowledged paternity, her mother's dead, and you're the other parent. As far as the State of Illinois is concerned, she's yours. Let's go get her."

"I'm not adopting a kitten at the SPCA," he said. "Come to think of it, you probably have to do more to adopt a kitten. I'm not . . . I'm not a dad. I'm single. Don't you have some— paperwork? A bloody *interview?* A brochure? Something?"

She smiled, which was the last thing he'd have expected. "You're the first person I've ever heard request *more* bureaucracy. You do realize that's exactly the thought in every dad's mind when the nurse hands the baby over at the hospital curb, and he tries to put her in the car seat for the first time and realizes exactly how small she is and exactly how much she's his responsibility now. Nobody's ready to have a child, although some people are less ready than others. You learn as you go. Your own social services offers parenting classes, I'm sure. The fact that you're aware you need support is a good sign. You'll be fine."

He wouldn't be fine. This was a *girl.* He knew about having a little brother. He even knew how to change a nappy. What he didn't know was what he was going to do with a six-year-old girl. He was going to have to talk to her about boys. He was going to have to learn about clothes. He was going to have to fix her hair.

That wasn't the real problem. He knew that, too. He was panicking, was what it was. Getting himself out of the moment, watching the scoreboard instead of the field. He took a breath and refocused.

He could have called in the whanau. Somebody would have taken her, some auntie or cousin, once he'd explained that she wasn't his, but she was theirs. He didn't trust half of them, though, when it came down to it. Not with a life. Not with a child. His Nan had done her best, but she'd been too old and too tired to take charge of two more rambunctious boys, as well as two of their cousins—*male* cousins. Which had left the kids to sort it out themselves. He wasn't dropping Casey, determined stare or not, into *Lord of the Flies*. And then there'd have been telling Zora the truth about her husband, and leaving her to pick up yet more pieces. That was a no.

He put the papers back in his jacket pocket, because nobody was interested in reading about the fact that he owned his home, was gainfully employed, paid his debts, and had never been charged with a crime.

Maybe he'd hang onto them for dating purposes. That would move things along.

He was stalling again.

Jada said, "Come on. Let's go get your daughter."

He'd been mad to think he could do this.

Too late now.

$$\heartsuit\heartsuit\heartsuit$$

The foster home was well south of the central city, and it took a good forty minutes to get there. They drove past boarded-up shops, over cracked asphalt, past mounds of gray snow piled up in the gutters and bare trees whose limbs shook in the wind like old bones. Depressing as hell.

Some of his whanau may not have had any more money than this, but at least it was New Zealand. You saw some green, you could grow your own veggies, and there was always an uncle ready to take you out on the boat, for the price of some fish-gutting. It also wasn't covered by gray snow.

It wasn't like he'd never been cold before. He'd played his rugby in Christchurch. It froze in winter there, from time to time, but it was never like this.

The church had hell all wrong, he'd always thought. Hell wasn't heat. Heat was the off-season, long summer days spent on the boat fishing, clearing your mind of rugby and your body of ten months' worth of niggles and knocks. Or, even better, under the water, spearfishing for snapper or collecting paua, that most delectable and hard-won of kai moana—seafood. Heat was sitting on the beach afterwards, having a beer with your mates, with nowhere to go and all week to get there. Heat was a girl in a bikini and no makeup, brushing her wet hair back and smiling at you as she stepped out of the sea.

However hot it got, heat wasn't horrible. Horrible was darkness and cold, the bone-chilling, skin-burning freeze that killed everything green and alive and relaxed in the world.

That last winter, when he and Dylan had been living with their mum in Invercargill—that was his own definition of hell. He could still remember seeing his breath inside the house, on the day the electric company had shut off the power. He'd had to bring Dylan into his bed and pile both their blankets on top that winter, telling him what a nuisance he was the entire time.

"Why do you have to be such a baby?" he'd asked his brother one night, the coldest one yet, as he'd got out of bed, savage with fury and shivering in the freezing night, to find them each another pair of socks and to rearrange their jackets over them. "You're bloody useless. If you don't stop crying, I'm not going to take you with me when I get rich and get out of here. I'm going to leave you alone."

The next day, he'd rung up their Nan and asked her to

come get them. He'd stood on the cracked yellow lino of the kitchen floor, the icy fingers of cold whistling in from around the window frames, held the chilly, hard piece of plastic to his ear, and waited to see if she'd answer. When he'd listened to it ring, watched a roach crawling over a stack of dirty plates, waving its antennae, and wondered if she'd pick up—that moment was still the coldest he'd ever been. Except maybe for the days afterwards, when he hadn't known whether she would come. And the night he'd told his three-year-old brother he'd leave him alone, and Dylan had cried like his heart was breaking.

It was hard to pick a winner. All those times had sucked.

He'd never been back to Invercargill since. When he'd been offered a coaching job in Leicester, in the north of England, after his two-year stint in Japan, he hadn't taken it. Leicester was the better club, no question, but he'd taken Toulon instead, on the Riviera. He'd told himself he could make more impact there. It had been true, but that wasn't the reason he'd done it. He'd done it because it was warmer.

He also still hated cockroaches. And disorder. And unwashed dishes. Possibly also tears, especially if they were his own. Tears were giving up, and he didn't give up.

They turned onto another street, and the neighborhood got a bit better. The house, when they pulled up to it, was small and white, not too unlike his Nan's house in Nelson. Nothing flash, but trying its best.

He followed Jada up the walk. She said, "You need a better coat. Also gloves and a hat."

"Nah," he said. "If I ignore it, it doesn't exist, that's the idea. Besides, I'm flying out tonight."

"You could lose your fingers to frostbite by then." She laughed. That was her version of humor, apparently. She rang the bell, and Rhys stood beside her on the concrete porch and focused on the way his breath emerged in icy puffs. The peephole on the front of the door darkened, and after a rattle of chains, the door opened. A smell of overheated floral air freshener wafted out, and the woman behind it, who was holding a curly-haired baby on her hip, said, "Hi. You must be here for Casey."

"Yes," Jada said.

The woman pushed the door open a little more with one hand. "Come on in." She held out a hand, the one that wasn't holding the baby, to Rhys. "Tiana Hooper."

The girl was sitting on the couch, a green-flowered thing with a crocheted blanket draped over it. To either side, little tables were covered by doilies, and the coffee table had a glass top. With a crocheted doily-thing underneath it. The carpet was pink, and above the couch, glass shelves held a collection of porcelain birds that would have rained down in a shower of splinters the first time there was an earthquake.

The girl sat rigid, wearing jeans, trainers, and a blue T-shirt, printed with a flying horse with gold sparkles in its mane and tail and the word "Magical" written underneath, a shirt that looked much too insubstantial for the weather. On her lap, she held a backpack and a doll, one hand clutching each, and there were two white rubbish bags at her feet and a navy-blue puffer jacket beside her. Her hair was loose, not in a ponytail or even fastened with the clips, or whatever you called them, that she'd worn in the school photo. The clips had had bows on.

Somebody had brushed her thick, wavy hair today, but that was all. Rhys got a flash of how he and Dylan had used to look, their impossible hair always too long and too tangled. When you went to school looking like that, it sent a message that didn't help you a bit. How much worse would it be for a girl?

Casey's mum had known that, clearly. That had been the reason for the bows on the hair clips, and the neat ponytail.

"This is Casey," Tiana said, joggling the toddler. "And this is your dad, Casey, here to take you home."

"Hi," Rhys said. *You can do this,* he told himself. *This is not a mistake. This is the only solution.*

Casey studied him, but she didn't get up. "Are you going to take me back to my house in your car?" she asked.

"No," he said. "I don't have a car here, and we're going to my house."

She said, "I want to go back to my house instead, please. You can call an Uber, if you don't have a car. That's what my mommy does, if she's late and she has to go to work and she doesn't have time to go on the El. It's a school day. I could go back to my school for the afternoon part. My lunchbox is still in my cubby, because I forgot it. It has a sandwich in it, and cookies. I could eat lunch there."

He'd been here sixty seconds, and he was already in trouble. "We can't do that," he said. No point in lying to her. "I don't live here. I live in New Zealand, so that's where we need to go." Surely somebody had told her that. Hadn't they? What were these people thinking?

"I never heard of that," she said. "Is it on the north side?"

"No. It's a different country. We're going to fly there."

"I can't fly."

What? Why? Did she have some condition he didn't know about? He glanced at Jada. She shrugged. Very helpful.

"Why can't you fly?" he asked when nothing else was forthcoming.

Casey looked at him like he was stupid. "Because I don't have wings."

He laughed, and she didn't. Oh. It hadn't been a joke. "We're going on a plane. The plane flies, not us. You must have seen that in . . . in cartoons." That was where *he'd* first seen it. He hadn't been on a plane until he'd made the First XV at seventeen. He'd known what they were, though, hadn't he, at six? He couldn't remember.

"Is my mommy coming too?" she asked.

His heart did something odd, like a sponge that somebody was squeezing out. And nobody else was saying anything. How was he meant to cope with this? Surely, somebody had told her. He was going to operate on that assumption, anyway.

"No," he decided to say, and sat down beside her, next to the puffy coat. He wasn't a good liar, and anyway, she looked to him like she didn't appreciate lying. Or he told himself that, because he had no clue, otherwise. "Your mum's gone. She died, remember? That happens sometimes. I had to leave my mum when I was a couple years older than you. My Nan—my grandma—took my brother and me in. We went to a new house, and I went to a new school. Good as gold."

Not exactly, but close enough. Besides, he wasn't a worn-out sixty-five-year-old with an addict for a daughter. He was a forty-year-old rugby coach, he was tough, he had a grand total of one child to look after, and he had the means to do it properly.

Casey looked at him measuringly. "If my mommy isn't going to be there," she announced, "I don't want to go."

What did he say now? "Where are you planning to go instead?" he asked.

She wasn't solid, not really. She was slim, like her mother. And her father. But when she set her jaw, she *looked* solid. She said, "I'm going to stay here and wait for my mommy. She said she would never leave. She *promised*. If I go away from here, she won't know where I am. She has to know where I am, so she can come get me."

He was about to tear up. He could feel it coming, and that wouldn't do anybody any good, least of all him.

He was still trying to work out how to answer her when Tiana said, "I'm afraid you can't stay here, Casey. I'm your foster mother. I told you that. 'Foster' means, 'for a little while, until there's another place for you to go.' Now, there's another place. Your mommy's in Heaven now, like we talked about, with the angels, but you have a daddy, and he's going to take you home, to a brand-new house. Isn't that exciting?"

Casey looked Rhys over. "No," she said.

*This* hadn't occurred to him. People generally did what he said. Correction—people *always* did what he said. He considered shouting, "I'm the rescuer here, damn it! Let's go, and smartly." He didn't think it would work, though. He cast about for something—anything—to say, and finally lit on the backpack in her lap. It was blue, printed with Hawaiian flowers, and featured a Polynesian girl with her hand on her hip and a confident smile on her face. At the top, the word was spelled out. *Moana.*

That was the doll from the film, too, he realized, that she was holding. He may have been under a rock in terms of popular culture, but he recognized this.

If you couldn't break the line, you found another way. You sidestepped. He touched the backpack lightly and said, "Moana, eh."

Tiana shifted position. She and the social worker were still standing, and the baby was starting to fuss. He looked up at them and said, "Maybe you could give us ten minutes."

Jada looked at her watch. He told her, "If you need to leave, go on. I'll find my own way back."

"I have a few minutes," she said.

"Come have a cup of coffee," Tiana said. She asked Rhys, "Would you like one?"

It would be served in a cup and saucer, he had no doubt. Possibly on a doily. It would also be weak. Chicago coffee was rubbish. "No, thanks," he said. "I'm good." He might be in the Twilight Zone, but he was working on a plan. After that, he stopped paying attention to them and asked Casey, "Do you know what this is?" He touched the silvery disk on the doll's necklace.

"It's a necklace," she said flatly. Her expression said, *Obviously,* and he had to smile.

"It's a paua shell," he said. "Or it's meant to be. Moana's traveling from the homeland, across the seas, with Maui's help." Which covered everything he knew about the film. "She's going to New Zealand. She's going to become a Maori."

She wasn't looking at him like he was stupid anymore, anyway. She was just looking at him like he was crazy. "That's not in the movie."

"No, it's not. But it's something you know in your heart if you're Maori. I'll bet you knew it already." He reached inside his own shirt and pulled out the pounamu pendant on its black braided cord. "Just like I do. See, I have the hei matau. The fish hook pendant, for the sea and for determination. Mine has a muri paraoa as well, a whale tail, on the other end, for speed and strength and protectiveness. That's all the important things. This was carved from a jade boulder that came from Tasman Bay, which is where I come from as well. It touches my skin and roots me to my family, to the ancestors, to our mountain and our river. Moana has a pendant, too. It reminds her where she came from, and who her people are."

There you were. Logic. Rationality. And a bit of magic as well, maybe. You could need magic, if your mum had died. That might be the reason for the T-shirt.

Casey's eyes had flecks of gold amidst the green and were as extravagantly dark-lashed as Dylan's had been. Right now, they were fixed on his, like nobody had ever told her to look down, to look away, and she wouldn't have listened if they had. There was as much intensity in her slim form as in any player about to run out onto the field, too, when she said, "My mommy said that. She said I was Maori, like Moana, and someday, Maui would come across the ocean for us and take us home. Nobody else said that, though."

"Except me," he said. "That's because I'm your dad. You see how that works?" First time he'd said the D-word.

"I don't think so," she said, and he thought, *Now what?* She went on to tell him. "I think you're Maui."

"Nah, sorry," he said. "I'm not him. Maui is much bigger. He's also a demigod. I'm not even a *semi*-god."

"He fished up the ocean with a fish hook," she pointed out. "And you have a fish hook."

"Because I'm Maori. Not because I'm *Maui*. Every Maori has a pendant."

"I don't."

"That's because it has to be a gift. Nobody's given you yours yet, that's all."

She wasn't getting heated. She was just frowning. Ferociously. Her eyebrows were as straight and as black as his, too. She said,

"That doesn't make sense. If everybody has one, I would have one. It makes sense that you're Maui. You're big like Maui, and your hair's like his."

"Because I was a rugby player," he said, *not* pulling on said hair. Also, if his hair looked like Maui's in that film, he needed to have it cut. He'd better not let her see his tattoo for a while, either. "That's why I'm big. They play rugby in New Zealand. Girls, too. When you go to school, you can play. I have a feeling rugby will suit you."

She appeared to be thinking that over. "What about rabbits?"

"What *about* rabbits?" He thought that was a pretty smart parry to a rubbish question.

"Do you have rabbits at your house?"

"Uh . . . no. Why would I have rabbits?"

"Oh." Her thin shoulders drooped. "I had rabbits ever since I was little. Hoppy and Fluffy. Tiana said they went to live on a farm, and a farm is nice, because they could eat real grass, but I can't have a rabbit here, Tiana said. Plus, it's temp—temp—"

"Temporary," he said. "It's not temporary anymore. When you go to New Zealand with me, it's permanent. That's the opposite. It means you're going home to stay. Like Moana."

She clutched her doll a little tighter. "So can I have rabbits?"

A man had to recognize defeat. "Yes. You can have rabbits."

"Three?"

A man had to recognize manipulation, too. "No. You can have two." Compassion was all well and good, but drawing the line would be important, too. Setting limits. Being firm.

Fortunately, he was good at that.

# cinderella's sparkles

He'd been a father for about two hours. He was already wondering how he was going to make it through the day.

At the moment, they were in an Uber, headed north from the Children and Family Services building, where they'd left Jada. He'd told the driver to take them to the airport, but he was realizing that it may not have been the best plan.

Casey hadn't said much on the drive into the city, and he hadn't been able to think of any conversation starters. Jada had played some overly bouncy music on the car stereo instead, which had been grating to the nerves, but, he was belatedly realizing, better than silence. It was twelve-thirty in the afternoon, and trying to keep a kid occupied for six hours until takeoff in all the atmospheric charm of O'Hare Airport was probably going to be beyond him. Keeping her occupied for *three* hours was probably going to be beyond him, for that matter, but he'd tackle that later.

He should have hung onto the hotel room for another day. Maybe he should check in again, in fact. It was mad, but so was every other plan he could come up with, and they needed some kind of . . . base. Also, he needed to see what Casey had in those bags and remedy any omissions now, because when they got back to Auckland, he needed to get her into school and himself back to work. They'd do their shopping today, when he had time to spare. A much better idea. He told the driver, "Change of plan. Take us to a department store instead of the airport. One that's near the Hilton, if possible."

She looked at him in the rearview mirror. Suspiciously, he'd call that, like he was cheating her out of her fare, which he probably was. The airport would have been a much pricier ride. "Which Hilton?" she asked.

"The one downtown."

"There are four of them downtown. Which one do you want to go to?"

"I don't care. The one nearest the department store that you're taking us to." He knew about carrying your clothes in rubbish bags, and he needed to do better. He told Casey, "We'll buy you a suitcase and whatever else you need, and then we'll go to a hotel and have a rest before the airport."

Would they think it was odd that he was checking in with a six-year-old girl, though? Should he get Casey her own room?

No. Kids that age couldn't stay in a hotel room alone. She was his daughter. Supposedly. He was overthinking this.

Casey asked, "Do they have lunch there?"

Oh. He tended to ignore meals when he had something more important to do. He guessed you couldn't do that with kids. "Right," he said. "We'll go to the hotel first, drop off your things, and have lunch. We could even order room service. You'll like that. Afterwards, we'll go shopping. Good, eh."

He sounded like that music Jada had been playing, like any minute, he was going to jump up, clap his hands, and shout, "Let's have *fun!*" He was going to have to find a happy medium between his Game Face and his Nearly-Dad Face, because that level of cheerfulness wasn't sustainable. He told the driver, "Another change of plan. Hilton first."

She muttered something and scrutinized him in the mirror again, and he said, "Charge me what you'd have charged for driving to the airport, then." He'd probably lose his own New Zealand citizenship for that kind of rash spending, but there you were.

"I could go to my school," Casey said. "And get my lunchbox. Then I could have my lunch that my mommy made me. I don't want to go to a hotel. My mommy said I shouldn't go places without her, and I already went to Tiana's house."

The driver looked in the mirror again. He wished she'd watch the road, which was bound to be icy, because it had started to snow, huge, wet flakes smacking the windscreen and sticking there. He considered telling Casey that her lunch, if it had still existed, would have grown an entire bacterial colony over the past weeks and probably forced the evacuation of the school, but he didn't. She was missing familiarity, that was all, like a nineteen-year-old rugby player from the wop-wops, away from home for the first time. What did those boys miss most? Food. Always, it was food. "What's your favorite thing to eat?" he asked. "We'll have that. Uh . . ." He tried to think what his favorite had been, at six. They probably didn't have whitebait fritters in Chicago. "Hamburger. Hot dog. Ice cream. You'd like an ice cream, surely." They had ice cream cones everywhere in the States, didn't they? That was one cultural advantage the country had over New Zealand.

Wait. In winter? Maybe not.

The driver hit the brakes hard enough to jolt them against their seatbelts, then swung into a service station and pulled up to the pumps with a screech of tires and announced, "I need gas."

He thought, *Shouldn't you have considered that before you picked up a ride?* She was out of the car and on her phone now, and she hadn't even got the nozzle in the pump yet. He was regretting the "airport fare" idea already.

Never mind. They'd spend a few minutes of their six hours here, which was fine. *Stay centered,* he told himself. *Keep your focus. You can only live through one minute at a time. There's no speeding it up.*

Casey said, "We could have pizza for lunch. That's my favorite. It's very expensive to eat it at a restaurant, though. It's better to cook things at home. That way they have more flavor."

Huh. He was beginning to like India Hawk, even though

she'd complicated his life. She'd clearly done her best, which was all you could ask. "You're right," he said. "But we're not at home yet, so we'll eat in a restaurant today. Pizza it is." His nutrition plan was another thing, apparently, that was going out the window. Just for today, until he got this sorted. Then it would be back to normal. "We'll get some lunch, and then we'll make a plan. Life's always easier with a plan."

Which all sounded solid enough, but the journey was taking forever, even after the driver got back into the car. She kept taking turns that surely weren't necessary. At least, they didn't seem to be getting anywhere. He told her, "We weren't this far from downtown. We were nearly there when we started."

"Road construction," she said. "Alternate route."

"I don't think so." He held on tight to his temper. "I already told you I'd pay the airport fare. The little girl's hungry, and if you don't have us at the hotel in five minutes, I'll be filing a complaint."

"Yeah, right," she said, making another turn. "I don't think you'll be filing anything today. I'd say you're *done*. Uh-huh. I'd say so."

He considered sniffing at his armpits. Either he smelled, or he'd lost all his Influence Factor on the way over the Pacific, because he certainly wasn't impressing anybody in Chicago so far. He'd *growled* that, and she hadn't cared a bit.

The thought flew from his mind in an instant when the woman pulled abruptly across three lanes of traffic as if she were trying out as a stunt driver. Rhys shoved his arm out to brace himself and threw the other across Casey, who stiffened, said, "Hey!" and was drowned out by a chorus of angry hoots from behind them.

"What the *hell?*" he was saying just as the driver slammed on the brakes again, making his and Casey's heads rock forward and slam back against the headrests. When that stopped, he asked Casey, "You OK?"

"Yeah." She clutched her doll closer and stage-whispered, "She drives really fast."

To top it off, the woman had stopped in a "No Parking" zone, which looked to be a very bad idea, as it was already occupied by an idling police car, its revolving lights painting the gloomy day with flashes of red and blue. It was also, though, not his car and not his problem. "We're here," she said. "The Hilton. That'll be twenty-four dollars."

Rhys pulled out his credit card and handed it over. Yes, it was too much, but as far as he was concerned, he couldn't get out of this mad city fast enough. The pizza had better be good, that was all he had to say.

The driver ran his card and handed it back as a cop got out of the car ahead, plodded forward through the gathering storm, and rapped on Rhys's window.

"Yeah, yeah, buddy," the driver muttered. "Least you could do is make sure I get paid."

Rhys signed the slip, then handed it and the pen back. "I've found my Chicago visitor experience lacking, so far," he told the woman. "You could pass that on to the tourist board for me."

She didn't say anything, possibly because the cop was tapping on the window again with a black-gloved hand, beckoning to him, and a second cop was coming to join him. Rhys said, "Thanks heaps for parking here, too. Extremely convenient. Don't bother to get out, please." He opened the door and told Casey, "Let's go. Pizza ahead." Sounding jolly again, but what could you do. He'd get his suitcase and Casey's rubbish bags out of the boot, and . . .

The cop took a step closer, put his hand on the butt of his weapon, and said, "Sir, can we have a word with you?"

Rhys said, "We'll be out of your way in a minute. Just checking into the hotel."

The Uber driver leaned across the seat and buzzed the window down. "Ask him why he calls her 'the little girl' instead of her name," she yelled. "Ain't no man in the world would say that, if he's talking about his daughter. Ask her about her school, too. Ask her about her mom."

"Thanks, ma'am," the cop said. "We've got it. We appreciate the call."

♡♡♡

Forty minutes later, the server slid twelve inches of high-calorie heaven onto a table that was fortunately now serving only two. At least the cops had let him order Casey's pizza before the interrogation had started, although probably only because she'd looked at them with those mountain-stream eyes and said, in a tiny voice, "I'm really, really hungry." They hadn't been any more resistant to those eyes than Rhys himself, which was why they were in this overheated, tomato-scented space, down the street from the Hilton and bustling with midday diners. It was wide enough for only two rows of booths, and had also turned out to be an excellent place to imprison an overlarge, irate Kiwi.

Never mind. He and Casey were free once more. They also had pizza. He put a mile-high slice onto her plate, then two onto his own, and contemplated the wisdom of his preferred path from here, which was to dive face-first into every single remaining yeasty, high-topped, cheese-and-tomato-sauce-laden slice, and carbo-load his way into a caloric stupor where he wouldn't care anymore.

It hadn't been the best forty minutes of his life, but at least it was over. The cops hadn't appeared exceptionally impressed with Casey's brand-new passport, or by his explanation that he was her father, either, especially once *Casey* had explained, at another table but loud enough for Rhys to hear, that she was *supposed* to be at school, because it was a school day, and she didn't even have her lunchbox, but she had to go with that man instead.

In the end, he'd had to produce Jada's name, and then wait until the social worker got back from lunch and deigned to return her calls. Sitting in a booth with a cop beside you, blocking your exit, and another across from you, both of them eyeing you alertly for signs of imminent flight, wasn't the most relaxed environment he'd ever experienced. He'd wanted to tell Jada, "I told you I needed more documentation than this," but he hadn't even got the chance.

"All right?" he asked Casey now.

"Yes," she said, sticking her fork into the middle of her pizza in an awkward sort of way and hacking off a bite. "Except I thought they were going to arrest you. That's what policemen do."

"Maybe they just wanted lunch. Did you think of that?" Bloody hell, this pizza was *good.* Sausage and all. He'd just sit here for a minute and inhale. Aromatherapy for men.

"Policemen don't eat *lunch,"* she said. "They only come if somebody did a crime. Then they take you to jail, which is like being in a cage, except not nice like a rabbit cage. And a lady police came to my school with Elizabeth when my mommy died, so that's two things. Arresting and telling bad news. They do that on TV, too, so I know it's true. But they didn't even take their handcuffs out. I thought they would do that. Handcuffs are the main *part."*

He kept eating. "Maybe we should invite them back to have another go, if you're disappointed. I haven't been terrorized nearly enough today." Casey was sawing away at her pizza with a knife and fork, but not making terrific progress on the dense crust. "Here," he said, and reached over to cut it into pieces. The last time he'd done that had surely been for Dylan. At least he knew how to do *something* semi-parental. "Who's Elizabeth?"

"She's my mom's friend. The police lady didn't know I was supposed to take my lunchbox. Elizabeth didn't know, either, but that's because Elizabeth doesn't have any kids. She says that kids make you fat and poor, but my mom said it was just poor, for her." She studied Rhys with what he could swear was a critical eye. "You're *kind* of fat, but not exactly. That's why I think you're really Maui and not my dad. You don't look like a dad. Besides, people don't just be dads all of a sudden. Your dad has you from when you're a baby. He only

61

sometimes lives with you, but you still know he's your *dad.*"

"Excuse me," he said, deciding that this was the easier part of the debate, "but I am not fat. I weigh less now than I did when I was playing, and my waist is three centimeters smaller. I'm big."

"Oh. But you're *kind* of. Like, your arms are fat."

"They're not fat. They're muscular. They're . . . never mind." He tried to remember what they'd been talking about. He was also rethinking the pizza, given all the talk about his excess weight, except that somehow, he'd finished both slices and had started on a third. A fourth might be in the cards, too. "That lunchbox has come up a fair few times. Maybe we'd better look for a new one of those as well as a suitcase. You'll need one for school in New Zealand, I guess. I don't actually know." Add that question to the list.

"They might not have one that has Moana," she said.

"But they might. Or maybe they'll have something you like even better."

She eyed him skeptically and gave a world-weary sigh. Her hair was mussed. He was going to have to work out what to do about that. And how you did it. He ate some more pizza.

"I can't like anything *better,*" she said. "It's *Moana.* That's my *name.*"

"Yeh," he said, "but your name's also Casey. Maybe there'll be one with a locomotive on."

"What?"

"Casey Jones. He was a . . . Never mind. We'll do our best." Time to establish some more of those boundaries. "We'll find something practical, that we both like. A mutual decision, that's the idea."

The department store, when they got there, did not in fact have a Moana lunchbox. Only natural, as the film had come out ages ago. He said, "Never mind. We'll find something better. Or we can wait until we get to New Zealand, and order it online. Might have to wait a bit, that's all."

"Oh," Casey said, her voice small again. She glanced up at him, then looked down. "OK."

He clearly still wasn't up to standard. "Or," he said, "maybe there's something else you'd like. Look, this one has, uh, girls on."

"Those are Disney *princesses,*" she said. "Not *girls.*"

"Huh." He studied them. "Nah. You're right. Too blonde. We're Maori. We'll hold out for Moana. Let's go look at suitcases instead."

*See?* he told himself. *You handled it. You're fine.* And when Casey spied the enormous pink hard-sided suitcase with an embossed pattern all over it, looking like somebody's fever-dream of a magnified diamond, which was nothing any reasonable man would have bought a six-year-old? Or anybody? He did his best to handle that, too.

He knew when Casey saw it, because she stopped, gasped in dramatic fashion, ran over to touch it, and said, "This is the best one. I *love* it."

"It's not made for kids," he said, and hefted it with a grimace. "Definitely not. Probably weighs as much as you do. It's made for . . . dunno *who* it's made for. Nobody with any style sense, that's for sure. A YouTube star, maybe." The tag said "Rose Gold," but as far as he was concerned, it was pink.

"But it's on sale. See? S-A-L-E. If it has a yellow tag on it, it's on sale, so you can buy it. It's saving money!"

"It's still a hundred twenty-nine dollars and ninety-nine cents, it's too big for you twice over, and God knows *I'm* not using it. No. It's not saving money if you get the wrong thing, and you have to go out afterwards and buy the right thing after all. It's the opposite. It usually means spending twice as much money."

"But I *love* it." She was on her knees, now, stroking her hand over the shiny surface. "It's *beautiful.* It's a princess suitcase, like Cinderella has. It's the best one there could ever, ever be."

He retreated to logic and command. His happy place. "No. It's impractical. Besides, Cinderella doesn't have a suitcase."

"Yes, she does. Because she goes to live in the castle, so she has to take her clothes."

63

For somebody whose own clothes were currently in rubbish bags, she proved impossible to budge, even after he took the time to explain it to her. "She doesn't have any clothes she'd want to take, surely. That's the whole idea. Her dresses are rags, but she's whisked away by the prince, and all her troubles are over. Which isn't how it works, by the way. There's no rescue, just hard work." Wait. He probably shouldn't be telling her that right now, since he actually *was* rescuing her.

Fortunately or otherwise, Casey didn't care about his life lesson. "She does too have clothes," she insisted. "She has the most beautiful dress in the world, and it's blue and sparkly. It's a ball gown. You have to take a ball gown, because it's very, very special."

"She changes back, though," he said, "when the coach becomes a pumpkin. The clock strikes twelve, and she's wearing her old clothes again. All she has left is her shoe. Which doesn't make sense, actually. If everything else vanished, wouldn't the shoes vanish as well?"

"Because it's *magic,*" Casey said. "And when Fairy Godmother comes, at the end, she waves her magic wand and changes Cinderella back again, and she has her ball gown again, and her crown." She bobbed her head in triumph. "So she does too."

Did he consider saying that in that case, Cinderella would have been *wearing* the only item of clothing worth taking with her, and therefore would have had nothing to pack? Yes, but he *didn't* say it, did he? He sidestepped. "Look at this one over here. It's made for kids, which you are, so there you go. It's round, which is cute, it's pink, it has unicorns on, and you could pull it yourself, because it doesn't weigh forty Kg's before you've even packed it."

He had now referred to a suitcase as "cute." His life was officially changed.

It didn't work. "I don't want that one, though," she said. "I want *this* one. Please. It's *shiny.* It's the best one ever, and I *love* it. My mommy says I can have it. She says you should always choose pretty things, especially if they're on sale."

That was how he ended up walking through the airport doors pushing one suitcase in bombproof black fabric, the kind that would bump up and down endless kilometers of conveyer belt and endure all the indignities of international air travel for years on end and still come out looking exactly the same. And one that assaulted his eyeballs, and that Casey had kept her anxious hand on all the way, as if it would kick up its heels otherwise and run away to join the forest of magical tacky sparkle-suitcases. When they checked in and it headed down the conveyer belt, she craned her neck and watched it go.

All in all, though, he hadn't done so badly, had he? She wasn't crying, and he hadn't been arrested. By the time they boarded, once Casey got over the excitement of flying and they'd had dinner, she'd surely be ready to fall asleep. How much of a sixteen-hour flight could a six-year-old girl sleep through? Nine hours, maybe? Ten, he devoutly hoped. That wasn't too much to ask after the day she'd had. And when they got to Auckland and he got her settled in school, which was going to be the first day, Wednesday, because he had a team to coach, he'd get some . . . advice. Some help.

The school would have recommendations. They'd be fine.

His optimism lasted all the way to Security.

# neck-septions

Casey didn't complain, not exactly. She just asked.

When they queued up for Security, she asked, "How come we're stopping?"

"Because they need to check us," he said. "To make sure we're safe."

"How come?"

"Because sometimes, people might do bad things. Bring a knife or something." He wasn't going to say "bomb" in a security queue. He wasn't a fool.

"Oh." She digested that, and the queue moved forward again. "Did you bring a knife?"

"No."

"It's a good thing your fish hook isn't big," she said. "Maybe they'd arrest you, if you had a fish hook as big as Maui's."

"You could at least not sound so hopeful." He preferred not to talk about being arrested in a security queue, also, especially as they were near the front now, with a TSA agent a couple meters away. "Just feel lucky that we're in the fast lane," he told her, putting his backpack into a tub and reaching for hers. "The one benefit of frequent travel is that you don't have to take off your shoes. Shove your doll in there. Your coat as well."

"I don't want to."

"You have to. They need to scan it."

"Why?"

"They scan everything, in case there's a weapon anywhere."

"My *doll* doesn't have a weapon. That would be silly. She's *Moana.*" She was clutching the doll tighter. He wasn't getting it out of her arms, it was clear, without a battle.

He sighed and waved the couple behind them past. His laptop, which was all of two months old and held every single bit of proprietary information his brain and the Blues possessed, headed into the scanner. He had backups, of course, and even if somebody walked off with it, the chances of them being from a rival Super Rugby team were slim to nil. He told himself that, even as he wanted to dive in after it. "See?" he told Casey instead. "Look over there. That old lady is getting scanned in her wheelchair. She looks about a hundred. Does she have a weapon? I'm guessing 'no.' It's a rule, that's all."

"Moana is scared, though," Casey said. "She doesn't like the dark. She doesn't want to go in the tunnel."

"It's dark for a minute," Rhys said. "Less than a minute. A couple seconds." Casey stared at him, absolutely unmoved, and he cast about for something else. "And there are, uh, X-ray beams that will light her up."

An entire family: mum, dad, two kids, and a baby in a pushchair, were passing them now, and the TSA agent was scrutinizing Rhys in a frankly suspicious manner. He recognized that look by now. He'd seen it about five times today.

"It *looks* dark, though," Casey said.

Rhys had always thought his stubbornness, his absolute refusal to give in or give up, was a positive. He was beginning to see the downside.

"I promise," he said. "X-rays. Call it a . . . doll scanner. We'll go through this big people-scanner ourselves, first you and then me, Moana will get scanned in the doll scanner, and then you can pick her up on the other side and give her a cuddle."

"OK," Casey said. "But she likes it better if I hold her hand."

*Oh.* Casey handed Moana over, and took a huge breath as Rhys set the doll in the tub. That had taken some courage. "We'll put her looking up," he said, "so she can see the X-rays." Then he stepped back into the queue behind the family and took Casey's hand. It was small and warm, and it clutched his tight. He got that squeezing sensation again, too, around his . . . chest area.

The only problem was, after he'd urged her into the scanning machine, which she was *not* daunted by, oddly enough, and had gone through himself, the TSA agent on the other side said, "Please step this way, sir."

That was what you got, he guessed, when you lingered too long. "One moment," he said.

"Right now, sir," the agent said.

The last thing Rhys needed was temper. It appeared anyway. His temper was a bloody inconvenient beast. "I need to see to my daughter first." Casey was, in fact, hopping up and down, trying to look into the bins to find Moana. "She needs to get her doll."

"Sir," the agent said.

Another agent handed Casey her doll, jacket, and backpack, so that was good, but she was looking around now. Looking for *him.* He said, "One moment. I just need to get her."

"I can't allow that, sir," the agent said.

Rhys was fifteen seconds from exploding. He could feel it starting to happen. "You can take me into a room and strip me naked," he said. "I've got hours to spare. You can do a cavity search. Whatever you like. Be my guest. It's nothing that won't have happened to me before at the base of a scrum, I promise you. But my daughter's over there. She's just lost her mum, she's never been in an airport, and she's scared. I need to get her first."

He got her. Possibly, the agent didn't want trouble. Or possibly, he'd seen Casey's eyes. They had some superpowers. She didn't appear especially traumatized, though, as she watched him be checked over. Pity his own heart was beating like a hammer, and so was the blood in his temples. It was a good thing a blood pressure check wasn't included, because he'd have failed.

"What's that?" Casey asked the agent as he scanned Rhys's palms, and then his laptop and phone, after patting him down in a way that would normally happen around the third date.

"We're checking for traces of explosives," the man said.

"You mean, like he'd explode?" Casey said. "People don't *explode,* though. He has a really big fish hook, that's all. I think he has powers, even though he says he doesn't, but not *exploding.*"

The agent subjected Rhys to some more penetrating gaze. "Could you show me the fish hook, sir?"

Rhys sighed and pulled the pendant out from under his shirt. "You already saw it." He didn't tell the fella not to touch it, even though he wanted to. That wouldn't end well. "And for the record, I don't have powers."

"No, sir." The agent handed him his backpack and laptop. "Have a nice day. You too, young lady."

He'd never been more glad to head toward an airline lounge, even though it was taking twice as long as usual. He was used to walking fast, but Casey's legs were too short for that. He was holding her hand again, which helped him moderate his speed, but the way she slowed for things like the giant-pretzel vendor didn't help.

"We could get one of those," she said, watching as an employee brushed an entire gym workout's worth of melted butter onto the top of a twisted knot of absolutely nutrient-free dough, then sprinkled it with a day's ration of coarse salt.

"We could," he said, "if we wanted to watch our cholesterol and sodium levels rise in real time."

"Huh?"

"It's not healthy."

"It's kind of like pizza, though. It has dough, see? That's how my mommy makes pizza. With dough."

"Pizza isn't healthy, either. And neither are cookies," he decided to add, since they were now walking past a shop selling those, and she was eyeing them in a way that boded no good at all. They were practically the size of her head. He could feel his waistline expanding just looking at them. That was the good thing about holding her hand. At least you could keep moving.

"If it's not healthy, how come you ate five pieces?" she asked.

"I was making an exception. Exceptions are allowed."

"We could make a neck— neck—"

"An exception."

"A neck-seption. For cookies. My mommy puts cookies in my lunch, because it's dessert."

"No. No more exceptions. We'll get a cookie at the lounge. *One* cookie. One *small* cookie." And zero giant pretzels.

When they were finally in the SAS lounge, which wasn't much more than some wi-fi that he needed, some food and beverages in which he wouldn't be indulging, and less noise than the gate area, he found them seats at a table, hauled out his laptop and notebook, and told her, "Good news. Security took so long, it is now only two hours until our flight is called."

"Oh. Are we going to wait here?"

"Yeh. It's an airline lounge. More comfortable than outside, eh. You can watch the planes and check out how we're going to fly."

She was shifting in her seat like it wasn't comfortable at all. "Something wrong?" he asked.

"I have to go to the bathroom."

He should have foreseen that. She'd gone at the hotel, but that had been simple. "Uh . . ." he said. "Fine." It would be down a corridor. Some corridor. He couldn't leave her to find it by herself. He closed his laptop, shoved it and his notebook into his backpack again, and went with her. "I'll wait for you here," he said when they were outside the door. "Give me Moana and your backpack. I'll hold them for you."

Was that OK? It had better be OK. What else would he do?

Five minutes later, with a stop for, yes, a cookie on the way back, and he was pulling out his backpack again. He needed to catch up with Finn about team selection for Saturday's match before nightfall in New Zealand, and time was running short.

He was typing when he felt the pull of the tractor beam. Which was, of course, Casey's eyes on him. He raised his own. "What?"

"What do I do?" she asked.

"Uh . . . We wait. Two hours, like I said, then we can board the plane. There'll be a TV on there." That gave him an idea. "You can watch now, if you like."

She craned around and looked at the set on one wall. "It's not a show for kids."

He looked himself. News. Something was blowing up. "Play with your doll, then," he suggested.

She stared at him like he was stupid. He was getting used to that, too. "I can't just *play* with her. I can't even change her clothes, and I don't have my room or my special rug or my bunnies or anything, so there's no magic."

"Right." He closed his laptop again. Sacrifices had to be made. "Do you have a better idea?"

"You could be the monster," she said, "and I could be Moana."

Not happening. He'd be facing the police again for sure. He'd also become aware of the occasional filthy look from another passenger. What did they think people with kids should do, then? Disappear? "We don't have, uh, room," he said. "For me to be the monster. I require space. What else?"

"I could do a coloring book."

"Good. Do that."

"Except I don't have one. Or I could play with a L.O.L. Surprise House. It has eighty-five surprises." She sighed in a heartfelt way.

"Let me guess. You don't have that, either."

"No. I just have Moana. But you won't be the monster."

"Fine. Let's go find you something to do." He stashed his

laptop again and stood up, and she jumped up and put her hand into his.

Three stops and forty minutes later, they still didn't have a coloring book. They had, however, on the advice of the motherly lady at the last bookstore, ended up at the museum shop where they'd seen the dinosaur models.

It was a prehistoric-animal sticker set, in the end, not a coloring book. "I want *this* one," Casey said, picking it up and hugging it to her. "Because I can make worlds. Look. There's a lake and a forest and *everything.* And you can move the animals around. This is the best sticker set *ever.*"

"Good," he said. "Fine." Educational, quiet, and non-messy. Good to go.

She was lingering, though, at another shelf. "Look, you can make a crystal! It's so, so beautiful. It's like a *jewel.*" She was holding that box to her now, too. It made for a juggling act, considering Moana and the sticker book. "It's the best thing ever. It's—"

"Pink," he said. "I noticed. But you can't grow a crystal on a plane. Once we're on board, there'll be movies." They had a whole section for kids, didn't they? "You can watch all of them you want."

"My mommy says only half an hour a day. Except it could be a neck-seption."

"That's it," he said. "Definitely an exception. Everybody gets to watch movies on the plane." Except coaches who needed to catch up, because they had to hit the ground running the next day. Coaches had work to do.

He bought the crystal thing. You made a night light with it, he'd found on further study, and she was afraid of the dark. It only made sense. He also bought her an enormous book about prehistoric creatures, because it was educational, too, and it was quiet. She could look at the pictures, even if she couldn't read it. It had two hundred eight pages. There were a lot of pictures. He bought her an Antarctic Dinosaurs T-shirt as well. She was going to need clothes. It was summer in New Zealand, and not much in those bags of hers had been suitable. Her summer clothes had probably been too small for her, he realized, and her unfortunate pink suitcase was three-quarters empty.

The shirt had nothing to do with sparkles, flying horses, or pink. It was black, and she was captivated all the same. The dinosaur was big, it was roaring, and that seemed good enough for her. Which was fortunate, when he came to think about it, since she was going to have to live with him.

He did not, however, buy her a hatching dinosaur egg, grizzly-bear-paw slipper-boots, or a plush gold-sequined snake that was two meters long. Every man had his limit, and a sequined snake was his. "You're reaching," he told her when she held it up and opened her mouth to say, "I *love* it. It's the best snake *ever.*" He didn't even need to hear it.

Snake or not, she was set for the flight, at least once he handed over his card and signed away eighty-nine dollars. Problem solved.

$$\heartsuit\heartsuit\heartsuit$$

Sleep didn't come gradually that night. That day. Whatever it was, in real time. His body had no idea anymore. Instead, sleep slammed him right between the eyes. The last thing he remembered, he'd been working on his laptop, wearing his noise-canceling headphones and enjoying, in a masochistic sort of way, the feel of a long-haul jetliner at night, the collective weight of hundreds of sleeping bodies and the pleasure of being one of the only souls still awake. He hadn't made his seat into a bed, because he still felt perfectly alert, despite the beer he'd had before takeoff, once he'd got Casey settled. And the wine he'd had with dinner, once he'd got her settled again, after she'd told him, "Moana's not scared. She's just lonesome." They'd worked out, eventually, that Moana would be less lonesome if Rhys were in the seat in front of Casey rather than behind her, since she'd be able to see his head, at least while he was sitting up. Or, rather, Moana would be able to.

The flight attendants had been awesome, as usual. When he'd told Ilona, a veteran of Business Premier long-haul whom he'd first met in his playing days, "This is my daughter, Casey. It's her first flight," she hadn't blinked. She certainly hadn't looked like she'd be rushing to alert the media, however interested New Zealand would be in this story. Instead, she'd said, "Hi, Casey. Would you like to come into the cockpit before we take off, and meet the pilots?"

"Yes, please," Casey said, like somebody who knew what a cockpit was. Casey was nothing if not a quick learner.

"After that," Ilona said, "maybe we could find you a snack."

"Do you have any cookies?" A quick learner, indeed.

"I think we *do* have a cookie," Ilona said. "Let's go see."

Casey cast a triumphant glance at Rhys as she headed up the aisle with Ilona's hand on her shoulder, and he had to smile. She was getting another neck-seption, and he was going to finish this beer.

Tomorrow, though, once they got home? The regime would be back in place, as per usual. "Start as you mean to go on," that was his motto. Tomorrow, it would be back to discipline. A scheduled, organized, orderly life.

Meanwhile, he'd work a bit more, knock this out, and still catch six hours of sleep before breakfast.

That was one second. The next, he was being poked in the arm by a white horse with sparkling wings. It kept shoving its nose into him, no matter how many times he pushed it away.

Wait. It wasn't a horse. It was a lizard. It opened its mouth, showed its teeth, and poked him again.

*Dinosaur.*

*"Aaargh!"* It was a roar, or a yell, except that he couldn't hear it. His knees knocked into something hard, and his arm bashed against something else. His funny bone, that had been. The shock of the nerve being whacked reverberated all through his body and made his eyes water.

*Plane,* he realized. *Casey.* She'd been beside his seat, but when he'd yelled, she'd jumped back. She was hovering almost out of sight behind him, and he got his headphones off and his seatbelt unfastened, shoved his table back, ignored his elbow, twisted around, and asked, "What? Problem?"

Her hair was a tangled mess around her little face, and she was in her stockinged feet, the way she'd been when she'd gone to sleep after dinner, once Ilona had helped her make up her bed. When Rhys had assumed she was set for the night.

"I have to go to the bathroom," she said.

"Oh." He shoved his feet into his shoes and got himself out of the seat. His body felt like it weighed four hundred pounds. The last few days of travel had caught up at last, it seemed. Or maybe that was lack of sleep, no workout, two—possibly three, depending how you counted—drinks, and two-thirds of a deep-dish sausage pizza.

He said, "Straight up the aisle. I'm right behind you," and put a hand on her shoulder for good measure, since the plane was rocking a bit. He stopped at the toilet, and she stopped with him.

A second. Two. She turned around to look at him. He asked, "What?"

He realized what was different. She didn't have Moana. She stared up at him, and finally, he crouched down to her level and asked again, "What?"

"Where's the bathroom?" she asked.

"It's right here," he said, glad it was nothing more extreme. *Why did my mummy die,* or some other terrible middle-of-the-night question he wouldn't be able to answer. "Didn't you go earlier?"

"No," she said. "I didn't know where." She was wriggling. "I have to go really bad."

"Easy-peasy," he said, then stood up and opened the door. "Here you are." He should have taken her, he guessed. No, he *definitely* should have taken her. What had he been thinking? About having his dinner, that was what, and feeling virtuous for turning down the second dinner tray offered by Ilona, who appeared to think he was still playing and needed the calories. About finally getting to work, and about how good that glass of Pinot Noir was tasting, especially after Ilona topped it up.

Never mind. He was here now. Except she wasn't going in. And she was wriggling worse, her face screwing up in concentration.

He was in trouble.

"Go on," he said, waggling the door. "It's empty, see? Nobody in there but you. All yours."

She went inside, and he pulled the door closed with relief. He'd barely done it when he saw the handle shake. He opened it again and asked, "What?"

She said, "I opened up the toilet, and there was a very loud noise. I think the nairplane has a hole in it. I think you can fall down. Can I go in a regular bathroom? Please?"

He said, "You can't fall down. It's a bit loud, that's all. It's safe."

Her shoulders heaved, and her face crumpled. He was still holding the door open, and she was yanking on her jeans, her other hand fumbling to open the toilet seat. Dancing up and down on her toes in her stockinged feet, and, finally, starting to cry. He swore, stepped inside, and lifted her onto the seat just as she got her trousers down.

And still, she cried. Both hands clutching the seat, her jeans around her knees, her shoulders shaking, her eyes squeezed closed, and the tears streaming down her face. It was pathetic. It *hurt.*

He crouched down, put his hands on her skinny shoulders, and said, "It's OK. Don't cry. It's OK now." A lame response from a bloody clueless fella, because all she did was cry harder. Still nearly silently, shaking with sobs.

He tried to think what to do. He couldn't. He wished with all his heart for a flight attendant. A friendly mum. *Somebody.* There was nobody here but the two of them, though, so he did the only thing he could think of. He wrapped his arms around her, pulled her head into his chest, and waited for her to cry herself out. And tried to tell himself that he could handle this.

♡♡♡

When she was dressed again, and he'd helped her wash her hands and face and blow her nose, wishing once again that he knew what to do about her hair, he felt a bit better. It wasn't rocket science. It was one little girl who'd had to use the toilet. All he had to do was pay more attention. He'd be fine.

He said, "Better?"

She nodded, not looking up for once. Well, everybody had their low times, in the middle of the night, when the bad thoughts came. She said, "Except my feet are sticky."

Oh, bloody *hell.* This floor was disgusting. He got one of her socks off, then the other, stuffed them in the rubbish, and said, "Good job we didn't buy the pink sloth ones. You'd have been sad to see those go."

She said, still sniffling some, "But now my feet are *very* sticky."

"I reckon they are, but we can fix that." He picked her up, propped her against his shoulder, and stuck her feet into the sink, then pushed the button to turn on the tap.

She said, wiggling her toes, "You're not supposed to wash your *feet* in the *sink.*"

"We won't tell." He grinned at her in the mirror. She smiled back, first tentatively, then wider. Her nose was red, her cheeks were still tear-stained, and still, she smiled.

Something inside him went *Click,* like a locked door sliding open. Something small, but, at the same time, like he'd just been driven back in the tackle by a South African. Both things couldn't be true, but they were.

She looked so much like him, but it was more than that. It was that she *felt* like him. Even though she wasn't his. She hadn't cried once, and then, finally, she had. If she had to do that, he had to hold her.

He dried her feet, then mopped up her face some more and said, "I'm going to carry you out of here, so you don't get disgusting again."

She put her arm around his neck and said, "Because you're Maui." Then she rested her head against his shoulder and asked, "Do I have to sleep on a nairplane every night?"

"No," he said. "Just tonight. I have a regular bedroom for you at home. You'll see." She closed her eyes, and he smiled, opened the door, and ceded the space to an older, solidly built fella who muttered, "About time."

"Sorry, mate," Rhys said.

The man gave him a second look. A sharper one. "Aren't you Rhys Fletcher?"

"Yeh."

He had his mouth open to say, "See ya," but the man beat him to it. "I see you've got your hands full," he said. "Good luck at the Blues. See if you can keep any more of those fellas from heading overseas, will you?"

"Yeh," Rhys said. "Cheers, mate." He headed back to Casey's seat, but when he would have set her down on her bed, she hung on tighter.

"My mommy always reads me a story at night," she said. "So I don't have bad dreams."

"Have you been having bad dreams since your mum's been gone?" he asked.

Her arms tightened around his neck, and he felt her nod against his chest. "Well," he said over the lump in his throat, "I reckon we'd better read a story, then." He reached over and got the dinosaur book from the pocket beside her seat.

When he straightened, Ilona was behind him. He said, "One sec," then stepped back and into his seat so she could get by.

"All right?" she asked.

"Yeh. Bit of a rough patch, that's all. We're just going to read a story."

"Aw," she said. "The poor wee thing. Bit scary, on a plane for the first time. She's got such a look of you, hasn't she? Buckle up, though, will you? We're likely to hit a rough patch up ahead."

She knew he wasn't married anymore, he was sure. She

also probably knew that he and Victoria hadn't had kids. She was, in fact, putting two and two together, like everybody else would be.

Nothing but what he'd expected. He was all good. He didn't live his life for the media.

He did buckle them in, although it was a tight fit with Casey in his lap. After that, he switched on his overhead light, got his blanket out of the plastic wrap, draped it over the two of them, reclined his seat, then opened the book at random and began to read.

*A Velociraptor runs on her hind legs, her small, nimble forelegs with their razor-sharp middle claws held in front of her bounding body,* he murmured, as close to Casey's ear as he could manage, since you hardly wanted to shout this sort of thing at the whole plane. *She is hunting with her pack, and the stakes are higher today, because she has a nest full of young to feed. When the pack finds a herd of grazing Protoceratops, they quickly single one out: an older male, wandering at the back of the herd. One by one, they leap to the attack, forcing the much larger animal to turn in circles, trying to face them head-on with his armored neck frill, leaving his vulnerable body unprotected. He delivers a savage blow with his heavy tail, and a Velociraptor falls, but another leaps into its place, biting into the four-legged herbivore's belly with its dozens of saw-like teeth.*

Huh. A bit bloodthirsty. He stopped, and Casey sighed and murmured, "Read more."

No accounting for taste, he guessed.

*Today,* he read on, *the pack wins the battle, and our Velociraptor mother gorges on the unlucky Protoceratops, perhaps regurgitating part of her meal later, back at her nest, to feed her young, just as many birds do now. Tomorrow, the outcome may be different. A broken bone from a crashing tail or a dispute with another of its kind, and our Velociraptor's life in the fiercely competitive world of the late Cretaceous could come to a sudden end.*

"Sounds like rugby," he said.

Casey didn't answer. She was asleep.

# around the corner

"I'd enjoy family time so much more," Zora's brother Hayden complained on the phone on Thursday night, two days after Rhys had cancelled on her, "if it involved more margaritas and dancing and fewer school recitals and jigsaw puzzles. And I'm not even *mentioning* compulsory P.E. A treetop adventure park? You know what a devoted uncle I am, but allow me to say that I cannot wait until Isaiah's old enough to think that 'Sunday' means 'brunch' and not 'something I'd rather do at the gym, if I have to do it at all.' Here's an idea. Maybe the two of you would like to go to a gallery opening instead. Very avant-garde, and I may have a wee thing for the artist. Picture black-rimmed specs and bright blue eyes. Anyway, I thought you were going to see Sexy Rhys's new place on Sunday. He's bound to think that swinging from ropes is a brilliant way to spend his day off. Why don't you invite him instead?"

"He cancelled."

"Oh." A pause, and a different, more cautious tone when Hayden asked, "Why?"

"He said he was leaving town for a few days."

"I thought he was coaching the Blues. Aren't they playing their opener at Eden Park next week? Which shows you how much I love you, that I know that. I only *do* know it because I checked. And I only *checked* because you told me he was living here, in the same boringly leafy suburb as you, oddly enough, and that he'd asked you over to 'give me advice about my furniture.' I wondered at the time, 'Why is she telling me all this?'"

"I told you why. Because Isaiah dented his car, and I wanted to know how obligated I was."

"Yeh. See, I didn't *quite* believe you. Or him. *Everybody* was lying, in my humble opinion, except possibly Isaiah. No man with that many scars on his forehead invites a woman over because he wants advice on where to put his furniture. He doesn't care where he puts his furniture, as long as the couch faces the TV and the bed's big enough."

"Uncalled-for and stereotypical hetero-normativity." She thought that was pretty good.

"Except not, because I'd bet money it's true. So you're meant to believe that he's leaving town, even though he's got *just* a bit on the line here, being the new coach and all. He's sorted out where to put his couch and TV and doesn't need your opinion after all, so never mind?"

"That's what he said. So, you see—I need something to do on Sunday."

Hayden sighed. "Right. I will climb trees and buy the hamburgers and be an uncle, just because I love both of you, and somebody has to do it. I'd also love to tell Rhys Fletcher that he's as dodgy as his brother. I'd say I'd threaten bodily harm next time I see him, or at least hint at it, except that he'd kill me, so I won't. I'll tell you instead. Some men get off on jerking your chain. I wouldn't have said he was one of them. Too straightforward, I'd have said, but I'd have been wrong, because jerking women's chain seems to be a genetic trait."

"Dylan wasn't—" she started.

"Dylan was. You can tell Isaiah whatever you like. Don't try to tell me."

She rang off and wished she could believe her brother, that Rhys had been messing with her. The truth was, though, that he'd regretted making the date—the friendly breakfast invitation—as soon as he'd done it.

He'd been able to tell, that was why. He'd thought it over and had realized, *Wait. Something was off there.*

She'd been fine until he'd accidentally grabbed her, and she hadn't jumped away. His hands had closed over her in the dark, and she'd been . . .

Face it. She'd wanted, for that frozen moment, for his hand to move on her breast, his other hand to brush her hair away, and his mouth to come down on her neck. In that sensitive spot just below the hairline, where nobody's lips had touched her in so very long. That place that would make you shiver. She'd all but felt it happening.

It had been absolutely dark in the kitchen. So dark that you could pretend not to know who was behind you, except that the hard man behind her could never be anybody but Rhys, which meant that the anonymous, swept-away body she was hoping for was . . . herself.

And he'd jumped back like he'd been burned.

Then she'd made it worse by holding his wrist and wiping the spilled Indian food off his arm, laughing up at him like he was hers. Like it was foreplay. She'd shuddered later that night, thinking about it. For two reasons, unfortunately. Only one was embarrassment. The other was a rush of heat that flooded her body and refused to listen to reason.

She'd felt like she had her life together. She *did* have her life together. Whose life turned out the way they'd planned it? Nobody's. You rolled with life, or life rolled you.

She was a good mother, she was a good florist, and her business was growing, if slowly. She owned a home, and she made the mortgage payment every month without holding her breath and checking her bank balance, thanks to her decision to downsize. She'd installed her own Pink Batts and learned how to change out her own kitchen faucet, she'd spent last night researching how you retiled a kitchen floor—how hard could it be?—and if she'd thought she could do it without killing herself, she'd have learned to replace her own roof. And if she was tired, after ten long years, of being the only adult in the room—well, everybody was tired of something. You made your choices, at twenty and for all the years since, and you lived with them.

No matter what Hayden thought, nobody had twisted her arm.

♡♡♡

Just like nobody was twisting her arm now, except that they were. For all Hayden's complaining, he and Isaiah had conquered the first three courses in the treetop adventure park and, when she was thinking longingly of a lovely coffee and muffin, had moved on to the fourth one. The toughest one. Isaiah had said, "We can't leave *now,* Mum! This is the most fun part!" And Hayden, the rat, had said, "Yeh, Mum. Where's your sense of adventure?" Now, she was facing the highest, most wobbly swing bridge in the history of swing bridges, staring at a narrow wooden plank, barely wider than her foot, that you were meant to balance on whilst holding onto rope handrails, and reminding herself that she'd be clipped in the whole way, while her treacherous brother and son beat on their knees at the other side and chanted, "Zo-*ra!* Zo-*ra!*" At Hayden's instigation, she was sure. He was getting his revenge for being dragged along, and it *was* revenge, because she was going to have a heart attack.

"Afternoon," she heard from behind her.

"Oh," she said, and turned. "Hi."

Alistair Corcoran. Client. Plastic surgeon. Single father, as he'd happened to mention. And right now, welcome distraction.

He smiled. "Stuck?"

"Oh, no," she said. "A tiny attack of nerves, that's all. And my son and brother on the other side, being disgusted with me."

He laughed, but not in a bad way, so she smiled back.

*"Dad,"* a preteen girl, standing behind him on the platform, said with a sigh.

"Go on," Zora said, waving her past. She made a "Shoo" motion at Hayden and Isaiah, too. She had a perfect excuse for waiting now.

"This is my daughter, Ruby," Alistair said. "Ruby, this is Zora, who does the flowers for the office."

Ruby looked at Zora with absolutely zero enthusiasm, said, "Hello," and asked her father, "Are you coming?"

"In a moment," he said, and she sighed again, clipped in, and started across the bridge.

"Sorry," Alistair told Zora. "I think that was a divorced-dad thing. Electra could come into it, possibly. Also, she's eleven."

"No worries. You have a son as well, don't you?"

"I do. Six years old, and disgusted at not being tall enough to be allowed on this one. He's having an ice cream down below to console himself."

"Right," she said. "Well, I guess we'd better go on, then, or we'll keep everyone waiting."

She headed across, when Ruby was done. *Mind over matter.* The plank wobbled horribly, which she was sure meant something like, "Your core strength is sadly lacking." Hayden was right. Why would you choose recreation that accused you? It was like going shopping with a friend who pointed out your cellulite.

She made it, though. She had to, since Alistair was behind her. Speaking of cellulite.

How could you get naked with a plastic surgeon? You'd always be wondering whether he was thinking, when he touched your thighs, *If I offered her a discount, would she let me take care of that? Or would I have to offer it for free? A little liposuction . . .*

One extremely long, stomach-dropping swoop on a flying fox, a scramble across a ship's-net-type thing that was going to make every muscle ache tomorrow, and a final flying fox to the ground, and they were done. She may have staggered, coming off. Hayden may have laughed, too. Alistair didn't. He said, when he brought up the rear, "Good work, Zora. My florist turns out to be not only beautiful, but brave as well."

Ruby rolled her eyes, Zora could swear Hayden did, too, and Zora said, "Your florist is glad to be done."

"Coffee?" Alistair asked. "Lunch? I think we've all earned it."

Zora said, "You have no idea how I've been waiting for those words," and muttered to Hayden, while they walked to the cars, "Stop it. You keep saying I should get out."

He muttered back, "Not with somebody who wears plaid shorts."

Lunch, on the patio of a tiny café, was short and decidedly non-date-like, possibly due to Ruby's laser-like stare, and possibly because William, Alistair's son, was decidedly drooping. As they were finishing their coffee, though, Alistair said, "I feel lucky I ran into you, Zora, since I haven't been able to graduate past offering you a coffee in the office until now. I'm thinking dinner would be nice, though. Next Friday?"

"Yes," Zora said. "Fine." He had confidence, asking in front of everybody. Confidence was good.

He smiled. "Fortunately, I have your number. I'll text you, shall I?"

"Please," she said, and thought, *See? You can do this.*

In the car, though, Hayden sighed.

"What?" she asked, then checked the rearview mirror. Isaiah was watching a movie on her phone, with headphones in. Good. Hayden could be seriously inappropriate. "Who was saying I needed to get out? Who's been *badgering* me to get out?"

"He was wearing a golf shirt," Hayden complained.

"He has kind eyes," she countered.

"And a bald spot. Also a daughter who'll tell all her friends you're the wicked stepmother and hate you forever."

"I'm not marrying him. I'm going to dinner with him. I haven't been to dinner with a man in . . . Memory fails."

"Tell me what he does for a job. Wait. Rodeo cowboy. Firefighter. Volcanologist. Stunt driver."

"Are you finished?"

"Nearly. Demolition expert. There, I'm finished."

"And they say *women* are too picky. He's a plastic surgeon. Ha. Got you. He wears a white coat and tailored trousers. He subscribes to my top-end package *and* pays the bills on time, which is no surprise, since he has an office in Remuera and another on the North Shore, and whenever I deliver his flowers, he invites me into his absolutely gorgeous staff lounge—which has gray leather chairs, like his waiting room, probably made from the foreskin of a whale—offers me a coffee, and chats me up."

"Bite your tongue," he said. "Greenpeace is shocked. And yet, with all that, you've never said yes."

She was silent for a moment, and finally asked, "Can't steady and trustworthy be good, too? A man who you can be absolutely sure is never going to text you a photo of his junk or text, 'R U Up?' because he's bored and thinks you should stop by and fix that?"

"Maybe," he said, "if he's hot enough for you."

They were headed across the Harbour Bridge. To the left, sailboats tacked for the marina and home, and above them, white clouds scudded across a blue sky. It had been a gorgeous day. Another school term had started, summer was coming to an end, and you could think that was sad, if you'd made the most of your summer. Which she hadn't. Even though she lived in one of the most beautiful places in the world, and she knew it.

At ten o'clock this morning, on her way to collect Hayden, she'd delivered flowers for a wedding. The bride had been older than her, in her mid-thirties at least, far from model-thin, and wearing the kind of strapless white meringue that did nobody any favors. Her groom had had a bald spot of his own, and they'd both shone like somebody had lit them up. The bride had looked at her groom as if she'd never heard of cynicism, and he'd looked at her like he was marrying his best friend, his lover, and the light of his life.

"My taste for exciting, glamorous men hasn't necessarily steered me right so far," she said. "Maybe it's time to try something new."

"Once isn't a pattern," he said. "Once is a mistake."

She froze, then checked on Isaiah again. Hayden looked back, too. "He isn't listening," he said. "And you know—

every single time doesn't have to be True Love. Nobody's keeping score, and if they were, I'd say you've ticked all the boxes. You took care of your husband even when it got gruesome, and God knows he didn't deserve it. You're supporting yourself and Isaiah. You cook dinner every night and never run out of milk or bread. You're my role model for adulting. I'm going to say that, and then you're going to forget it, please, and not use it against me. But there's such a thing as having fun, too. Real fun, not forcing yourself to run about at the tops of trees when it scares you, because you think you should. And, yeh, I noticed. You're not even thirty-one yet, and sometimes, I think *you* think you're sixty. So I'm going to ask you. What do you want? Really want? What do you lie awake at night and wish for? Don't tell me 'security.' I don't believe you. Tell me the dirty thing, the secret thing. Tell me, and then go for it, because whatever it is, you need it, and you deserve it."

*Whoa.* She couldn't say this. Could she?

Hayden waited.

"I want . . ." she said, and forced herself to go on. "I want . . . I haven't worn a bikini in years. Summer's almost gone, and yet I just thought that anyway. I want to wear a bikini again, and not to care what anybody thinks about it. I want to start unbuttoning my shirt for a man, and to have him take over, because he can't wait. I want to lie down on the bed, have him come down over me, and know that he wants what he sees, and he can't believe he's getting it. I want to be thrilled. I want to lose my mind. And I can't believe I'm telling you this. But it's here." She clutched at her chest with one hand. "Sometimes, I feel like I'm screaming with it."

"You want to get laid," Hayden said. "So why not go out and do it? Why not go dancing, give into temptation for once, and get your freak on? Why not take a chance, and make a mistake?"

"Because," she said, "what I want most of all? I want to be in love. For real."

"Ah," he said. "Harder."

"Yeh." Now that it was here, it wouldn't stop. "I want my breath to catch. I want my heart to stop beating because he looked at me. I want his to do the same thing. I want to *believe* it. And I don't think I'm ever going to get it."

They were off the bridge now and nearly to Grey Lynn and Hayden's apartment. His life couldn't be more different from hers, and yet, as he looked at her, she thought he understood.

"I wouldn't be too sure," he said. "Saying it's the first step to getting it."

The tears were there, right behind her eyes. "You think?"

"Yeh," he said. "I do. It could be just around the corner. And if it comes? Maybe you'll see it. Maybe you'll open the door."

She turned into his street and pulled over, and he reached into the back seat, ruffled Isaiah's hair, and said, "See ya, mate."

Isaiah said—too loudly, because he was still wearing his headphones—"Bye. I had a very good time."

Hayden's smile was crooked, and he reached across the van, gave Zora a cuddle, and said, "Buy a bikini. Don't worry that summer's nearly over. Don't think that it costs too much. Buy it anyway. And don't listen to me. Listen to your heart instead. Walk around the corner. Open the door."

# princess flowers

She was in her flower shed, three days later, when her phone rang. Of course, she was hand-tying an arrangement at the time, a thanks-for-your-business gift for her most profitable client. It was the most inconvenient moment to be interrupted. She glanced at the screen.

*Rhys*

She should let voicemail pick up. She wasn't in a good place to talk to him, seeing as her unresolved sexual tension appeared to be an explosive force that could detonate at any time, and it had only got worse since Sunday.

She hadn't seen *that* coming. Or, more accurately, she hadn't seen it coming *back,* whatever she'd told Hayden. Maybe that was due to saying "yes" to Alistair and contemplating the daunting prospect of a man actually, possibly, kissing her on the lips, except it wasn't. She could contemplate that without any flutters at all. Alistair wasn't the problem.

And the fact that Rhys had clearly noticed was . . . what was the word?

Oh, yeh. "Humiliating." Or, possibly, "disastrous," if you looked at the issue on a continuing basis, since she was, as usual, about as mysterious and inscrutable as a puddle. If she saw him again, she was going to give it away, but how could she avoid seeing him again?

All of that went through her mind even as she set down the bouquet and picked up the phone. She'd be casual, that was all. Friendly. *Sisterly.*

"Hi," she said, focusing on making it easy-breezy. It came out as more of a shout. Whoops.

"Hi," Rhys said, sounding, as always, like he was talking while frowning, or after having chewed a bag of nails. "Can I come talk to you for a few minutes?"

"Uh . . . of course. Tonight, you mean?" Her heart needed to stop it. Right now. *Stop it,* she commanded. *You are a mother. A businesswoman. A solo entity. He's your husband's brother.* She was as successful as usual, too. Meaning, not at all.

"No," he said. "I was thinking about this afternoon, if you can. I could use some advice."

Oh. It was his new house after all, whatever Hayden had thought. He *had* said he needed advice, even though Rhys had never seemed like the type to ask anybody for advice about anything except, perhaps, his tackling technique. He was, as Dylan had complained enough times, a "bloody perfectionist" about rugby, a man who'd never heard of "good enough." She'd never thought he'd fuss about interior decoration, but it could be something else. Where to shop. Needing a plumber. His love life.

Please, not his love life.

"I'm arranging flowers at the moment," she said. "I could pop by tonight, though. With Isaiah," she hastened to add. "Aren't you at training, though?"

"If you can arrange and talk at the same time," he said, "I'll come there."

"Now? Oh. All right." He hadn't even answered the question about training. Why was that? It was *Wednesday.* Wednesday was the toughest training day, when you set the foundations for the game ahead. Why wouldn't he be there?

She knew coaches could get sacked, but before their first game, their first *season?* Surely not. That couldn't be performance. It would have to be something else. She hadn't seen even a rumor, though. Wouldn't it have come out?

If that was what it was, how much of a blow would it be to a man that proud? He'd come all the way from France to take this job, and had bought a house, presumably. Besides, nobody had ever sacked Rhys Fletcher from anything. They'd probably be afraid to. It had taken broken bones even to sideline him, back in his playing days, and his bones hadn't broken easily. Come to think of it, it had taken *major* broken bones. She could swear there'd been a rib or two in there that he'd ignored, and probably a finger taped to its neighbor, too.

"I need to leave at two in order to make my deliveries," she said, because it was the one thing she could grab hold of. "When were you thinking?"

"Right now."

She was wearing the following: a singlet, short shorts, a white chef's apron stained with dirt and plant juices, and jandals. It would be a reasonable enough look to make her deliveries to a few spas on a casual New Zealand summer day, once she got rid of the apron, pulled on an oversized cream cotton jacket, added some earrings, and fixed her hair. At the moment, that was piled on top of her head with a clip, she was sweating, and she was wearing zero makeup. In ten minutes, though, she could be presentable. "Fine," she said. "I'll be in my shed."

"See you." He rang off, and she stuck her flowers back into water as hastily as she could without damage and headed for the door.

She opened it, and there he was, his shoulders blocking out the light and the usual look on his face, like whatever he was doing next, he was already roaring his way toward it.

She stepped back and said, "Oh. You meant *now* now."

"Yeh. We were outside. Too soon?" He was still frowning, and he was holding somebody's hand. A girl of five or six, her curly dark hair wild around her face, her brows straight and dark, and her gaze intense.

A gaze that came from black-lashed hazel eyes.

It was hard to breathe. Zora's body had frozen up, and her mind couldn't put the pieces together.

"Hi," she said when she got her breath back. "I'm Zora. What's your name?" The girl was clutching a fashion-sized doll close to her body, and was wearing a pair of jeans that were a bit too short and surely warm for the day, and a black T-shirt that was too big, featuring a roaring dinosaur. Zora would have thought she was a boy, except that she so clearly wasn't.

"Casey Moana Hawk," the girl said.

"My daughter," Rhys said, absolutely unnecessarily.

"Come in. I was just fixing my flowers. Or go on into the house and make a cup of tea," Zora told Rhys, "and get something to eat as well, if you like. The door's open. I'd offer to help, but . . ." She cast a hand out at the arrangements on the work table. "It's my spa day."

*Get it together. Focus. This isn't about you.*

"I thought that generally involved nail varnish and a massage," Rhys said, with a hint of a smile, as if he had no idea what kind of blow he'd just dealt her. "Nah, we're good. We just had lunch."

"It was a sandwich," Casey said. "But I couldn't have a cookie, even though they had lots of cookies."

Zora wasn't sure how to answer that. She looked at Rhys, who told the girl, "You had two cookies yesterday, and a chocolate tart on the plane as well."

"That was *yesterday,* though," she said.

"Also," he said, "you didn't even finish your sandwich. You said you were full."

"That was my *regular* stomach," she said. "I still had room in my *dessert* stomach."

The corner of his mouth twitched, but he said gravely, "You've got me there. We'd better tell Zora about our day, and ask her our questions, because she looks busy."

"I am," Zora said. "But glad to have company." She wasn't.

Not Rhys, too. She'd always thought he was solid. That when he said something, it was true, and when he stood by somebody, it was real. He hadn't let Dylan down, ever. But a woman was different? A woman didn't count?

If this girl was—what? Five? Six? He'd have been engaged to Victoria, or married to her, when she was born. He'd asked

Victoria to marry him, had told her he loved her, and Victoria had known—she'd *known,* Zora was as sure of that as she'd ever been sure of anything—that his word was good. And then he'd gone on tour and thrown all that trust away.

Dylan had said it didn't mean anything, that everybody did it. She hadn't believed it was true, but here the truth was, literally staring her in the face. She said, hearing her voice shake and unable to prevent it, "Would you like to get up on the stool and watch, Casey?"

"Yes, please," the girl said, and Zora dragged it over, then got herself back into territory she knew something about. Flowers. She began with her bucket of hydrangeas, cutting them far up the stems and arranging them at the base of three round vases, letting the touch of the blossoms, the sweet-clove scent of the stock, the need to pay attention, distract her and soothe her, the same way they had at the very beginning. Which had been so much worse a time than this, however bad this felt, and she'd got through that, hadn't she? "My son used to use this when he helped me," she told Casey. "But he's got so tall now, he doesn't really need it. Isaiah's eight. How old are you? You'd be cousins, I guess. And to Maori, that's a big thing." She was talking too much, when really, all she had were a thousand questions, sitting like a leaden lump in her belly. Or maybe a fiery lump, because there was something else in there, too.

Face it. It was rage.

"I'm six," Casey said. "I'm in first grade, but they don't have it here. They say it's Year Two, but that would be second grade, because two and second are the same. But you have to do more things in second grade. It's really hard. I have a friend who's in second grade, and she says you have to read long words. I only know short words. My new school is a bad word, too."

"Titirangi Primary," Rhys said.

Zora had to smile, even through the rage. Her head was so confused. That accent was American. *What?* She said, "Isaiah's a pupil there as well. Never mind, you'll get used to saying it. It's Maori, that's all, and the bad words aren't the same in Maori. Titirangi means 'Fringe of heaven.' Really, it means 'Fringes of cloud in the sky,' but heaven sounds better. A new school could make you feel a bit nervous, but I'm guessing that after a few days, you'll find a spot where you fit. Most of the kids are pretty nice, I've found, and Isaiah will look out for you, too."

Whatever Rhys had done, it wasn't this little girl's fault. There were dark shadows under her eyes, her hair needed major taming, and all the same, she stood on her stool like she'd been planted here, and here was where she was staying.

"I wouldn't be nervous if I had rabbits," Casey said. "You can pet rabbits if you're sad, and they're very soft."

♡♡♡

Something was wrong. Everything Zora said was fine. It was just the look in her eyes, like the shutters had come down. That could be, though, because she'd caught the look in *his*.

When she'd opened the door, he'd thought at first, for one heart-stopping moment, that she wasn't wearing anything but the apron. Then she'd turned around, he'd seen the ribbed white singlet, the delicate blue ribbons of her bra straps beneath it, the tiny flowered shorts with their ruffled edges, the soft skin of her inner thighs and the slimness of her ankles, and he'd had another difficult moment. She wasn't any athletic hardbody, and there was no doubt she was little. But so nicely made.

This was about Casey, though. He'd tried to think who to ask, and Zora was the first person he'd thought of, possibly because she was the best mum he'd ever seen.

He still remembered how she'd looked when he'd come to see his nephew for the first time. She'd held the baby against her shoulder, her hand cradling his head with so much tenderness, it had made his heart twist. He'd seen the softness in her eyes and had wanted, with a pain that stabbed him right in the chest, for that to be his. Except that, of course, it wasn't. She was somebody's mum now. Somebody's wife.

His brother's.

*Right. Focusing.* He watched her shove pink and lavender blooms into the mound of white flowers she'd arranged in the vases—straight into the midst of the other flowers' multiple tiny blossoms, which wouldn't have been how he'd have thought you'd do it, but looked good anyway—and said, "Casey's moved here with me from Chicago, as her mum's died, which means our lives have undergone a . . . shift, you could call it. We're both having a new start. We went to enroll her in school today, and came up against a couple obstacles. And I told you," he said to Casey, "that we're working into the rabbits. We need to make sure they have a home first. We need to make sure *we* have a home first. The rabbits are coming."

Casey sighed in a martyred sort of way, like the drama queen she was. "I get to wear a uniform at school," she told Zora. "It's green, and you have to wear the same thing every day, because that's the rules, but you can wear a skirt or you can wear shorts. And you have to wear a special hat every day outside, because the sun is very strong, and it's the summer, but you still have to go to school. I never heard of going to school in the summer. What are you making?"

"My weekly floral arrangements for a chain of day spas," Zora said. "My Wednesday job. It has to be very special, because a spa is where you go to feel more beautiful. I've got the calla lilies and eucalyptus done for the front desks, in those vases at the back, which are more elegant, but I thought, this time, I'd do something more special for the lounges. This is hydrangeas, lisianthus, and orchids, with snowberries and blackberries, and some stock so it smells lovely."

"It's very pretty," Casey said.

"It is, isn't it? It's not sleek and modern, not like calla lilies, but I thought we'd try it anyway. One of the buildings used to be a bank, and it always looks like a palace to me. The table and the benchtops are made of limestone, and there are these gorgeous marble columns that are sort of cream and brown. They make me think about a throne room, or someplace else very beautiful. The couches are white, and the chandeliers are gold. I thought I'd go with something purely romantic, so you're lounging in your dressing gown, waiting for your facial or relaxing after your massage, sipping water with slices of cucumber in it and feeling like a princess."

"Like Cinderella," Casey said.

"Or something even better. A Russian princess, in the Marble Palace in St. Petersburg, wearing gold and rubies in her hair. And here." She picked up a cream-colored flower, cut it off short, threaded it through with a pin, and fastened it to Casey's black T-shirt. "Now you can pretend, too. This is lisianthus. So pretty."

"A bit like I always thought you looked," Rhys said. "A Russian princess."

Zora glanced at him, clearly startled, then laughed. "You did not."

Well, this was awkward. "Your eyes, I reckon," he muttered.

"So you're enrolled in school, and you have a uniform," Zora said to Casey, ignoring him. She was arranging stems of greenery like she knew exactly where they should go. Not stuck around the edge like he'd have assumed, but more haphazardly. "Sounds like you're well on your way. When did you get here?"

"This morning," Rhys said.

She set down her clippers. "This *morning?* As in, you flew here this morning? From the States?"

"From Chicago. That's where Casey was living with her mum."

"Did you even stop at your house?" Zora asked.

"Yeh, of course. We had to, didn't we, to drop off the bags."

Zora was all but rolling her eyes. Why? What should he have done instead? Casey needed to go to school, and he needed to go to work. Which reminded him. "But we have a wee problem," he said.

"You don't say. I can't imagine."

"School doesn't start until nine," he said, "and it ends at three. There are no spots open right now in after-school care, let alone what you do in the morning. Casey's on the waiting list, but meanwhile . . ."

"Because it's not the right time," Casey said. "All the kids have already started in Year Two, and I'm only halfway in first grade."

"I thought you might have some suggestions," Rhys said. "Know of someplace decent I could take her. I can't just bung her in anywhere. That's no good. Besides, I've realized that I'm going to need to get somebody to stay at the house, for when I'm off with the team, so I probably shouldn't make any commitments, day-care-wise."

Casey looked up at him, and he realized that he should have said something about that. What, though? *By the way, I realize I'm the only parent you now have, and you don't know me, but I'll only be around half the time?*

"You know what?" Zora told Casey. "Let's go pick you some mandarins. I have a tree. They're better than cookies, I think. There's a lovely hammock in the garden where you can lie and eat them while you listen to the birds. You could even take a nap, if you like."

"I don't take naps," Casey said. "I'm not a baby."

"Of course not," Zora said. "You're six. You can have a wee rest, though."

"Or I could help you with your princess flowers," Casey said.

"Next time," Zora said, "I promise I'll let you help with the princess flowers. Just now, though, I need to talk to your dad."

Rhys did not have a good feeling.

# a disaster as a liar

Rhys leaned up against one end of the long table with his arms folded, his usual stance, and watched Zora work.

She wasn't lighting into him the way he'd expected. In fact, she wasn't saying anything. Gathering her forces, he suspected.

Outside, the air was warm, the breeze soft, and Casey, when he'd peeked out there to check, was lying in the hammock, one ankle over her knee and her dinosaur book in her lap, looking right at home and not one bit tentative.

If not for that moment in the airplane toilet, he wouldn't have known what was under the toughness. He *did* know, though, and he needed to get her set, so she wouldn't have to worry and she wouldn't have to cry. Worrying was his job, not hers, and if she did have to cry, he needed to be there when she did.

Her mum must have been something. She must have been special. And yet they'd been two more people Dylan had thrown away.

All of that was why he was here, in the cool of the shed, which was scented the same way Zora's van had been, a mix of spicy and sweet. Zora's motions were absolutely assured as she cut the stems of more white and lavender multi-petaled flowers that looked a bit like roses, but weren't, then arranged them the same way she'd done with the others, straight into the midst of the other flowers. She started on some deeper purple orchids, and the whole thing looked even better. He said, "You don't do it symmetrically."

"No." She glanced at him, then away. "It looks better like this. Less formal. More of a cottage garden effect. Lush and romantic, that's the idea, especially when I add the snowberries and a few blackberries. Texture and color and contrast, and making it all blend together as a whole."

"I believe you. It looks good. I just didn't realize how it . . . worked." He'd never thought about flowers much. Flowers were what you sent when you were gone on tour, or what you brought home on Friday night. At which time you picked them up from the shop, already put together and wrapped in plastic. Flowers were easy points, but they didn't normally have this kind of—well, sensuality. The way she'd arranged them, the ones she'd chosen—it was as different from a dozen red roses and some ferns as a gold chain around a woman's neck was different from a rope of pearls hanging down her bare back.

The ones she'd already done were interesting, too. Frankly sexual, if you asked him. The lilies, or whatever they were, had a fuzzy yellow nub inside, and a single folded, heart-shaped white petal opening around it in a delicate frill. That was nice, and so were the eucalyptus leaves around them, their solid gray-green contrasting with the fragility of the pussy flowers.

Whoops. *Do not say "pussy,"* he reminded himself. It had been too long since he'd been married, probably. He was losing his civilization skills.

He could get behind giving something sexy like that, though, or like the other thing she was doing, with the orchids and all. For a Russian princess, she'd said, with gold and rubies in her hair. There was a word for it. "Sumptuous," maybe. He could try saying that, if he didn't think she'd laugh. Better than "pussy," anyway.

Instead of saying either, he asked, "What is it about pearls?"

"What?" She looked startled again.

"Why do pearls look like something your grandmother would have on, if you wear them in the front, and nothing like that if you wear them in the back?"

"Pardon?" She was staring at him like he'd lost his mind. "Do you wear pearls often? Are you asking for fashion advice?"

"Sorry. Train of thought derailed. Never mind." He shook his head, trying to clear it. He was getting fuzzy.

"To answer your question," she said, "I don't know anybody who does after-school child care."

Her movements had got a bit stabby, surely, with the flowers. They were getting into it, then. "Oh." That was all he could think of to say. He tried to summon up some energy, and some thought. He blanked. "Well, I'll . . . Dunno what I'll do, actually." He rubbed a hand over his jaw. When he'd found out about Casey, he'd thought, *I'll go get her. I'll handle it.* He hadn't realized how much "handling" it was going to take. He hadn't thought it through, either because he hadn't wanted to, or because he hadn't known what would be involved. Or both.

She turned away from the flowers with a sigh and set a palm on the table. "I'll watch her. Of course I'll watch her, until you find somebody."

"You will?" He blinked. He wasn't going to say, "That's not necessary." He was running out of choices.

"Of course I will. That little girl, losing her mum, having to move to a new country . . ." She went back to the flowers again, tweaking and arranging, perfecting what he'd have thought was finished. "How often have you visited her? How often has she visited you?"

"Uh . . . never. I found out about her mum dying early last week, and I went and got her. And here we are."

Her hands stopped, then started up again. "You've *never* seen her?"

No good way to dress this one up. "No."

"And yet she's clearly yours. Did you know about her? I don't know why I'm asking. Which answer is going to be better? Neither. They're both bloody awful. In one, you're absolutely thoughtless, and in the other, you're absolutely uncaring." She said the last bit like she was talking to herself.

Oh, bugger. He hadn't even thought of what she'd think of him. He hadn't thought about counting backward, or what any rugby player's wife would imagine. What *Dylan's* wife would imagine. He was working out how to answer when she said, sounding calmer, if no happier, "I don't want to know, not really. I don't need to, not to look after her. Now that I know you'd never even *seen* her." She was lying to herself, because she was clearly getting worked up again. She apparently did need to know.

"I did know she was mine," he said. "I, uh, paid. Child support. But her mum, uh . . . I . . . it was complicated."

He should have thought of a better lie. Some story of how her mum had refused him access, but he'd sent Casey long, loving letters and bought her a pony for her fifth birthday. Except that Casey would have rubbished it, so there you were. He was stuck with the almost-truth.

"I can imagine," Zora said. "Does Victoria know?"

He was casting about for a lie. *Some* lie. The problem was, he was a disaster as a liar. When they'd been kids, even as Dylan was smiling charmingly and spinning a much preferable story, Rhys had always been caught, flat-footed and stolid, with the unpalatable truth. What had happened to the feijoas off the neighbor's tree? A possum had got up in the tree, Dylan would say, and a cat had gone after it. They'd had a royal battle, and half the fruits had been knocked down, but the possum had got away. Dylan had tried to pick the feijoas up and put them in a sack, but the other kids had come along and started eating them, and they hadn't listened when he'd told them to stop.

That time, their Nan had sighed and looked at Rhys, and he'd said, "We picked them and ate them."

They'd got a hiding, and Dylan had told Rhys tearfully, afterwards, "She was *believing* me. Why do you always have to tell?" He couldn't have explained. He was built that way, that was all. He had no twisty spaces inside.

Except, now, he looked like he did have them. And he *still* couldn't think of a lie. If that wasn't the worst of both worlds, he didn't know what was.

"No," he said. "Victoria doesn't know. Reckon she will now, because I'll have to tell her."

"Well, yes," Zora said, back to tweaking her flowers, "I'd say so. You wouldn't want her to base her life, all her memories, on a lie. You wouldn't want her to . . ."

Her hands were trembling. He wanted to take hold of one of them, to pull her in and hold her close, the same way he'd done once before, almost the only time he'd ever touched her. He wanted to wrap his arms around her and tell her, *Yeh, he was a bastard, but he loved you. Just not enough. You deserved better.*

"You're right," he said instead. He didn't say, "I'm sorry." That had been Dylan's other talent: apologizing like his heart was broken to have broken yours, and he'd never do it again. He'd always meant it, too, Rhys would swear. At the time. He was sure Zora had heard that enough, so instead, he said, "I'll take her home, I guess, and get her things unpacked. Sort out dinner and so forth. I'll bring her tomorrow. Seven-thirty OK?"

Zora sighed. "Rhys. I can tell she's exhausted, but how much sleep have *you* had?"

He ran his hand over his jaw again. He'd shaved to meet the social worker, whose name he somehow couldn't bring up anymore, but not since then. His eyes felt as scratchy as his face, and his muscles ached from lack of use and the discomforts of travel. "Oh, not so much. I'm good, but Casey's a bit tired, you're right."

"You're not good," she said. "You're both practically falling over, and are you telling me you've got *nothing* for her at home?"

"I barely have anything for *me* at home," he admitted. He had sheets on his bed, and that was about it. He wasn't sure that his milk wouldn't have gone off by now. How long had he been gone? And Casey needed . . . He was blanking again. He couldn't even think what she needed.

Zora said, "Help me carry these to the van. I'll make my deliveries, and I'll pick up a few things for her on the way back. Am I guessing that you don't have anything for her hair?"

"There's a brush. I told her to brush it."

She stared at him, then laughed. "Rhys. *You* have to brush it. She'll never get through all that hair. What clothes does she have to wear after school?"

"A few things. Mostly winter jumpers and jeans, a couple dresses. Warm ones, though. It was winter there."

"What size is she?"

"Uh . . . not sure. Small?"

She didn't roll her eyes, but he suspected she wanted to. "Take the flowers to the van and shove them into the pasteboard holders back there so they won't spill. I'll find out."

"How?"

"I'll look at the tags, of course."

When he came back from loading the van, though, and went to find Zora, Casey was fast asleep, turned onto her side with her face buried in the fabric folds of the hammock and her fist still clutching Moana tight. Zora had picked up the dinosaur book and was holding it, looking down at the girl. Thinking what, Rhys had no idea. He said, keeping his voice down, "Can you guess, on the clothes?"

"Yeh. I can. Let her sleep. Except that I need these." She eased off Casey's trainers and peeked inside. Looking for the size, he guessed.

He hesitated, then said, "I don't want her to wake up and be scared. That happened on the plane. I'll put her on your couch instead. At least if she wakes up, I'll be there."

He lifted her into his arms. She made a protesting sound, nothing but a broken-off murmur, snuggled into him more tightly, her head on his shoulder, and went limp again. Zora followed behind him with the book and set it on the coffee table while he laid Casey gently down on the couch and pulled a cotton throw over her. Zora said, keeping her voice down,

"If I'm not back before Isaiah comes home, tell him I'll be here soon. We'll talk about the rest later."

♡♡♡

She delivered her flowers with the radio turned up, and when that didn't work, she sang along. No point in thinking too much, or, rather, a wonderful time to think about the six hundred dollars every week's spa-flowers subscription brought her. The lovely thing about Anna Pemberly, the owner, was that she wanted everything high-end. "No carnations" and "use your own judgment"— those were six words that brought joy to a florist's heart.

When she'd finished her deliveries and was wandering the girls' aisles at Cotton On in New Lynn, though, the thoughts came back. And as always when it came to Rhys, they were confused.

He'd never seen his daughter, and yet he'd picked her up like she was precious. When he'd covered her with the blanket, Zora's heart had melted a little. There was still the cheating and lying he'd done, though, not to mention the non-visiting, and how to reconcile that with everything she'd supposed him to be. It wasn't her business, but how could she help thinking about it?

Never mind. She forced herself to focus instead on the unexpected pleasure of shopping for little-girl clothes, of balancing Casey's dinosaur T-shirt against her fascination with the princess flowers, and doing her best to shop for both sides of her. Casey wasn't hers, but she'd pretend, just for a few minutes. Both Casey and Rhys clearly needed the help, and for once, she didn't even have to worry about the budget.

She was late getting back, as she'd expected, once she'd made another stop at Pak 'n' Save. She saw them all as soon as she pulled into the drive, and once she did, she got out to get a better look.

Casey, still with the flower pinned to her dinosaur shirt,

was running full-tilt across the grass, her curly hair bouncing around her shoulders and a rugby ball under her arm. Rhys was just behind her, calling, "Chuck it over." She did, in a wild pass that made Zora smile, and Rhys adjusted his stride, stuck a hand out and caught the ball like it had Velcro on it, and flicked it behind his back, one-handed, to Isaiah. "Good one," he called, when her son caught it. Isaiah turned and ran in the other direction, since they were all about to crash into the bushes, but Casey tripped. Rhys scooped her up in one big arm before she could fall, turned around just that fast, set her down again, and said something. Probably, knowing Rhys, something like, "No forward passes." Casey took off, and Rhys jogged over to Zora with a grin on his face, looking like a buccaneer taking a night off from ferocity, and said, "Hi. How'd you go? Here, let me get those."

He reached for her grocery bags, and she handed them over. "I thought you'd need dinner," she said, ignoring, as best she could, that other side of *him,* the one she'd never seen before, that was making her go a bit goopy inside. Not to mention the size of his arms in the white T-shirt, or the contrast it made with his golden-brown skin and the blue-black tattoo. He must have had it on under the long-sleeved dress shirt he'd been wearing earlier. She also didn't look at his rear view when he leaped up the stairs into the house, taking them two at a time, or the breadth of his shoulders. Much.

"Some of this is for you," she said when he'd set the groceries down on the benchtop. "Milk, bread, butter, eggs, bacon. The essentials. You said you didn't have anything," she reminded him when he looked surprised. "So I thought, as I had to pop by anyway to get a few things for tonight . . ."

"Good of you," he said. "Anything else out in the van?"

She couldn't help laughing. "Heaps. There was dinner, and then there was Casey. I could've gone a little wild."

"I'll go get it," he said, "and then we can sort out what I owe you."

When he came back, he was carrying at least eight bags at

once. "Bring in the vases as well?" he asked. "I noticed you had a collection out there."

"Yes, please. Put them in the shed." What a luxury it was to have somebody to carry in your groceries and help empty out your van. Bonus points for looking so good doing it.

Five minutes, and Rhys was back. "I gave them a bit of a scrub," he said, "and put them in the rack to dry. They looked like they needed it."

"Oh." Well, *this* was confusing. "I was thinking how nice it was to have that kind of help, but now, you're just spoiling me."

His eyes were so warm, and she was getting a little lost in the green and gold of them, and the contrast with his hair and skin. "Could be. Could be you deserve some spoiling, too. What can I do?"

"Take the skin off the chicken breasts, if you're offering. Never my favorite thing." That hadn't been flirty. He was concerned, that was all. He'd said as much. His sense of responsibility was as oversized as the rest of him, even for somebody who didn't belong to him. Like, say, her.

"I'm offering." He moved around her and washed his hands at the sink, careful not to touch her in the confined space, she noticed. Which was good. The other night had been unfortunate, but this was a new start. Not that she needed one, now that she knew enough about him to get over her inconvenient near-obsession.

It would have been easier, though, if he hadn't smelled so good when he got close. Like cedar and sandalwood and clean man. It was faint, but it was there. She hadn't noticed it the other night, probably because the house had smelled like curry, but she was noticing it now.

She said, still unpacking groceries, "You took a shower when you got home."

He looked up, then smiled. Slowly. Bloody hell, but he had a good smile, sexy and warm. "Yeh," he said, "I did. But then, I've been bathing regularly ever since I turned thirty."

She had to laugh. "Sorry. That came out wrong. It's just

that you, ah . . . that you smell good, so I . . ." She waved a bag of spinach about in a random matter. "I'm, ah, a florist, so . . ." This was not going well.

"Shower gel," he said. "Somebody bought me some once, and it seemed to be appreciated, so I've kept on. You haven't discovered my secret perfume habit, no worries. It works, though, you think?"

"Yes," she said. "Nice. Manly." She so needed to find another subject. Also, "it seemed to be appreciated?" That was a reminder, if she'd needed one, that he'd never suffered for lack of female attention. He'd said he'd taken his ring off fast, once he and Victoria had split. She'd just bet. "Casey woke up, eh." Another dead obvious statement, but what could you do. She wasn't in her best form.

"She did. We both did, in fact, when Isaiah came home." He dumped the chicken skins in the rubbish and handed her the packet with the meat. "Seems I sat down and more or less passed out."

"I shouldn't wonder. So you decided to play rugby. Make a cup of tea, if you like."

"It seemed like a good way to wake up. And I will, thanks. D'you want one?"

"Sure." It was nice to work in a kitchen with somebody. She'd forgotten that, too, or maybe she'd never known it. Dylan hadn't been much for cooking.

"Isaiah's playing on the wing, he told me," Rhys said. "He's fast, but that's no surprise. Got good hands, too."

"You'd know, I guess. He enjoys it, but it's not a passion. Which is maybe just as well."

"Rugby can be a ticket out," he said, "but Isaiah doesn't need a ticket."

"No. He doesn't." Not like Rhys had, or Dylan. Why was Dylan always "less so?" Because Rhys had been older, probably, and protective. Always.

They'd been with their mum, first, and then their grandmother, their dad's mum. And finally, Rhys had gone with his dad across the ditch to Aussie, because Tana Fletcher had been doing construction on the Gold Coast, and had taken his near-teenage son to live with him. Abruptly, Dylan had said, and unexpectedly. Dylan had felt left out and left behind, but Zora suspected that Rhys had been the one who'd been alone.

He'd picked up Rugby League out there as easily as he'd played Union until then, and by the age of nineteen, he'd already begun to establish himself as a battering ram, impossible to put away. The newspapers, Dylan had told her, half-proud and half-resentful, had been full of him, and so had the nightclubs, because Rhys had worked hard and played harder, throwing himself into the higher-profile League scene the same way he threw himself into everything.

It wasn't easy to see the partier in the solid man leaning against her kitchen cabinets, his muscular arms crossed over his broad chest, talking about his nephew and focusing on this moment, this issue, this responsibility. Casey was proof, though, that the partier was still there.

He was silent for a minute, and she finished putting away the groceries, lined up the ingredients for tonight's dinner with more precision than required, and wondered what to say next.

"You've done a good job with him," he said. "I've always thought so. You're a great mum."

"Thank you." It was nice. It just wasn't exactly sexy.

Fortunately, Isaiah and Casey chose that minute to burst through the door. "Mum!" Isaiah said, toeing off his trainers. "Casey moved here all the way from Chicago, and she's my cousin, did you know? I didn't know I *had* a cousin. Chicago is the biggest city in Illinois, but it's not the capital. It's far north, so it's very cold, compared to here. Because of latitude, and also, it's on one of the biggest lakes in the world. It's called Lake Michigan, even though Chicago isn't in Michigan, it's in Illinois."

"Geography is another fascination," Zora told Rhys.

"You need to take your shoes off," Isaiah told Casey.

"How come?" she asked.

"Because it's in the house."

"It's a New Zealand thing," Zora said. "A Maori thing. Besides, I have some surprises to show you, and you may need to have your shoes off to fully appreciate them. Let's go into the lounge. Rhys, you could bring those shopping bags from Cotton On."

She'd tried to restrain herself, thinking that Rhys could take Casey shopping later, but the clothes had been so cute. A pair of denim shorts with lace filling in the V-shaped cutouts on either side, a blue pair with flowers, and a red pair with different flowers, just because you could never have too many flowers. A pair of gray capri leggings with pink butterflies flying across the bottoms, and a pink pair with flowers, because . . . see the note on flowers. A red T-shirt with a glittery star on the front, a black-and-white-polka-dotted long-sleeve one with a message spelled out in pink, *Girls Can,* that would be perfect with the pink leggings, an adorable gray one with an enormous picture of Mickey Mouse printed across the front, and another one, that she hadn't been able to resist and that she hoped wasn't too girly for Casey, that was white with pink trim and featured a sparkling unicorn rearing up on its hind legs, its extravagant mane and tail curling like Casey's own hair. And matching socks for all of it, of course. You needed matching socks, and Rhys would never know it.

The unicorn shirt was the one Casey grabbed. "I *love* it," she said. "I want to wear it tomorrow, for when I go to school in Year Two, but I have to wear a uniform instead. There's even a different uniform for P.E. So I have to wear *two* uniforms."

"You change when you get home," Isaiah said. "Like me. You can wear it then."

"Except I'm supposed to come here after school," Casey said. "It's like day care. You don't change in day care."

"Of course you do," Zora said. "It's not day care. It's your auntie's house, which is me, just like Isaiah is your cousin. You'll have to change, if you're going to help me with my flowers and play outside." However she felt about Rhys, how could she take it out on this little girl? "You leave a few things here for now. The unicorn shirt, and which shorts?"

"These ones," Casey said, looking excited, pointing to the jean shorts with lace. Zora guessed the princess flowers hadn't been a momentary fascination.

"Best for last," she announced. "I saw that you had trainers for running, and I assumed your . . ." She had to stop for a second to say it. "Your dad bought your school shoes, but girls need fun shoes, too." She pulled them out of a bag. A pair of sparkly silver trainers that made Casey's eyes go wide, and a pair of pale-blue jellies. "Also," she said, "togs, because you never know when you'll need to take a swim." She'd chosen a blue-and-white-striped top with sleeves, for sun protection, and boy-shorts bottoms. The top was adorned with a red anchor, so the whole thing looked like a sailor suit. Fun, but practical, too. And a pair of cute shortie PJ's, with Mickey and Minnie on the top and yellow polka dots below.

"She'll need more, obviously," she told Rhys, who looked at her like a deer in the headlights at the thought, "but this will get her started. And—" One more bag. "Hair. I got clips, and elastics and scrunchies, and some pretty bows that will look gorgeous on a high pony, as well as a new brush and comb, just in case, and a spray bottle that you can fill with warm water, helpful for styling. And I thought, Casey, since we have time before dinner, we could give your dad a lesson in how to fix your hair."

# not your life

Twenty minutes later, Casey sighed and said, "You're not very good at this."

"Oi," Rhys said. "I'm a beginner. You don't coach a beginner like that. Give a fella a chance to practice. Nobody's good first time out of the chute."

"You're still pulling," Casey informed him. She made a face that was surely more dramatic than the occasion warranted. *"Ow."*

She was standing on a kitchen chair, in front of the bathroom mirror. She was half his height and about a fifth of his weight, but there was no question which of them thought she was the Queen Bee here. He should work on that. He'd do better tomorrow, when they were rested.

Zora said, "You'll want to grab her hair tighter up above so you can work the tangles out below without pulling." She put her hand over his. "Up here. See?"

"You could sound less amused," he told her.

"Oh," she said, "I don't think I could." She was laughing at him, in fact, in the mirror, and she was much too close. She'd said he smelled good? So did she. It wasn't anything strong, just faintly floral, which made sense. Roses, maybe. He wasn't going to tell her so. Very bad idea.

Isaiah said, "You could get your hair cut very short, Casey, and then you wouldn't have to do all that. Girls have short hair sometimes."

Casey rolled her eyes. Zora rolled hers, too. They were a

matched set. "No, she couldn't," Zora explained, "because then she won't be able to use all her hair clips and bows." Which sounded like a wonderful idea to Rhys. Taming Casey's hair was like pruning blackberries.

"Right," he said, "that's the tangles out, I think. It's a bit . . . wild, though." He looked at Casey's hair dubiously. It was, in fact, standing out almost horizontally from her head.

"We'll use this for now," Zora said, slapping a bottle of something into his hand like a nurse in the operating theater, which summed up how this felt. Generally, though, you had some training before you tried surgery for the first time. "But you'll want to pick up some shampoo and conditioner for her. Detangler, also, and a curl cream."

"A *what?*"

"I'll write it down. Brands, maybe, and where to buy the good stuff. I'll text it to you, so when you're panicking in the store, you can text me back." She was laughing at him again.

"I'm going to be making a special shopping trip, aren't I?" he asked.

"Oh, probably." She didn't have to sound so happy about it.

He spritzed Casey's head with the stuff in the bottle, and Zora said, "Put your hand over her forehead so it doesn't get in her eyes. That's a detangler, and it adds shine. It's what I use on my own hair. Don't brush any more, either. That's how you get frizz. Work it in gently with the comb instead. You'll want to comb her hair after you wash it, using the detangler, and then use a bit of the conditioning cream as you work her style. You brush as little as possible, like making pancakes."

He set the bottle down and met Isaiah's gaze in the mirror. The boy gave an exaggerated shrug and made an *"I don't know"* face, and Rhys said, "The pancake reference is lost on us."

"Men think, when they cook anything, that they should stir it thoroughly," Zora said. "Like they're mixing paint. But if you're making pancakes or muffins, you only stir it a bit, and leave some lumps. The texture's better. Call it 'a light hand.' Otherwise, you may as well be cooking up wallpaper paste. That's how you work with this kind of hair, too."

"I like muffins," Casey said, to his absolute non-surprise. "Do you know how to make muffins?" she asked Rhys. "I like chocolate chip ones the best."

"No," he said, combing the detangler into her overabundance of hair, which kept trying to fly away. It was soft, though, like holding a baby duck. "I don't. I just found out that I need four products in order to comb your hair. I'm reeling here. How long is all of this going to take me? I'm going to have to set my alarm earlier."

"Whingeing," Zora said.

"Yeh. Tell me what to do next. I'm definitely going to need the text, too. And possibly a step-by-step guide."

"Text how to make muffins, too," Casey piped up.

"She can text it," Rhys said, "but I'm not doing it. There's a limit, and doing your hair is mine. This is madness. I comb my hair, rub some stuff into it if I'm feeling flash, and I'm done. Groomed." He met Zora's gaze again. "Don't say it."

"What?" She was trying not to smile, and it wasn't working.

"Not *well* groomed. No worries, I'm getting my hair cut."

"Oh, I don't know," she said. "The wild-man look's working for you, I'd say. You present a complete picture."

"Your hair's kind of messy, though," Casey said. "Maybe Zora can give you lessons, too."

"Thank you," he said. "Your feedback is noted. I'll point out here that I used to have a bar of soap in the shower and call it good. I'm practically a metrosexual now. I'm aggrieved at your vote of no confidence."

When Casey climbed down from her stool, her hair *was* in a plait, and it *did* have clips at the sides. Of course, Casey had poked at various non-smooth spots and said dubiously, "It has some lumps in it," but he'd answered, "I'll do better tomorrow." He *was* going to have to set his alarm earlier.

Zora told him, "Take it out of that plait before bed and do a loose one, low down. It'll be more comfortable for her to sleep with, and you won't have to detangle so much in the morning."

"I just put it in," Rhys said. "Now I have to take it out?"

"But think how much more you'll appreciate the effort women go to," Zora said. "Just wait until it's makeup time. Also, I didn't buy any dresses. You have so many surprises in store." Sounding saucy again, the way she'd used to be, and it made him smile.

"Don't tell me," he said. "I'm a man with lessons to learn, it's clear."

"Come on, Casey," Isaiah said. "Let's do a puzzle. I'm glad I don't have long hair. Girls are weird."

Rhys blew his breath out, once they'd left the room, cleaned up the explosion of hair elastics, bows, and clips that had somehow happened on the counter, and asked Zora, "Here's one that's been bothering me. Do I need to help her do the hair-washing and so forth?"

"Yes," Zora said, "you do. She won't get all the shampoo and conditioner washed out by herself, or the other products worked in properly. You teach her as you go, though. Coach her, so she can do it herself later on. Could be a few years before she can do it all."

A few *years?* What were they coaching here, Olympic gymnastics? "Right," he said. "But . . ." He wasn't sure how to say this. The bath was small, and Zora was right there, watching him in the mirror. She wasn't wearing the apron anymore, or the jacket she'd thrown on before going out, either. Nothing but that white singlet, which wasn't as high-cut or as opaque as it might have been, the flirty, floaty little shorts, and bare feet. Her bra straps were showing again, and so was her pale-blue bra. Faintly, but he could see it through her shirt. Her toenails, he'd happened to notice, were painted the delicate pink of the inside of a conch shell. Her fingernails weren't, because she worked with her hands, he guessed, but her hands were pretty anyway, and her feet were prettier.

He had it bad. Also, he'd forgotten what he'd been talking about.

She wasn't looking at him, or she was. They were both looking in the mirror. He never let himself stare at her like this, but right now, there was nowhere else to look.

It took her a minute to answer. Maybe she'd forgotten, too. He could see her breasts rising and falling with her breath. It wasn't that he meant to look, but there she was. Rounded arms, dark waves of hair that looked so soft, that sexy fringe over her eyes, and, bloody hell, that sweet, kissable mouth. She had the best mouth he'd ever seen. How could he not stare at that?

Finally, she said, "Pardon?" Oh. She'd noticed him staring.

"Uh . . . right. Helping Casey with her hair."

She turned away. He was sorry, and he was glad. Mostly, though, he was sorry. "Come on in and help me with dinner," she said, "if you have any energy left. And, yeh, you can help her in the bath, or the shower. You're her dad. It's all right, and it's your job. If you'd had her all along, it would be nothing but natural. Although I don't think Dylan ever gave Isaiah his bath."

Rhys didn't want to hear about his brother. He didn't want to *think* about his brother, or the chances Dylan had missed all down the road. He especially didn't want to think about how he'd have done it differently, if all of them had been his. He followed Zora into the kitchen, washed his hands, accepted the plastic wrap and meat mallet from her, and took out his frustrations on three unfortunate chicken breasts. He pounded one all the way through, in fact, ripping it to shreds before he realized he was going too hard and eased off. Zora filled a huge soup kettle with water, but when she went to lift it out of the sink, he stepped over and said, "Let me."

"I can do it," she said.

"I know you can. But please let me."

She did, and he felt obscurely better. She turned the fire on under the kettle, put the lid on, and said, "Pasta with pesto sauce, breaded chicken breasts sliced into strips on top, spinach salad with dried cherries and almonds. Twenty-five minutes. OK?"

"Brilliant," he said.

"You can bread the chicken, then."

He did it, following her instructions, while she made salad dressing, and tried not to feel too cozy. He said, though, while he was carefully pressing his extremely well-pounded chicken breasts into a Parmesan-cheese coating, "Thanks for the help with Casey. I want to do it right."

$\heartsuit\heartsuit\heartsuit$

She could've said, "Pity you didn't think of that six years ago," but she couldn't bring herself to. He was thinking of it now, and what good would it do to bring up the past? She said, treading cautiously, "It's hard to realize what parenting means, all the changes it brings, until you do it for yourself. And you didn't have the best models."

"You're excusing me," he said. "Don't."

His tone was harsh, and she flinched. He said, "Sorry. But she was in foster care for weeks. She's braver than any kid ought to have to be."

"I'll bet she's not braver than you were." She was looking down, toasting almonds. That was the only reason she could say it. "Dylan told me how much of the time you took care of him. Here. Put those chicken breasts in the pans." She waggled the frying pans to swirl the butter around a bit more evenly.

He did it, then took the spatula she handed him. "I was bloody impatient with Dylan, most of the time. Resentful as hell. I don't want Casey to feel that. That edge, so a kid feels like a nuisance, and like she should tone herself down. She's got a big personality, the kind that faces the world head-on. It's a good personality. She should be able to keep it."

"Confidence," Zora said. "I think her mother did a good job."

"So do I." He sounded grim again. Why?

Zora hesitated, then asked, "How did she die?"

116

"Suddenly. Hit by a car."

"Poor thing. And poor Casey."

"Yeh."

"Which is why," she said, "you're so concerned, obviously."

"That, and that I like her," he said, which was so unexpected, she laughed. "What?" he asked.

"Nothing. I just think it's awesome." She slid the dried pasta into the pot and stirred. Standing so close to Rhys jangled her nerves, and it felt right at the same time.

She'd had another of those uncomfortable moments when she'd looked in the mirror at him, there in the bath. The size of him, the intensity of his eyes, the unruliness of his dark hair, and the scruff on his hard jaw. The strength of his arms. And then there was that dimple in his chin.

If it had been somebody else standing there, if it had been a movie, he would have put his hand on her jaw, tipped her head up, brushed her hair aside, leaned down, and kissed her. Gently. Tenderly. He'd be tender, she somehow knew, because he knew his strength, and it would thrill him to take it easy with a woman. And if that was devastating in such a rough man—it was no secret that she had a thing for hard men. She may not have known that when she was twenty. She knew it now.

It wasn't a movie, though. It was her absolutely regular, all-too-real life, and this wasn't a love story.

"Thirty dollars a day OK?" he asked.

"What?" She stopped stirring pasta. The fraught moment had been on one side only, clearly.

"To pay you to watch her. I looked it up. It could be four hours a day, by the time I get back, and that's what it costs." He flipped the chicken. "That looks about right, doesn't it?"

"Yes. You don't have to pay me, Rhys."

"I do, or I can't ask. Especially as I'm about to ask you to take her on Saturday as well. It dawned on me, sometime today, that I'll be gone from noon until late, and that it's only a couple days away. A week after that, we're on the road for twelve days. If I don't have somebody hired by then, I'll be stuck, and I'll be asking again."

"Oh."

"And before you say anything—I know you're not my personal daycare provider. Short term, that's all, until I can hire a nanny. And I'll appreciate the hell out of it."

"We can start," she said, "and see how we go. She's Isaiah's cousin, and looking after her won't be much harder than looking after Isaiah. And honestly?" She sighed and admitted it. "I can use the money. I'd like to do it for nothing. I'm a bit ashamed to ask for pay, but I will anyway. I need it."

Rhys had turned off the fire under his chicken and, without her asking, slid the cutlets onto a cutting board. When she started to lift the pasta pot, he said, "Thought I said to let me do that," She glanced at him, startled, and he said, "That's my coach voice. How'd I do?"

"Very authoritative. Go on, then." Her heart was beating harder, just from standing here with him, just from being honest.

He wasn't her dream man. Her dream man was solid as rock, strong to the core, and absolutely trustworthy. Her dream man had mana. He just happened to look and sound like Rhys Fletcher.

He drained the pasta in the sink, then turned to her and said, "Yes. Please. Please look after her. I told you that I couldn't let you do it without paying you for it, and that was the truth. You'll ease my mind, though, because there couldn't be anyone better."

"I'm not a perfect mother," she said.

"Oh," he said, "I think you are. I've always thought so."

She'd lost her breath, somehow, even though that was perhaps the least sexy thing anyone had ever said to her. She said, "If you'll cut that chicken into strips and go get the kids, then, I'll put the dressing on the salad and the pesto on the pasta, and we'll be set." And thought, *Not your man. Not your life. No.*

# the sense it makes

Zora said, during a dinner that felt weirdly intimate and oddly comfortable to Rhys, which must be his fatigue talking, "You may want to stay over tonight, Casey. I'm guessing your dad has your school uniform in the car. Changes always make a person tired, and you've had heaps of changes. You could sleep on Isaiah's bottom bunk. That's fun."

Casey didn't answer. She just looked at Rhys, and he wondered what that meant, and what he was meant to say. Having Casey stay here sounded good to him. She'd be in bed faster, and he'd have a night to regroup and no hair to do in the morning. He could focus on the job, which would be a brilliant idea right now. But that too-somber look on her little face—what did it mean?

That she had no expectations anymore, that was what. That she was waiting to see what life was going to do to her next, and that she knew she had no choice.

He asked her, "What do you think?" Nobody had ever asked *him* that. They'd just told him. But hadn't he been thinking, these past days, that he didn't want her to have a childhood like his?

"I thought I was going to live with you now," Casey said. She still hadn't called him "Dad," he realized. He wondered how that would feel.

"You are," he said. "But I have to work, so you're going to spend some time with Zora and Isaiah." He hesitated, then told her. Better to be straightforward, surely. "I spend a week or two at a time away from home, because I'm a rugby coach. When the team travels, so do I. And that's a lot."

"Oh." She ate some more noodles, working hard on it, like she did on everything, and thinking things through, like she also did. "Are you a teacher?"

A *teacher?* "Uh . . . no. Just a coach."

"Coaches are teachers, though. Like, at my school, they have a soccer coach for the big kids, but really, she's a teacher. She doesn't go away, though. She's always there. I think she lives at school."

"Teachers don't live at school," Isaiah said. "They live in houses. Or apartments, because teachers don't make a lot of money. Coaches make a lot of money, I think. All Blacks make heaps, and they have flash cars, so I think coaches must, too. They're the boss, and the boss always makes the most money. Uncle Rhys was an All Black for a really long time, even though he isn't now, so he probably saved heaps of money from that. My dad was an All Black, too, but only a little bit, and then he died. That's why we only have a little house."

Casey studied Rhys. Dubious, he'd call that look. "You're not black, though," she said. "You're not even kind of brown. Lots of black people are just kind of brown. My friend Charliece is a black person, and she's brown. Her hair's a lot curlier than mine, too. So I don't think you're a black person."

"It's a team," Rhys said. "Called the All Blacks, because they wear black uniforms. You can be any color to be on it. You just have to be the best at rugby." He debated explaining that Maori wore their brown on the inside, no matter how they looked on the outside, but it was a pretty subtle concept, and one his brain wasn't up to right now.

Casey's eyes got wide, and she forgot to eat the noodles on her fork. "The Chicago Bears have a coach. Are you that?"

"No," he said. "That's American football. This is New Zealand football, the kind we were playing before, out on the lawn. Different."

"Oh." She heaved a sigh and stuffed some more noodles into her mouth. He'd disappointed her again.

Isaiah said, "Being an All Black is better. It's the best thing."

Casey studied Rhys some more, and he could hear it without her saying it. *Yeh, right.* He had to smile.

Zora asked Rhys, "Do you have sheets for Casey's bed, or do you need to borrow some?"

"Oh." He rubbed his face with a palm and tried to think. "I do somewhere. In a box. Some box. I have a fair bit of unpacking still to do."

"What size is the bed?" she asked.

"Normal."

She sighed, looking exactly like Casey. Rhys looked at Isaiah, who shrugged again. Somebody here was on his wavelength, anyway. Pity he was eight.

Zora said, too patiently, "Listen carefully. Twin size— single bed. Full size—not as big as a queen. Queen size— most common. King size—big. Probably what you have in all those hotel room. Which is it?"

"I have a king size."

"Surprising nobody," she muttered, which made him smile.

"The other two bedrooms have something smaller. I had a woman who bought extra furniture for me, since the house is bigger than I've had, but I haven't paid much attention yet."

"I have an extra set of queen sheets," she said. "Even if it's a full, queen sheets will work. Just tuck more of them in."

"Good. Fine. We'll go home, then," he told Casey, "and make the best of things. We'll be camping out a bit for now, because it's a new house for me—for us—but we can make it more, uh, cozy. Eventually."

"OK," she said, and focused on stabbing a dried cherry. "If it has a rabbit house, it will be more cozy. Because rabbits are—"

"Yeh," he said. "Soft. I got it. For now, we'll get sheets on your bed. One step at a time."

Zora popped her head into Isaiah's room an hour later, holding a laundry basket, to find him on the floor, working on his jigsaw puzzle in his PJ's, which were navy and gray and absolutely plain. Last year, he'd rejected anything with a design, even *Star Wars,* as "babyish." She missed the Ninja Turtles and superheroes and rocket ships. She was proud of who he was growing up to be, but she still missed her baby.

"Do you want me to read to you tonight?" she asked.

"No, thanks," he said. "I'm reading a very interesting book about a teacher who taught somebody who was blind and deaf, in the olden days. She had to think how to help her to communicate. She finally figured out how, though, by putting her hand in some water and spelling the word for 'water' in sign language into her hand at the same time. That's very interesting, because if you couldn't hear anything *and* you couldn't see anything, you wouldn't even know that things had names. You wouldn't know how to think about them, or what was happening at all. You wouldn't have any words in your head, or any sentences. So I think that teacher was very smart. Except she was poor. When she was a kid, she was in an orphanage with her brother, and her brother died. She never had a home or a family or anything until she taught that girl. Then she got famous, but the girl got more famous, because she was the one who was blind and deaf. I think the teacher should have got more famous."

"I think the girl was Helen Keller," Zora said.

"The teacher's name was Annie," Isaiah said. "They were American, like Casey. It would be weird to be American."

"And to come to New Zealand, too." Zora decided to sit down on the floor. "You could help me fold this laundry."

Isaiah did, carefully picking out his own clothes. He'd told her that touching "girl underwear" was "weird." Apparently, even his mum's counted.

Zora said, after a minute, "It's a sudden thing for everybody, having Casey here."

Isaiah didn't look up, just continued folding his T-shirts in the way he liked, which consisted of putting a shirt flat on the floor and then folding it into a tiny rectangle, the way absolutely nobody else would have. He said it was neater. Now, he said, "Yeh."

She said, "I guess you know how she feels. Her mum died, just like your dad."

"I didn't have to go anywhere, though," he said, "because I was already here."

"That's right." She wondered, as always, how much to say. Isaiah was so grown up in some ways, so relentlessly logical, and still a little boy in others. She settled on, "And I was already here, too, with you. I knew how to be a mum. Uncle Rhys doesn't know how to be a dad. They both need some help, and they're our whanau."

"I know," Isaiah said. "I thought he didn't like us, but now he acts like he does."

"It's all pretty confusing. And it could be especially confusing," she decided to say, "because it's been just you and me for a long time now. And you could think, if I'm caring for Casey as well, that I don't love you as much. It could be odd to have to share your mum like that. Uncle Rhys is paying me thirty dollars a day, so it's a job, but it's more than that. Casey's my niece, and I'm going to love her, too. I feel like I've already started."

Isaiah shrugged. Boy shrugs usually meant, *You're getting close,* so she went ahead. "Here's the thing, though. I don't think love works like that. I don't think it's subtraction. It's more like addition, or multiplication, even. I think people have lots of different rooms in their hearts. You only see the room you're in, but that doesn't mean there aren't more. Or maybe love is like seeds, just waiting to grow into flowers. Maybe love is potential, and you always have more potential. That's how a mum can have lots of kids, and love every one of them with her whole heart. You wouldn't think that was possible, but it is."

"That doesn't make sense," Isaiah said.

"I don't think hearts always make sense. Or maybe we just don't understand the sense they make."

"It could be like space," Isaiah said. "Like there are more things that we don't know yet, but scientists can learn them."

She smiled and put her hand on his head, smoothing his dark hair. "It could be exactly like that. But there's one thing I do know for sure. I know that when they put you in my arms after you were born, I put my hand on your head just like this, and I thought—where did this love come from? How did I not know this existed? I knew that nothing could ever make that love any less, because that flower bloomed whole and bright and perfect just as it was. I knew who you were from the beginning, too. I could *see* you being clever and thoughtful and serious, even when you were a baby. I'm glad I have you to help me with Casey, and that you've got such a caring heart. Even though you may be sad sometimes, if I'm not paying enough attention to you. If that happens, though, I guess you'll tell me. You can say, 'Mum, I need your attention now,' and I'll listen."

"Just like you say," Isaiah said with his wicked little grin, the one time when he looked like his dad, 'Isaiah, I need some quiet time now.'"

She laughed, leaned over, and kissed his head, and for once, he didn't shift under that. "Yeh. Exactly like that. We'll love each other enough to tell the truth, even if it feels hard. That's our deal."

# hard line

When Rhys pulled into the driveway, Casey asked, "How come your house looks like the doctor's office?"

Still asking. Still stroppy. His body and mind might feel as battered as after a one-point loss to South Africa, but he liked this kid. A lot. He said, "It's an unobtrusive entrance," then pulled into the garage and cut off her view of the low wooden structure. Its narrow vertical windows were the only thing visible on the front—well, actually, the back of the house—in the purely rectangular, absolutely plain façade, and that was fine by him. Anonymous was good.

He considered explaining that New Zealand had only four and a half million people, and that he couldn't buy groceries or get a coffee without having a chat with half of them, but he saved it for another day, climbed out of the car, and said, "The good stuff doesn't always show on the outside. Life lesson. Or just say that not all houses look alike. You saw the inside this morning. That didn't look like a doctor's office, did it?"

"Other people's houses still look like *houses,* though," she insisted. "Or mopartments. They have curtains, and you don't have any curtains. And they have pretty things in them. You don't have any pretty things. My real house is a mopartment, but it doesn't look like your house, either."

He didn't know how to answer that, so he didn't. She waited, shifting from foot to foot, while he hauled her school uniform, the clothes Zora had bought, the groceries, the bag of hair paraphernalia, and the borrowed sheets out of the back of the car. He'd always been a minimalist sort of fella. It looked like that was another part of his life that was about to blow up. He grabbed one last bag and told her, "Run on ahead, if you're that impatient." She was practically hopping up and down now.

"I have to go to the bathroom really bad," she said.

Not this again. "Why didn't you go at Zora's?" he asked. It wasn't easy to juggle everything and still get the door into the house open. It was dark in here, but he could hear Casey jumping around. He also couldn't remember where the light switch was, though, especially since he was fumbling around for it and trying to get his trainers off while still holding his bags.

"Because Isaiah was there," she said. "You can't tell about going to the bathroom to boys." When he got the light on, she sat on the floor and started untying her shoelaces. One of them was in a knot, and she tugged at it. "And you're supposed to remind me."

"Next time," he said, "go on and ask. Ask Zora. Ask whoever. You can ask to use the bathroom, surely. We went through this on the plane, remember?" He tried to remember where the bathroom was up here. He'd spent less than a week in the house, and putting Casey's suitcase into one of the bedrooms this morning marked the sum total of his exploration of the upper level thus far.

He was heading down the passage to turn the lights on, toting a collection of purchases that would have done justice to a Maharani visiting a neighboring state, when he realized Casey wasn't with him and looked back.

She was still on the floor in the entry, one shoe off and one on, looking stricken.

"What's wrong?" he asked.

"I wet my pants." Her chin was wobbling. "I tried really hard not to, but a little bit came out anyway. And then it all came out, and I couldn't make it stop."

She was going to cry. Bloody *hell*. This day just kept giving.

"Stay there," he told her. "I'll get towels."

He found her bedroom, tossed everything but the groceries onto the bare mattress, went into the bathroom, once he remembered where it was, and realized there were no towels up here. Of course there weren't. There wasn't even any toilet paper up here. He had to go all the way down the stairs and around the house to his own ensuite bath to get both. When he came back, Casey *was* crying. Silently, not even trying to wipe the tears away. And still sitting exactly where he'd left her.

He'd said to stay there, and she'd had no choice but to mind him, even if it meant sitting in a puddle with her jeans soaked, feeling like she'd failed, knowing he was mad, and wondering if he was going to throw her away.

It was right there: the memory of Dylan, his shorts wet and the pee still dripping into the grass, standing in the middle of the yard and crying, while the cousins laughed and Rhys raged, hot with frustration and embarrassment, "Why do you have to be such a baby? You're useless. Go change before Nan sees. You aren't playing with us anymore, either. Stay in the house, baby." The satisfaction and the shame when Dylan had run away, and the hollow spot in the pit of his stomach.

You could always do better. Time to start. He said, "Here. Let's get that wet kit off," then crouched down and stripped her T-shirt and jeans off her, the ones she'd been wearing for two days now. In Chicago in the winter snow, and in Auckland in summer. At a foster home, at a restaurant being questioned by the police, at an airport, on a plane, at her aunt's, at a new school where she'd be the newest of all and had the wrong accent, and in the not-halfway-unpacked house of a strange man who wasn't really her father, and who knew it. She was looking over his shoulder now, for once not meeting his gaze, trying to suppress the sobs, and failing. Like somebody who'd been pushed too far, and was finally giving up.

He'd never been able to stand giving up, and he couldn't stand watching her do it, either. He got his hands under her arms, pulled her to her feet, and said, "No worries. It happens. Everything washes the same whether you pee on it or not."

Her undies were blue, with dots on, and on the front, they said *Friday.* Just as wrong in New Zealand as they'd have been in Chicago, where it was now Tuesday. There'd been nobody to tell her which ones to wear, he guessed, or nobody who'd cared enough to do it. Her mum had probably helped her pick out her clothes. At night, maybe, before she'd read her a story.

"Next time," he said, knowing his voice was too gruff but unable to keep it from being any other way, "ask *me* about the toilet. That's a Dad job." He got a towel wrapped around her. That was better. She looked safer. Warmer.

"You won't . . ." She'd stopped crying, but she was looking down, like she didn't want him to see her face. "You won't be there. Because you have to go to . . . work." A sniff. "And then you're going away."

"You ask Auntie Zora, then, or your teacher. You ask Isaiah. He's your cousin." And kinder than Rhys had ever been, because he had Zora in him.

"What if I wet my pants again at my new school, in Year Two, though? Everybody will laugh."

She looked at him at last. Those eyes. Too scared, and too tired. He should probably get on her level to answer, so he crouched down, kept a hand on her shoulder, and said, "Fair point. Let's think about it. First of all, you won't do that, because you'll ask your teacher when you first need to go. And if it *does* happen, and somebody laughs, you say, 'So what? Bet you lot have all peed your pants as well. I don't have to go anymore, anyway, which means I can kick your arses.' They can try to embarrass you, and they probably will. That doesn't mean you have to show it. You turn it around onto them, that's all."

Her expression could only be called skeptical, but that was an improvement over "defeated." He lifted a corner of the towel and wiped her face, and that was better, too.

"That's not the right thing to say, I don't think," she said.

"You're not supposed to say to do fighting."

She was probably right. Zora would no doubt have offered up something better. He tried to think of what it would be, blanked, and gave up. "That's because I'm the dad," he said. "That's the *dad* thing to say. Never let them see you're scared."

"Oh," she said. "What if I *am* scared, though?"

"Then you tell me, and we'll make a plan, like we just did. We'll strategize, eh. Because, again, I'm the dad. That's my job, to help you when you're scared."

She looked more dubious than ever. "It is?"

"Yeh. It is." At least it should be. He was in guessing territory here, because he'd never had much of a dad himself until he was a teenager, and there hadn't been heaps of sharing of feelings going on. Well, other than anger. His dad had been good at that one. "Come on. Let's get you into the bath."

*One thing at a time, mate.* He didn't have to wash her hair tonight, or if he *did* have to, he was pretending he didn't know that. Four more things, then. Shower. PJs. Plait hair. Put sheets on bed. Ten minutes, and he'd be done. He got her into the shower, stuffed her dirty things into the washing machine and started it, then found the PJs in one of Zora's carrier bags and the Thursday undies—pink with white stripes—in Casey's suitcase, and took them into the bathroom. He could at least make sure she had the right undies.

*See?* he told himself. *You don't know how to do it, but you're doing it anyway. Parenting.* More or less. Not too unlike sharing a hotel room with a nineteen-year-old kid when you were thirty-two, and letting him watch you and follow your example, except that Casey was younger. And a girl. And his daughter.

But other than that.

She was standing directly under the tap, her eyes screwed shut and her hair and face soaking wet. He poked his head around the glass partition and asked, "What are you doing?

You weren't meant to wash your hair."

"I couldn't help it," she said. "The water comes from on the top. It's getting in my mouth. I don't think showers are very nice."

He turned the tap off, getting fairly wet himself in the process, grabbed the towel again, rubbed it over her face and hair, and said, "You keep your head out. You don't stand directly under it." He thought about what she'd looked like when he'd turned the tap on and told her to get in. Hesitant, he'd call that. "Have you taken a shower before?"

She shook her head. "Tomorrow," he said, "I'll show you how." He was over the am-I-supposed-to-see-her-naked part of the question, at least. Clearly, there was no choice.

He'd be fixing her hair again tonight after all. Which was fine. They were fine. Two-a-day trainings were normal.

By the time she'd got herself dressed, he had her clothes put away from the various boxes and bags and was getting the sheets on the bed. "See?" he told her when she came in from the bathroom. "They have flowers on. Nice and girly. I'm going downstairs and getting a blanket for you now." From off of his bed, since everything else was still in boxes. "And then we'll comb your hair and I'll practice my new plaiting skills." After that, he could get to bed himself. His eyelids felt lined with sandpaper, his muscles felt like he was dragging them along, and his focus kept wavering, which was what happened when you'd managed maybe six hours of sleep out of the past forty-eight.

"OK," Casey said. "Maybe I could go with you."

He was almost out the door. "I'll be back in a second."

She stood planted there, her damp hair already frizzing around her face and Mickey and Minnie dancing on her PJ top, all of her looking tiny against the too-large bed. There wasn't even a carpet in here, and he hadn't asked the decorator to hang any art on the walls. For good reason, he'd thought. Decorator-chosen art was always something rubbish—a mass of intertwined driftwood fastened, for some unknown reason, to an open wood frame, or a red "X" covering a sloppily painted white background. If somebody had painted your shed as messily as that, you'd have refused to pay him, but if they did it on a painting, you paid extra. Go figure. He'd had both of those in his house in France, and had never been able to work out why. The driftwood had looked like a giant spider crouching on the wall, especially in the dusk. Casey's walls might be bare, but at least they wouldn't give a person nightmares. So why did she look like she'd be having nightmares anyway?

"What?" he asked.

"Nothing."

He crouched down beside her again. "What?"

"It's kind of scary in your house. Because it's a jungle outside of it, like *Jumanji*. Are there wild animals?"

He held out his hand. "Come on, then. We'll go get the blanket together. No wild animals. Nothing but birds. It's New Zealand. Very safe place. We'll have a look around in the morning, and I'll show you. It's called, 'Prime hillside property, your own slice of heaven, set amongst native bush.' Means there are trees, that's all, and that you pay extra for them."

"Jungly trees. Like in dinosaur times."

"Fern trees and palms, but no dinosaurs, and nothing else scary, either."

Which was all fine. But when she was in bed at last, and he was standing by the door, about to turn off the light and wondering whether he'd manage to get his own clothes off or just fall in a heap across his bed, she clutched Moana closer and asked, "Could you leave all the lights on?"

"You can't sleep like that, surely."

"But if it gets very scary, I could find where you were. Your bedroom is a very far ways away, and your steps have holes in them. My mommy's bedroom is next door, so if I have a bad dream, I can go find her."

"Right," he said. "I'll read you a story from the dinosaur book for the bad dreams. After that, I'll turn your bedroom light off, but I'll leave the door open and the light in the passage on. If it gets very scary, you *can* come find where I am." She had to be at least as tired as he was. Surely she wouldn't wake up.

Also, what were the builders thinking, putting a floating staircase into a house where people might have kids? The steps looked flash enough, each riser carved out of pale-gray wood, the bottoms shaped like waves. The acrylic panel was more secure than your average railing, too, even if it didn't look it, but Casey was right. There was open space between every riser. You might not actually be able to fall through, but you'd *feel* like you could. It was a stupid design.

"OK," she said. "But maybe I could sleep on the couch instead, so it wouldn't be so far and there wouldn't be holes, and I could find you."

When he finally allowed his eyes to close, at a point where he couldn't have held them open five more minutes, he was wrapped in his duvet on the floor beside her bed, with her arm hanging over the side and the tips of her fingers brushing his hair. Making sure he was still there, that he hadn't left her.

It was better for her to be in her own bed than on the couch, that was all. He was helping her get used to things, and it was just for tonight. After that, they'd be fine. One day at a time.

*I need to get a carpet down here,* he thought. *But no rabbits in the house. Absolutely not. Hard line.* And fell asleep.

# character is destiny

Rhys was always first to training. How would the players care if the coach didn't care more? On Thursday, though, Finn beat him in, and so did almost a dozen of the players. The skipper, Hugh Latimer, was amongst them. Hugh and his wife had twin babies, as well as two other kids, yet here he was.

Rhys was beginning to get the idea that just getting to work on time, when you had kids, was an accomplishment, what with checking a forest of jungly trees for lurking wild animals, plaiting hair, helping a six-year-old into all the pieces of her new school uniform, cooking breakfast, checking that you'd filled out various pieces of paperwork and she had them in her backpack, and having to wait for her to run back inside, when you'd finally made it into the car for the short drive to Zora's house, for her sparkly trainers.

"You can wear your school shoes for today, surely," he'd said.

"Not with my *unicorn* shirt," she'd said. "Because it has sparkles, and the shoes have sparkles, so they match. You have to *match.*"

Needless to say, he was late. The gym resounded with the clank of metal plates, the soft thuds of impossibly fast feet running intricate patterns marked onto the floor with tape, and the driving beat of the music that kept the adrenaline pumping. He headed over to Finn, who was casting an eye over the squad, each of them going through his own individualized workout routine, and asked, "How're they going?"

"Not bad," Finn said, making a note on his clipboard. "Give me a minute, and I'll fill you in." He took in Rhys's appearance, which probably wasn't anything to write home about, and decided to add, "You look like hell. Family troubles not sorted, then?"

"Not quite." Rhys passed a hand over his jaw. He'd meant to shave. He hadn't had time. He had time to say this, though, and he needed to. To everybody, and soon. Why hadn't he told Finn before, at least? Some kind of magical thinking, maybe, believing that it wasn't really happening until it actually did. Not a mindset you encouraged, if you were a coach. Or if you wanted to be any kind of man. He said, "I went to Chicago to get my daughter. Her mum died, so she's with me now. It's been a bit of an effort to get things in order."

Finn didn't actually stare slack-jawed at him. It just felt that way. After a moment, he asked, "Where is she now?"

"School. At least she will be soon. She's six. Staying with Zora, Dylan's wife, before and after school. Going to the same school as Dylan's boy, which is handy."

"Her first day there?"

"Yeh." Finn was still looking at him too sharply. "What, I should've taken her? I thought that, after."

"Maybe. Not easy being a single dad, though."

"You'd know, I reckon." Finn had been a widower with two kids when he'd met his wife. Now, he had four.

"I'll ask this," Finn said, and Rhys braced for it. "When was your last workout?"

Not the question he'd been expecting. He tried to remember, and blanked. Too many travel days and time changes. "A while back."

"After training, then," Finn said, "we'll run ourselves through."

Rhys said, "I'm guessing that reminding you that I'm meant to be in charge here isn't going to stop you. Or saying that it'll have me collecting Casey even later."

Finn gripped him by the shoulder and shook it. "Nah,

mate. It's not. Also, you're stiff as iron. How are you going to think like that? There's no problem that a good workout doesn't help you solve. You're not going to be much chop as a dad if you let yourself get unfit and grumpy, and you'll be even more of a bastard as a coach."

"Right," Rhys said. "Fine." He'd text Zora and tell her six-thirty, and he'd pick up a takeaway for himself and Casey, and something for Zora and Isaiah as well. That would make up for the lateness, he hoped. He hadn't expected this parenting thing to be so . . . all-consuming, and it had been, what? A few days?

Spontaneity, he was beginning to realize, was a thing of the past. He'd never thought he had much of that. In fact, though, he'd had heaps. If he'd had somewhere to go or something to do, he'd just gone, or had done it. He hadn't realized that was unusual.

On the other hand, when he'd crouched down to say goodbye to Casey this morning in Zora's kitchen, she'd asked him, "Are you coming back?"

He'd said, "Yeh, I am. You live with me now, remember? If you aren't sure what to do at school today, or if anything bothers you, you can make a note in your mind and tell me tonight, and we'll make a plan."

"A statagee."

"Strategy. That's right. A strategy always helps." He'd smoothed a hand over her hair, which wasn't quite as lumpy today, and given her a kiss that barely felt awkward at all, and she'd put her arms around his neck and pressed her cheek to his. And he'd thought fuzzily, *That's all right, then,* and ignored the way his chest had tightened.

He definitely needed a workout.

♡♡♡

Nobody pushed you harder than Finn. At nearly six that evening, when Rhys was sweating freely and doing his third set of pull-ups with an enormous weight chained to his waist, everything else was gone from his mind but this fairly extreme moment. And when he dropped to the ground at last, unclipped the weight, and put it back on the stack with arms that shook, he said, "That's why I retired, you sadistic bastard."

"Nah," Finn said. "Good for you. Last one." He headed over to a set of inclined benches, hooked his legs under, and started doing crunches, and Rhys wiped his face on the bottom of his T-shirt and followed suit.

"So your daughter's six," Finn said, curling his upper body off the bench yet again. "From Chicago."

"Yeh. Casey." Rhys didn't feel like talking, and not just because he didn't feel like explaining. He didn't feel like *talking*. It must be all the pizza. It felt like every slice had settled in his abs and was burning to get out.

"Didn't realize you'd been to Chicago seven years ago," Finn said, not even sounding out of breath, "other than with the ABs."

"I wasn't. That was when."

"What was when? What happened?"

Rhys curled back down, breathed a moment, and said, "With the ABs. What d'you think happened? It wasn't a bloody romance. I was with Victoria. It was a night."

"Before or after the game? And you're three reps behind. Keep up."

Rhys laced his hands behind his neck again and grimly pressed on. "What does it matter? She's here. She's six. She's mine."

"Maybe you forget," Finn said, "that I was your roomie in Chicago. I remember a hockey game, a couple nights before ours, maybe, because we were pretty relaxed. I remember a curfew the night before, and having a few beers after the game in some bar. And I remember walking back to the hotel with you. It was bloody cold. Windy, too. It may have been snowing. I even remember you ringing Victoria, because I went and took a shower I didn't need and wished she wouldn't talk so long. I wanted to go to bed. So unless you hooked up in the toilets somewhere in there, or became a different man from the bloke I'd known for ten years . . ." He swung his feet out from under the bar and stood up. "I don't think so."

Rhys said, "You don't need to know the details." He did his three more reps and got to his feet, possibly not as smoothly as he ever had in his life. Tonight, he and Casey were keeping to the schedule. Home, dinner, bath, bed. He needed sleep, and so did she.

Finn tossed him a towel. "Does Zora know the truth?"

Rhys buried his face in white cotton, then scrubbed the rough fabric over his head. "No. Hasn't she had enough to cope with?"

"The whanau? Victoria?"

"No. My name's on there. I'm the dad. And as for the rest—I'm still waiting for all the dominoes to fall. It'll happen, no worries."

"But you didn't know before."

"If I'd known before," Rhys said, the anger rising on the words as he tossed the towel into the barrel, "I'd have made sure Dylan did better. He never even saw her. Didn't make arrangements for her. It's two and a half years now."

He was furious. He was *filthy*. And he had nobody to take it out on. Why hadn't Dylan told him? He could have handled it, then. He could have taken care of all of it. Casey's mum would never have been hit in that crossing, wouldn't have been running from one job to the next, trying to keep the two of them afloat.

"He'd have had to tell you, though, to make arrangements," Finn said. And, yes, that was probably why Dylan hadn't. "Or Zora, but more likely you. Always one for skating away from the tough ones, Dylan."

"I'm in the showers," Rhys said, and walked away.

When they were changing, though, his body settling down into the shaky-gelatin aftermath of a hard workout, calming his mind, he asked Finn the important question, at least for now. "If you know, who else will?"

"Nobody," Finn said. "They'll be surprised, maybe. Think less of you, probably."

"Cheers," Rhys said, pulling a clean T-shirt over his head and tugging it down. "I think I knew that."

"I think you did, too," Finn said. "And that you did it anyway. Nobody's going to suss out the truth, though. It won't occur to them that there's another explanation, because nobody but you would do this. Character is destiny. That's what they say. Could be true."

This conversation was making Rhys itchy. Besides, he needed to go get Casey. First day of Year Two, where you had to read big words, and she wouldn't know any of the kids. Maybe he wanted to see Zora as well, or maybe he just needed to get out of here. "Not true," he said, tossed another towel, and laced up his shoes. "You'd have done it."

"Nah, mate," Finn said. "I don't think so. In fact, I know so. I've come up short on tests heaps easier than this one. I think this is all you."

# spark. or not.

Feeding Rhys and Casey on Wednesday night had been fine, Zora thought on Friday. It had been the right thing to do, and it was good for her to get used to being around Rhys anyway. Maybe then her heart wouldn't start pounding just at the sight of him coming up her walk, his long legs eating up the ground like he'd rather be running, or like he was eager to get here. To collect Casey, of course. Or at the way he'd looked last night walking out to the car again, holding Casey's hand while she skipped along beside him. What was it about a dad and his little girl that made you go all goopy inside?

However much of a reluctant, uninvolved dad and lying, cheating bastard he'd been? Yeh, there was that.

At the moment, she was studying her appearance in the bedroom mirror, touching up her eye makeup, slicking on ruby lipstick she'd bought specially for the occasion, wondering if it was too obvious a shade, rumpling her hair a bit more, and trying not to feel either (A) cross, (B) jumpy, or (C) stupid, with approximately (0) success.

She wasn't used to trying to look sexy. Was this the right amount of it? For that matter, was the idea of her looking sexy ridiculous under any conditions? She had no idea anymore. She wished she could ask somebody.

Elegance, she'd reckoned, and not much skin showing. Especially not if that skin might be striped by a few silvery stretch marks.

Including on her breasts. And Alistair was a plastic surgeon.

Gah.

Getting used to Rhys being around was one thing, but that he was here for *this? Damn* Hayden for inviting him to stay to help babysit. Her brother had done it for mischief, she'd swear it.

Never mind. She'd said yes to Alistair, so ready or not, here she went. She wasn't getting naked in front of anybody tonight anyway. Call it a dry run. She gave a final tweak to her skirt and headed out into the lounge.

The kids didn't look up from their cards. Hayden did, though, and so did Rhys, and she wished she knew what he was thinking. Rhys, not Hayden. His hard face had gone even harder, back to that stony expression she remembered from their first meeting, when she'd thought he didn't like her, or he didn't approve of her. She'd seen that expression enough in the following years to recognize it, and she was seeing it again now.

Well, bugger that. She wasn't twenty years old, she'd been the best wife she could manage, she wasn't married anymore, and she wasn't begging for Rhys Fletcher's approval.

Hayden whistled, and the kids finally quit studying their cards and looked up, too.

"*Very* nice," her brother said. "On the hot side for a first date, though. The *absolutely* first date, in fact," he told Rhys, "believe it or not. How many years has it been since your last first date, Zora? Ten? Eleven?"

She knew which emotion she was feeling now. It was cross. Why did he have to share? "I do not look that hot," she said, and forced herself not to make it a question. She glanced at Rhys, but he wasn't telling, so she went to "defiant" instead. A much more comfortable spot than "scream and run." She told Hayden, "You're the one who said I should get out there again. Red's the best color for a first date. I read it online. You're not used to seeing me in heels, that's all." The dress might be sleeveless and the bodice fitted, but the neckline was square and not very low, and the skirt didn't hit very far at all above her knees. "I can't wear anything longer or fuller, and you know it. It would swallow me up." She tried to pretend that Rhys wasn't listening. It wasn't easy. "I'm short, in case you haven't noticed. I'm not wearing stilettos, and kitten heels are on nobody's list of erotic attire. Also—cardigan." She slipped into the cropped blush-pink sweater. "Practically office wear, except for the dangly earrings. In fact, that's what he'll probably think. 'Why didn't she change her clothes, at least?'"

Hayden's glance at Rhys was pure mischief. "What do you think?"

"I think," Rhys said, "that if she were in my office, I wouldn't be getting any work done."

He was still staring at her. *Was* this too much? She'd thought it was perfect. She'd looked it *up*. The dress wasn't fire-engine red. It was closer to burgundy, and although the fabric was on the silky side, it wasn't skin-tight. Surely men weren't *that* single-minded, anyway.

"You don't work in an office, Uncle Rhys," Isaiah said. "You work with all men. Also, Saturday night is when people go out on dates, and rugby games are always on Saturday nights. Sometimes they go on Friday nights, too, but it's Friday night *now*, and you're not on a date."

"Sounds like you know, mate," Rhys said. He had that not-smiling-but-amused look on his face again, at least, instead of the stoniness.

"Because my dad said it to my mum once. She asked him to take her on a date and he said no, because of rugby. He said, 'Can't take you Friday, and can't take you Saturday. Both date nights are out, and all I want to do on Sunday is put my feet up and have you cook me dinner. D'you mind if we just stay in?'" Another thing Zora could have lived without Rhys hearing. Isaiah wasn't done, either. He asked Hayden, "What's 'erotic'?"

"Sexy," Hayden said.

Isaiah made a face. "Yuck."

"Hmm," Hayden said, his eyes lit with mischief again. "I think Uncle Rhys goes out on dates. I'm guessing he's somewhat of an expert in that area, in fact. He seems to be saying you look hot, Zora. Good news, unless it's not."

Casey said, "It's your turn," with a nudge at Rhys's leg, because she was on the floor and he was on the couch.

He shoved a handful of Jaffas into the middle of the coffee table without looking at his cards, then tossed in two pineapple lumps and said, "I raise you two lumps."

Isaiah sighed and shook his head.

"What?" Rhys asked.

"I don't think you've got good enough cards for betting that much," Isaiah said. "I think I'm going to win."

"Excuse me?" Rhys asked. "Who learned how to play poker tonight, and who's spent half his life in hotel rooms with nothing else to do?"

"I don't think you were very good at it," Isaiah said. "I see your two pineapple lumps and raise you three more. That's fifty points," he told Casey. "You should only bet that if you have very good cards. Do you want me to look at them and tell you what to do?"

"Yes," Casey said. "Because I forget."

Isaiah scooted over and studied her cards. "You should fold. That means stop and lay down your cards."

"But then I'll lose all my candy," she protested.

"You're going to lose your candy anyway," he said. "Except it's called 'lollies.' My hand's better than yours, so I'm going to win. You still have more lollies left, though, and besides, I'll share with you."

Hayden sighed and muttered, "Ringers. I'm surrounded by ringers. I fold." He tossed down his hand, and Isaiah gave a satisfied smile. His hand was practically poised over the pile of lollies in the middle of the table. Black licorice, chocolate Jaffas, pink marshmallows, and pineapple lumps. The stakes.

"Do you want to fold, too, Uncle Rhys?" he asked politely. "Or do you want to bet some more?"

The doorbell rang, and Zora jumped. Literally. Why was she so bloody nervous? Also, why did she want to get onto the floor, sit back on her knees, and have her card-shark son deal her in instead of going on this date?

Hayden said, "That's either the pizza or the plastic surgeon. I wonder which."

♡♡♡

It was the plastic surgeon. Zora brought him into the lounge, and Rhys relaxed his hands, shuffled the cards, and wondered for the hundredth time why he'd accepted Hayden's invitation. He had a game to coach tomorrow night, pizza *still* wasn't on his diet plan, despite the way it kept appearing in his life, and he wouldn't have called himself a masochist. Before.

He kept his eyes off Zora's soft mass of dark hair, and all the way off the deep-red lipstick that emphasized her full lips. Any man who looked at that mouth across a dinner table would be imagining kissing the lipstick slowly off of her. Unless he was thinking about the traces she could leave on him, and all the places he wanted to see that mouth go.

Unfortunately, if he didn't look at her eyes or her mouth, or at her breasts, he had to look at her pretty legs, or at those shoes. They were chocolate-colored suede, the heel was narrow, and a wide strap ran diagonally across the instep, from the pointed toe nearly to the curve at the back. Whatever she said, anything "kitten" was sexy as hell, and those shoes were . . . He forgot to think what.

Her feet were small, like the rest of her. He wondered if she'd painted her toenails to match her lipstick. You could hold one of her slim ankles with one hand, while the other slipped that shoe right off her foot. After that, you could do the other one. Her legs were bare, her skirt was short, and . . .

He wanted to tell her that, yes, everything about her look was too sexy for a first date, or any date. He wanted to shove this fella out the door and tell Hayden to take over the kid-minding duties. After that, he wanted to take Zora out someplace where the lights were low and the tablecloths were white, watch her drink a couple glasses of deep-red wine, open her car door for her, drive her somewhere dark and out of the way, turn the radio to something low and slow, and find out how long it would take him to kiss off all that red lipstick, and how much he could make her sigh while he did it.

He wanted to make out with his sister-in-law in the back of a car. He wanted to do more than that. Also, he hated the plastic surgeon on sight. He was wearing a perfectly tailored deep-gray suit and white dress shirt, his black shoes were beautifully polished, and he clearly didn't care that he was balding, because his hair was cut short and made no attempt to disguise his V-shaped hairline. Despite a skinny build that would go down in the first tackle and stay down, he looked like a man who'd done everything he could to make an impression on a woman, and who was confident he could do it. He was also eating Zora up, virtually speaking, in a way that told Rhys what kind of impression he'd like her to make on *him*. Which had to do with that mouth, because that was what he was staring at.

Why were you so rarely allowed to throw a punch, or even to raise your voice, in social settings? That was a decided drawback to modern life.

Zora was introducing him and Hayden, and Rhys shook hands with the bloke and didn't squeeze too hard, because that was a dick move. Nobody said he had to smile, though. The guy's name was Alistair. He even *sounded* like a plastic surgeon.

"Where are you two off to?" Hayden asked brightly. "Better be someplace good enough for my sister. That's me coming over all big-brotherly, even though I'm younger, and even though that's Rhys as well, and he'd probably do it better. Wait. He'd *definitely* do it better. Jump in here anytime, mate."

Rhys didn't.

Alistair blinked, but said, "I booked us into Sid at the French Café. That suit you?" he asked Zora. "And by the way—you look very beautiful."

Which was what Rhys should have said, instead of staring at her and then looking away again and not saying anything at all. "Thank you," she said. "That sounds lovely. I've heard the food's gorgeous." She was flustered, he thought. As if he'd summoned the idea, she glanced at him, then away, and her hand went up to smooth her hair. "Also," she told Alistair, "Rhys isn't my brother. He's my brother-in-law. My late husband's brother."

"Oh," Alistair said. "The reason for the surname being the same. I recognized the name, and you, of course," he told Rhys. "But I didn't realize . . ." He shifted tack like the smooth bastard he was. "That you were a widow, Zora."

"Yes," Zora said. She picked up her evening bag from the coffee table and bent and kissed Isaiah and then, after a second, Casey, who didn't seem to mind a bit. "Don't stay up too late," she told them. "Also—four lollies max. *After* pizza."

"Mum." Isaiah sighed. "I *won* them."

"And yet four is still your maximum," she said. "Because I'm the mum. See you later."

♡♡♡

A couple hours later, Hayden stood up, stretched, and said, "I'm not saying you're boring, mate, but it's barely nine o'clock, I'm falling asleep here, and it's Friday night. Why does Zora's life always make me feel like I've skipped a few decades and am suddenly fifty and wearing a sweater vest?"

"If you're asking me if you can leave," Rhys said, "the answer's 'yes.' I'll stay."

"I told Zora I'd mind Isaiah, of course," Hayden said in a musing sort of way. "On the other hand, they're both asleep, and Casey *is* your daughter, isn't she?"

His brown eyes were shrewd, but Rhys didn't take the bait, just stared calmly back and said, "Yes."

"Then," Hayden said, "I think I'll leave. See ya. Tell Zora

I'll expect a post-mortem tomorrow. What d'you reckon he makes a major move? The plaid shorts threw me off initially, but seen in his natural element, I'm getting a different vibe. Zora's such a baby. The article probably said men liked red dresses best, not that you should *wear* a red dress. It was short as well. Why won't she ever ask for my advice? The mind boggles. And I'm off."

Rhys thought, *Good,* and pulled out his notebook. He needed to organize his mind before the game. Perfect opportunity.

This time, Casey had agreed to spend the night. They'd played poker until the pizza was gone, by which point, Isaiah had won all Rhys's lollies anyway, and was well on his way to winning Hayden's. He only hadn't won Casey's because he'd helped her keep them. After that, Isaiah had said, while Rhys loaded dishes into the dishwasher, "If you stay over, Casey, we can watch a movie until bedtime. You can borrow my PJs that are too small. They're Star Wars."

She looked at Rhys, and he said, "It's your choice. We can go home now if you'd rather."

She said, "Will you come and get me tomorrow?"

"Yeh," he said. "I will."

"Do you promise?"

His heart did that squeezing thing again. "I promise. And I keep my promises. You'll see."

"I have to stay here tomorrow night," she said, "because you have to do your job."

"That's right. Tomorrow, though, we'll bring your own PJs. For tonight, you can choose. We'll go home now and put you to bed—*straight* to bed—or you can stay up a bit longer, watch a movie with Isaiah, and do a practice run at staying over."

She chose to stay, "because Isaiah has cartoon movies, and you don't." Fair point.

At least they didn't have to watch *Moana* again. Casey had been fairly devastated last night, in the form of her face crumpling up in the way Rhys couldn't stand, to find that her

*Moana* DVD wouldn't play in New Zealand. They'd had to go out after dinner—the night when he'd planned on both of them being in bed by eight-thirty—to hunt down a region-friendly copy, and then she'd had to watch it, "to make sure it works." She'd looked too small sitting on the couch alone, her second night in his house, which had meant he'd had to watch it with her, which hadn't been the plan at all. They'd both fallen asleep on the couch, but she'd felt relaxed in his arms this time, which was surely better.

Never mind. She'd slept in her own bed, eventually, and he'd slept in his. That was a start. He'd begin instilling discipline next week, when she was used to him, and they had their routine down.

They'd ended up watching some cartoon movie about a Yeti tonight, which was silly, but the kids had liked it. And when Casey had leaned into him on the couch, then had fallen asleep against him in her robot-intensive PJs? It hadn't been such a bad Friday night, especially when he'd carried her to bed and tucked her in, and she'd turned toward him with her eyes nearly closed, wrapped her arms around his neck, and asked sleepily, "Do you really promise to come tomorrow?"

"I promise." He hesitated a moment, then leaned down and kissed her cheek. "Good night, Casey Moana."

She sighed and closed her eyes. "Night."

"Night, mate," he told Isaiah. "Well done on helping Casey with her cards tonight, even though I'm still calling beginner's luck. Next time, it's revenge."

Isaiah climbed up the ladder and scrambled into the top bunk. "No," he said. "I think I'm just better." And Rhys had to laugh. The boy went on, "I have to help her, I guess. Because I'm older."

"Yeh. I was an older brother once, myself."

"With my dad." Isaiah had turned toward him, resting on his elbow, his eyes sober. "You were his big brother."

"I was. I looked after him, but I didn't always do it kindly. You do better at that. A good heart matters, eh. Probably makes you miss him, too."

Isaiah looked thoughtful. "I don't think I miss him. He wasn't at home very much until he got sick. Mostly it was just Mum, and she's still here."

"Tossed the rugby ball with you and all, though," Rhys said.

"Mostly Mum does that," Isaiah said. "I don't remember Dad doing it. So I don't think it happened very many times."

Not much of an epitaph.

Now, both kids were asleep, Hayden had left, and Zora still wasn't home. It had been three hours. How long were they planning to spend over this dinner? Or had that fella taken her somewhere else after? Rhys wasn't sitting up here all night. He had work to do.

He was just thinking it when he heard something outside. A car, switching off. A door slamming, and then another. He'd been making a note, but his head went up, and he listened.

Thirty seconds. Sixty. More. What were they doing out there?

Never mind. He knew.

The house was silent except for the occasional barely-ticking-over sound of a fridge motor humming into life, the random pop of a not-that-well-built house settling. Surely those were voices, though, just at the edge of his hearing. He set his notebook down, headed toward the kitchen, thought better of it, and sat on the couch again.

A door opening, another soft word, and footsteps, and he *did* stand up. Zora came through the world's tiniest dining room and into the lounge carrying her purse in one hand. When she saw him, though, she stopped short.

"Oh," she said. "Hayden gone?"

"Yeh. Off to find some nightlife." Her lipstick was smeared, surely. "Casey wanted to stay the night. I hope that's OK."

"Of course." She bent and pulled off first one shoe, then the other, stood up again with them in one hand, and smiled at him. "I'm not used to heels, although I should probably wear them more. Makes me taller, eh. I'm not sure these were right, though. Too businesslike, you think? I'm out of practice."

She sounded breathless. Also, her lipstick was *definitely* smeared. He said, "Nah. I was thinking that they looked good. That *you* looked good. Pretty. I thought."

Yes, he was Captain Suave. She smiled a little and said, "You're more complimentary than Hayden, anyway." Her hand went up to pull back her tousled hair from her face, and then she shook her head and the hair settled around her again, so what had been the point, other than to heat his blood a little more? "Would you like a beer?"

"Depends," he said. "Are you going to have one?"

"Yes." She set the shoes down beside an armchair. "I had wine with dinner, and I have a wedding to do tomorrow, but I want a beer anyway. Decompressing. Should a date require decompressing?"

"If it's your first one in years, it probably does. Sit down, though. I'll get them."

He brought back the bottles and a glass, but she waved the glass away and said, "Bottle's fine." She'd sat on the couch, so he sat down beside her, took a sip of beer, and said, "So."

She tucked her legs up under her, and, yes, her toenail varnish was deep red. "So. That's me started, I guess. Back out there in the world. Was it hard for you to do?"

Was he supposed to lie? He said, "No." Still rubbish at lying, then. He considered telling her that he was having a hard time moving on now, and didn't. Very bad idea.

She said, "Oh," and twirled the bottle in her fingers.

"Something wrong? Did he do something he shouldn't have?" He tried to keep his hands from tightening, and failed.

"No. He kissed me a fair amount, that was all. And dropped his hand a bit low on my back, possibly. I didn't give him any signals not to. Beforehand, at least. I wanted to . . . see, I guess."

She sighed. What did that mean? She had her hand in her hair again, at the back of her neck this time, was looking away

149

from him, and he could smell her scent. More than roses tonight. Something spicier and darker. Exactly how far down was "a bit low on my back?" He'd *known* there was something shady about that bloke. Doctors. Arrogant bastards.

He should get up and leave. He didn't need this frustration. He had a game tomorrow. Instead, he asked, "And did you see?"

She looked down at her beer bottle like she'd forgotten she was holding it. "Maybe I'm just not in practice. I thought that earlier tonight, when I was getting dressed. Or maybe I've lost it."

"Lost what?"

She raised her eyes to his. "Whatever it is. The spark." A long moment. "Desire."

He watched his hand move, willed it back, and for once in his life, absolutely failed to control himself. He was touching her hair, twining a curl around his finger. "Or maybe," he said, "he wasn't the right one."

He wished she didn't have those eyes. He was in big, big trouble. "I think that's pretty well established," she said, and, yes, she definitely *was* breathless, and his heart was thudding like a jackhammer. "He's a nice man. He has beautiful office furniture, and I'm sure he could fix all my problem areas. Of course, for him to do that, I'd have to show them to him. Not happening. If I've got a spark, it's not with him." She shifted and looked away, he dropped his hand, and she stood up. Moment over.

"You know—" she said, "I don't think I want this beer. I think I'll go to bed. Come for breakfast tomorrow, when you come to get Casey. I'll be running to get those arrangements done, but we all have to eat. If you want to help cook it— even better. You don't mind showing yourself out, do you?"

# promises kept

Eight days later, and Rhys had officially made it through more than a week as Casey's dad. It was getting easier with practice and discipline, exactly like everything else in the world.

*You see?* he told himself every single night. *You can do this.*

Eight mornings of hair combing and teaching Casey to read the names of the days, so she could choose the right undies. She'd learned to take a shower, and he'd learned to wash her hair, as well as the many other required steps. He'd even done two plaits this morning, which had involved parting her hair and creating something called a "French braid," which may have required a YouTube video and a bit of coaching on the phone from Zora, but he'd done it, hadn't he? He'd fastened the plaits with twin red barrettes with sparkly stars on. The whole thing made Casey, in her green-plaid uniform skirt, look cute and cared for, which would help at school, surely, especially as she'd made a friend, a girl named Esme who had a puppy. Which Rhys was hearing about constantly.

"No puppies," he'd said, just last night. "Absolutely not. Hard line."

Casey had sighed, and he'd been able to predict the words before they'd made it out of her mouth. There was no reason in the world he had to fall for those big eyes, either. "If I had *rabbits,*" she'd told him, scrambling up onto her bed beside him in her Mickey and Minnie PJs to read stories, "I wouldn't want a puppy, because the puppy might chase the rabbits. If

I had rabbits, I would never be lonesome."

Zora had smiled at him this morning, though, when he'd dropped Casey off at her place, and said, "Oh, well done on the plaits, Rhys. She looks adorable." Which shouldn't matter as much as it did, but there was something about winning a woman's approval that got you every time.

There'd been eight evenings, too, of sitting against Casey's headboard at bedtime with her cuddled up beside him, and having her read to him from the "hard books" she was working to master in Year Two, because she needed to get up to speed, helping her do it was his job, and he always did his job. After that, he'd read to her from the dinosaur book, which remained altogether too focused on combat, but which she loved anyway. A rugby girl through and through.

Then there were the eight breakfasts and eight dinners, most of the dinners, somehow, eaten with Zora and Isaiah.

It was too easy to say "yes" when Zora invited the two of them to stay, and so much cozier in her tiny, warm kitchen than in his own perfectly appointed one, helping her cook something that tasted better than he ever managed for himself. You could say that he was getting cooking lessons, which was helpful in his new role, and Casey was getting time with the whanau. He and Zora hadn't had a repeat of the moment on the couch, because she'd obviously regretted it, and he didn't stay past washing-up time, so what could be wrong with eating dinner with both kids at the table? They didn't talk about Zora's personal life, or about Rhys's, or, ever, about Dylan. They didn't talk about rugby, and the break was welcome. It was easy to get too caught up in it, for a player or a coach. The harder the pressure got, the more you needed time away. They didn't talk about what Victoria would say when she learned about Casey, or what anybody else would, either. They talked to the kids, he had a chance to relax and to laugh and so did she, and it was quite possibly the best part of his day.

And if those dinners were what he thought about every single night when his car was aimed like an arrow, straight toward the little house at the edge of the hills, and what he resolved to put an end to every single night when he was driving Casey home? He had a plan for that, too. When he kissed Casey good-night and headed downstairs to get in an hour of thinking time before the next day's training, he'd remind himself, *It's a transition period, that's all, for both of you. Next week, you're leaving for twelve days. Heaps of time to meet somebody pretty in a bar, or there's that reporter over there, the blonde. Chemistry there. Invite her for a drink this time, and see how it goes. Sydney's only a three-hour flight. Once you've got somebody else, you'll be over this obsession. You can cook your own dinners, and Zora can find somebody to help her rekindle the spark. You're not helping her do that, hanging about like this. You're getting in each other's way for nothing, just because it's so easy to fall into that softness. After this trip, you'll be able to start saying no.*

For now, though? He never said no.

After the first couple of dinners, he'd begun stopping by the shops on the way home from his workouts—the ones Finn had been doing along with him every afternoon, "because nobody ever got more effective by losing their structure," which was speaking his language—and buying a few things for Zora to make the next night. He had to pick up groceries for breakfast and Casey's lunch anyway, he'd reckoned, and it only took a few more minutes to drop another item or two into the trolley. It was the least he could do.

The first time, it had been tender, buttery rounds of eye fillet that you barely needed a table knife to cut, baby potatoes, and asparagus. She'd loved those. Another night, a packet of just-baked ciabatta rolls together with ground Fossil Farms venison that had made the best burgers he'd ever tasted. That one had been a solid hit until Isaiah had let it slip to Casey that they were eating Bambi's mother, which had produced stricken, accusing eyes, followed by a logical discussion initiated by Zora and taken up by Isaiah about animal welfare, the merits and drawbacks of vegetarianism, and free-range meats versus factory farming. If Casey had ended up deciding to be a vegan, Rhys would have put his foot down absolutely. Hard line. Fortunately, though, she'd eaten the burger, "because the deers had a happy life." Casey was a practical girl.

There'd been the bag of avocadoes as well, that had cost two dollars apiece and had left Zora exclaiming helplessly, but had her face lighting up, too, which he called success. For tonight, when he'd texted her and said, *Picking up something quick for us to make,* because telling her ahead of time was surely better, it was a bottle of walnut oil, and another of balsamic vinegar flavored with herbs, along with a couple racks of lamb. He'd reckoned the vinegar had to be good, because it cost four times as much as the other kind, and the shop assistant at the gourmet place had recommended it and the walnut oil to go with his baby lettuces. He'd picked up a six-pack of craft beer as well, because Zora liked it as much as he did.

There was no side to her, he'd realized. She was happier with a burger and a beer on the deck, he'd swear, than she'd been going out to that flash restaurant with the plastic surgeon. And if he still burned to take her out himself, to have her put on that red dress just for him and to wonder what she was wearing under it, to be allowed to tell her exactly how smoking hot she looked, to smile down at her and put his hand lightly onto her lower back, but not too low, as he ushered her through the place—so what? He knew he wasn't going to get it, and you couldn't help your fantasies. His fantasies were unruly bastards. But he could cook the steaks or the burgers on the barbecue and eat them looking out onto the peace of her pretty garden in the lingering warmth of the day, drinking beer from the bottle and smiling at Isaiah's efforts to teach Casey how to sing the national anthem in Maori. And that wasn't bad at all.

Well, it was torture, but still—it wasn't bad.

Tonight, Zora opened the bags he'd brought, saw the lamb, and had said, *"Rhys,"* in the same way another woman would have if you'd brought her a diamond necklace. He said,

"It looked like exactly what I wanted, and I thought it might be exactly what you wanted, too. Tomorrow's your hard day, after all. Friday's the deliveries to houses, right? And you have wedding flowers on Saturday as well. I'd say lamb is necessary. Anyway, I told you I'd bring something quick for tonight. This is it."

She raised her hands, then let them fall onto her thighs with a slap, laughed helplessly, and said, "If you're going to keep doing this, I need to plan for it instead of holding my breath and wondering what's coming my way next. I'll start giving you a list, once you come home from Aussie. You may as well buy the entire dinner while you're at it. You're practically doing it now."

"Definitely," he said, though he wasn't paying perfect attention. He was, in fact, busy appreciating the hell out of the skirt she had on tonight, a fluttery little thing with blue flowers that went with her snug blue T-shirt. She'd painted her toenails a ruby red, though. That color was his favorite so far, and he was able to see it, because her feet were bare.

He was getting as obsessed with her feet and ankles as some fella from Victorian England, possibly because it was the one part of her body that he allowed himself to look at openly. Painting her toenails was her girly indulgence, he had the feeling, and if he had an image of her sitting on the bed in some kind of shortie PJs that showed every bit of her thighs, wielding that tiny little brush and blowing on her toes to dry them faster? That was his problem.

That blonde Aussie reporter, or somebody nice-looking in a bar, definitely. Somebody with a good smile and some softness to her, but not a brunette, and not short, either. He needed to draw a firm line under this and move on. For now, he said, "There's also the question of whether you'd cook fish for me, if I brought it home to you. I'll have some time to teach Casey to fish when I get back from Aussie. I can take Isaiah as well. Seems like a good idea. I'll take you, too, if you'd like to come."

"Fresh fish? *Really* fresh? Oh, yeh." She sighed, leaned up against the kitchen bench, and looked like he'd just given her the best treat in the world. "Keep talking, boy. If you clean it? I'll take that. But I don't need to go. You can take the kids, some lovely, lazy Sunday, and I'll stay home and . . . have a bubble bath." She smiled, slow and sweet, and he tried not to imagine her there, her hair pinned up on top of her head, a scented candle burning, soft music playing, and a glass of wine beside her, every delicious bit of her enjoying the luxury of time alone and maybe, just maybe, anticipating him coming home.

He failed absolutely in the not-picturing department. No surprise.

"A fisherman always cleans his own fish," he said. "Fillets it, too, especially if he's bringing it back to somebody special. I may have mentioned that I spent a fair bit of my childhood on a fishing boat."

"Am I special?" she asked.

"I think you know you are." He barely knew what he was saying. Her body was swaying toward him, he'd swear it. In another second, he was going to have his hand at her waist. He wasn't going to be able to help it.

"Why do you have to clean fish? They're getting washed all the time, because they live in the water." Oh. That was Casey, who'd been sitting with Isaiah in the red stools on the other side of the kitchen bench, working on her maths. Despite her terror of Year Two big words, it was the maths that had proven more daunting. They were fortunate that Isaiah was a good tutor.

Rhys went back to the salad dressing he was mixing from his too-expensive oil and vinegar, wrenching his mind off bubble baths and bare, wet skin. "'Cleaning's a whaddayacallit," he said. "A nicer way to say you gut the fish and take its head and tail off. Fillet it as well, if it's a big one like a snapper or a kingfish. We'll think positive, eh. Handing it over and expecting your—a woman—or, uh, your mate— to clean it as well as cook it, to deal with the nasty bits, is a rubbish move that gets you nowhere."

"A euphemism," Zora said. "Cleaning it, I mean." She had some pink in her cheeks, for some reason.

"That's right."

"You take out its guts?" Isaiah asked. He and Casey looked at each other and said, "Eww," bang on cue, which made Rhys smile.

"Yeh," Rhys said. "Can't eat the guts or the head, can you? And your mum doesn't want to look at those anyway. You've been fishing, surely, with your dad. He wasn't as keen as me as a kid, but he knew how."

"No," Isaiah said. "I don't think he went fishing. Or maybe I don't remember that."

Rhys cast a quick look at Zora, but she just opened the oven and asked him, "D'you want to take the roasting pan out for me? After that, we'll give it ten minutes to rest while the veggies finish, and then I'll have you slice chops."

He maneuvered the heavy pan out, setting it carefully down on a rack. "Cheers for asking me. That's points for you."

"Do I need points?"

"No," he said. "You don't." And fell a little deeper into her mouth and her eyes, even though she barely had on any makeup, she wasn't wearing a red dress, and she wasn't even trying. He didn't need a red dress or sexy shoes or lipstick or anything else. He just needed his hands on her. And his mouth. And his body. She was short, which meant that you should want her on top. It wasn't that he *didn't* want her on top. It was just that he wanted to be on top of her even more. On his elbows, with his hands in her hair while he kissed her mouth, and then made his slow way south. Taking the scenic route. Taking his time.

She hadn't been loved right in too long. She hadn't had anything she should have had in too long. He wanted to give it to her.

"Your dad went fishing," Zora said to Isaiah. "With his mates. He didn't always catch anything, that's all." Her voice tightened on the words, and Rhys thought, *Fishing, or something else that took him away from home,* and opened the oven again to check on the red potatoes and carrots roasting in there, just to keep from showing his face.

"Well," he told Isaiah when he'd closed the door again, "we can fix that. We'll go out early on a Sunday morning, the three of us, rain or shine. Out on the wharf for starters, so the two of you can learn how. That's a date."

"Mm," Zora said. "Lay the table, please, kids."

"You're going away for a very long time on Tuesday," Casey said, opening the silverware drawer and counting out knives and forks with all her concentration. "That's after Saturday, when we're all going to watch the rugby game, because you're the coach. But you're coming back."

"That's right," Rhys said.

"And you don't have to go to work on Sunday," she said. "Because the game will be over. So we can do fun things."

"Also right. I wonder where this conversation is heading?"

"We could go to a rabbit store and buy rabbits," she said. "Then I wouldn't be lonesome for you while you're gone."

"There's no such thing as a rabbit store, I don't think," Isaiah said. "Rabbits don't do anything useful, like lay eggs like chickens, or find lost people like dogs, or catch mice like cats. That's probably why people have other animals instead of rabbits."

"People do so have rabbits," Casey said. "Lots of people do. So there has to be a rabbit store."

"Maybe they only have that in the United States," Isaiah said. "Not in New Zealand. Rabbits are only useful for eating. I've seen them in the butcher's before. Parts of them, anyway, because they're butchered."

"They are not," Casey said. "You don't eat rabbits."

"You didn't think people ate deer, either," Isaiah said. "But they do."

"People do have pet rabbits," Zora said firmly. "We won't talk right now about butchering, Isaiah."

Casey didn't look tearful, like another girl would have. She looked fierce, like she'd defend her nonexistent rabbits to the death. She might not be Rhys's, and yet she most definitely was.

He looked at her with as much sternness as he could summon, and she looked back at him with those killer eyes and sighed, all the way from her skinny chest. She was wearing the red shirt tonight, the one with the sparkly heart. A heart that knew what it wanted.

"Rabbits are my replacement, eh," he said. "Good to know. You'll be happy to know that I've been researching hutches, then. I may possibly have ordered one, and a pen as well. They're arriving—when was that? Oh, yeh. Tomorrow. In about a hundred boxes, I'm guessing, requiring assembly. Of course, I've spoilt the surprise now."

Her mouth opened, and for once, she seemed stuck for something to say. "Yeh," he said. "I see that I *did* surprise you. I told you, I keep my promises."

She ran straight at him like the world's most ambitious tackler. He pivoted, got her around the waist, swung her into the air, and pulled her in. She was still holding the silverware, but she wrapped her arms around him anyway, bashing him in the back with it in the process, buried her face in his neck, and said, "I love you very, very much."

There was something in his eye, maybe. Zora was smiling, but her eyes were bright. "Rhys," she said, "that's so . . . that's very sweet."

"Except for two things," he said, hanging onto Casey, who felt exactly right there, in his arms. "First, that we still need to get some rabbits, or there's no point. Maybe Isaiah wants to come help us put the hutch together tomorrow evening, and have dinner at *my* house for a change. He could even stay over and give Auntie Zora a night to herself. And maybe Zora *and* Isaiah want to go bunny-shopping with us on Sunday, what d'you reckon? I could take us out for that brekkie I promised weeks ago. After that, there's the wee issue of my absence. I had an idea about that. Just temporary, of course, until we get our situation sorted and get you a nanny." Which would be progressing faster if he'd actually done anything about it.

"Hmm." Zora was looking skeptical now. "I can't wait." He wondered if she'd guessed about the non-nanny-hunting. He'd meant to do it. He just hadn't managed it yet. Which was unlike him, and which would change, once he got back from Aussie with his head on straight.

"Of course," he said, "there's bunny-visiting instead, but that would be so much extra work. Every morning and every night, probably, and who knows what kind of vicious, feral beasts you'd have at the end of it, with nobody to pat them? Killers, most likely. I'd have to pay Zora much more for that, too, even than I'm doing for full-time care, and I'm a cheap fella. Or there's another way. It seemed to me"—this part, he said cautiously, because this wasn't the precise way he'd meant to broach this idea—"that you and Isaiah may want to do some commuting, Zora. Flowers-wise, instead of bunny-wise. Or not, because I have a shed myself, as it happens. I've also got this flash house. It's a fair size."

"His house looks like a doctor's office," Casey said. "Except it's not. It doesn't have a bathtub for kids, and it has scary stairs, but it's very jungly, which is a good thing, because we could play soldiers in the jungle, Isaiah."

"All true," Rhys said. "Good kitchen, also, which the decorator outfitted with the basics, fortunately. The only issue is that it has, ah, three bedrooms. The master has a view you may like, though, and, of course, I wouldn't be there. That would be the idea."

"I'm sleeping in your bed, that what you're saying?" Zora asked. "Rhys—"

"With clean sheets, so it's like I've never been there at all. And as I mentioned," he hurried on, wondering exactly how shot down he'd feel when she quite rightly rejected the entire mad idea, "the house comes with a shed, and I don't have anything in it. It even has a sink outside it, under a shelter. I confess I was thinking of it more in terms of that fish-gutting, but I haven't had a chance to put it to use yet, so it's pristine as far as flower arranging goes. I'm a dead loss as a Kiwi bloke just now. Been gone from the homeland too long, and haven't had a chance to acquire much of anything in the way of tools, or even any tackle for camping and fishing and that. If you wanted to shift the floral operation over entirely during my absences, the buckets and clippers and all, that would work."

Zora did that thing again where she lifted her hands, then slapped them against her thighs. Her palms left a faint pink mark on her skin. He couldn't help but notice. "Kids," she said, "go do . . . something in Isaiah's room." She reached out and took the somewhat grubby silverware from Casey's hand. "We'll call you when it's time for dinner."

"I'm very hungry, though," Isaiah said as Rhys set Casey on her feet. His eyes went from his mother to Rhys, and he looked off-balance for once.

Zora wrapped an arm around his shoulders. "Uncle Rhys and I need to talk for a few minutes. We'll eat dinner very soon, and we'll talk about everything we decide. I'll answer all your questions then. I promise."

# past tense

Zora waited until the kids had left the room and asked Rhys, "Why, exactly?"

"Because it's—" He stopped.

She needed to get him to slice the lamb. She needed to lay the table. She needed to hear his answer.

Hayden had rung the night before and said, "Just to let you know, I'll come cut your grass again on Sunday. Also, I could take Isaiah to Kelly Tarlton's afterwards, if you like, especially as Mum and Dad have invited us to dinner. Well, they've invited me, and I'm sure you and Isaiah are about to be summoned as well. I'll fulfill all my family obligations in one day, and learn some natural history at the aquarium at the same time, because that's so valuable in my life. Did you know that Antarctica is both the windiest and the driest continent on Earth? You wouldn't think it, with all the ice, but it's true. Your son knows it, and so do I. It also has an active volcano. Ask me how I know. They have new rescued sea turtles at Kelly's, too. I may have had a voicemail about them."

"No on the grass," she'd said. "Rhys did it, and I'm guessing he'll do it next time. He was here on Monday to drop off Casey, and he noticed it was getting long, so . . . For that matter, I can cut my own grass. Why do men always think they have to cut the grass? No man ever says, 'I see you need dinner cooked. Why don't I take care of that?' Which generally takes longer than cutting the grass, and you have to do it every single night." It helped if a man did your grocery

162

shopping, though, especially when he brought the kind of melt-in-your-mouth steaks that cost fifty dollars a kilogram, which you couldn't indulge in no matter how many flower subscriptions you sold, not if you were saving for a new van. And then barbecued them for you. And then talked to you like he wanted to be there, and smiled with his eyes.

All right, *some* men *did* take care of dinner.

"Wait," Hayden said. "What's that note I'm hearing? Why aren't you interested in my turtles? Wait again. *I'm* not interested in my turtles. Why aren't *you* interested in my turtles?"

"What note?" she said. "There's no note. The date didn't go anywhere, just like I told you. I'm the same as ever, and I'm fine. I'll say yes to Kelly Tarlton's all the same, though. Do you mind taking Casey as well? She'd love to see the penguins, and I'd kill for a couple hours alone. Face mask, pedicure, very long bath, architecture magazines. Heaven."

"So many avenues to explore," Hayden said. "First—Mr. Plaid Shorts wasn't interested? Too right he was interested."

"But I wasn't." She was just glad Rhys and Casey had left and weren't hearing this. "No spark."

"Mm-hmm," Hayden said. "Surprising me not at all."

"Would it—" She stopped, then tried again. "What would a man think—other than you—if I told him that? That there was no spark with somebody? If I mentioned that I—"

"Oh, boy," Hayden breathed. "If you mentioned that you what?"

"Had sort of lost my—desire. I can't believe I said it," she hurried on. *"Why* did I say it? Too much to drink, possibly." Or the look in Rhys's eyes. She hadn't melted once during all that kissing, but the minute he'd looked at her? Oh, yeh. She'd done more than melt. She'd burned.

"Let me get this straight," Hayden said. "Who did you say this to? Not to Dr. Plaid, because we both know what he'd say. 'Thanks for nothing, see you at the office, and by the way, you're getting saddlebags.'"

"I am not getting saddlebags. I exercise." She ran her hand

down the back of her thighs to make sure. Her tummy and bum were possibly not as tiny as they might have been, but she wasn't getting saddlebags. She had good legs. It was her best *thing.*

"But if you said this to, say, Rhys Fletcher?" Hayden went on. "As in, 'Why can't I get excited anymore, even when a man kisses me for hours and uses his tongue the way I like? Why didn't I get that panty-melting buzz tonight? Is there something wrong with me, Rhys? Will I never be satisfied by a man's touch again?'"

"Ugh," she moaned, then rolled over and hit her forehead against the mattress. "Ugh. Ugh. And I did not say the thing about the tongue. It's bad, though, isn't it?"

"To the most competitive man in the world? Possibly. Or not. Not bad at all, unless you didn't mean him to take it as a challenge."

"I thought so. *Bugger.*"

*"Did* he take it as a challenge? I wouldn't have thought it, and yet I would. So many interesting cross-currents there. Most upright fella in the world, I'd have said. Boringly so, if he weren't so smoldering hot. Mana up to the eyeballs. Your brother-in-law, too. Don't tell me I have to defend your honor, please. I'm too young to die."

"No. Of course not. I may have embarrassed myself a bit, that's all. Oh, well. It was one time, on one night. We're friendly. I'm helping with Casey, as you know. And by the way? The most upright fella in the world doesn't run around on his fiancée and make babies with somebody else, and then waltz off and go on with his life."

"Is there more than one baby now?"

"No. Figure of speech." She was feeling more than cross.

"He's doing all right by her now, it seems," Hayden said. "Back to fully honorable status, I'd say. Exactly how friendly are you?"

"Never mind. I'm sorry I told you. Kelly Tarlton's on Sunday sounds awesome. Thanks."

Now, she knew she'd be ringing him up and canceling

Kelly's, because they were shopping for rabbits on Sunday instead, and she wanted to do it. Seeing Rhys and Casey together did something healing to her heart, maybe, despite the lying-and-cheating aspect, and her heart needed healing. She told Rhys, "Go on and slice that lamb now," and got the veggies out of the oven. "And tell me again why moving into your house makes more sense than us staying here."

He picked up the carving knife and fork and got to work. He'd got his hair cut on Tuesday. Although it was as dark and thick as ever, it was more under control now, like the rest of him, the hair pushed back from his forehead, furrowed both by lines and scar tissue, with its distinctive hairline that was exactly like Casey's. His hair fell only to his chin, and he'd shaved, too. Chin dimple present and accounted for, and if anything, more visible muscle than ever. She wished he wouldn't wear white T-shirts that showed his tattoo, his golden-dark skin, and the swell of his biceps. He'd been working out more, he'd mentioned, but surely it wouldn't show that fast. Maybe she'd just had more occasion to look, especially since her eyes were about at the level of his chest. Which meant she looked at his chest a lot.

"Could be that staying at my house doesn't make sense, of course," he said, "other than the rabbits, if we end up with rabbits. But I think we'll end up with rabbits. Or it could be that I thought it might be a treat. Which doesn't sound good until I say that your bath is surely not big enough for you to stretch out, and mine is, and has a view besides. I don't care—I've never used it—but I thought you might. Like going on holiday to a posh hotel, possibly, since I won't be there. A holiday with two kids and your job still to do, but you can't have everything, eh."

She stared at him. "How did you know that I was thinking about lying in the bath?"

He stopped carving lamb. "What? Uh . . . you told me. A bubble bath, and painting your toenails."

She had not told him about her toenails. She'd never have done that. It was her one indulgent time, at night, which for some reason, was fantasy time, too, or had become so. Whatever she'd told Hayden, whatever she'd told Rhys, her buzz was back.

She needed to find somebody, obviously. That had to be why she was reacting so inappropriately. How did you find somebody when you never went out? It was a daunting prospect. "Never mind," she said. "We'll do the rabbit-minding, one way or another. Although I don't know anything about rabbits, fair warning. If I kill one, you'd better tell me how to get a replacement fast."

He smiled. "No worries. I've researched. Also, I expect Casey will put us both right."

♡♡♡

Going to a Blues game again was weird. More than weird. Surreal.

She hadn't been for four years, not since Dylan had left New Zealand to play a final season in England, and hadn't taken her with him. "It's for less than a year," he'd said, "and Isaiah's in school. I'll visit."

It hadn't been hard to convince her. She hadn't wanted to go. Dylan wanted to pretend to be single, and she wanted to actually *be* single. Going to the games had been hard for a couple years by then. Smiling and cheering with the other wives and girlfriends, and wondering how late Dylan would come home. It wasn't a time in her life that she wanted to revisit.

As she walked up staircase after staircase in Eden Park, holding Isaiah by one hand and Casey by the other, she thought that however hard her life sometimes felt now, it was so much better than the last time she'd taken these stairs. She didn't have to pretend anything anymore, to anyone. She might have had to put a bucket in the corner of her bedroom last night when it had rained and the water had dripped through the roof, but she had heaps of buckets. Her van might be making a worrisome knocking noise, but she was going shopping for a new one in another month or two. Her life might not be one bit glamorous, and nobody would see her photo in the newspaper and envy her, but she was free to live her own life and not be lied to, and what could be more enviable than that?

Casey asked, when they were through the doors and headed down to their section, "Where is he?"

Zora didn't ask who "he" was. She knew. There was some reason Casey didn't call him "Dad," or by his name, either. She was in in-between land, still. "Your dad?" she asked, keeping it calm. "He's up in the coaching box." She turned with Casey and pointed up to the glassed-in boxes above them.

"Oh," Casey said. "But the Chicago Bears coach is always down there next to where they're playing, because he has to yell at people."

Zora laughed despite her tension. "Rugby's a bit different. All the coach can do during the game is watch. If he has to yell, he has about ten minutes at halftime to do it. Otherwise, the players make the decisions themselves, while they're out there."

"Oh," Casey said, and considered. "They must be very smart."

"Uncle Rhys was," Isaiah said, absolutely unexpectedly. "That's why he was an All Black, and why he's the coach. He had spectacular on-field vision. That's what this one article said. That means he can tell what's happening, and what he thinks is going to happen next, and he's usually right. I read about it. My dad wasn't as good as Uncle Rhys. He was good at running, but he made mistakes. Uncle Rhys didn't make mistakes."

Wow. Zora needed to address that. How, though? "This is us," she said. At least she hoped it was. Three seats empty at the end of the row, and next to them, the one face she knew best, and the one she knew would be welcoming. Jenna Douglas, married to Rhys's assistant coach, Finn, and still sitting with the wives and girlfriends, because they were still her friends.

Other than Jenna, though, this definitely felt awkward. Most of the wives had called, when they'd heard about Dylan's illness, had asked her out to lunch, to see a movie, offered to watch Isaiah for an afternoon. Everybody had been kind. She'd wondered, at the time, *Did you know? Did everybody know?* Besides, she'd had a five-year-old whose world was changing too much, and a husband who was hurting and scared and so afraid she'd leave him alone. The world of rugby, of strong bodies and mending injuries and training as hard as you could to earn your starting place, had seemed far away, like she was looking at it through wavy glass.

Dylan hadn't even wanted to watch the games on TV anymore, after a while. After he'd known this was it, and there was no coming back. Instead, he'd wanted her to read to him. Murder mysteries, and funny things. P.G. Wodehouse, humor from decades ago, and still funny. Oddly, those quiet moments had been the closest she'd felt to him in years, when she'd seen the man she'd fallen in love with once again, funny and sweet and needing her so much. She'd resented him, she'd felt sorry for him, and she'd loved him, in an exasperated, hopeless, pitying way that was nothing like anything she'd felt before.

None of which was necessary to think about now, except that maybe it was. She needed to remember the good parts, too. Bitterness got you nowhere. She was so tired of bitterness, of feeling cold. She needed sweetness and laughter and warmth and *life,* and so did Isaiah.

Jenna's face lit up on seeing her, and she jumped up, hugged her with one arm while she juggled a chubby-cheeked two-year-old in a Blues jersey in the other, and said, "Finn told me you'd be here. What a lovely surprise. I saved you seats at the end, by me. And you're Isaiah. I haven't seen you since you were a little fella. And Casey, too. Hi. I'm Jenna. My husband works with your dad. Is this your first rugby game?"

"Yes," Casey said. "It's supposed to be kind of like

football, but it doesn't look like football at all."

Jenna said, "You're American. Me, too. Never mind. If you sit by me, I'll tell you what I know about it."

"OK," Casey said. She had on her stolid look again, and Zora put a hand on her shoulder.

"Isaiah," Jenna said, "scoot on past and sit with Harry. Just don't expect him to be too excited. He watches more closely than he used to, but he still isn't impressed by rugby. How about you?"

"I like to play it best," Isaiah said. He could be shy with strangers, but you couldn't be shy with Jenna. It was something about her voice, maybe, or the way she remembered everybody's name. "I don't watch too much on TV, because Mum doesn't like to. Come on, Casey. I'll explain."

Wonderful. Zora had been outed even before she'd sat down.

"Thanks," Zora said, taking a seat at the end of the row, while Jenna scooted one over toward her. "I heard you'd had another baby. Congratulations, though I'm a bit late there. What's his name?"

"Ethan." Jenna joggled him, and he didn't pay too much attention. He had a dump truck in one hand and a police cruiser in the other, and was engaged in running them into each other on his trouser leg and making them crash, and then laughing. "He's a happy guy most of the time, and a good sleeper, fortunately, aren't you, buddy? Good at taking your nap?"

Ethan said, "No nap," forcefully enough that Zora laughed.

"Or not," Jenna said. "What can I say? He's two."

"Time for another one, maybe?" Zora asked teasingly.

Jenna was the one laughing this time. "Two girls and two boys already. Some people love art. Some people love jewelry, or luxury travel, or expensive cars. That one, I'll never understand. I love babies."

Casey said, on Jenna's other side, "He's not exactly a baby, though, because he talks."

"That's true," Jenna said. "There you are, then. Look out,

Finn. I don't have a baby anymore. Danger time."

"How come they're going inside?" Casey asked, scrutinizing the field. "Is it over? I thought there was going to be tackling."

"They've been warming up," Zora said. "They'll be coming out again and playing soon."

"They don't have helmets on, either," Casey said. "And they're wearing shorts. Football players don't wear *shorts.*"

"They're too tough for that, is the idea," Jenna said. "No helmets. No pads."

Zora murmured, "Just balls," and both of them laughed this time. A stupid joke, but true.

"I'm glad you came," Jenna told her. "I was happy when Finn told me you were bringing Casey. I missed you, when Dylan left for the UK. Maybe because you're low-key, like me." She smiled. "Truth coming out, even after all this time. And I was so sorry, of course, to hear about Dylan. That was a shocker. They get hurt all the time, of course, but . . ."

"Yeh," Zora said. "Thank you for reaching out. I just couldn't, at the time."

Jenna touched her hand. "We all do what we have to do. If you haven't been in that spot, you can't judge, surely. Finn told me about your flower business, though. That's exciting."

"Earning a living," Zora said, "but I like it."

"Is it awkward if I subscribe?" Jenna asked. "Flower arranging isn't something I've ever really mastered. Funny, what you do well and what you don't. My Christmas trees generally feature things my kids made in school. I found out that people have theme trees, and I realized that the whole idea had just gone . . ." She passed a hand over her head. "Whoosh. My interior design skills are slim to none, in fact. I could use some beautification, if that's all right. I could spread the word, too. And don't worry, nobody will be signing up out of pity, or whatever you're imagining. Your arrangements are stunning, unless what's on the website is a cruel hoax."

Zora was laughing. "Not a cruel hoax. And if you saw my house . . . I've got a bucket in the corner of my bedroom. My roof leaks. Also, my kitchen is red. I don't mean red accents. I mean it's *red.*"

"Well, red can be . . . homey? Warm?"

"Or bizarre," Zora said. "At this point, I'm clinging to it out of stubbornness. I'm oddly fond of my red kitchen. And dining room. We're *extremely* red."

"Mm. Finn says Rhys's new place is flash, though."

"I don't know," Zora said. "I'm seeing it tomorrow."

"Could be strange," Jenna said, "having him back in your life. And Casey now, too. Nice, I'm sure, but different. I always liked Rhys, maybe because he's like Finn. The kind of man that appeals to me, I suppose. Wait. That came out wrong. I mean—"

"Big," Zora said. "Hard-tackling. Scary, if you don't know better. Hard man. Good dad."

"Is he?" Jenna asked, her face lighting up. "I'm glad. I was surprised, when Finn told me. We were all surprised. It's been a topic, you could say. Not surprised about the 'good dad' part. Only surprised that it was . . . uh, him. Or that it took him so long to . . . that . . . Oh, dear. I've boxed myself in."

"Yeh," Zora said, and finally relaxed, just as the announcer's voice swelled, the torches below sent out gouts of flame, and the team ran out onto the field. "I was surprised, too. But I think I'm getting used to it."

# bathsheba

Zora pulled the van to a stop in Rhys's driveway at exactly nine o'clock on Sunday morning. It felt like an occasion. It felt too momentous. It had been going to see the rugby, probably, and all those complicated feelings it brought up, especially her attraction to men who ran hard, tackled their hearts out, and battled as long as they could draw breath.

She wasn't nearly as modern a woman as she ought to be. She also didn't seem to have learned much over the past ten years.

"It does look like a doctor's office," she told Casey. "A bit." Well, that would make it easier to resist the temptation, mad as it was, to stay here with the kids while Rhys was gone. She'd envisioned something totally glam, multiple levels of spectacular high-end housing. Instead, she was looking at a dark-wood rectangle with four tall, narrow windows and a door for a two-car garage. Otherwise? A concrete pad for cars, and a flat patch of tiny stones overlaid by more concrete pavers leading to an absolutely plain front door, with a few small bushes to break the monotony.

She wasn't overly materialistic, she hoped. If she ever had been, she'd got over it. Rhys was a practical man, and this looked as low-maintenance as you could get. There was probably some back garden on the downhill slope, anyway. There had to be, if there was a rabbit hutch down there. Better views, too, surely. Scenic Drive was the most tree-intensive and winding of streets, with views that justified its name and a price tag to match, and wound around a ridgetop and into the Waitakeres, the mountains that lay between Auckland and the rough, wild western shores of the Tasman Sea. Nobody would build a house up here with a view of only a few trees.

"Come on," Casey told her, climbing out. "I'll show you my room." She raced over to one of the narrow windows, and Isaiah went with her. Casey put her hands around her eyes and peered inside. "It's kind of plain," she told Zora, "but it's going to get better."

Zora took a look. That was no joke, about it being plain. A queen-size bed and bedside table, a wall of built-in white shelving and desk, and that was all.

"The next one is mine," Isaiah said. "Except the bath is in between." With glass-block windows, so you couldn't see in. Which made sense. And—yes. "Isaiah's room" was another queen-size bed and some more white shelving.

The door opened behind her, and there was Rhys, dressed in rugby shorts and a gray T-shirt in the end-of-summer weather, and with the kind of breadth to his shoulders and warmth in his eyes that could cause breathing problems. A warmth that was meant for Casey, because she ran to him, and he swung her up into his arms, gave her a cuddle, and asked, "How did you like your first rugby match, then? Ready to join the team at school?"

"Yes," she said, her arms tight around his neck and her face pressed to his. "Because it's very fierce and fast. Except I need you to teach me."

He laughed, a warmer, more relaxed sound than Zora had ever imagined coming from him, until the past few weeks. "I could do that," he said, "along with Isaiah. How you goin', mate? Have a good time, did you?"

"Yeh," Isaiah said. "Except the Blues lost."

Rhys made a face. "You aren't supposed to mention that, not straight off the bat."

"Did you yell at people?" Casey asked hopefully.

Some more smile. "Nah. I'll yell at them tomorrow, no worries. Or, rather, I'll go over where we fell short and what we need to do better next week. Here's a secret. Losing's on me, too. On me most of all, you could say. Winning's my job. If we didn't win, I need to do my job better."

"Nobody wins every time," Isaiah objected. "Even the All Blacks have only about eighty percent of winning. That means they lose two times out of every ten games they play," he told Casey. "And ninety percent winning for the last ten years. That's nine times out of ten, and one time, they lose."

"If you keep saying the L-word," Rhys said, "I'll lose all my happy feelings and won't be in the mood to buy bunnies at all. That would be tragic." He looked, finally, at Zora, and his expression, instead of hardening the way it sometimes did, got . . . what? More intense, maybe, but not harder, not this time. "Hey," he said, and there was that smile again, around his eyes. "All right?"

Dylan had always been moody and grumpy after a loss. Zora said, "Hi" back, then got stuck.

"Come inside," he said.

Oh. Good idea.

An entry that was nothing but oversized gray tiles underfoot and walls of uncompromising white, and a stairwell leading down. She saw what Casey meant about the scary stairs. The staircase was curved, and it was mostly clear acrylic, with gorgeous pale-gray stair treads standing as if by magic, like something in a story. And when she took that turn? It was *really* magic.

"Rhys," she said helplessly. "Wow."

"Good, eh," he said.

"Yeh. You could say that."

It was like being in a treehouse. The entire front—back—whatever—of the house was glass from end to end and floor to ceiling, looking out on an endless section of native bush marching down the hill to the sea, all palms, tree ferns, cabbage trees, and pohutukawa. There'd be ferns under there, too, she knew, all of it looking as misty and magical as it had hundreds of years before. Jungly trees, Casey had said, and they were. The sky was a clear, impossible blue today, except for a few drifts of white cloud, and the sun dazzled, shining on the flat stretch of water far below.

"Sea view," she said. "Harbour view, at any rate."

"Yeh. I like seeing the sea. Never got over that one." He'd set Casey down, and she and Isaiah ran through an open glass panel and down the stairs from this level's third room. That was an enormous deck, furnished with comfortable-looking couches as well as a dining set, all of it in dark wicker, that stretched the width of the lounge with its black leather couches, the dining area, and a clean, modern kitchen done in white and shades of gray. The deck railing was entirely acrylic again, so you seemed to be perched on the edge of forever. If you had a fear of heights, it would be scary. If you didn't, it would be magic.

"All roofed over," she said. "So open, and so private. I love it. Must be spectacular at night, with the city lights. Of course," she tried to joke, "I'm pretty spectacular too these days, with my red tile and all."

His eyes went to "alert" again, or maybe they went to "more alert," since Rhys could never look any other way. "Not sensitive of me, maybe, showing the place off to you?"

"No. Not at all." She laughed and ran a hand through her hair, wishing all the same that she'd worn something other than shorts, a sea-blue top, and sandals that she'd kicked off at the door. She'd thought the top was cute, with its pintucks, cap sleeves, and buttons down the front, but she'd resisted dressing up too much. What would Rhys have thought if she'd turned up in a mini? That she was trying too hard, which would make him wonder why.

Especially since she'd somehow changed into short skirts after work every day this week. They made her feel sexy, and she'd wanted to feel that way. Today, though, they were shopping for rabbits. Sitting on the grass, probably. And she needed to stop trying to be sexy for Rhys, or imagining that he was looking at her legs. Or looking at his shoulders and his mouth, and picturing his . . .

*No. Stop.* Anyway, here she was, dressed in shorts and

nowhere near glamorous enough for this house. "No," she said again. "I want to see where you're living. Where Casey's living. Of course I do. It's a beautiful house. It's a spectacular house. It shouldn't feel the least bit cozy or homey, not with nothing but gray carpeting to soften it, no curtains or pictures on the wall, but it does. It must be the trees."

"Yeh," he said. "What I thought. This is my first house, believe it or not. I'm forty, and all I've had before are condos. Time for a change, in all kinds of ways."

"Victoria liked the low-maintenance high-rises, Dylan said."

"She did. But come see this bath. This may be why I bought the place, even though I never use it. Could be I had a vision. Call it a fantasy, maybe."

The master bedroom was part of the wall of glass that stretched on two sides, looking out on both the view and into the rest of the house. Roller shades hung at the top of the windows, and here, too, there were no curtains. And on the other side of a king-sized bed, dressed in white and sitting against a charcoal wall, there was a bathroom.

"Gorgeous," she said when she stepped inside. It was an ensuite, that was all, of the ultra-high-end variety, except for one thing: the pedestal bath that stood in front of the wall of glass and looked out over bush, city, and sea. "You'd feel exposed, but in such a sexy way. A bit of David and Bathsheba on the roof, maybe."

His green-gold eyes got a little warmer, or maybe a little more hawklike. She wasn't sure what to call it. She just knew he was focused. "I don't know about that, other than that I agree, it's sexy."

"Not a very nice story." She shouldn't have said the "sexy" bit. It had just slipped out. She leaned back against the long gray-marbled white counter with its two white vessel sinks. "Is this floor heated?"

"Yes. Not now. Too warm out." He was leaning himself, one hip against the wall, his arms folded. She wondered if he knew how good that stance made him look, biceps and forearms and chest and tattoo and all, and if that was why he did it, but dismissed the thought. Rhys wasn't one bit vain. Another difference from Dylan. Rhys's face, its nose broken one too many times, his jaw too square, his brows too thick and dark and his brow ridges too pronounced, told you that you could judge him by what he did, not how he looked, not that he cared a bit how you judged him at all. He said, "Tell me the story."

She wished she hadn't said anything about it. This wasn't going to come out well. "Maori usually go to church," she said instead. "You and Dylan seem to have missed out on that."

"Some. Call our upbringing 'irregular.' Never mind. Educate me."

Was it hot in here? She had a hand at the back of her neck, the other one tracing over smooth benchtop and the edges of those gorgeous sinks. They were like broken pieces of shell, tumbled in the sea until their edges were smooth. The whole house was like that. Nothing but gray and white with a few splashes of charcoal, all of it organic, full of texture, and belonging as much to the sea as to the land.

"King David," she said, and quoted, "'And it came to pass in an eveningtide, that David arose from off his bed, and walked upon the roof of the king's house: and from the roof he saw a woman washing herself; and the woman was very beautiful to look upon.' That's the only pretty part of the story, if having him spy on her while she was naked can be called 'pretty.' Something about it I always remembered, because it was hotter than anything else in church, probably, like every boy hears the Song of Solomon and thinks, 'I want that.'" She smiled, or she tried to. "That song 'Hallelujah'? You must have heard that. That's what it's about, David and Bathsheba."

"Mm," Rhys said. "I have. Hell of a sexy song. I thought it was about orgasm."

"That too. About love and sex and being overwhelmed beyond reason. And maybe about more than that." Why were they talking about orgasm? She was so far out on the edge.

This was disastrous. She was going to embarrass herself and him in the worst possible way. She couldn't go on.

He prompted, "Then what happened? In the story?"

She was going on. "What d'you think happened? If it hadn't been bad, there'd have been no story. He was the king. She was the wife of one of his generals, and he knew it. And still, he sent for her, and he slept with her. They don't tell you whether she wanted it, but I'm guessing she was torn. The heart of a lion, the courage of twenty, and the strength to build himself into a king, all the way from nothing? Anyway—however she felt about it, he did it, and he got her pregnant. After that, he sent her husband off to the front lines to be killed. Once that was done, he married his widow. Not too loyal. Not too virtuous. You couldn't call it anything, in fact—" She had to stop and take a breath. "But betrayal."

"Or," he said, "you could call it overpowering. Stronger than reason. Stronger than everything you've ever been taught is right."

She swallowed. It wasn't easy. "Strong as sin."

"That desire you talked about," he said. "When the spark turns to flame. When it takes you in the fire, and you can't help but burn."

She was burning now. "I—"

He took a step toward her. Just one. And she was right over the edge. She asked him, "Do you know what I wanted last night?"

Oh, no. She wasn't saying this.

"No," he said. "I know what I did, though." He wasn't touching her, but his chest was rising and falling like he was in the gym. "I know what had me running for two hours this morning to try to shake it loose, and it wasn't just the game I lost. It was what I want that I can't have."

Her own breath was so shallow, she was nearly panting. "I wanted," she said, then gathered her courage around her like a cloak of feathers and went on. "I wanted to watch you play, just once, and be allowed to do it all the way, to feel everything I felt, with no shame and no holding back. Almost every time I did watch, you were playing against the Blues."

"Playing against Dylan." His hand came out, exactly as it had on the couch a few nights ago. When she'd thought, *No. You're imagining things.* Now, she knew she hadn't been, when he took a curl between his fingers and rubbed. "Or watching with him, maybe."

She couldn't move. He had her pinned with those eyes. "Loyalty," she said. It was almost a whisper.

"Sin," he said, and the word fell from that sensual mouth like a pebble into a pond, sending its ripples through her body. She knew how Bathsheba had felt, when she'd become aware of the king's eyes on her. How she'd turned her head and drawn the sponge over the back of her neck, down her arm, warm and languid, and thought, *He's the king. What can I do?* The dark thrill when she'd walked to him across a bedchamber, and he'd put his hand out, brushed the white gown from her shoulder, and exposed her. How she'd closed her eyes, and how she'd shuddered.

His hand moved from her hair. Slowly. His palm cupped her face, turned it up to his, and it was so gentle, it hurt. Her eyes closed, and he said, "Zora. Look at me."

Oh, God. There was no escaping this. Her lids fluttered open, and he dropped his head. And when his lips brushed over hers . . . they tingled, and the desire went down her body like a flaming arrow.

Strong as sin.

Another kiss, his lips firmer now, and his arm around her back, pulling her in. The faint scent of cedar and sandalwood, the moisture in the air from the shower he'd taken, cleaning up for her. The warmth coming off the skin of a man who'd run for two hours on a forest track, trying to get her out of his blood, and hadn't been able to do it.

"Mum?"

Rhys stepped back. Barely. He didn't turn around, though. She slipped out from under him, and he stood there, both big palms on the white benchtop, his dark head bent, his breath coming hard. She knew why he hadn't turned around.

Because he couldn't. That arrow had been as hot going through him as it had been in her.

They were both there. Isaiah and Casey. Casey was looking at Rhys, or at his reflection. Isaiah was looking at her. They were both looking worried.

"Hi," she said. "Good house, eh. I can see why you like it, Casey. But you know what I haven't seen yet? Where you're planning to put these rabbits. Take me down and show that to me. After that, I think Uncle Rhys has plans for the day. I guess we'll all be surprised."

She knew she had been.

# absolutely not

Rhys was standing in a front garden in Mount Eden, watching Casey fall in love, and not thinking about Zora.

That was a lie. He was *trying* not to think about Zora. How it had felt to finally kiss that sweet, soft mouth, after ten years of imagining it. The intake of breath that he'd felt under his mouth, the triumph of knowing he was making it happen, and the silk of her cheek under his palm. He'd still barely touched her, and he knew exactly how she'd feel under his hands, and most intoxicating of all—how she'd respond to him. That was the beauty of imagining things for ten years, except not. Imagining wasn't enough anymore.

He didn't tell himself the thing about the reporter in Sydney again. He didn't want a blonde.

"I *love* him," Casey was saying, and he refocused. "He's so, so aborable. He's the cutest one ever, except all of them are. They're like babies, even though they're grownups. They're better than dolls."

"He" was a rabbit. A Mini Cashmere Lop rabbit, to be exact, less than a kilogram of fuzzy cuteness, currently being cradled in Casey's arms as she sat on the grass, and nibbling a baby carrot out of her fingers. He was adorable, right enough, a mound of impossibly plush, cream-colored fur, his head round and his little ears hanging down. No stuffed toy in the world could possibly be as cuddly as this, and Casey was toast.

Beside Casey, Isaiah was cuddling another rabbit, this one a rich brown, and Zora held a third, a dappled black and white. All of them, though, were exactly as sweetly fuzzy, exactly as round, exactly as droopy-eared, and exactly as tiny.

"We have another couple of places still to visit," Rhys reminded Casey. "And then we'll decide."

Three pairs of eyes turned to him. All of them were reproachful. The current owner of the rabbits, an older woman with short white hair cut in a combative style and an air about her like a dealer in Oriental carpets that boded no good at all, said, "That's fine, then. If you're finished looking, go on and put them back in the pen, as I have another couple coming who are very keen."

Casey didn't put her rabbit back in the pen. She held him tighter and said, "Marshmallow doesn't want to go with somebody else. He wants to come home with me. And Cinnamon is sad, because nobody's holding him."

Fine. Rhys picked up the fourth rabbit, who was, well, cinnamon-colored. How much trouble was he in that Casey and Isaiah had already named them? Marshmallow, Cinnamon, Cocoa, and Oreo. Heaps of trouble, that was how much. The tiny animal's nose twitched, and he snuggled into Rhys's palm as if he wanted to be there. Rhys gave him a careful stroke, feeling like he was about to squash him and resisting the cuteness with everything he had.

He was a hard man. *Famously* a hard man. He did not cuddle bunnies. If anybody asked him to kiss one, he was refusing, no matter how Casey looked at him. "They're smaller than I had in mind," he told the woman, whose name was Nora. "Delicate, maybe."

She snorted. "And small's a bad thing? I don't think so. About the most sought-after pet rabbit in the world just now. Most rabbit breeds don't want to be held, but these ones love it. Perfect temperament for kids this age, if they can be gentle."

"Also," Rhys continued doggedly, "they're all male. Not so good. Could be aggressive." Anything less aggressive than the tiny furball currently eating a stalk of hay out of his hand couldn't be imagined, but you never knew.

"Male rabbits are calmer," Nora said. "More desirable. Less likely to nip. Like I said—if you don't want them, that's all well and good. It's three weeks still until we move. I'll have no trouble selling them in that time. If I find the right family." She eyed Rhys in what he could only call a suspicious fashion. "You're an All Black, I understand. You could be violent."

*Violent?* He could be violent? "I was an All Black, yeh," he said, although there was no "was" about it. Once an All Black, always an All Black. He'd never forgotten his All Black number, his spot in the long line of proud men that stretched back over a hundred years, and he never would. The digits, and his name, were stitched into every one of the black jerseys tucked into a corner of a closet—a fraction of the seventy-nine he'd earned. He'd kept only the most memorable ones, and had given the rest away to various charities. He didn't live in the past, and his number wasn't tattooed on any part of him but his mind. "These days," he said, "I'm a coach." He didn't address the "violent" part. What the hell?

Nora said, "Coach of the Blues, my husband says."

"That's right."

She said, "I liked the fella they had before. He was a neighbor, just in the next street. They should have kept him on."

"Aleke Fiso," Isaiah said. "He went to coach Wales, though. And Uncle Rhys isn't violent. Violent means hitting people at regular times, not in rugby. He doesn't hit. I don't think he hit people in rugby, even. Not with his hand."

"You're right," Rhys said. "Hitting with your hand is generally frowned upon."

"Or Finn Douglas," Nora said, as if he hadn't spoken. "I see his wife at the dairy from time to time. She's lovely. Natural as you please. Why didn't he get the job?"

Rhys didn't answer that one, either. Coach selection was like any other kind of selection. The public wasn't polled, and there was no point in arguing with the armchair critics who were convinced that they could put together a better squad. There was nothing that would satisfy them anyway. If you won every game, they'd ask why you hadn't won them more convincingly, or how on earth you imagined you'd win the next one with those rubbish selections.

"Presumably," Zora said, with a spark in her eye that didn't bode well, "because he wasn't the best choice, and Rhys is."

"Didn't win last night, I hear," Nora said.

"You may not want to sell your rabbits to me, then," Rhys said. "Understandable. Let's go, Casey. Two more places to visit."

"I never said that," Nora said. "When did I say that?" Which was no surprise at all. In about thirty minutes, once he'd parted with too much money, he'd be "that lovely new coach, over at the Blues. You can tell he adores his little girl. Of course, they only select the solid ones for the All Blacks. You could see it in him."

"If these look good to you," he told Casey, setting Cinnamon down again, "choose the two you want, and let's go." There were probably things he should look for, rabbit diseases, ear malformations, whatever. They all looked fine to him, though. They looked like rabbits. Small ones.

"I can't only pick *two*," she said. "They'll be lonely. They're *brothers.*"

"They are not brothers," he said. "They're four rabbits of varying ages who happen to live in the same hutch."

"They're each other's *family*," she said. "They'd be sad. Can't I have them all? Please? They're very small. They'll hardly take up any room. We could fit *more* than this."

"I said two." He could feel the control slipping right through his fingers. "I distinctly said two rabbits. We could buy about forty guinea pigs for the price of two of these rabbits, by the way. Guinea pigs are soft." Why hadn't he thought of that? Guinea pigs were also fairly interchangeable. If one of them turned up its toes in the night for mysterious reasons, he could substitute another one, with Casey none the wiser.

"But these are so *little*," she said. "They'll fit. *Please.* I'll do everything for them. I'll give them hay and fill up their pellets and change their water bottle every day, and empty their tray and wash it out again every single week like you showed me, except you might have to help, because it's very big and heavy. And I'll give them toys and play with them and make sure they are very, very loved. They can be our family, and I won't be lonesome when you're—"

"Fine," he said. "Fine. Four rabbits."

"Four hundred dollars," Nora said brightly. "Only because they aren't babies, you understand. Otherwise, it would be six hundred."

"Three hundred," Rhys said, on principle. He had the feeling even that was too dear. She'd marked him as a sucker the moment she'd seen Casey's eyes. Also, he'd had no idea in the world that rabbits could cost this much until he'd started looking around and had realized how much Casey would love the lop-eared ones. He should have bought her regular rabbits anyway. Normal, cheap, everyday rabbits. She would've been thrilled.

Too late now.

Nora shrugged. "I'll show them to the other couple," she said. "If there are any left, you can have them for a hundred dollars apiece."

Casey let out a strangled cry of protest, and Rhys surrendered. "Fine," he said. "Four hundred."

Nora said, "I'm selling the hutch as well."

It was a wooden affair, and none too flash. She probably had it priced at nine hundred dollars. "No, thanks," he said. "We've got one."

She said, "There's an indoor cage, too, dead easy to clean, all plastic and wire, built on two levels. The deluxe size, that is. Good for if the kids want to have the bunnies in the house overnight. They use their litter box, of course, but you don't want them running around the house unsupervised, do you?"

"I don't want them running around the house at all," he said. "No, thanks."

Casey said, "Can't we get an indoor house too? Please? They could be outside on the grass during the day, like we said, and I could bring them in when I got home from school so they could sleep in my room with me. If it was at night, and I had a bad dream, I could hear them munching their hay, and it would be very, very nice. Especially if you were gone a long way, to Nostralia."

"Australia," Isaiah corrected her. "I think an indoor cage is a very good idea, Uncle Rhys. Rabbits can chew on things, if you let them out. They can even chew electric cords and electrocute themselves. That would be dangerous. It could start a fire."

"If you don't let them in the house at all," Rhys said, "your electric cords are completely safe, and so are you. How about that?"

When he was loading up the back of the BMW with a two-level wire and plastic rabbit cage with four twitching-nosed, hundred-dollar bundles of fur inside, he told Zora, busy putting a bag of hay, another of green rabbit pellets, and a collection of miscellaneous items into the boot beside him, "Don't say it."

"What?" Her own nose was twitching, he'd swear, exactly like the rabbits', like she was restraining herself with immense difficulty from bursting into laughter. "That you paid full retail price for a used rabbit cage?"

"Because I don't have to look for it. Get it all set up today, that's the idea. I'm leaving Tuesday, in case I didn't mention it."

"Pity you didn't buy the protective tubing for your electric cords, then," she said sweetly. "Or the rabbit toys."

"I am not paying higher than retail value for some plastic tubing and a half-chewed ball of sea grass. One trip to the hardware store, and we're done. Besides, I was out of cash."

"Mm." She was trying so hard not to laugh. "Five hundred dollars. D'you want a flower subscription, by the way? My Supreme package is twenty percent off if you pay annually."

"I'm opening the door for you," he said, doing just that, and watching her hop up into his passenger seat with a pretty spectacular flash of thigh, "because I enjoy being a gentleman.

Not because I enjoy being teased."

"No?" She fluttered her lashes at him. "And yet I could swear you do. Four rabbits, Rhys. Four fluffy little bunnies, with an indoor *and* an outdoor home. What happens when I share that with Jenna? What happens when Finn finds out?"

"I may have four rabbits," he said. "But he has four kids." And considered the argument won. Or quit while he was behind. One or the other.

# or the shower head

"So," Zora's mother asked that night, over a dinner of chicken, rice, and vegetables that wasn't exactly gourmet, but that Zora hadn't had to cook, at least, "what kinds of new and exciting things are happening in your life, darling?"

Hayden looked at her with the usual glint in his eye. Their mum never asked *him* that. She was of the "Don't ask, don't tell" mindset when it came to Hayden's much more interesting life. Anyway, Zora's presence here with Isaiah, and the arrangement of hydrangeas, zinnias, and spray roses spilling out of a sterling-and-ceramic vase in the center of her mother's starched white linen tablecloth, looking perfectly feminine and just bloody fine in shades of blush and pale green, represented everything about her life she wanted to share. She had a son, and he was awesome. She did flowers, and she was good at it. She was organized enough to bring one of those floral arrangements to dinner. Boom. Done.

She thought about saying, *I kissed my brother-in-law,* or possibly, *I found out that every man in the world apparently cheats, including the one I thought had mana. I can't figure out why I can't stay angrier about that, or why I'm wishing I was cooking dinner with him tonight, that I was looking at him and he was looking at me with all that heat and humor, and that we were both wondering what would happen once we put the kids to bed. Why do I keep conveniently mislaying my grip on the truth, when the evidence is right there in thoroughly lovable six-year-old form, and nobody's even* trying *to deny it? Why is my body always so much more persuasive than my mind?*

188

*What is* wrong *with me?* Or maybe she should say, *I could be having sex tonight, for the first time in almost three years, with the only man in the world who burns me down, and who doesn't seem any more able to resist me than I'm able to resist him. I'll bet he knows exactly how to do it. I'll bet he'd hold me down and make me come until my legs shook. I'll bet he'd make me scream. But I can't do any of that, for reasons listed above.*

This was why flowers worked so well for her. Flowers were pure, like children. Adults, though? Adults were complicated. Also twisty, deceptive, and confusing. And once you added sex to the mix? That was when she got herself into real trouble. Every single time, like she'd never learned a thing.

She'd waited too long to answer, because Isaiah said, "I got a new cousin. That's new and exciting. Her name is Casey Moana Hawk, which sounds very cool. Her name's going to get changed so it's the same as ours, though, and we'll all be Fletcher then. I think it's better to have your names the same. That way, you know which family you belong to. I kind of wish my name could be Hawk, though. Also, Mum's earning more than a hundred and fifty extra dollars a week, and maybe even two hundred dollars, so we can probably buy her new van sooner. That's very exciting."

"Taking your points in order," Hayden said, the mischief all but shining out of him, "there is the sad reality that having everybody's name be the same *generally* means that one partner is giving up her name entirely. Unless their names are already the same, somehow, which would make everything so much easier. Is the price of inclusion too high, I wonder? What do you think, Zora? Although I agree. In fact, I think we should *all* change our name to Hawk. Much cooler. Hayden Hawk. I sound like a brand. Definitely an option."

"Oh." Isaiah appeared to be considering that idea. "Is that how it happens? Does one person have to change?"

"Yes," Zora said. Another somewhat dull subject that she could think about logically. Yay. "Uncle Hayden and I are the same family, but we have different surnames."

"Because you got married to Dad."

"That's right. It's a debate you could have, or you could decide that everybody gets to choose for themselves. You can hyphenate your kids' names, so your name would be Isaiah Allen-Fletcher, and my name would still be Zora Allen. Or you can choose just the dad's surname, or the mum's. Casey has her mum's surname. Some people even give the boys the mum's name and the girls the dad's, or the other way around, but then the kids have different surnames."

"That would be weird," Isaiah said. "I didn't think of that."

"Don't be ridiculous," Zora's mother said. "All this chopping and changing. If a tradition has been good enough for everybody for hundreds of years, it's good enough now. Isaiah's right. You're one family, and a family has a surname."

Hayden murmured on Isaiah's other side, "Shot down once more, kid. Keep thinking it through, though. Much more attractive to the ladies." He glanced at Zora, and she read the thought in his eyes perfectly. *I need wine.* There was never wine on offer, or coffee, either, at their parents' house. Sometimes, it felt like a cruel deprivation. Orthopedic surgeons needed steady hands, though, and in this house, her dad's needs ruled.

Their mother continued, "What cousin is this, Isaiah? A real cousin, or a Maori cousin?"

"Maori cousins *are* real cousins," Zora said, for approximately the seventy-third time. "Different definition, that's all."

"She's both kinds of cousin," Isaiah said. "She's Maori, like me, and Uncle Rhys is her dad. He was my dad's brother, and that makes her my cousin. I didn't know she was, and Casey didn't know he was her dad, either, but then her mum died and Uncle Rhys came, and she found out. Now she comes to our house every day, and I have to help her with school and things." He shrugged and stabbed another piece of chicken, then, at a look from Zora, picked up his knife and cut it properly. "I guess I have to, though, like Uncle Rhys says. He says a good heart matters, so you have to be kind. But Casey has rabbits now and likes to watch movies, so I don't mind."

"Dylan's brother suddenly has a secret daughter?" Her mum's brown eyes had sharpened. "I thought he was divorced."

"Getting there," Zora said. "He and Victoria are in the waiting period for the divorce. Didn't I tell you that?"

"That didn't take him long," her dad said. "No grass growing under his feet. No surprise there."

"Casey's six." Zora kept her voice level. This was the first of many times she'd be explaining this. You could call it a test.

Her mother looked up, and her dad did, too. Her dad laughed, in fact, and said, "That's not what you'd call careful. Who'd have thought Rhys Fletcher would be that reckless? Rugby players aren't always known for their self-discipline, though, I guess."

"Rugby players are exactly known for their self-discipline," Zora said. Well, not Dylan, maybe, but Rhys? Also, her dad wasn't saying, "Maori aren't known for their self-discipline," but that was what he meant. Isaiah was Maori. She'd pointed that out to her parents, and still, they did it.

"Casey came from Chicago," Isaiah said. "Which is in the United States, but Uncle Rhys brought her home to live with him. Mum and I are living at Uncle Rhys's house starting on Tuesday, and Casey got rabbits today, so she needs help to take care of them, because Uncle Rhys is about to leave for Australia."

"*Excuse* me?" Zora's mum said.

"We'll be there caring for Casey," Zora said, "while Rhys is in Australia, like Isaiah said. Rhys is coaching the Blues now, and he's bought a place in Titirangi, so it's convenient for all of us. Extra money for Isaiah and me, and Casey's a darling."

"You're a child-minder now?" her mum asked.

"No. I'm helping out with my niece, which is no hardship at all, and Rhys is paying me for it, which is a wonderful bonus."

"In other news," Hayden had to put in, "Zora had a date recently. With a doctor. Not just a doctor. A *surgeon*. Absolute parental approval territory. Life returns, eh."

Both her parents sprang into hyper-alertness. "What kind of surgeon?" her dad asked.

"Plastic," Hayden said, while Zora shot daggers at him. "Alistair something. Plaid shorts. It didn't work out, though. One and done. You have to kiss a lot of frogs, I guess, but at least she's begun the kissing."

"Alastair Corcoran, by any chance?" her dad asked, and at Zora's reluctant nod, said, "Good surgeon. Does very well for himself indeed, only ten years or so in, and not a bad fella. Well done, Zora."

"Except that it didn't work out," Zora said, doing her best to keep it light. "Maybe Hayden went out this week. We could ask him about it. Bound to be more entertaining than hearing about my life, unless you want to talk about flowers. So few people ever want to talk about flowers."

"Well, I think getting out there is a wonderful idea," her mum said firmly. "Past time, I'd say, kissing or not."

Isaiah said, "Mum *is* kissing, though. She kissed Uncle Rhys today, in the bathroom. Casey and I saw."

The clock on the wall turned over the seconds. *Tick, tick, tick.* In the silence, four pairs of eyes swiveled toward Zora. Her father looked startled. Her mum looked disapproving. Hayden looked amused and expectant. Isaiah looked apprehensive, like he shouldn't have said it.

Zora smiled—at least she thought she was smiling, because her face felt frozen—and said, "Family's different, Isaiah. Your Nana and Uncle Hayden are talking about a different kind of kissing."

"Oh," Isaiah said, and looked doubtful. She didn't lie to him, except that she just had. What else could she have said, though? It was one time. One slip. It was over.

Rhys hadn't mentioned it again, but then, it wasn't the sort of thing you discussed amongst the play rugs at Bunnings Hardware, when Casey was deciding between the town and the castle, because Rhys had noticed that she needed a carpet, and, in typical Rhys fashion, had taken steps to fix that.

How would she have brought it up? *Sorry I projected my sexual frustration onto you. Please excuse the orgasm topic. I'll try much harder in future not to imagine your hands slowly pushing my legs apart and your mouth moving up my inner thigh, and I'll also stop wondering whether you can actually be as big as you felt against me, because I don't need to know. But since we're talking, can you possibly be as absolutely physical and completely sexual a man, or as determined to work at pleasing a woman until she loses all her strength, as I've been imagining? Just tell me once, and then I'll drop the subject.*

Obviously, he *was* that sexual, or he wouldn't have responded the way he had. Also obviously, he'd thought better of it once he'd had a chance to think it through, whatever he'd said at the time, or he'd have addressed it himself. Rhys wasn't exactly the retiring, tactful sort.

It was such a good thing that he was leaving.

She thought the subject was closed here, too. When she and her mum were doing the washing-up, though, just the two of them, her mum returned to the topic. She started out with the oblique approach. "I'm glad to hear you're dating again. Dylan was a lovely man, but two years is long enough."

"My mandated mourning period's over, is it?" Zora asked.

"Don't be silly. You're the one who mentioned dating. And really, darling, your life is so precarious. That can't be pleasant, worrying about the bills every month. Isaiah needs a father, too."

Zora took a breath. Why hadn't she said this before, as much as she'd been thinking about it? She always stayed in her lane with her parents, but she was thirty years old, and a mother herself. Maybe it was time to change lanes. She said, "Dylan cheated on me, you know." There the words were, right out there. "Often, I think. I suspected it for a long time, and around the time he got ill, I found some old text messages. I wasn't even looking for them. I didn't want to know, and I found out. Anyway, there's no such thing as not letting yourself know. You always know. I stayed anyway, all the way until he died, but I'm all done with that kind of loyalty. I'm not putting myself into that position again."

She was so tired of dragging this around, and wondering whether it had been her own failing that'd had Dylan looking elsewhere. She needed to put it where it belonged and move on, and to do that, she needed to say it. The day she'd found those texts had been a terrible one, the kind of day when the sun turned red in the sky, when time froze and all the blood drained from your head, and you'd forever remember standing in the kitchen, your hand gripping the phone until your knuckles turned white, as you stared down at the screen and every last damning piece slipped into place, and you realized your entire life had been built on a lie.

It had been a bad day, but there'd been so many bad days, and it was *over.*

Her mum stopped scrubbing at the roasting pan. "Oh. Well," she added after a minute, "it happens."

"It *happens?*" Not the reaction Zora had expected. Where was the outrage? Where was the mother-daughter bonding?

"Of course it does. You're not a baby. He didn't marry any of those other girls, did he? Didn't ask for a divorce, either, unless I'm very much mistaken, and I don't think I am, because he loved you, and he wanted to be married to you. That was plain to see. I may not have approved at the time, but you had a lovely life together, until the last bit, and everybody admired what you did for him. You say you don't want to be loyal anymore, but that's what marriage is. It's not loyalty to somebody perfect, it's loyalty to somebody who isn't. He didn't buy enough life insurance, of course, and that's a pity, but then, you didn't see to it that he did. And there are two sides to every story."

Zora's mouth was trembling so hard, it was difficult to form the words. "No. There are not two sides. We took vows. He broke his. How is that two sides?" She'd been wiping crystal glasses with a tea towel. She stopped, because otherwise, she was going to break something. Her hands were shaking. "Did Dad cheat, is that what you're saying? *Does* Dad cheat?"

Yes, she'd said it. Talk about getting out of your lane.

"If he does," her mother said, her voice tightening, but her hands never stopping, "I don't worry about it. I take care to keep myself looking my best, and thirty-four years after we met, he's still coming home to me." She shot a glance at Zora's shorts and blue shirt, which she hadn't bothered to change. For rebellious reasons, maybe. "A doctor's always going to notice that. What am I saying? Any man's going to notice that. You may want to pay more attention to your diet, darling. You're getting a wee bit bigger in the derrière, I've noticed. We both tend to be bottom-heavy, if we don't watch it, because you have my face and figure, for better or worse. I've found measuring to be very helpful. Weigh yourself every morning, and measure your waist and hips once a week. It's so much easier to lose one Kg than it is ten, and to shift those wee fat deposits when they *are* wee."

"Why would I care?" Zora asked. "If he's going to cheat anyway, what's the point in my perfection?" She was furious, but she was also fascinated. Had she been raised by dinosaurs? Apparently so. No wonder she kept having trouble with her attitude toward Rhys, and remembering exactly what Casey's presence in his life meant. It was subliminal messaging, that was what. She was going to share this with Hayden as soon as they got back to her place. *With* wine. If he thought cheating was OK, too, or that it was her fault, because she wasn't hot enough, she was . . . she was going to throw him out and drink the whole bottle by herself, and to hell with her five o'clock start tomorrow morning. Everybody in the world could think it was OK. She still wasn't going to, even if she was alone forever.

"You don't want to be alone forever, surely," her mother said, and there was Zora's problem, right there. She was absolutely transparent. "You adored Dylan. So did I. So did everybody. He wasn't perfect, but he had so many fine qualities, and your life was so much easier than it is now. You weren't meant to go through the world without somebody to help you. I can hear you now, thinking, 'You and Dad should help me more, then,' but your dad *did* help, with advice that, I'll point out, you haven't taken, because you sold that beautiful house anyway. If we helped you financially, we'd be passing the problem down, wouldn't we? Next thing you know, Isaiah would be looking for a handout."

"My life is fine." Zora was going to explode. Physically explode. They'd be picking bits of her off the walls. "I've been lucky. I was well off, and then I was less well off, but come on, Mum. I own a home. I own a business. I have a wonderful son with a brilliant mind and a kind heart. People would kill for my life. And I've never asked you for a handout. Never *once*. Also, a man who lies to me isn't somebody I'm going to adore, not anymore. How would my life possibly be better with another man like that? I paid attention, with Dylan. I paid all the attention that *got* paid. I made all the decisions about our life, about our house, and about Isaiah. I didn't gain weight, either, whatever you say. Not that it would be any excuse, because I would've gained it having his *baby*. I didn't cheat. Why is it OK if Dylan did? Why is it OK that he worked at rugby, and nothing else? And not always even that? Why is it OK that he didn't work at *me?*"

It was so wrong, she'd thought, to feel contempt for your husband. She'd always run from it, had shoved it down and stamped on top of it. Now, she faced it. "He wasn't a grownup," she said. "I was. And if I let myself see that, if I admit how angry I was about it, I don't think I'm the one with a problem. I think that's healthy. I do. I don't want to go through my life angry, but I need to say it in order to let it go."

"It may be healthy," her mum said, beginning to lose her equilibrium at last, "but it's not going to get you anywhere in another relationship. It's idealism, is what it is, and it's not one bit realistic. You weren't a star. You weren't living in hotels half the time, far from your wife and child, handsome and talented and so charming, with women throwing themselves at you everywhere you went. Men need release, and they can separate the emotional from the physical so much better than we can. If you know that he cheated, you probably confronted him with it, didn't you? I'm sure you did. And he told you it didn't mean anything, because it didn't. He told you that you were the only woman he loved. You can blow up at me all you like, but it doesn't make it any less true. Dylan was a loving, kind, generous husband."

"Men need *release?* That's the reason? Don't women need release, too? It doesn't take another person to get it. That's what they make shower heads for."

No scrubbing happening anymore. "Zora Adrianne." Her mum's voice was sharp. "Nobody—and I mean nobody—wants a woman with that kind of mouth."

"Oh, I don't know." Zora was feeling absolutely reckless, driving with the top down, throwing caution to the winds for the second time today. It felt good. In fact, she wanted to laugh. Could be hysteria. "I think I know some men who do. Maybe they aren't lovely. Maybe they're even a bit rough around the edges. An honest man I can be honest with, though? He'll do."

Her mother turned to face her. There was judgment there, and Zora didn't care. "Who's your example, then? Rhys Fletcher, whom you're kissing in the bathroom? I'm not even going to *ask* about that. I'm just going to hope it's what you told Isaiah, because anything else would be shameful. Yes, I'm going to say the word. Shameful. And don't get on your high horse with me. You can hardly get more rough around the edges than Rhys Fletcher, and you just told me that, surprise! He has a daughter. How will his wife feel when she hears about that? Except that she already knows, and obviously, if the girl's six, that wasn't the thing that ended their marriage. Why? Because she accepted the good and the bad together."

Zora was having trouble breathing. She tried to say something, but it wouldn't come out.

Her mother put a hand on her shoulder and softened her tone. "All I'm asking, darling, is that you consider being a little more practical. Yes, you were hurt, and I understand that, but it was years ago. It's over and done. Marriage is a partnership. All partnerships involve compromise. You get something, and you give something. I'm not saying not to pursue your career. I was never more upset than when you gave up your architecture, was I? Art was my own dream, and I couldn't have been happier to know you were going to be doing something so close to that. I told you not to get pregnant, too, but you did anyway. You made your own choices, like we all do. Dylan was your choice. You had your eyes open, I thought. That's fine. Keep them open. Don't cut off your nose to spite your face now. Don't look for perfection and overlook somebody good enough, who can give you what you need. Just make him somebody suitable next time, somebody you have a real future with, for Isaiah's sake. You've got what I can only call a lowbrow side, darling, and it's not your best side. A plastic surgeon isn't going to look like a Maori rugby star. Nobody gets everything, so take care what you put highest on your list."

"I thought Dylan was lovely," Zora said, when she could say anything. "What happened to that?"

"You didn't seem to think so," her mum said, in a stunning display of illogic. "And who knows who it'll be next time?"

Zora tried to think of an answer. She couldn't. "I'm not looking for perfection," she finally told her mother. "I'm not looking for anything at all. I've got everything in the world I need. Right down to the shower head."

# outside forces

Rhys headed up the wide stone steps of Finn's house in Mount Eden at nine the next morning, and because he didn't feel like jumping up them two at a time, he did just that. The body went where the mind took it.

Finn answered the door with his youngest kid, dressed only in a nappy, in one big arm. He took a long look at Rhys and asked, "Why do you look as buggered as you did a week ago?"

Rhys could have answered, *Because I couldn't sleep.* Instead, he said, "Never mind. Let's go over those plans."

Jenna appeared in the doorway. "Hi, Rhys," she said, and he bent down, kissed her cheek, and thought again what a nice woman she was. She said, "I met Casey on Saturday, did Zora tell you? What a sweetheart. Congratulations. That sounds funny to say, when she's six, but kids come to you in all sorts of ways. Wonderful to see Zora again, too." After that, she smiled some more, took the toddler from Finn, and headed back into the house, and Rhys thought, *I'm surrounded by mums and dads and kids, and it's all right. When did that happen? And how is it that I'm almost there, but I feel nowhere close?*

Finn said, "Let's go golfing."

"We're not going golfing," Rhys said. "Too much to do, mate."

"We'll talk while we golf. Efficient, eh. Nine holes. Got your clubs in your boot?"

"If I wanted to golf," Rhys said, "I'd have had you meet me in Titirangi. Ten minutes from my house."

"Yeh," Finn said. "Hang on a sec. I'll get my clubs."

Did Rhys feel more relaxed, a few hours and quite a few tree-shaded Remuera Golf Club kilometers later, headed up Finn's steps again? Yes, he did, and also yes, they'd talked over most of what they needed to. Finn opened the door and said, "Let's see what we can scare up for lunch. We'll fuel up, and then we'll finish this," and Rhys threw up his mental hands, went in and made a sandwich, and took it into the lounge with Finn along with a cup of tea, his laptop, and his notebook. He did have to move a naked baby doll over on the couch in order to sit down, however.

"I want to try swapping the wings around," he was saying twenty minutes later, his sandwich forgotten on the coffee table. "I think Kevvie could give us more on the right."

"You sure?" Finn asked, frowning. "He's gone well on the left so far."

"I'd like to see him on the openside, find out what he can do there. He's got more finesse than Matt, and Matt's going to be better at bashing his way up the guts. He's young and raw, but he's got the power, and we need to give him his head to use it. If it doesn't go, we'll swap them back. Let's talk about the lineout."

He'd started to chart a set piece, sketching fast, explaining, when a little girl wandered into the room. Her curly ginger hair was in a high ponytail that looked neat, but not any neater than Rhys was managing himself now, and her top had a unicorn on it. Unicorns were a thing, it seemed, because ever since he'd found Casey, he'd seen them everywhere. The little girl headed straight for his couch, climbed up on it beside him, picked up the baby doll, and said, "Daddy, my baby has lost her bottle."

Rhys paused in his sketching.

Finn said, "Say 'Excuse me,' Lily."

"'Scuse me," she said. "My baby has lost her bottle." She turned big, accusing green eyes onto Rhys. He was doomed to be followed by accusing little-girl eyes, it seemed. "I think it's under your bottom."

Rhys stood up and turned around. Yes, there was a tiny, white-plastic bottle in the corner of the cushion. He handed it to Lily, and she said, "Thank you. She needs her milk, because it's her lunchtime, and she's a baby." Which was logical.

"She needs clothes to eat lunch, surely," Rhys said.

"No," Lily said. "She's 'posed to be naked, because she is going swimming very soon. She doesn't have any togs, because they got losted, so she has to be naked. But first she has to drink milk. And then she can go swimming."

"She's a girl, eh," Rhys said.

"Yes. Because she doesn't have a penis. Boys have a penis, but dolls never have a penis. So dolls are all girls."

Finn said, "There you are, mate. Can't argue with that."

Jenna came into the room fast and said, "Sorry. Lily got away from me. Come play in the kitchen, sweetie. Daddy's busy working."

"OK," Lily said, "but I have to kiss him first." Another scramble up onto the other couch, a smacking kiss and a rub of her hand down Finn's hard cheek, and she took off, dragging the doll by one arm. The girl doll.

"Can I bring you boys another cup of tea?" Jenna asked.

"Nah," Finn said. "I'll make it, once we've finished. Pretty soon now."

She took off after her daughter, and Finn said to Rhys, "Normally, this would be the moment when I ask you how it's going with Casey, but I'm waiting until that cup of tea."

*Or,* Rhys thought, *this would be the moment when I ask you why it is that I used to feel lucky not to be married and have four kids, and now I realize that I'm not actually as lucky as I thought. Except that it's not a question I can ask.*

♡♡♡

Zora turned the van eastward. Five o'clock had come early this morning. Extremely early. Exceptionally early. That was what you got when your brother had had other plans for his Sunday night, the way somebody with a social life tended to do, and instead of getting some reassurance from an actual live person, you'd lain on the couch, drunk half a bottle of wine, laughed, cried, steamed up, and let yourself believe that a man could be devoted to a woman, absolutely and forever.

All right, only in *Pride and Prejudice,* which was set in the nineteenth century and involved fictional people, but it still counted, sort of. Jane Austen had believed it, and other people believed it enough to still buy the book and watch the movie two hundred years later, so there you were. Besides, seeing Mr. Darcy be so hopelessly attracted, so nobly determined to make things right, and so smolderingly hot was good for her. About the only company she had right now was her dirty fantasies and her apparently outmoded standards, so she might as well spend the night with the one person who shared them, even if that was Jane Austen and she was dead.

It had been a drunken thought, but her own.

She may have cried some at the end. She may also have crossed her legs when Elizabeth's eyes had met Darcy's over the piano, his hard face had softened at last, and both of them had known that there couldn't ever be anybody else. Also that all Darcy wanted at that moment was to draw Elizabeth down on his bed, shove her bodice down with a slow hand, and show her everything her body could possibly feel for hours on end, and all Elizabeth wanted was something vaguely like that, too, which she wouldn't even have been able to fantasize adequately about, because she'd never had sex. And all *Zora* had wanted was to believe that Mr. Darcy had been as attentive, intense, and careful a lover, and Elizabeth as gorgeously shocked and satisfied, on their fictional, completely nonexistent wedding night as she imagined them.

Also, at least the BBC, unlike her mum, her dad, Rhys, Dylan, and probably Hayden, was willing to tell her, *Yes, cheating's a dealbreaker.*

She'd got up at five o'clock anyway. She might not be good at everything, but she was good at soldiering on. If ninety percent of life was showing up, she had ninety percent taped. And when Rhys had brought Casey over before school, she'd focused on the girl, not on him.

It had been fine. It *would* be fine. Rhys's face had been back to "shut down," anyway, like Mr. Darcy's pre-revelation, so that told her what she needed to know. Tomorrow, she'd drive him to the airport, since he'd insisted that it was better if she have his car, "just in case," and then she'd have twelve days to take care of bunnies and kids and get herself right again.

In his bed. In his bath, too, in front of the windows as the sun set over the mountains.

*And it came to pass in an eveningtide, that David arose from off his bed, and walked upon the roof of the king's house: and from the roof he saw a woman washing herself; and the woman was very beautiful to look upon.*

He wouldn't *be* there, and she wasn't all that beautiful. What was her *problem?* Other than the kind of insistent need that couldn't be cured by a shower head?

Now, she had the van loaded down with her Monday subscription deliveries, and was turning up a quiet street in Mount Eden to drop off the first of them, which was to Jenna and Finn Douglas's address. Jenna had asked for her flowers on Mondays rather than Fridays, unlike the rest of her residential customers, "because Finn will never notice flowers on Friday, and neither will I. Too many game thoughts for him, and too many kids in the house at the weekend for me. We always end up with extras, somehow. My quiet time's during the week. I want them then."

She saw a silver BMW SUV with a dent in the front fender parked out front, and nearly turned around again. She felt scrubbed raw, and she wasn't sure she could face Rhys. Even though, for once, she was wearing makeup and looking relatively polished, in leggings and an embroidered tunic. Business-delivery mode.

*Harden up,* she told herself, then took the arrangement out of the back of the van, climbed the steps, and rang the doorbell. *You won't even see him. You'll hand over the flowers to Jenna and leave.*

Jenna answered the door, smiled like the sun at sight of the flowers, and said, "I'm feeling so brilliant for asking you for these. I still hate it when Finn leaves on one of these trips, but those are going to console me. So beautiful. Thank you."

"I'm glad you like them," Zora said. She always felt a little shy, the first time she delivered to a new client. She'd gone with the same thing she'd done for her mum last night, because she'd loved how it had turned out. She'd thought about sunflowers, something more late-summery and androgynous, but she'd done the blush-and-pale-green instead. It was prettier, that was all. It was gorgeous and lush and feminine and special. Men liked pretty things, too, especially if they could tell themselves that their appreciation had to do with appreciating a woman.

That was a confused thought. Probably the wine talking, still, or the relentlessly sexual thoughts that kept intruding, three years' worth of them arriving in one hard rush.

"Do you have time for a cup of tea?" Jenna asked. "Ten minutes?"

"Sure," Zora said. She knew Rhys was in there. She said yes anyway. Ten minutes.

Jenna's littler kids were playing with a train set in the lounge when she walked through the house, and Rhys and Finn were sitting at the kitchen table. Having a cup of tea, what else. When Rhys saw her, he stood up, and her heart did some kind of flip and flutter, like she hadn't seen him a few hours earlier.

"Hi," he said. Smiling with his eyes all the way. She'd surprised him, clearly, because he didn't have that blank look he so often did when he looked at her.

"Zora's brought me my first flower delivery," Jenna said. "I didn't tell you that I subscribed, Finn. Surprise! I subscribed. I need pretty things, I decided, and isn't this gorgeous?"

"You do need pretty things," Finn said. "I've got no

problem with that. Hi, Zora." He kissed her cheek. Rhys didn't. "Good to see you again. Thanks for making my wife happy. Always a good thing."

His face was even craggier than it had been when he'd been playing with Dylan, his body was exactly as rock-solid, and both he and Rhys looked like they could lace up their boots right now and run onto the field, and like they were just hoping somebody wouldn't turn up in time so they could do it. That was a lot of rugby muscle for one kitchen, she thought confusedly. The confusion was possibly because Rhys was still looking at her, and Rhys's eyes made her knees go weak.

"Do you have a prettier vase?" she asked Jenna, who was filling the electric jug at the sink. "Since I'm here, I may as well do that for you. I deliver them in jars so people can do their own vases, but . . ." She was babbling. She knew it. She needed to get her hands busy, and fast.

Ten minutes. Floral arranging, cup of tea, and out. And if she tingled the whole ten minutes? Nobody had to know.

$$\heartsuit\heartsuit\heartsuit$$

Zora had left. Rhys needed to leave, too. He'd just finish this tea first.

She'd seemed rattled, hadn't she? Or was that him? He didn't know. She hadn't said anything the day before about what had happened. In fact, she'd barely looked at him, either yesterday afternoon when he'd dropped her and Isaiah off, or this morning, either, which told him everything.

He shouldn't have talked about orgasms. He'd known it at the time. It had slipped out, that was all, and everything else had seemed inevitable, exactly like that story she'd told. Like once you saw that woman naked in the moonlight, you had no choice.

Finn said, ". . . it's going."

"Pardon?" Rhys blinked.

Finn exchanged a glance with Jenna. "I was asking you

how it was going with Casey. Saying I'd meant to ask you sooner."

"Oh. Fine. Zora's watching her. I told you that, though. She's a good mum, and good to Casey, too. Better, I thought, for her to be with whanau."

"Yes," Jenna said. "I'm sure. To have other people who love her. Does she talk about her mum?"

"No," Rhys said, then hesitated. "Should she? I've wondered."

Jenna said, "You'll have to excuse my interest. This is what I used to do, teach Year One. Do you want to know what I think? Or no? If it's no, that's all right."

Finn took her hand under the table. Rhys couldn't see it happen, exactly, but he could tell it had. "Yes," Rhys told her. "I do."

"Kids go along with what happens in their lives," Jenna said. "First, because they don't have a choice, and second, because they haven't had the life experience we have, so they don't compare their lives to what they expected, the way we do. That's a good thing in some ways, because it means they can roll with the punches better, and a not-so-good thing in others, because they have no perspective. They don't know that it gets better."

"Meaning," Rhys said slowly, "that I should give her perspective, maybe."

Jenna smiled at him approvingly. "Yes. That would be helpful. Gentle perspective. You don't . . . shove their noses in it. You sort of slide in sideways. Reading is good, for example. Stories, so they can make the connection. Do you read?"

What, was he literate? What did she think? She laughed and said, "I mean, do you read with her, ever."

"Oh. Yeh. At bedtime. We've read a dinosaur book, though, mostly." They'd read a dinosaur book always. He should've bought something else, he realized now. He still thought that social worker should have given him a brochure. There should be a rule book. Everything else had rule books, and kids were trickier than anything else. You needed guidelines even more, and you had exactly zero. He'd buy a parenting book, maybe. Heaps of time in hotel rooms to read it.

"That's a good thing, that you're already reading," Jenna said, which meant he'd done something right, anyway, even if it had happened by accident. "You could read books about mothers and kids, maybe. Fathers and kids, too, though those are harder to come by. She'll be worried about you leaving. Tomorrow may not be easy for her."

"I know she's worried," he said. "She asks if I'm coming back every time I leave."

"And you do come back, which is the most important thing. But . . . hang on a second."

She jumped up and headed into the other room, and Rhys lifted his brows at Finn. Finn said, "She has a plan, mate. No worries, she'll tell you what it is. She's brilliant at this."

Jenna came back holding a hardback book. A slim one, with not many pages to it, and with—what else?—rabbits on the front. She handed it to Rhys. "This one. Borrow it. You may have to read it more than once. Kids like to hear their favorites every night. It's meant for younger kids, but I'm guessing it'll work for her."

He read the title aloud. *The Runaway Bunny.* You must know Casey. We got rabbits today. Four of them. She has a bit of a thing about rabbits."

"Even better," she said. "Look for more bunny books, then. Or better yet—I'll send you a list. And you got rabbits for her? That was a great thought. Are you surprised that you're such a good dad?"

His hands stilled in the act of opening the book. "I'm not a good dad."

"Oh," she said, "I think you are. Anyway, it's the baby bunny who talks about running away in this one, but the mother bunny tells him, over and over again, that no matter where he goes, she'll be there, too, because he's her little bunny. That security message is one kids need anyway, and for a girl who's lost her mother and is in a new place with a new dad, especially if she's been in foster care, the way Finn said? It's a message she'll need to hear even more. That you'll come back, and that she'll never be alone."

"Thanks." He tried to think of something else, but he didn't have it. "If you have other ideas, other books, definitely let me know. A parenting book, I was just thinking. Is there a *Fatherhood for Dummies?* That's the level I need."

"I do have another idea," she said. "This is a good one. Why don't you and Zora bring Isaiah and Casey to us this evening, after dinner, say, and let them stay over tonight? That could help, too, for when you're gone, to know she has other people besides you and Zora. A rugby team's a family, too. She won't know that, but if she comes here and stays with us, she'll find out."

"Wait," he said. "I'm leaving tomorrow, but I should bring her to another new place tonight?"

"With Isaiah," she said. "He was so sweet at the game. When she had to go to the toilet, he took her, and he held her hand so she wouldn't get lost. He's her buffer, and her guide. So, yes, I think so. I think you should bring them over, and pick them up in the morning, and show her again that you'll come back."

♡♡♡

Finn closed the door behind Rhys, then headed back into the kitchen. Jenna had the mixer out already, was pulling out her measuring cups, but he got in there early, coming up behind her, wrapping his arms around her, and kissing her neck. She jumped, laughed, and sighed, and he smiled and pulled her down into his lap and kissed her neck some more. He palmed a breast, too. It was right there, and it was one of his favorite things to hold.

"I'm going to miss you," he said. "Is it nap time yet?"

She was humming. "Half an hour." She sounded a little breathless.

"Also," he said, because it wasn't nap time yet, "I'm expecting to hear exactly why it's a good idea to have six kids here tonight. That explanation made no sense."

She turned around so she could see him, wrapped her arms around his neck, kissed his jaw, and smiled at him. He did love his wife. "Because they're dying for each other."

That distracted him for a minute. "Who? Drago and Zora? She's his sister-in-law."

"Mm-hmm. Doesn't matter. He couldn't take his eyes off her, and she couldn't look at him. Something's going on there. Rhys is a volcano. Everything's under the surface, but it's about to blow, and I think it needs to. So—he'll either get an evening to be serious and prepare more, which he needs like a hole in the head, if you ask me, or he'll grab his chance and let the explosion happen. I can't tell which it'll be, but I can offer the opportunity. I like Zora. I like her a lot. I think she's had a rotten time, and I think Rhys is a lot like you, which means he just might be the man she deserves, and vice versa. Sometimes it takes two tries to get it right."

"I can't argue with that," he said. "I can't argue with any of that, in fact. Not a volcano, though. A dragon. Been holding his fire, you think?"

"What was he like, really?" she asked. "Dylan?"

He made a face. "Not too bad. All show and no go, that's all."

She eyed him soberly. "Did he cheat?"

"Yeh." Not a subject he enjoyed discussing with her. She trusted him, like he trusted her, but still . . . not something you brought up.

"Did Rhys?"

"No."

He didn't realize what he'd said until she asked the question. "So whose is Casey?"

His head came up, and he stared at her. She said, "You knew the answer to that one already."

"I was his roomie on that tour," Finn said. "And I knew him. I know him. Then and now. He won't want anyone to know, though. Not something that little girl needs to ever find out."

"Not with the abandonment issues she has to have already, no. Or Zora."

"No. Or Zora."

She was silent a moment. "And what I'm seeing between them? Is that from before? Or is it new?"

"It's not from before. That's not Drago. Not possible. At least, not acting on it, however he felt. He looked out for Dylan. He was the big brother."

"That's what I thought. And by the way—I love you."

"I'm pretty fond of you as well," he said, and then laughed and gave her a slap on the bum. "Or I'm over the moon about you. One or the other. I'll tell you tonight, when it's dark and I'm not embarrassed to say it. *When* I have six kids in my house, because my beautiful wife can't help but try to make everybody's life work out better."

"What do you think," she asked, not in any kind of rush to get up again, which he appreciated, "about having another baby?"

"I think I'd enjoy trying."

She laughed, but said, "Seriously, Finn. Too many? Ridiculous? I said four, remember."

"And I said six. If we're going to breed a team of All Blacks, we'd better get our skates on."

"Hmm." She rubbed her cheek against his and kissed his mouth with the kind of enthusiasm a man had to enjoy, worked her way across to his ear, took the lobe between her teeth, then whispered, "We could have to add on to the house again."

He laughed out loud. "Fortunately, I know a builder."

The sound of running feet, and Lily and Ethan came skidding into the kitchen. "Oh," his daughter said. "Kissing again."

Jenna smiled and stood up. "Because Daddy's leaving on his trip tomorrow, and I'll miss him very much, so I have to kiss him now."

"Because you love him *soooo* much," Lily said, and she may have rolled her eyes. Could four-year-olds roll their eyes? He had the sauciest daughters in the world.

"That's right, "Jenna said. "That's what mummies and daddies do. Now. Who wants a glass of milk before nap time?"

# how to be casual

If Zora had been tired this morning, she was giddy with it now. Also—confused. Was she ever confused.

At six o'clock, while Isaiah was eating his breakfast-for-dinner, which was a nice way of saying that she'd fixed him five minutes' worth of eggs on toast, she gave up and rang Hayden.

"Matricide is illegal," he announced the second he picked up. "Just to forestall you."

"I'm over it," she said. "On to a new problem. I need advice, and you're the only one I can trust. Also, you can't tell anybody I asked."

"I am not telling you how to give a good blow job," he said. "Awkward."

She held the phone away from her face, then put it back. "No. That's disgusting. I need to know what to wear to go out with Rhys."

A long silence. "I think I prefer the blow job."

"That's the problem. Exactly. You're thinking I'm doing something, or *he's* doing something, and you're going to have to tell me not to. No worries. Nobody's doing anything. I need to let him know that *I* know that nobody's doing anything. The kids are going to a friend's house for the night, that's all, and Rhys suggested that we could have dinner. To discuss things. Casey. The house. Rabbit care. Et cetera."

"You need advice on what to wear to discuss rabbit care?"

"You're enjoying this. Stop it and listen. He's leaving

212

tomorrow, and he suggested he and I should go out to dinner, because we always make dinner at my house. Or he stays for dinner with me, or whatever. Family time, with the kids. So he said, let's go to a restaurant instead for once, let somebody else do the washing-up, and I said fine, and *he* said, I hear The Grove is nice. Suit you? And *I* said—"

"You said, 'So you *do* want to do the horizontal tango with me, and it's not just my imagination, even though it's practically incest, but since I want the same thing, and I've got a dangerous appetite for hot Maori rugby players, let's go, boy.' Except that you didn't say that. You want to be ladylike, in case somehow you've read it wrong, and he just wants to give you a sisterly treat. I can set you right there, anyway. He's not giving you a sisterly treat. Or rather—he *is*, but that's not the one he has in mind."

"Never mind. I knew I shouldn't have asked you. I'm hanging up. I'm not going to be ready no matter what I do. At least I don't have Casey, because Rhys collected her from school. He only rang me a few hours ago, though, and it's my busy day, so I only got home forty-five minutes ago, and there was Isaiah's dinner and getting him ready to go and taking a shower, and . . . Also, you realize he cheated on Victoria."

"Did he?" Hayden wasn't laughing anymore, at least. "You sure?"

"Well, obviously. Casey."

"They weren't . . . taking a break, or something?"

"No. They were engaged."

"Oh. Huh."

"Right. So what I want to know is—what in my closet is appropriate for not being a date, but going someplace flash? A trouser suit, obviously, but I don't own a trouser suit. I haven't done my makeup, even. Tone it down, right? Pink lipstick. No, peach. No, nude."

"You don't own a suit at all," Hayden said. "Which is oddly fortunate. I can see you marching out there in your navy trouser suit and sensible court shoes, hair pinned up in a French twist and peach lipstick on, killing his buzz stone dead. Also, I'm looking up The Grove, since nobody's ever taken *me* there, and it's not sisterly. Not possible. Seven-course degustation with premium wine pairing? Five hundred thirty dollars for two. I'm telling you that, because I'll bet you *twenty* dollars that he's not going to let you look at the menu to see. He'll be wearing a suit, though, I'll bet. What is it about a hard man in a suit that's so hot? No tie, the shirt won't be white, and the top two buttons will be unbuttoned. He's putting a jacket on for you, though. I'll give you another tip—he doesn't do that for his sister. A straight man wears a suit to dinner because he's hoping to get laid."

"Oh, God." She sank down on the bed and buried her head in her hand. "See, that's exactly what I can't do. He's not the right man, he's my brother-in-law, he's Casey's dad, I'm caring for her, he's paying me . . ." She wished she had a paper bag to blow into. "And everybody in Auckland will see. Tell me not to drink wine. I'll offer to be the designated driver."

"About forty people in Auckland will see. It's a small restaurant. I'd ask you how he got a booking with no notice, but I know how. He's Rhys Fletcher. He's not going to let you be the designated driver, either. He's going to turn up in a taxi, and he's going to give you that smoldery look over his wine glass and tell you you're beautiful. You'll be lucky if you make it into the house and aren't doing it against the wall. If you want to send a message, tell him you'd rather go out for a kebab. Otherwise, you're never going to hold out. And, no, you cannot wear the red dress. How long do you have now?"

She looked at her watch. "Twenty-five minutes."

"Right. Switch to your camera, open up your closet, and let's go."

$$\heartsuit\heartsuit\heartsuit$$

Rhys headed up the walk in the slanting shadows of late evening, holding Casey's hand, and told himself, *Slow down, boy.*

He hadn't meant to do it like this. He'd meant to be casual about it. When he'd rung Zora and told her the sleepover idea, she'd been on the road, making her deliveries, and had sounded startled, or distracted, or something. He'd needed to go down to Queen Street and buy Casey the thing he had in mind, pick up the parenting book before he collected her from school, and then spend some rabbit-intensive time with her. He'd needed to pack for the trip and change his sheets for Zora, too. Instead, he'd been going online and checking out restaurants. And, somehow, choosing a flash one had rattled her again.

It made perfect sense. They needed some quiet time together to talk about the things Jenna had said today, about his schedule for the next couple weeks, about anything she might need him to do for her around her house before he left. You needed a quiet place for that, not to be screaming at each other in some Viaduct bar, before you downed a hamburger at a table half a meter from your neighbor. And if he wanted to give her a better night than the plastic surgeon had? He was a competitive bloke. That wasn't news. Besides, she didn't get much pampering these days, from what he could see, and he'd swear she'd given up on expecting it. The plastic surgeon had been her first date, and she hadn't seemed to know exactly how to go about it. He was giving her some practice. *Safe* practice.

Isaiah answered the door. "Hi," he said. "Mum's still getting ready. She kind of screamed when you knocked, and slammed the bathroom door, so I don't think she's very close."

"No worries," Rhys said. "We'll wait for her. Hang on, and I'll pop out and tell the driver."

"We came in a different car," Casey told Isaiah, "even though our real car isn't even broken down."

When Rhys got back, Zora still wasn't out of the bathroom, and Isaiah and Casey were sitting on the couch. Isaiah was shuffling a pack of cards with a deceptive lack of expertise, like an octopus blending into the sea floor, making itself look harmless to its unsuspecting prey. "D'you want to play poker while we wait?" he asked hopefully.

"No," Rhys said. "I want to board the plane tomorrow with money in my wallet. What other games do you know?"

"We could play Go Fish," Isaiah said. "That's a kid's game, though."

"Well, as you're a kid, that works."

Ten minutes later, Casey was asking, "Do you have any fours?" and Isaiah was saying, "You asked that two times ago, and you know Uncle Rhys probably doesn't, because there are only four fours in the whole deck, and he only took two cards since you asked him. Ask him if he has any twos or sevens, if you have any of those. That's what he asked for the last two times."

"Oh," Casey said. "Do you have any twos?" she asked Rhys. He handed them over with a sigh, and she smiled happily, set down her four twos with a flourish, and said, "I'm beating you so far." And Zora came out of the bathroom.

She wasn't wearing the red dress, but she was wearing the chocolate-brown shoes again, with a blue dress this time. High in the neck, but the sleeves barely covered her shoulders, it nipped in very nicely indeed at the waist, the skirt ended in a couple layers of flounce and was short, and her lipstick was a deep, pinky red. All of which worked for him.

He wondered what color her toes were tonight. Her toenail varnish, he was beginning to suspect, was a signal to her state of mind. And, possibly, the state of her heart.

"Hi," he said, and stood up.

"Hi," she said. "Sorry I'm late." Her cheeks were flushed, or she was wearing makeup so they looked that way, but he thought they were flushed. Because she was rushed, or because she knew she was beautiful. Her eyes were shaded with smoky brown, and her hair had that rumpled-bed look he loved.

"Never mind," he said. "It was your busy day, and my easy one. I like your dress."

"It's one I wear to weddings. You look very nice. Suit, eh. You shaved, too."

216

"Yeh." Gray suit, blue shirt. Appropriate, he'd thought. Looking like he'd made an effort.

"Are we going?" Isaiah asked, looking from one of them to the other. "Because otherwise, we should finish our game."

"Yeh, mate,' Rhys said. "We're going. Pretend you already won. Bring the cards, if you like. Ask Finn if he can teach you to play poker. That seems to draw the suckers in."

"How come you're both being all fancy?" Casey asked.

"We're not being fancy," Rhys said when Zora didn't answer. "We're going out to dinner, that's all."

"Oh," Casey said. "My mom says that high heels means you're going on a hot date. High heels hurt her feet, because she stands up all day being a waitress, and Zora stands up all day doing flowers and doesn't wear high heels, either. So I thought it was a hot date. That means you kiss at the end."

"Ew," Isaiah said.

"Kissing is romantic," Casey informed him. "Like, they kiss at the end of movies, because it's romantic."

"Shall we go?" Zora asked. "Otherwise, we'll be late."

# in your heart

Once again today, Zora was in a car pulling up at Finn's house. This time, she wasn't driving. Rhys had said, when she'd seen the car and driver, "Better, I thought. We may want wine. They do these pairings." Score one for Hayden. Score two, three, and four, actually, because Rhys *was* wearing a suit, and a blue shirt with it, and the top two buttons were undone. The jacket and trousers were tailored to his shoulders and his chest and his thighs and every other outsized part of him, his hair was neat, and he was clean-shaven, and still, the dark energy all but pulsed out of him. You know that tattoo was under there, you knew that *body* was under there, and you could almost see his fire.

Dragon.

Now, she opened her car door, and Rhys said, "Hang on a second, everybody." He asked the driver, "Could you turn on the overhead lights?"

"Sure," the woman said, and did it, and Zora turned in her seat to see what was going on.

Rhys pulled a tiny pouch out of his pocket, but he wasn't looking at her. He was looking at Casey, sitting in the middle. "I'm giving this to you now," he said, "because there's some leaving coming up, and then there's more leaving. Leaving, and coming back. So I thought you might need it."

He set the flax kete—the woven pouch—in her hand, and she asked doubtfully, "What is it?"

"I told you that every Maori has a pendant," he said. "And

that it has to be a present. Remember?"

"I don't have one," Isaiah said. "So not every Maori does."

Rhys's gaze flicked to Isaiah, then to Zora. She said, "You're right, love. You should have one. We'll have to take care of that."

Casey asked, "Is this mine?"

"Yeh," Rhys said. He showed her how to loosen the fastening, drew out the thing inside, and laid it in her palm.

It was small, because Casey was small, but it was gorgeous, and like nothing Zora had seen before. One twist cradling another one inside it, with a koru at the heart of the smaller one. The graceful curves were carved from a luminescent mid-green jade, with drifts of lighter green like the path of feathers drawn through the stone, the arcs of color within echoing the graceful lines of the carving.

Rhys told Casey, "Ahakoa he iti he pounamu. 'It is small, but it is greenstone.' Means it's precious, given from my heart, and meant to be worn near yours." He drew his own pendant out from under his collar and said, "I've got the fish hook, remember?"

"Like Maui," Casey said. "But you have a whale tail, too."

"That's right. Strength and determination and protectiveness. That means I protect you." Which had Zora putting a hand on her own heart.

"Mine isn't a fish hook, though," Casey said.

"No. Everybody has their own special one, with its own meaning. Yours is a rau kumara, and it's a twist inside another twist. The twist is for people bound together, who'll always come back again. For you and your mum, and for you and me. It tells you that the people in your life who love you will always be part of you, even if you can't touch them any more. You have them in your heart, and nothing can ever take away the people in your heart. He hono tangata e kore e motu; ka pa he taura waka e motu. That's Maori, too. Means, 'One can cut a canoe rope, but the bond between two hearts can never be severed.' That's a saying you could remember."

Casey traced the curve of the larger twist with her finger,

then touched the smaller one nestled inside it. "It looks like my mommy is holding me."

"Because she is. Always. The little twist has a koru at its heart, see? That's for strength and starting over, and that part is you." He drew the braided cord over Casey's neck, pulled on the ends to tighten it, and said, "You wear it between your collarbones, just below the hollow of your throat, because that's a special place, an open place, where you can feel your breath and your blood. When you're lonesome, when you're sad, you put your hand on your pendant, feel how it's warm from your skin, and remember that you're a strong girl who knows how to start over. Remember that your mum's still there in your heart, and that you're in mine, and I'm coming back."

Casey said, "OK." It was a whisper. The driver, Zora saw, was wiping tears away with the heel of her hand. She caught Zora's eye and mouthed, "Oh, my God," and Zora had to agree.

Rhys stroked his hand over Casey's hair, plaited into a single French braid tonight, and said, "I'm coming back. Tomorrow, twelve days from tomorrow, and every time. You can count on it."

"Because you keep your promises," Casey said. "And you're my dad."

"That's right. Because I'm your dad."

"OK," she said again.

Rhys kissed the top of her head, and his voice was a little rough when he said, "Let's go, then. We'll get you sorted with Finn and Jenna, and then I'll take Auntie Zora out to dinner."

"You give lots of things," Casey said. "But nobody gives you things."

"Oh," he said, "I wouldn't say that. I wouldn't say that at all."

Zora didn't say much on the way to the restaurant, and Rhys was glad. He'd well and truly choked himself up there. He'd meant to give Casey her pendant, and to say a few things that might help her believe in the runaway bunny idea. He hadn't meant to lay himself so raw, in front of an Uber driver and all.

When Rhys had followed Zora's swaying hips and pretty legs across the room and avoided looking at anybody, because he didn't want to have a chat tonight with anyone but Zora, and she'd slid into her chair, though, half-hidden behind a discreet wall in the cozily elegant, dimly lit space of The Grove, he said, "You could show Casey how to get her pendant off at night, maybe. Not safe to have that cord round her neck while she sleeps."

"I'll do that," she said, smoothing her white serviette across her lap. "And you're right, she probably will want to sleep in it. I think you convinced her that it was magic. You just about convinced *me*. That was good, Rhys. That was so good."

"I didn't quite mean to say all that. It just came out. Can't even remember exactly what I *did* say."

Her eyes went soft, and her hand came out to cover his. He wished she'd worn the red dress, but he didn't hate this one. It showed her arms and her legs, at least. If she'd had the red one on, though, her lipstick would have matched. A Russian princess, with rubies in her hair and pearls down her back. "You did gorgeously," she told him. "I think I cried. I *know* I cried. The driver cried, too. It was beautiful. The pendant, and everything you said. When did you think of that?"

"First day. She didn't want to go with me, in Chicago, since she'd never met me, so we talked about it. She's watched *Moana* too many times, in case you don't know. She thought I was Maui, especially once she saw *my* pendant. I think she's given up on that one now, at least."

"Well, I can see that. You *are* fairly Maui-like. Temperament. Size. Demigod. And so forth." A smile. "Fully Maui, I'd say. Or fully dragon. Or both."

Wait, what had they been talking about?

The waiter came over with a pitcher of water, and Zora took her hand away. Before she could look at her menu, Rhys said, "They have a tasting menu. We could do that, if you like. Fewer decisions. Those wine pairings, too. Nobody's driving, all I have to do tomorrow is get on a plane, and Isaiah said that Tuesday is your easy day. What d'you reckon? Time to indulge a little, let yourself be spoilt for once?"

"Oh," she said with a breathless laugh, "why not. I'll just sit here and be . . . surprised."

He handed the menus back to the waiter, then told Zora, once the man had left, "Surely, letting yourself be surprised is good, if somebody wants to dedicate himself to pleasing you."

That had come out too intense, probably. Too bad. He was over her in the bathroom again, his hand on her cheek, her mouth under his. She was wearing the spicy-sweet perfume again tonight, too. He'd smelled it when he'd taken her hand to help her out of the car, and she'd stepped out in those delicate little shoes, swayed a wee bit close, and said, "Thank you," on a breath.

She didn't say anything, and he wondered if he'd gone too far, and hoped she couldn't read his mind, or wished she could. One or the other. She said, "I was just thinking that last night. Drinking wine then, too, if I have to confess the truth, when I shouldn't have. Watching a movie with too much redemption. I didn't get enough sleep, either. Depending how many of those pairings we do, you may have to carry me out."

He shouldn't answer that. He should ask her instead why Isaiah didn't have a pendant from his dad. If Rhys had been dying, he'd have made sure his son had a moment like that to remember, and something to touch to remind him that his father was still with him. He needed to fix that. He needed to talk to Zora about it. It should come from both of them, maybe. From him, because he was the uncle, and he was the one who was Maori, the link to the whanau and the iwi, and from her, because she was the mother.

222

He didn't talk to her about it. Instead, he said, "I'll carry you out, no worries. Go on and enjoy yourself. I didn't sleep so well last night myself. Could have been too eventful a day for sleep, possibly."

After that, he ate a tempura soft-shell crab in a dollop of custard that tasted like the sea, watched her tip her head back and slip a Waiheke oyster into her mouth, swallow it down, and smile at him, and lost a little more of his equilibrium. The sparkling wine, crisp and light as the sunlight shining like diamonds on the wave tips of Tasman Bay, didn't help.

Another fifteen minutes, and he watched her eat a forkful of butternut ravioli, silky pasta layered with scampi and tiny cubes of pumpkin, and close her eyes before reaching for her latest wine glass, tasting the creamy, fruity Viognier, and giving him another slow smile.

"I am drowning in food lust," she said when they were eating perfectly crunchy asparagus in a mustard vinaigrette, topped with a generous swirl of Comte cheese foam, and sipping on a massively intense Marlborough Sauvignon Blanc that knocked you out with tropical fruit. "You're pacing yourself on the wine, and I'm trying. If only it weren't so bloody delicious."

"You *do* seem a little drunk," he teased. The music was more than classical, a rising and falling chorus of voices, winding together like ribbons, that belonged in church, but that sounded like a dance, too, slow, urgent, and sensual. "And I like this music. What is it?"

"Mm. Dunno. I like it too, though."

The waiter arrived again to take away plates, and Rhys asked, "What's the music, can you tell me?"

"I can find out," the waiter said. "Back in a minute with your next course, which is my favorite. Saddle of lamb, and a 2014 Pegasus Bay Pinot Noir from Canterbury that's just gorgeous. Velvety, I'd call it. Heaps of mouth feel. Silky. You'll see what you think, though."

He swanned off again, and Zora drank a little more of her Sauvignon Blanc and laughed at him with her witch's eyes.

223

"Silky," she said. "Mouth feel. Mm. Sounds sexy."

"It does," he said. "Like a woman in a red dress, maybe."

She made a face. "I *knew* I should have worn the red one. It's better, no matter what Hayden says."

Now, he was the one laughing. "Nah. You look beautiful. I can't help it if I like red best, just like all those other blokes who answered the question. We're programmed, that's all."

The waiter came back, eventually, with the lamb and the Pinot Noir. "The music was Palestrina," he said. "Whoever that is. And *Osculetur me,* whatever that is when it's at home. *Song of Solomon,* is the CD. Try this, though. and tell me what you think."

He waited, and Zora took a sip. Rhys couldn't let her drink alone, so he took his own sip. He didn't know about "silky," but the wine was rich, all right, asking you to dive down into its ruby depths, take your time, and explore. Possibly for hours.

"Gorgeous," Zora said with a sigh. "Thanks." He looked at her red mouth, thought about slipping off one of those shoes and holding her foot in his hand, and burned. The waiter left, and she looked at Rhys and said, "I'm loving this. Thank you."

"So many courses to go," he said. "Who knows what they are? Are you still up for being surprised?"

"Right now," she said, "I'm up for everything. I'm meant to be asking you serious questions about life and love and kids and . . ." She waved her wine glass. "Life choices. I don't want to. I want to enjoy myself. That's why I'm *really* wearing this dress instead of the red one, if I'm honest. You can't see my waist in it."

He knew he was smiling more than he ever let himself, and he couldn't help it. Maybe he was a little drunk, too, but it wasn't on the wine. "I've seen your waist," he said. "Your waist is fine. So is the rest of you."

"I'm also not wearing a control garment," she said. "I asked Hayden, and he said no. Besides, I don't have one."

Now, he was laughing. "What the hell is a control

garment? Do I want to know?"

"Makes my bum look smaller." She lifted her glass to him, took another sip, and smiled, absolutely deliciously. "But— flared skirt, and you can't see my bum anyway, because I'm sitting on it. Also, as I mentioned, I don't own a control garment, so you would've been out of luck in any case. Not because I don't need it, but because I don't go on dates, except with the plastic surgeon. He didn't get a control garment, either. Sad. That was rebellion, probably. I wanted him to look at my problem areas, and I wanted to say, 'Sez you, mate,' when he did." She sighed. "I have a rebellion issue. Always have had. My secret side, that is. Not so secret, I guess, because there's my life and all, proving the point. And I know this isn't a date. It's practice, that's all."

He'd just thought it was practice for her. What had that been, an hour or two ago? He said, "It's not practice. And you don't need to make your bum look smaller."

"My mum says I do." She took another sip of wine. "Which is sad, don't you think? My mum thinks I'm a nasty, nasty girl."

♡♡♡

She was floating along, except that wasn't the right word. Floating was something you did on clouds, and she wasn't on a cloud. She was in the bath, the warm water pouring over her, stretching out luxuriously and letting it come. Or, possibly, drowning in Rhys's eyes, which, if they'd ever been hard or cold, weren't that way now.

He was looking at her across the piano, that was what it was. She felt it. She *knew* it. The cool touch of the wine on her tongue, the layers of it, the rich taste in her mouth . . . she knew it. She said, "Kiss me. That's what the song means."

He blinked those dark-lashed, green-gold eyes. Slowly. "Pardon?"

"It's Latin. Song of Solomon."

"Ah. 'Let him kiss me with the kisses of his mouth, for your love is sweeter than wine.'" When she must have looked gobsmacked, he said, "I looked it up. No excuses, eh. You said it was sexy, so I looked it up. I know another part as well. 'Behold, thou art fair, my love; behold thou art fair, thou hast doves' eyes.'"

She shuddered. She couldn't help it. He saw, and she knew he recognized it for what it was: a hot rush that had gone straight down her body and settled in her core. The buzz had become a hum, insistent and too warm. A smoke alarm was going off, somewhere in the back of her mind, and she wasn't listening. She wanted to burn.

His eyes got hotter, and he lost the smile. "My beloved is mine," she said, letting the words fall out and lie there, exposed, "and I am his: he feedeth among the lilies." She tried to smile herself, but wasn't sure it was working. "That one got me thinking, when I was fourteen or so. Rebellious even in church, eh."

"There's so much more to you," he said, "than a mum."

Her hand was on his, somehow. "And there's so much more to you than rugby. Could be most people never look deeper."

He looked down at his plate like he wasn't seeing it, then up at her again. "Right," he said, then sat up, pulled out his phone, and texted something, and she thought, *What?* He put the phone away and began working his way through the lamb, and she thought, *All righty, then. That's told me.* She tried not to look at the breadth of his shoulders in the open suit coat, at the way his blue shirt lay over his deep chest, and failed.

She'd had too much to drink. She might have embarrassed herself forever with him. The smoke alarm was louder now, more insistent.

*Then don't ask me out, boy,* she thought, *and tell me I should've worn the red dress,* and drank a little more wine. *This is me, and if you don't like it? That's not my problem.*

Another drunken thought. But her own.

Five minutes later, the waiter took away the lamb and the

glasses, and Rhys asked her, "How much do you want the sweet courses?"

"Uh . . . pardon?"

"I probably shouldn't eat them," he said.

"Oh, no," the waiter protested. "They're lovely, truly. Pressed strawberries, buffalo milk, and lime, and a figgy pudding like you've never tasted in your *life.*"

Zora said, "I don't . . . I don't need them." She was having trouble talking. She was having trouble *breathing.* She wasn't going to do this. Not possible. She also considered saying that pressed strawberries and buffalo milk didn't sound nearly as lovely as, say, chocolate torte with salted-caramel drizzle, but she didn't, because that was how this moment felt. Like rich dark chocolate and warm salted caramel, melting on your tongue.

"Could you bring me the check, please?" Rhys asked. "Or better yet . . ." He reached into his back pocket, which involved some straining of the shirt over his chest that the waiter eyed as much as Zora did, then pulled out a credit card and handed it over. "I've got a car waiting," he told the bloke. "So—quick as you can. And if you have a back door . . ."

The waiter looked around, then said, "Oh. Of course," and took off.

"What?" Zora asked, looking around herself.

"Somebody gearing up to come over for a chat," Rhys said. "Telling me we shouldn't have lost, and what I'd better do in Aussie to keep it from happening again."

"Oh," she said. "Going out must be awkward."

He smiled, the hard planes of his face easing with it, though his eyes still burned. "Not in France, so you could say that I'm just not used to it anymore. And it's not something you can resent, not when it comes along with the thing you've wanted most in your life. But I don't want any of it tonight. I want to go out the back door and get in the car with you. If that's what you want."

"That's . . ." She cleared her throat. "That's what I want."

# the perfect man

This time, Rhys didn't open the front passenger door. Instead, he opened the back door, and when she slid in, he slid in after her.

She thought, *Touch me. Please. Now.*

The driver turned the key, then looked at them in the rearview mirror and said, "Fasten your seatbelt, please."

Oh. Zora almost laughed, and then she didn't.

One red light after another, the car gliding through quiet Monday-night streets, then merging onto the motorway, and Rhys still didn't say anything. He didn't even touch her hand.

Did she have this all wrong? Was it the most massive case of wishful thinking in the history of time? Or, possibly, just alcohol-induced lust? Food-induced, music-induced, hopelessly-spoiled-induced, soaked-undies-induced lust? She'd tumbled into bed with somebody the first time out exactly once in her life, and she'd been drinking too much then, too. That had been Dylan, and look how *that* had turned out.

Rhys had quoted the Song of bloody *Solomon* to her. Like he'd meant it, too. What was he doing that for, if he didn't want to touch her?

She shot a look at him. He was leaning a little forward, his hands on his knees. Looking like he was on the bench in the sixtieth minute, and the team was down by ten. Like he was waiting to get the call, knowing he couldn't go in until then, but with every hard muscle tensed in anticipation of the moment when he'd finally run onto the field, make that first contact, and start earning the win.

He turned his head and looked at her. They were on the motorway, it was dark in the back of the car, and she couldn't see the expression on his face.

"Wait," he said.

She shivered. Same as before, all the way down her body, and he was still watching.

Titirangi, now. Around the roundabout and down her road. One street. Two. Three. She unzipped her purse and took out her keys, then tugged the zip closed. It wouldn't go. Her hands were shaking. She left it open.

The car pulled into the driveway, and Rhys said, "Thanks."

"No worries," the man behind the wheel said. "Good night."

She got out on her side, and heard the *thunk* of the door as Rhys got out on his. The stripe of light washed across her as the car reversed. The engine noise faded, and the light was gone, and she kept walking.

A hand on her arm, stopping her, turning her. Then his hand was at the back of her neck, his other one was underneath her, and he was lifting her with one arm and taking her mouth.

It wasn't anything like the first time. It was hunger. It was greed. His mouth slanting over hers, his tongue licking into her, the taste of chocolate and spice swirling into her head. *Pinot Noir,* she thought fuzzily, but then she couldn't think at all, because she was almost off her feet, he was bending her back over his arm, his hand was in her hair, tugging her head back, and his other hand was around her upper thigh. It was so big and so warm, and his fingers gripped her hard.

That hand, that mouth were all she could think about. All she could feel.

Another of those full-body shudders, and he lifted his mouth from hers and said, "Keys."

She couldn't remember. Then she realized that they were in her hand, digging into him, probably, where she'd been gripping his back. She held them up, and he took them from her, took her hand, and headed up the walk.

When he had the key in the lock, she put a palm against the door and said, "Rhys. Wait."

She didn't want to say it. She'd never wanted anything less. But it was the last chance, and the smoke alarm was shrieking.

"Once," she said.

His hand was still on the key. He didn't turn it. Instead, he turned his head to look at her. Slowly. "Pardon?"

"Tonight," she said. "Because I want it so much. I know it's the wrong thing, and I'm sure you do, too, but . . . I can't help it. I've never been able to help it. Tonight, because I can't do anything else. But we both know it's wrong, and I can't, anymore. I can't, with the lying. So just tonight."

A long moment, and he said, "No."

"Rhys." She tried to laugh, but it wouldn't come out. "You know how to do one night. I know you do."

"How?"

"Uh . . . Casey's mum? Most of your life experiences? Dylan shared more than you may know."

"And that's the same as you and me?"

"Isn't it?"

Two seconds. Three. "Judge me for the man I am," he said. "Not the man I used to be."

She hauled in a breath. "I want to. It's all I want. But I can't do it anymore. I can't live with wondering what's true, and what's a lie. But I need it tonight. Please."

His chest lifted and fell with his breath, and the hiss of distant cars, the rustle of wind in the palms was the only sound in the dark night. "No," he said, and picked up her hand, and she thought, *Yes. Finally. Please.*

He dropped the keys into her hand, curled her fingers around them, then turned and strode down the steps. Up the walk. Down the drive.

Gone.

She almost went after him. She didn't. What would she say?

This was the right choice. She knew it. It just didn't feel like it. She'd been so ready to do it. Or to be more exact: she'd felt like she couldn't go another minute without doing it. She'd been so unwilling to say anything to slow it down. Which was exactly like every other time in her life, when her insistent body had overridden her cautious mind. She was supposed to be wiser now, though. She'd meant to be. She *had* been.

So why did it feel so bad?

She went into the house, turned on the kitchen light, and slipped her shoes off. She had to put her hand against the wall to do it. She wasn't exactly drunk, but she wasn't exactly sober, either.

The roof creaked, the refrigerator motor turned on with a click and a hum, the lino was cold under her bare feet, and she shivered in the night air. She got her phone out of her purse, texted Hayden, *Help.* And waited.

No answer. Monday night. Nine-forty-five. Why wasn't he answering? She pressed the button to call him, thinking, *Pick up. I need to talk to you. I can't do this alone. Not anymore. Not again.*

One ring. Two.

No. This was the wrong answer.

She pressed the button again, and the phone stopped ringing. She clicked on an app instead, then entered the address.

*Wait time: 20 minutes.*

She couldn't wait twenty minutes. She couldn't wait *five* minutes. But she'd had too much to drink. There was no way she could drive.

*Judge me for the man I am, not the man I used to be.*

She grabbed her keys, pulled her shoes on again, and slammed the door on her way out.

231

It was nine hundred meters between Zora's house and his. His stride was close to a meter long. Call it a thousand steps. He took them fast, and then, when that wasn't enough, he ran them.

He wasn't thinking, or if he was, he wasn't letting the hornet-buzz of thoughts land. He didn't want to see them. He sure as hell didn't want to listen to them.

Inside the house, he took off his shoes and socks, his movements jerky and savage, then stripped off his jacket and threw it across a kitchen chair on the way out to the deck.

The trees below were a patch of dappled green darkness like jungle camouflage. Beyond them, lights shone gold from houses and streets, until you reached the strip of absolute black that was Manakau Harbour. And he was burning with a fury that couldn't be denied anymore. At Zora, for saying it, for believing it, even though it was what he'd told her to believe. At himself, for not telling her, and not being willing to live with the consequences, once he'd made his choice. And, above all, at Dylan, who'd taken a laughing, excited, beautiful girl of twenty and turned her into a woman who couldn't believe.

He wanted to hit his brother, to shout at him, to let him know exactly what he thought of him. But Dylan was dead.

*I'm not going to take you with me when I get rich and get out of here. I'm going to leave you alone.*

*Go in the house, baby. You're useless.*

He lowered his head to his hands and rested it there, pressing his forehead into the darkness, and breathed. He breathed because he couldn't hit anything, and because he couldn't have the one thing he needed most, and he'd needed it for so long. And then he stood up, arched his back, opened his mouth and let the pain out.

*"Aaarrrrggggghhhh."*

The howl reverberated in the night. Two doors down, a dog barked, and another joined in. Rhys wanted to bark, too. He wanted to bay at the moon until the frustration and the fury and the pain were gone.

A musical chime. Not his phone. The doorbell.

Wonderful. He'd sounded like he was dying, probably violently, and the neighbors were checking. He stood still and waited. If he didn't answer, maybe they'd think it had come from another house. The last thing he wanted to do was open his door, show them who he was tonight, and have them see him, his shirt damp, his hair unkempt from where he'd grabbed it, and think it was about the loss. That he was wallowing in it, that he couldn't take the learnings and apply them to the next time. That he couldn't pick himself up again.

That he wasn't a winner.

Another chime. Doorbell again. He didn't move. *Go away. I can't. I'm at the bloody, bitter end. I can't.*

Another. Then three more.

Bloody *hell.* He shoved off the acrylic railing, raked his hand through his hair again to smooth it, went to the door, got his Polite Face on, and opened it.

Zora.

Her hair was tousled, and she was breathing hard. Her hand was on her chest, and her other hand clutched her keys, the same way she'd done when he'd left her.

She said, "You could . . . answer your door. And it's uphill to your house. I didn't realize . . . how much. Also, my feet hurt."

He looked down. Chocolate-brown suede shoes with a strap swooping from the outside of the pointed toe, crossing the arch of her foot, and landing at the inside of her ankle, at that soft, sensitive spot where her pulse beat.

"Did you walk?" he asked.

"I ran." She had her arms around herself. "Can I . . . come inside?"

He stepped back, let her in, and shut the door, and she said, "Judge the man I see."

He wasn't sure that was such a good idea anymore. "Yeh."

"I judge him, then. I see him. And I want him."

233

She couldn't breathe before he kissed her. After that, she *really* couldn't breathe.

A second, and then she was tipping, and off her feet. Because he'd picked her up.

"Rhys," she said, and he said, "Yeh," and headed down the stairs with her in his arms, past the kitchen, into the bedroom, where he got onto one knee on the bed, somehow while still holding her. *Bloody hell, boy,* she thought hazily, *you're that strong,* and then he was setting her down. Gently.

"Hang on," he said, then turned and hit a switch, and a light came on from above the padded headboard, directly onto the spot where she lay.

She said, "That might be too much."

He was frowning, his black brows drawn down, and she was swamped by a wave of pure lust. She wanted to put her tongue into the dimple in his chin. She wanted to lie over him, hold his head, and lick into his mouth. She wanted him to *touch* her. "Too much what?" he asked.

"Light."

"Oh." He smiled. Slowly. "Nah."

He was undoing shirt buttons, and she struggled onto her palm and turned to help him. He put out a hand and shoved her gently back down. "No," he said. "Not this time."

She was watching him strip the shirt down his arms. It fell to the floor, and she didn't care. The skin of his chest glistened, its dusting of black hair making her greedy to feel it. His tattoo covered the muscle of his shoulder and ended below his elbow, shining blue-black in the lamplight, and its spirals and chevrons had so much ground to cover.

He came down on a palm over her, and she put a hand out and drew it down his body. Over the bunched muscle of his shoulder. Over the swell of pectoral muscle, then drifting over the flat brown nipple, which had him sucking in a breath. Over the ridges of abdomen, and on down the trail of black hair below his navel. She got her hand on his belt buckle, and he said again, "No."

"Then kiss me, boy," she said, and he smiled. White teeth.

Chin dimple. All of it. He moved down her body, got a hand around her ankle, and she tensed. He was going to just dive in, then, and not even get her dress off? She wanted that, but she didn't. She wanted some more kissing. She wanted some slow, sweet loving.

He slipped her shoe slowly off, dropped it over the side of the bed, raised her foot to his mouth, and kissed the inside of her ankle, and she forgot to think about what she wanted. His thumb traced over the delicate skin, then across her instep, and he kissed her there, looked up, his dark hair brushing his jaw, and said, "Dark red nail varnish. My favorite."

"Yes." She barely knew what she was saying, because he'd set her foot down, touching her gently still, and was doing her other shoe, then running slow hands up her calves, then higher, his thumbs brushing the sensitive skin of her inner thighs, taking her skirt with them until it was all the way up her legs. He looked down at her and said, his chest rising and falling with his heavy breath, "You have the prettiest legs."

And then he came down over her, first on one palm, then the other, lowering himself down in the world's slowest press-up, and finally going to his elbows, until at last, his body was over hers, and he was kissing her mouth. Slowly, still, sucking her lower lip into his mouth, licking into her, not in any hurry at all. And she had her hands on the shifting planes of his back, the indentation that was his spine, supported by all that muscle. A hand, then, on his jaw, as he continued to kiss her. Blackberry and chocolate and plum, rich, dark, and deep.

Kisses sweeter than wine.

He kissed her cheek, and then she felt the gentle brush of lips on her closed eyelid. "Behold, thou art fair, my love," he murmured. "Behold, thou art fair, thou hast doves' eyes."

*Oh, God,* she thought. *Rhys. I am going to burn up and fly away.*

He brushed his lips over her other lid, then said, a laugh in his voice, "Sit up, though. I need this dress off."

She laughed herself, but it came out breathless. When she sat up and reached behind her for the zip, though, he brushed her fingers aside, got a hand on her shoulder, and lowered it himself, centimeter by centimeter. A brush of his lips at the top of her spine, and he was working his way on down as he pushed the bodice of the dress over her shoulders, down her arms. His hands stroked down with it, from her shoulders to her wrists, then came back up again, and he drew his hands down her back and sides, and sighed. She felt it, even though he was behind her.

She said, "I'm taking it off. Take off your trousers."

"You're anxious." There was a smile in his voice now, and he hadn't stopped kissing her spine. He was on his back, somehow, and she was still sitting up, feeling his hands gliding over her sides like he was learning her by touch, seeming in no hurry to get to the point.

"I've waited three years to feel this," she said.

"And yet . . ." His lips had moved to that most sensitive spot, just above her tailbone. He had a hand on her belly, his fingers splayed, pulling her back against him, and if he thought that belly wasn't flat enough, he wasn't saying so. "As I've waited ten, I think I'll take my time and do it right. I think I'll make you remember it."

She shuddered. The edge of roughness in his voice. The idea that he'd been waiting for her, that he'd wanted her, had burned for her, maybe, with the same shameful desire she'd felt for him. The hunger in his hands, the brush of his lips against her skin, and the aching slowness with which he explored her.

She said, "Not in a . . . rush? To get to the . . . good stuff?" It was a bit hard to breathe. Who knew that the small of your back could be so erotic?

"Sweetheart." There was that laugh again. "This *is* the good stuff."

"Oh." It was a breath.

He let go of her at last, though, and said, "All the same, let's get this off you. Naked is good. Naked is brilliant. And if I get to take everything off myself? It's even better." She pulled the dress over her head and dropped it as he worked the trousers down his hips, and then she turned around and gave him a hand. She pulled fine woolen fabric over hair-roughened thighs corded with muscle, down long calves and oversized feet, and then she got her fingers under the silky waistband of black boxer briefs.

*Wait.* Not yet. He'd waited? She'd waited, too. She lowered herself down, stroked her hands down his broad chest, teasingly, letting her fingers flirt with him, then kissed him through the soft fabric.

He jumped into her. She smiled, and he swore and said, "Zora—"

"Shh. Somebody told me this was the good part." She had her palm there, tracing over the length of him, and he was kissing him again, still through his briefs, all the way from bottom to top. He was on his elbows, watching her do it, and she looked up at him, the smile curving her lips. "Nice, eh," she said softly.

"Killing me," he said, but he didn't move to put an end to it. She got her fingers under the waistband again and peeled the briefs down slowly, a centimeter at a time.

She kissed him there, softly, a brush of butterfly wings, did it again, then sighed. "Oh," she said, "that's going to feel good."

His smile was slow. "Yeh. It is."

She got the things down his legs, and he was naked, but she wasn't. She put a hand to the front clasp of her bra, but his hand closed over it. "No," he said. "That's mine," and pushed her onto her back again.

When he kissed her neck, she shivered, and he slowed down and did it some more. When his hand finally traced over the edges of her low-cut bra, she shifted. When he flicked the clasp open and closed his mouth around her nipple, she moaned.

"You like that?" he asked, then sucked harder, and her back arched. A third time, and she was on her heels, stiffening, starting to go up. She cried out, he slid a hand right under her thong and rubbed once, and she came apart. He swore, slid all the way down her body, shoved the damp silk aside, and sucked her into his mouth. And she screamed.

♡♡♡

He was in some other zone. His mouth was on Zora, and she was having the strongest orgasm he'd ever felt, just that fast. Or like she'd been teetering on the edge, waiting for it, all night long. The edges of her hands were still on the mattress, but that was all. Her entire upper body was arching off the bed, and so were her legs, until the only parts of her touching the bed were those hands, the back of her head, her heels, and where he had her pinned with his mouth.

She shook. She shuddered and spasmed, and she didn't stop. She came like thunder and lightning, and he drank it all down.

She was still going, and he wasn't going to make it much longer. He'd wanted this to be slow. He'd wanted it to be easy. He needed it to be now. When the spasms turned to shudders, he rolled off her, pulled her thong down her legs, grabbed a condom from the bedside table, and rolled it onto himself with hands that weren't altogether steady.

"Tell me," he said, "if anything's too much." Then parted her thighs with his hands, spiking up hard just from doing that, and, as slowly as he could possibly do it, shoved his way home.

♡♡♡

She'd wondered, when he'd said it, why. When she felt him inside her, she knew.

She hadn't had sex in three years. She'd only had it at all with two people. She'd never felt anything like him. She was lighting up like there was a fire burning inside, and Rhys was kissing her hair, twining the fingers of one hand through hers, moving slow. Almost all the way out, as glacially slowly as he could go, then a hard thrust in, over and over. It was a long, long way in and out, he was stretching her so deliciously tight, and she was buzzing from the inside out, tingling all the way down her inner thighs. All the way to her *toes*. Like the best vibrator in the world, and every bit of him focused on making her feel it.

She was kissing his shoulder, his chest, her legs straightening again, her body tensing. He felt so good, but if she did what she needed . . .

He asked, "What?"

"Nothing." She was so out of practice. She needed to move, to give him something back, but she didn't want to move. She needed to lie back and *feel* it, and to touch herself, too, but how could you do that?

He stopped moving and pressed his forehead to hers. "What?"

"I . . . I need it harder. With more . . . touching." She wanted to explain. She didn't know how. *It's been three years, and I've done it the same way all that time. I'm not sure I can get there like this, and I need to get there again so badly.*

Selfish. Needy. But she *was* needy, and she wanted to be selfish. She wanted to be *pleasured*.

He smiled, then took her mouth in a slow, deep kiss and said, "Why didn't you say so? Turn over, sweetheart. We'll do it harder. With more touching."

A surge of excitement, and she did it. On her hands and knees, but he said, "Oh, no," lifted her hands, and slid them down the bed so her arms were all the way over her head, her upper body stretched out on the mattress, her thighs spread wide, her bum in the air.

Not the position you would want to assume the first time, or the way you'd want to have him see you after ten years, a pregnancy, and some weight shift past your best body. A posture that told you that all you could do was kneel there and let him look his fill, and then do whatever he wanted to you.

He made it hotter. "Here's the other thing," he said. "You have to hold still." He shoved a pillow up under her belly. "Except for grinding into that. You can touch yourself, too. Make yourself come. Give it up while I'm inside you. Make me feel it."

She started to say, "Wait," but he drove into her, and she called out. He did it again, and she started to rock.

He stopped. "No. Hold still."

"I can't."

He put a hand on the back of her neck. Lightly, but the shock of it went all the way through her body. "Do what I say," he told her. "Hold still."

The darkest, deepest thrill. She could have told him no. She didn't. It was torture, and it was incredible. The slide of him inside her, giving her that electric buzz, the friction of the pillow, and then her hand, when she got it down there. And holding still, so there was only this to feel.

A hard thrust in, and Rhys saying, "You're so bloody hot. You're so tight." A slow slide out, then another thrust. "I'm going to keep you . . . right here." Pulling out again. "For as long as I want to . . . fuck you. Don't you dare move."

The buzz was hard and hot, making her shudder. Now, she had to move. She couldn't help it.

His hand was at the back of her neck, brushing the hair away. And then he got his teeth there, bit down, and when she jerked, said, "Hold still." After that, he put his hand on her upper back, just below her neck, and held her there.

The heat of it. The pressure of her cheek against the mattress, his heavy body over hers, his hand holding her down. Her upper body was stretched out long, her pelvis grinding against the pillow and her hand, and he was buried all the way inside her, grinding there, too. Pressure everywhere, pushing her higher, gritty and dark.

The orgasm came on her like a dragon on the flock. Gliding over the hills and down the valleys with a growl like thunder, the vibration of it entering the soles of your feet and echoing up your body, centering between your legs, corkscrewing down into you, pinning you there, pulling you with it, deeper and deeper, driving you into the ground.

His hand was hard, and so was his breath in her ears. He was swearing, moving faster. "Come on," he said. "Come on. Do it. Give it up, or I'll fuck you harder."

"You . . . can't . . ." she tried to say. *You can't make me,* or something like that.

"I can," he said, and his voice was the dragon's. "And I will. Come on. Give it to me. It's mine."

The darkness was roaring in her head, and the dragon was on her. Vibrating into her bones, into her marrow, and she was catching fire.

He held her harder, his hand pressing her down, and she came. And came. And came. She burned to nothing. He plunged into her as the dragon took her in his claws and shook her senseless, and then he was groaning, gasping, driving all the way to the heart of her, pinning her down.

Shaking. Shuddering. Up in flames.

♡♡♡

Somewhere, some bloke was having sex and getting up again like bouncing out of the tackle. That bloke wasn't Rhys. He was lying over Zora, the fingers of one hand wrapped through hers where her hands were stretched above her head, his body still pressing her into the mattress. He was still inside her, too, and he needed to get out, because he couldn't get her pregnant.

The thought sent a thrill through him like skidding on black ice, and it shocked him out of his immobility. He rolled off her body, got rid of the condom, and got his sense back in a rush.

She was still face-down. He lay down beside her, got his arm around her, kissed the back of her head, and said, "Hey. All right?"

"Mm." She rolled over, finally, but not toward him. Away

241

from him. She straightened her legs, sighed, and said, "I should have cramp."

He laughed. It might have been relief. "And you don't?" He ran his hand down her back, over her gloriously round bum, and then focused there, because that was *nice*.

"No. Mm. That feels so good. Why does it all feel so good? It's like you light me up. I feel like I could come again right now. Like I could do it all night long." A thought that sent a thrill straight through his body. That she'd think it, and that she'd share it. He was such a lucky man.

He'd seen her right all along. The sweet exterior, and the wanton she was underneath it. He wanted to peel away those layers. He wanted to strip her down.

As if she could hear his thoughts, she said, "You held me down."

"I did. Bit you as well." He brushed the hair away from her nape and kissed her there, softly this time. "Having to hold still helps you keep your focus on what you're feeling and not on whether you're doing it right. It worked for me too, though, no worries. So did holding you down." He sighed. "Oh, yeh. That was nice. You are one gorgeous fuck."

This time, she rolled over to face him, and she was laughing. "Excuse me?"

"Shit. Sorry." He rolled onto his back, threw his forearm over his eyes, and laughed. "I didn't say 'pussy,' at least. Been reminding myself of that for weeks now."

"Except that you just did."

"Guilty. It may have been a while since I've minded my manners."

She was over him, now, draping herself over his chest and kissing his mouth, so he wrapped his hand around the back of her head and helped her do it. "I'd say, boy," she told him, "that it's been a lifetime since you minded your manners. I'm not sure you know how. Dragon. And you just told me you coached me through sex."

"Oi." He couldn't stop smiling. "Coached you pretty well, I'd say. It worked."

"You did." She kissed him again. "It had been a while, you know? I wasn't sure I could . . . How did you know what I was feeling, though?"

"Dunno. I just do. Some people know how to fly jets in combat or do nuclear physics. I know how to read bodies. And it made sense. Nobody's in their best form after three years out of the game. Training alone only gets you so far."

He smiled, and she laughed, but said, "It's so awkward to think about, I reckon you have to laugh. Feels like a taboo. It always has. Why is it such a thrill to break it? What does that say about the kind of woman I am?" She stroked a hand over his shoulder, down his arm, and kissed him there, her lips brushing over the design of his tattoo like she'd always wanted to do it. Then she moved on to his neck, and if he lit her up? She set him on fire. "Can we just stay with the thrill for tonight?"

"We can." He kept his hand moving down her back, over her backside, then back up again. Nice and slow. "Must be why that dinner was so bloody hot. I did well, though, I thought. Didn't start sharing my fantasies or anything, and it was tempting."

"Which would those be?"

He sighed. "How much time do you have?"

She smiled as seductively as any woman could possibly have done, bathing on the roof and watched by the wrong man. The powerful man, and that was him. All of it as taboo as you like, which only made it hotter. And then she kissed his neck some more and said, "All right. Now you have to tell one."

"The one I keep coming back to," he said, "is pretty basic. Just you on your knees. Naked. And I'm dressed. Why is that so bloody hot? I tried not to think it for years and thought it anyway, and now, it won't leave. Or possibly you turned nose-to-tail with me, so I can eat your gorgeous pussy—oops, sorry—at the same time. Yeh. That's been a feature. I'm still dressed, though, and you're still naked. Dunno why. That might not work in reality, as you're so tiny, but I could have thought almost as much about eating you as I have about holding your head in my hands while I push myself all the way down your throat. It's a close call, though. I could have a bit of a thing for your mouth. Possibly since the first night I met you. And now that I've seen everything, I've got a thing for more than that. We're going to need some pillows. The things I want you to do . . ."

"Oh, God." She buried her face in his neck. "I'm going to have to ask Hayden for his help after all."

He got up onto his elbows and stared at her. "Exactly how? And exactly *not.*"

Her shoulders were shaking with laughter. "Tonight. I was asking him for advice about what to wear to go out with you, and he thought I was asking him how to give a good blow job. Well, he didn't really think so. He just said he did. But I don't know how to, ah . . . deal with your . . . size. So maybe . . ."

"No," he said. "Absolutely not. Hayden is not coaching you. That's my job. It's exactly my job. And you see—" He smiled. He felt like he could keep smiling forever. "I'm the perfect man for the position."

# nobody listens

She'd used his toothbrush. She'd slept naked in his bed, and she hadn't even wondered if he still wanted her there. And when she'd rolled over in her sleep and had stirred into almost-wakefulness at the alien sensation of a warm, hard body beside her? He'd pulled her in, rolled over her, and kissed her mouth until she was sighing. He'd kissed a slow path down her body, then, feeling his way, and showed her that he knew exactly how to please her. Gentle, slow, and almost lazy, and she'd lain there with her eyes closed, his palms against her inner thighs and his mouth devouring her, the dragon melting her by slow, sweet degrees, until she'd drifted into the sweetest half-dreaming orgasm that had ever dissolved a woman's bones. After that, he'd rolled her over and taken her from behind again, lying flat this time, a pillow under her hips, her arms over her head, and the rest of her doing no work at all. He'd petted and pleasured and filled her until she'd gone over the edge again, with no worry at all that she couldn't get there, or that she couldn't do it right. All she had to do was take it.

No words spoken, and none necessary. A midnight lover, coming to you out of the silent dark, taking your breath, your sighs, your moans in payment for the pleasure he gave you. She couldn't even have said when sighing satisfaction had turned to sleep, except that she knew that she'd still been sprawled face-down on the bed, unable to muster the strength even to roll over, and he'd still been halfway over her, his arm draped across her body, like he needed to keep her there, guarded by his strong right arm. And she'd felt warm all the way through for the first time in years.

When she woke again, dawn had stolen into the room, and he'd stolen out. She could see him, though, out the wall of windows, standing at the acrylic railing and looking like he was perched at the edge of the ravine in the pearl-tinged light of early dawn. He was sipping from a mug, wearing another blue button-down shirt and charcoal-gray trousers. His travel-day wardrobe, she guessed. The coach, back to inscrutable hard-man toughness, wearing the mantle of responsibility like the feather cloak on a Maori chief.

She pulled on her clothes from the night before, used his toothbrush again, and headed out there.

"Hey," she said. "Brr. It's like being in the bush, bird calls and all. Nice. What time is it?"

"Six-thirty." He pulled her to him with one arm, kissed the top of her head, and handed her the mug. It was tea, and she wrapped her fingers around the porcelain for warmth and snuggled into him. A tui called, a long, musical warble, another answered, and the pearly light turned a little pinker. Rhys smelled clean and cedar-spiced once more, like he'd taken a shower, and she still smelled like sex.

Too bad. He was leaving in a few hours, and she had twelve long, cold days ahead to sleep alone in his bed, during which her rational, careful mind would no doubt be talking her into behaving sensibly. She wanted to smell musky and warm and sex-soaked for a little while more. Or maybe she wanted to smell that way until she dropped him at the airport, then come back and wash off the smell of him in his bath, and imagine him watching her do it.

"Couldn't sleep?" she asked.

"Something like that."

"Worried?" She hesitated. "That was intense, last night, but . . . I loved it. So you know. Or feeling guilty, maybe?"

"No. Not guilty. I can't seem to manage it. And I know you loved it. I'm feeling good. Feeling fit. I even remembered to open the hutch door for the bunnies. We'll go inside and make breakfast. I'll get you something warmer to wear."

She cooked eggs wearing a hoodie that reached below her hips, and a pair of fuzzy socks. It was a pretty silly look, but when she rolled up the sleeves, laughed, and said, "Fashion plate, eh," he said, "I like you like that. Something sexy about it, you in my clothes, just rolled out of bed, the smell of me still on you. A little messy. Nice. Mine." With some intensity, his eyes heating up again, so she had to kiss him, and all she'd wanted was for him to pull her down and make her burn some more. Except that they didn't have time.

So that was all very lovely and sweet and hot as hell. Until they walked up the path to her front door a little later, and her front door was ajar.

Not just ajar. Something was wrong with the frame. It was bent. Twisted. Broken.

♡♡♡

Rhys said, "Shit," then thought, *Zora.* "Stay here," he told her.

She grabbed his arm and said, "They could still be here. They could be in the house. We should call the police. Where's my phone? Oh, no. I left it in there."

He said again, "Stay here." The hell with calling the police. The hot fury was rising, filling his belly, his chest. He hoped they *were* still in there.

He didn't creep along and peer around corners. He ran. Surprise was always the best approach. Surprise meant your opponent had no time to react, and most people's reflexes were rubbish anyway. He leaped up the stairs in one stride and was bashing through the nearly-closed door in two more, his shoulder leading the way.

He was in the kitchen, and sensing movement. Two more strides, and he was around the corner and into the dining room, his arm already out for the fend even before he saw the figure, just starting to turn. Rubbish reflexes. He hit him bang in the chest, and the bloke flew backward and landed in a heap.

*Shit.*

He was over the prone figure, reaching for his hand, hauling him up, and the fella was wheezing, clutching at his chest, gasping.

"Sorry," Rhys said. "All right? Thought you were a burglar."

Hayden said, "What . . . the . . . *hell.*" Not very loudly at all. "Is that how you normally tackle? How the hell aren't you killing people?"

"Nah. That was a fend, that's all. If I'd tackled you, you'd have gone down much harder." He looked around. Nothing had been disturbed, if you didn't count Hayden's phone, which had clattered into a corner. He retrieved it, handed it over, and said, "Hope it isn't broken."

"I hope my *ribs* aren't broken," Hayden muttered. "I need a Panadol. And possibly an ambulance."

"Hang on," Rhys said. "What did they take?"

"What did *who* take?" Hayden's face changed. Rhys could swear it went white. "Bloody hell. Zora's not with you."

"What? Yeh, she is."

"No, I mean . . . Oh, bugger. She's gone." Hayden's voice was shaking, and he had a hand in his hair. "I'm calling the cops."

Rhys put out a hand and caught his wrist in mid-dial. "Hang on. She's with me."

He was saying it, then whirling at the sound of running footsteps. Zora, coming around the corner, holding a shovel over one shoulder. He got his hands out and caught her by the upper arms as she skidded to a stop, then took the shovel from her and said, "Thought I told you to stay outside."

"Oh, bugger," Hayden said again, sank onto a chair, and put his hands on his knees. "Zora."

She looked at him, but told Rhys, "I heard crashing. I was coming to rescue you."

"That was him tackling me," Hayden said.

"It was me pushing you a bit," Rhys corrected. "And I

didn't need rescuing," he told Zora. "I am never going to need rescuing. Next time, when I tell you to stay outside, *stay* outside."

She opened her mouth to say something, but appeared to be at a loss. He said, "Yeh. Don't say it. Pretend you listened, that you know I meant what I said, and that you'll be doing what I say next time."

"Lovely," Hayden said. "Meanwhile, I'm sitting here, battered to a pulp, probably got bruises on my hip and my back the size of dinner plates, and is anybody asking after me? No, they are not. If my ribs have snapped and punctured a lung, tell Mum and Dad I loved them. What the hell were you playing at, Zora? Do you know how worried I've been? Why didn't you have your phone? Where's Isaiah?"

"Finn Douglas's. I told you, the kids went to a friend's overnight. Did you call the police?"

"No, thank God. I'd look a fool then, wouldn't I?"

"What? My house has been burgled."

"No, it hasn't," Hayden said. "At least not that I know. Or is that why you left?"

She sank down beside him and glanced at Rhys, who was still holding the shovel. He set it against the wall, sat down with the others, and said, "I think we'd better back up. Zora's been with me. She's fine. What exactly do you think happened, Hayden?"

"I think," he said, looking fully aggrieved now, "that I got a text from my sister, later than she'd normally even be awake, that said, *Help.* And then I got a hangup call that I missed. I didn't see either of them until I woke up this morning, and when I rang her back, and texted her, she didn't answer. Over and over. Which alarmed me, because Zora always answers. Most reliable woman in the world. Then I rang *you,* because she said the two of you were going out last night, and *you* didn't answer, either. I got the bright idea to check her phone location and saw that she was here, so I called in to work to tell them I'd be late and drove forty minutes that should have been twenty in traffic snarled by the arms of Ursula, evil octopus queen, saw Zora's van in the drive, rang her doorbell, checked her phone again, imagined her in here, hurt or worse, probably by you, I'll just say, mate, because it didn't look good, had about ten years taken off my life, kicked the door in—your door's too easy to kick in, Zora—which I thought was pretty bloody heroic, found her purse and her phone on the kitchen bench, thought she was kidnapped, and lost ten more years. And *then,* in the midst of ringing the police, some arsehole came around the corner like Captain bloody America, punched me into next week, and probably broke my phone. Now, I'll be missing a meeting I should be at, about unsafe baby food, he says virtuously, I'll be hobbling for days, my sister's fine, and I have gray hair. Other than that, though, my morning was wonderful, thanks."

"You kicked down my *door,"* Zora said.

"Yeh. Points for me. Pulled a muscle in my groin. Thank you *very* much."

"You should've stretched," Rhys said.

"Excuse me? Before I kicked the door in to rescue my sister? Who the hell texts 'Help' to her loving brother and then waltzes off for the night without giving it a second thought?"

"I meant . . ." Zora was having some trouble going on. She glanced at Rhys, then away again. "I meant, help with my *problem.* Not *help* help. And I didn't mean to leave my phone and my purse. I was a bit drunk, maybe. A bit upset."

"Excuse me," Hayden said, "that I didn't adequately read the shades of nuance in your single-word message." He rubbed his chest and winced. "Do you have a glass of water, two Panadol, and an icepack? I feel I deserve them. I'm sorry I thought you were a murderer, Rhys, which is handsome of me, under the circumstances. Also, the dress looks good."

"The red one would've been better," Rhys said. He got up and put his hand on Zora's shoulder. "Stay there. I'll get it. Cup of tea all around, I think. And unless you aren't a lawyer anymore, Hayden, I'm guessing they'll live with you being an hour or two late."

Interesting, he thought, that for all his casual manner, Hayden was so concerned about both his firm and his sister. Interesting, and possibly touching, too, but not really surprising. Hayden had been there for all three days of Dylan's tangi. Zora's parents had come for one.

"It's nearly eight," Zora said. "We need to leave to get the kids in twenty minutes."

"I could think," Rhys said, "that you didn't want a cozy chat with Hayden and me. And yet I'd swear you didn't feel ashamed."

She was flushing, now, and looking more than cross. She was looking, in fact, pretty bloody adorable, and he wanted to kiss her. It was going to be a long time before he got tired of kissing that sweet, soft mouth. She'd come in to rescue him, too, armed with her shovel, fierce as you like. He hated that she'd done it, but he appreciated it all the same.

Right now, her sweet mouth was saying, "I wasn't planning on making an announcement. I was planning on keeping it to myself until I knew what it . . . what we . . ." She trailed to a stop.

"In that case," Hayden said, "you should've taken your phone. Because I think you just announced. I also think that Rhys should volunteer to have your door frame replaced. Seems like the least he could do."

"Already happening," Rhys said. "Along with better locks, so some wanker can't kick the door in. Seriously, though—well done, mate. Hang on. I'll get that ice."

# water damage

He was sitting on the hotel bed in Sydney, like he'd sat on hotel beds ten thousand times on ten thousand nights, but for once, he wasn't thinking about the next day. He was thinking about the text he'd sent Casey, via Zora, of the Air New Zealand plane out the window, painted all black with the silver fern along the side. He'd typed, *On our way. This is the special plane they made for the All Blacks. We'll have the same kind of seats you and I had, but we won't make them into beds, because it's only three hours. I'll miss reading you your bloodthirsty dinosaur story tonight. Auntie Zora will read to you instead, but don't make it too scary for her. Take good care of our rabbits. I expect to see four happy bunnies when I get home.*

And the answer Zora had sent back, a few hours earlier. *Casey says, "That's just our book. It's special. Auntie Zora reads me out of a different book. And Marshmallow still likes to be cuddled the most, but Isaiah and I are going to hold the other bunnies a lot so they get used to snuggling."* With a photo of Casey and Isaiah in Casey's room, sitting on her new "castle" play rug and holding bunnies, that may have made his heart swell a little.

It had all made him smile then, and it still did. If your special book was the dinosaur book? You might have a special kid.

He needed to buy her some rugby gear while he was here in Sydney. New shorts and trainers from the Adidas store, maybe, because all the ones Zora had bought her were rubbish. Good for looking cute, maybe, but not up to any kind of serious work. And some for Isaiah as well. He could take them to the park on Sunday morning, once he was back, and get Casey started on some basic skills. Isaiah's kicking wasn't where it should be, either. They could work on that.

Ten-thirty here, eight-thirty in Auckland. Zora would have the kids in bed. He should've called. That would've been better. Tomorrow, he'd call.

He was just thinking it when his phone dinged.

A video. His bath, with two candles on the wooden tray, their light flaring on camera, reflected in the black windows beyond. Water pouring in from the high, arched faucet, and a hand, a bare arm draping a towel over the rack. And that was all.

*Come on,* he typed. *You can't leave me there.*

A long wait. Was she doing this now, or had she recorded it earlier?

Now, he decided. Eight-thirty. She would've just got the kids to bed, and this was her relaxing time. Her time to take a bath and sit in the middle of his wide, white bed in her shortie PJs, painting her nails with that little brush and blowing on them to make them dry faster.

Another video, and he clicked, breathless as a teenager.

Her leg, sliding into the water, then another one, and the video scrambled, tilted crazily, until she was there. Her hair up in a clip, her bare shoulders. She was lowering herself into the water, he thought, because her face changed, looked surprised, a little alarmed. *Hot,* he thought, and then it relaxed, and she smiled. And the video ended.

Hell with this. He video called her.

"Hey," she said, and there was that smile again. "I thought you'd like to know that I'm using it."

"I'd like to know. You have a face like a Russian princess. I've always thought so. Made for rubies and pearls."

"Mm." Her smile was looking sleepy now. "Who knew you were so poetic? I love that. Are you missing me?"

"Yeh. I am." He tried to think what else to say, and couldn't. He wished she'd move the phone down. How did you ask for that when you'd been with a woman exactly one night? "Come on, baby, show me your tits" was on no woman's list of romantic phrases.

"I miss you, too," she said. "I didn't take a shower this morning, after I got home from the airport, because I smelled like you, and like sex, and I wanted to keep smelling that way. I'm not going to change the sheets for a while, either. I want to smell you on them. I want to smell you on *me.*"

Bloody *hell.*

"And then, of course," she said, "I had to meet the handyman who was coming to fix the door, so I couldn't take a shower anyway. Do you think he could smell it on me?"

He couldn't breathe. "Yeh," he said, "I expect he could. And that's not all right."

"No? What are you going to do about it?"

He wanted to be there. He *needed* to be there. He knew exactly what he was going to do about it. Except that he couldn't. He asked, "What are you doing now?"

"Washing myself." Her face had gone dreamier. Softer. "Thinking about you."

"Show me."

The phone moved down. Not far enough. The swells of her breasts, and a white facecloth moving over them, and down. And, finally, a flash of nipple, like it had happened by accident. It was a good flash. He cleared his throat and asked, "Are you painting your toenails tonight?"

"I will if you want me to," she said. Back to her face again, and he was glad, but he was sorry, too. "What color do you want me to do?"

"That pale pink you had on the first day. Like the inside of a shell. A secret color, I thought. Nice."

"Mm. I'll do that, then. I'll text you a photo, shall I?"

"Yeh." He cleared his throat. "Good." He didn't have a foot fetish, at least he never had. He just had a thing for her feet. And her breasts. And her bum. And her mouth, which he was looking at now.

"And in a few days," she said, "you can tell me what color you want, and I'll do that. Because you asked me to."

"Because I told you to," he said.

Some more secret smile. "Maybe so. And you can think about what would happen if you came home right now, and pulled me out of the tub. I'd be naked, and you'd be dressed. Almost like a fantasy. You could think about how I'd look on my knees. You'd be so hard for me to take, but I'd do my best."

Oh. Bloody. *Hell.* Her expression was changing, her eyes losing focus, and the image was getting a little shaky. As if the phone were moving, because she couldn't hold it still. "Is that making you come?" he asked.

"Yes." It was a gasp. "Oh. *Rhys.*"

He was a gentleman, or he tried to be. You met the lady's needs. He said, "I thought, this morning, that I shouldn't push it. That's why I didn't put you on your knees on that couch that's right there on the deck, tell you to hold onto the back, push your dress up, rip your undies off you, and solve our height problem, even though all I wanted to do was fuck your brains out."

She was making some noise. He said, "Yeh. Just like that. Just like you're imagining." He wasn't good at phone sex. He was better at actions than words, especially stringing together a whole narrative of touches and kisses and wardrobe details. But he could just about manage this. "I licked you and kissed you enough last night. Time for you to let me fuck you the way I want to."

*"Ahh."* It was a moan, and her eyes had closed.

"Open your eyes," he said. "Look at me."

It was an effort, he could tell. But she did it. He said, "Yeh. You'll do what I say, if you want it, won't you?"

"Yes." She was gasping. "Yes."

"Then open up, baby," he said, "and take it hard."

She closed her eyes again, her face twisted, the phone jerked and shook in her hand, and she hung up on him. Accidentally, he was fairly sure.

He was never going to make it twelve days. Not possible.

The next day, during lunch, Finn said, "What?"

Rhys jerked his attention back. "What?" Had he stopped in the middle of a sentence, or something? He couldn't remember.

This morning, at breakfast, when she wouldn't be awake yet, he'd texted Zora, *Until the day break, and the shadows flee away, I will get me to the mountain of myrrh, and to the hill of frankincense. That's what I meant to text last night. I may have been a bit less romantic than that, as it turned out. Pretend I said it.*

Ten minutes ago, she'd sent back a close-up photo of a deep-pink rose with dew coating its petals, and nothing else. You could call that photo distracting, though.

He asked Finn, "What do you give a woman, if you can't send her flowers?"

"And you can't send her flowers because . . . she's allergic?" Finn hazarded.

"Take it that I can't send her flowers, that's all."

"Ah," Finn said. "Because she's a florist, maybe. Coals to Newcastle, eh. Never tell me Jenna was right."

"What?"

"Mate." A smile broke through the craggy surface of Finn's face. "Why d'you think we took the kids the other night?"

"Oh." Rhys wondered whether he should be alarmed. Offended. Something. He decided on, "Well, tell her cheers for that."

"What do you want to give her?" Finn asked.

"A ring," Rhys said. He didn't mean to. It just slipped out.

Finn looked startled. Small wonder. "It's that bad?"

"Yeh. That one's out, obviously. Could put too much pressure on."

"You think? That could've been brewing for a while, then, I'm thinking."

"You could say that. You could say ten years."

Finn said, "So. No flowers, then. You could give her something else. Jewelry. Like that. Something small. No pressure, eh."

It was Friday, and Zora's hands were flying. She had three new home deliveries added to the list for today, which was good, and a wedding tomorrow, which was better. But it was a lot of deliveries to make in one afternoon.

Fourteen arrangements stood on her work tables: four standard, five premium, and best of all: Five supreme. Two of the new clients were Supremes. She loved Supremes. Not only did they pay the best, their arrangements were the most fun to do. Today, she was pairing the unabashed sensuality of cream, blush, and lavender roses with papery-white anemones, the deep-plum petals of ranunculus, and the open invitation of white clematis, all of it accented with more green and white: the tiny drops and delicate petals of snowberry, the fragility of maidenhair fern, the sturdy structure of eucalyptus, and the twining, trailing vines of jasmine winding through everything, trying to overtake it all.

Roses that lasted never had much scent, but the jasmine and clematis made up for it, their honeyed fragrance mingling in a gorgeously strong perfume. She'd cut the snowberry and clematis from her own garden, and the jasmine and maidenhair fern from Rhys's, which meant that she'd got all the greenery she'd needed, more than anybody would have had for sale in the markets. The arrangements were huge, drooping, and extravagant, and they looked as little like something from a floral service as an Indian banquet did from her mother's Sunday dinner of roast chicken and two veg.

If you were the same as everybody else, why would anybody choose you? Besides, she needed to express herself, to allow herself this burst of sensuality, and to offer it up to her clients like a gift. She was taking a chance again, as usual, as always, because otherwise, what was the point of having your own business?

Paying the mortgage, that was what. Doing the flowers as distinctively and as high-end as she could possibly manage was a business decision, that was all. She needed to be making good decisions now, because the rain had started bucketing down on her way home from taking Rhys to the airport three days ago, like having him wrenched from her was as bad as it felt, and it had kept doing it in fits and starts ever since. The bucket in her bedroom was filling faster, she could swear. There were probably leaks she couldn't see, drenching her Pink Batts, filling her crawl space with mold, and winter was coming. She needed to buy the van before she did the roof, but she couldn't.

She set her palms on the table and breathed in and out as the panic tried to set in. She'd wait two weeks, after another couple rounds of payments had come in, and do the roof on a credit card, that was all, so she had enough for the down payment on the van. And she'd do an extra arrangement for Jenna, she decided, and deliver it today. A surprise. Two of the Supreme subscriptions and one of the Deluxes had been from WAGs. She owed Jenna for that, and besides, you rewarded your customers for referrals.

The only solution to money worries was to keep moving. *That* was the point of owning your own business: that you could always do more. You didn't have to ask for more hours, then figure out how to get enough daycare to cover them. You could just *spend* more hours. Hours of shoving pink flyers under windscreen wipers in the carparks of day spas, along side streets in tony Parnell and fashionable Ponsonby, in an effort that might yield eighty dollars extra that week for ten hours of trudging, but she'd needed that eighty dollars, and she hadn't had money for ads.

She wasn't sticking flyers under windscreens anymore, and that was progress. She was good. She was *fine*. She put together Jenna's arrangement, and was adding some extra roses to it when her phone rang.

"Zora's Florals," she said, because she couldn't identify the caller.

"Hi," a woman's voice said at the other end. "I'm calling from Metalcrafters Roofing."

"Sorry," Zora said. "Not interested." She'd checked them out already. In fact, she'd had them out to give an estimate six months ago. They were the best, especially if you went with a metal roof, but they were too pricey.

"It'll last you at least twice as long," the bloke had said. "Well worth it on a per-year basis. Barely more than half the cost, looked at like that. The resale value on a metal roof is eighty-five percent. Which means spending four thousand, and getting . . ." He'd hauled out a calculator, and Zora had thought, *Isaiah could have done it in his head by now.* Of course, *she* couldn't have, but she wasn't selling roofs. "Thirty-four hundred back when you sell," he said. "Approximately. Very cost-effective on a per-year basis, metal roofing."

Which was all very well and good, unless you couldn't afford to think of it on a per-year basis. If you had to think of it on a how-much-can-I-spend-now-oh-my-God-not-nearly-that-much basis.

Now, she said, "I know I asked for an estimate. I told your representative when he rang up, though, that it was out of my price range." That should get rid of the caller fast.

A short silence on the other end, and she pulled guard petals off roses and didn't hang up, because they *had* given her that estimate. And maybe they were having a thirty-percent-off sale. A woman could dream.

"I'm a bit confused," the voice finally said. "I'm calling to select colors and schedule your install. We'd like to start on Wednesday, since there should be a break in the weather. Two or three days, and we're done. I gather next week is convenient for you, as you'll be away from home anyway."

"I think there's been a mistake," Zora said. "I don't have the money to install a new roof, period, at the moment, and I don't have the money to install a metal roof *ever.*"

"Ah," the woman said. "Huh. We have a credit card on file, so that's all taken care of. Hubby didn't let you know, maybe? Or maybe it was meant to be a surprise?"

Who gave a new roof to somebody as a surprise? Anything *less* of a surprise would be hard to imagine. A bit difficult to ignore a team of blokes taking the cover off from over your head.

"Whose credit card?" she asked. Only one answer, really.

Her parents. She should maintain her independence, probably. Pity she wanted a metal roof so badly. In mid-gray. Was it *very* bad if you accepted a roof? Did it give them room to criticize her life? She'd have to ask Hayden. She was very much afraid that the answer to that was "Yes."

"Ah . . ." There was some rustling of paper. "Rhys Fletcher. *That* Rhys Fletcher? Wait. Zora Fletcher. Sorry. Your—brother? was, ah, always a favorite of mine. Nice of him to shout you a new roof."

♡♡♡

Rhys got the call when he was in the hotel gym with Finn. Or, rather, he realized he'd missed the call, and rang Zora back.

She didn't bother saying hello. She said, "I'm driving. I'm probably going to crash now."

He said, "What? Put the phone down."

"Nah. You're on speaker. Rhys." She was laughing. He thought. Sort of. "I'm gobsmacked. I'm also telling you no. You can't buy me a roof."

"Why shouldn't I buy you a roof? You need a roof. Isaiah told me so."

"When?"

"First night, in the van. What does it matter when?"

"When you sleep with a woman," Zora said, in a too-reasonable tone that promised objections coming up, "you send her flowers. It's a lovely gift. A *normal* gift. A gift a woman knows how to interpret. It says, 'I would like to continue this relationship, because I find you attractive.' Which would be why it's customary."

"I couldn't send you flowers, though, could I? You're a florist. I call that unreasonable. What do today's look like, by the way? You could send me a photo."

"Today's what? Flowers? You do not want to see a photo of my flowers. And how do you know I'm doing them today?"

"It's Friday. Residential deliveries are on Friday. And yeh, I do want to see a photo of your flowers. Your flowers are dead sexy, and my work laptop's got some sort of filter on, so I can't get the good porn. I'm getting desperate here."

Finn was shaking his head, then stacking weights on the Universal machine, lying down on his back, and beginning to do chest presses, like a bloke who was saying, "She isn't going to let you buy her a new roof after one night." Which was what he *had* said, two days ago.

Zora made a noise, sort of a muffled scream, like it was coming from behind clenched teeth. "Earrings," she said. "Pearl studs. There you are. Romantic. Extravagant. Probably still well and truly over the top. *Definitely* well and truly over the top."

"Insulting," he said. He was beginning to enjoy this.

"Pardon bloody me? Insulting how? I just demanded *jewelry.*" She was either still narky, or she was laughing. Possibly both.

He climbed onto a leg press, adjusted the weights, and started in. "Pearl studs? That's what you call 'jewelry?' I can do better. You should *want* better."

She said, "What are you doing? Why are you breathing hard?"

"Because I'm pleasuring myself. Arguing with you does that to me. Or because I'm doing a bit of strength training. Take your pick."

"Right," she said. "Revisiting the roof idea. You don't think that's a bit excessive? A metal roof is four thousand *dollars,* even on my tiny place. I got an estimate."

"Really? They told me five thousand." He added another twenty Kg's of weight to the stack and started his second set. "Could be I went for higher quality, of course."

"Rhys," she said helplessly. "No."

"On the other hand," he said, "the thing I *wanted* to buy you was nine thousand five hundred. You could say that you were on a forty-percent discount. I *won't* say it, though. Crass, probably."

"There are letters all over the place to relationship gurus," she said. "With answers saying that early gift-giving is inappropriate. Red flag, they say."

"Mm. Are we nearly done here? Because this is a bit dull, and the chest press is calling my name. I could say that's for reasons of fitness, but the truth is that I'd like to come home looking jacked. I have a feeling I might get lucky if I do. How about if we agree that this would be a rubbish romantic gift, so I must be doing it for some other reason? We could say that you don't owe me anything, and that all I'm doing is making sure my daughter and nephew aren't sitting around all winter in a leaky, moldy house. Casey could get asthma. What kind of shape must those Pink Batts be in now?"

She said, "How do you know that? I was just *thinking* that."

"Because I'm brilliant." His voice softened. Finn might be listening, and he might not. He didn't care. "Or because I've thought about it, and Finn told me that you told Jenna that your roof was leaking. Come on, baby. Let me do this for you. Make me happy. It's one tiny little thing."

"It's five thousand *dollars.*"

"The bunny hutch was nearly a thousand."

He didn't hear anything for a long minute. "You spent a thousand . . . dollars . . . on a bunny hutch."

"Very easy to clean. Molded plastic. And there was the walk-in run, since Casey wasn't going to have the rabbits in the house. My plans have had a way of not quite working out lately. The rabbits haven't chewed through the electric cords yet and started any fires, I guess, because you would've told me." He switched to leg curls and started working, which might muffle his voice a bit, as he was lying face-down, but too bad. A man couldn't neglect his workout, not if he wanted a woman to touch him all over. And kiss him there, too, possibly. She'd seemed, that first time, like she'd wanted to undress him. He wanted to know if it were true.

Eight more days.

"You are insane," she said.

"I could be. Better take advantage of it."

"I have to . . . deliver these flowers. I . . . You're . . . I'll talk to you later."

She hung up on him again. On purpose this time.

He should be upset about that.

Nah.

# take it to the bank

Hayden turned up on Wednesday evening.

"I'm here, and I brought kebabs," he called into the strange, echoing space that was a house being re-roofed. "Although I could ask," he said when Zora came around the corner from the lounge, "why *you're* here. When am I going to get to see this flash house of Rhys's?"

"I wanted to make sure everything was buttoned up tight," she said, "and covered, of course, in case it does rain overnight." She took the food bag from him and set it on the plastic covering the kitchen benchtops, started opening boxes, and said, "Mm."

Isaiah skidded into the room, with Casey behind him. "Hey, mate," Hayden said, ruffling Isaiah's hair, then offering Casey a high-five, which she returned with relish.

"We're getting a much better roof than Mum planned," Isaiah informed him. "It costs almost two times as much, but it lasts more than two times as long, so that's less expensive, really, if you live in your house for fifty years. It's made out of metal."

"I see," Hayden said. "Where are we eating?"

"Lounge," Zora said. "Coffee table." Which meant, "On top of a different sheet of plastic."

"How did this happen, then?" Hayden asked Zora, when they were sitting on the floor and he'd begun tackling his lamb kebab. "I thought you couldn't afford to do your roof yet. Now you're doing a metal one? Business that good?"

She wished she hadn't shared quite so much with him. "No," she said. "Rhys is doing it, as Casey's here all the time. And Isaiah, of course."

"Wait," Hayden said, arrested in the midst of lamb pursuit. "Rhys is buying you a new roof?"

"Yes," Isaiah said. "Because he probably makes about five times as much as my mum does. Maybe ten times. She makes about fifty thousand dollars a year, once you take out how much she spends on the van and flowers and things. I don't know how much Uncle Rhys makes, but it's probably heaps more."

"Which isn't our business," Zora hurried to say. "And doesn't obligate Uncle Rhys to buy us anything, much less a roof. That isn't how money works. Also, love, we don't talk about how much money people make, remember?"

"Except he *wanted* to buy us a roof," Isaiah said. "He said so. You can do it if you *want* to. It was a present. Presents are OK. And it's Uncle Hayden. You can talk about how much money in your *family*."

"Not in your family, either," Zora said. She wasn't looking at Hayden. She couldn't. She got up and went back to the kitchen to get her mail instead. Two days' worth, since she hadn't come inside yesterday at all, and had only come over to do her spa flowers. Rhys's house was just so comfortable.

When she came back, Hayden said, "That's a pretty good present. I thought men usually sent flowers."

She wasn't listening. She'd ripped open the envelope from BNZ, and now, she was looking at the letter inside, unable to make sense of it. She'd never had an account there. This was a mistake, surely. Had she been hacked?

She couldn't get her breath. She needed to check her accounts *now,* but she couldn't. Her computer was at Rhys's. Oh. She could check on her phone. She stared at the few lines of text and fought the lightheadedness, the sudden panic.

"What is it?" Hayden asked. He picked up the ripped envelope where she'd set it on the coffee table. "BNZ. Addressed to Dylan. Is that still bothering you?"

"Is what bothering you, Mum?" Isaiah asked.

"Sometimes," Hayden told him, "seeing the name of somebody you've lost takes you by surprise."

"Oh," Isaiah said, exchanging a dubious glance with Casey. "But you heard their name all the time when they were still alive, so why would it be different if they're dead? Plus, Dad's name is the same as Mum's name."

"I don't know," Hayden said. "Hard to say."

"No," Zora said. "It's nothing. I'm fine." She folded the paper up again, avoiding Hayden's eye, and stuffed it back into the envelope. "Surprise, that's all. Like you say."

"Casey and me both have dead parents," Isaiah announced. "That's called being a half orphan. I read it in a book."

"It is?" Casey asked. "A norphan is if you don't have parents, though. Besides, I don't think you can be half of something. You're not half of a *person.*"

"You're right," Hayden said, when Zora didn't answer. "There's no such thing. You're an orphan, or you're not. You each have a parent who's alive. Nobody here is an orphan."

♡♡♡

She didn't have time for this, she thought the next morning. She had more than a day's worth of accumulated paperwork and bookkeeping to do, and only today to do it. Tomorrow was residential deliveries, then that wedding on Saturday, and then, on Sunday afternoon, Rhys was coming home. Paperwork was her least favorite thing, and if she didn't schedule it, it didn't happen. You couldn't run a business like that.

She was standing in front of the BNZ branch anyway, clutching a manila envelope and shifting from foot to foot. Five minutes to nine, and everybody was at their desk or behind the counter inside, so why couldn't they open up?

Finally, a thirtyish woman in a black pantsuit came

forward, unlocked a padlock, then unwound a chain between the handles before she pushed the door open and told Zora, "Come in."

Zora said, "I need to talk to somebody in, ah . . . customer service. A banker. Not a teller."

The woman said, "What is this about?" She was eyeing Zora a bit askance. She probably looked wild-eyed. Possibly like a bank robber. It couldn't be her clothes. She'd dressed in her most businesslike attire for this, which happened to be the blue dress she'd worn to go out with Rhys. She was short on businesslike attire. Also date attire. She was short, in fact, on everything but "Arrange flowers attire," which trended distinctly in the shorts and yoga-pants direction.

Never mind. She sat in a visitor's chair, handed over the letter, and waited some more.

The woman scrutinized the letter, then handed it back and said, "I'm afraid the account holder would have to come in himself."

"He can't exactly do that," Zora said, "as he's been dead for two years. I'm his widow. I'm also his sole beneficiary."

"Do you have paperwork showing that?" the woman asked.

"Trust me," Zora said. "I have paperwork showing everything."

She folded the letter up again and put it away. She didn't have to look. She knew what it said.

*Dear Customer,*

*This letter is to inform you that the account referenced above will be deemed dormant due to inactivity in sixty (60) days, as three years have elapsed since the last activity on the account. We have attempted without success to contact you at the email address and telephone number listed in conjunction with the account. If we do not hear from you within sixty days, your account will be deemed dormant, and additional service charges will apply.*

Twenty minutes later, the woman, whose name was Esther, and whose overdecorated fingernails made a *clackety-clack* noise on the keyboard every time she typed, which was heaps, had made copies of Dylan's birth and death certificates, his power of attorney, his will, his passport, and Zora's passport. And she was still typing. Zora had given up asking questions. She was just sitting, now, and trying not to let her mind descend into the hamster wheel.

*He didn't have any other accounts. His pay was deposited every two weeks into the joint account. You paid all the bills. You know what came in and out. You were the one who transferred funds into his personal account for him, and you checked that, too, to make sure he hadn't overdrawn it.*

*Except that he did have another account. He had this one. How? Where did the money come from?*

*There won't be anything here. It'll be something old, from before you were married, that he forgot, the way Dylan did. It'll be nothing.*

*You know it won't be nothing.* The prickling of the skin on her arms last night had told her that.

Finally, Esther said, "Right. That's all in order, then. We're able to transfer the funds to you now. Sign here, please, and here and here, and we'll send them electronically to your account at Kiwibank."

"Wait," Zora said. "What about seeing the history?"

"Once we transfer the funds, there is no history. The funds are in your account, and this account is closed."

"Before you do that, tell me what's in there."

"You'll have to sign first."

"Fine," Zora said, and signed.

Esther pushed a button on her keyboard, stood up, and said, "I can give you a statement, anyway. One moment."

It was probably thirty seconds. It felt like thirty minutes. Esther came back, sat down again—fussily, with some extra skirt-tucking—then pushed the sheet of paper across to Zora with her blue acrylic nails.

It was there in black and white. On the left side of the paper, the account number and *Dylan Ihaka Fletcher.* Ihaka.

"He will laugh," because to Dylan, everything had been a joke. Fun until it wasn't. On the right side,

*Balance*

*$127,218.65*

She was trying to get air, but she couldn't. Her chest was tightening, and her hands were tingling.

She was having a heart attack. Black spots appeared in her vision, and then it got wavy. She couldn't *breathe*.

Esther leaned across the desk. She was saying something. What was she saying?

"Put a finger on your nostril."

That couldn't be what she'd said. Too weird. She said it again, though, so Zora did it. Maybe it was the angels talking. Some Buddhist thing. Serenity.

She was seriously having a heart attack.

"Breathe," Esther said. "Short breaths."

She didn't want to. She wanted to gulp in air. She *needed* to gulp in air. But this was helping. Wasn't it? She couldn't tell.

"Keep doing it," Esther said. "You're hyperventilating, that's all. You're fine. Keep breathing. Short breaths."

She didn't know how long it was. She only knew that, when it was over, she had her head on Esther's desk, the hand under her face was shaking uncontrollably, and so was her knee.

"Here." A paper cup of water appeared on the desk a few centimeters from her eyes, and she sat up, took it in both hands, and tried to take a sip.

"Thanks," she said. "Sorry."

"No worries," Esther said, looking fully human at last. "My husband gets panic attacks. I thought that was it. I almost rang for an ambulance, but then I thought, no, too much of a coincidence. Because you'd been gulping air."

"Oh. Do you have a ... tissue?" She was sweating. Dripping, in fact. Some people really knew how to be businesslike.

She wasn't having a heart attack now. She was just approaching hysteria, or massive detachment, or something.

There was a name for that, when your mind got overwhelmed and separated. Whatever it was, it was happening.

Esther shoved a box across, and Zora wiped her face and hands, took another drink of water, looked at the paper again, and said, "I need to see all his account activity. I need online banking. Put me on the account. Set me up."

Esther said, "I'm not sure if I can do that."

"For banking purposes," Zora said, the heat rising from her chest to her throat, "I'm him. The lawyer explained it. I can ring her up right now and have her explain it to you. I can afford to pay her to do it. The surprises you, I'm sure. It surprises me too, but here we are. I have his power of attorney. We just went through this." Not panic this time. Rage. She breathed some more. This wasn't Esther's fault. "Please. It's my money. It's my account. I need to know."

Esther said, "Hang on. Let me check with the branch manager."

Another fifteen minutes, during which time her paperwork still wasn't getting done, and during which time she stared down at $127,218.65 and tried to make it make sense.

It only made sense one way. That Dylan had hidden money from her.

For years.

Why, exactly? Because he'd planned to leave her and Isaiah all along, and he'd wanted an extra slush fund when he did, that she wouldn't know about and he wouldn't have to share. What other answer was there?

When he was *dying?* When she was shaking out two more Oxycodone tablets, because the Fentanyl patch wasn't enough? When he was moaning with the pain, with the anxiety and the terror of knowing there was nothing else to do, nothing else to try, and no recovery possible? When all of that had been ripping at him with steel claws, shredding his bones, and she could practically see it happening? When he was holding her hand like it was all that he had to hang onto, and telling her, "Hurts. *Hurts.* I can't do it anymore. I can't.

Don't leave me. Please." And she was lying down beside him, wrapping her arms around him while he clung to her, while he tried not to cry and cried anyway, sobbing with pain and fear?

He'd still kept this secret?

How could that be true?

How could it not be?

# can't buy me love

Something was wrong.

Another man might have tried to deny it, but Rhys had learned a long time ago that problems didn't go away when you ran from them. Problems could always run faster than you could.

On Thursday night, he'd texted Zora from the hotel in Tokyo and hadn't had an answer for so long that he'd fallen asleep waiting. When he woke on Friday, there was a video message from Casey, dressed in her Mickey and Minnie PJs, her hair in its loose bedtime plait.

"I hope you have a very good Captain's Running tomorrow," she said, and he heard Isaiah in the background, saying, "Run." Casey said, "I *know,*" then faced forward again and said, "I think it's very hard when you can't yell at people, so maybe you should just say, 'Good job,' or something. Or give them a sticker." More talking from Isaiah, and Casey said, "Or you could stamp their hand, because then it's there to remind them for all day."

He went to breakfast with a smile on his face, but realized, when the Captain's Run was over and he *hadn't* given anyone a sticker, that Zora still hadn't texted herself. When dinner was done with and he was sitting on his bed again with nothing more to add and nothing left to do until tomorrow, the moment of truth when the team's training and their preparation would be tested in the only way that counted, she still hadn't. So he did. He texted, *How's the roof looking? Did they finish?*

Fifteen minutes, and he finally got an answer. Not the one he'd expected. *I found the money after all. Thank you for the offer.*

He didn't even think about texting again. He called.

Voicemail. He rang off and tried again, and this time, she answered.

"Rhys."

"Yeh." Something was wrong with her voice. Too tight. "What happened? Casey?"

"No. She's fine. I . . . Some things came up. I need to focus now, and I know you do, too. I'll be there on Sunday. I'll see you then."

"Wait," he said. "If something's wrong, tell me now. I can't fix it if you don't tell me."

"I know you think you can fix anything," she said. "You've fixed too much. You can't fix this. Not anymore."

"Wait," he said again. "What? Talk to me."

"I . . . I can't." Her voice was shaking, but he couldn't tell why. Sadness. Fear. Something. "I'll talk to you on Sunday. I can't do this on the phone. There are too many things to ask, and to say, and once I start . . . And not before your game. I'll help Casey text you tomorrow. You can send her one as well. Please don't text me."

She hung up on him for the third time, and left him there, staring at the screen, wondering why he felt like he'd just been driven back in the tackle with a shoulder to the solar plexus. He couldn't get his breath. He couldn't calm his thoughts. He breathed his way through them, and he still couldn't.

Something was wrong with *her,* or with Isaiah, and it was bad, because she was shutting down. The same way she'd done that afternoon at Dylan's tangi, when she'd reached the end of her rope, and he'd known she needed to be quiet, and to be alone. That was how she sounded now. Like she couldn't cope, and she had to cope anyway.

If it was Isaiah, it would be worse. That would be how she'd feel. She'd battle through anything for herself, but if it was Isaiah? She wouldn't be able to stand it, and she'd have to stand it anyway.

273

Wait. It couldn't be Isaiah. He'd sounded fine on the phone—well, in the background—and so had Casey.

If it wasn't Isaiah, it was Zora.

Cancer wasn't catching, no matter how it seemed when your Dad and grandmother had both died of it. No matter how it had felt when your brother had been diagnosed with testicular cancer, too, and it had ravaged him like it wasn't meant to do. Even though it was meant to be survivable. Everybody had said it was survivable.

He'd never reckoned he'd get it himself. He'd reckoned it would happen to somebody else he loved instead.

Zora was young, though, and she was strong.

*So was Dylan.*

He swung his legs over the edge of the bed, gripped the edge of the mattress with both hands, dropped his head, and held on.

He'd been in Japan when Dylan had called him with the news. He'd been here. In Tokyo. In this same hotel, the night before a game, lying on the bed and watching a movie. It was the same thing all over again, and he couldn't . . . he couldn't . . .

"It's bad, bro," his brother had said that night, and his voice had wavered. "I'm not going to be playing again."

"It's all right," Rhys had said instantly, so sure it would be. "Nobody plays forever anyway, and you've had a good run. You'll be all good. You'll do treatments."

Dylan had been released from his English club anyway. If he'd been playing again, it wouldn't have been at Super level. Time to do something else, Rhys had thought. Time to man up and move on. Dylan had a wife and son to support, and the house he'd bought had been too much of a stretch. He'd been talking about TV, about becoming a commentator, but Dylan was always talking about something. Which was, of course, why he'd be a good commentator.

"They're going to take one of my balls," Dylan said, and Rhys's mind caromed back to the moment, back to where his focus was supposed to be. "And they're going to do radiation on the other one. It's going to make me sterile. Zora . . . she wanted another kid. She used to, anyway."

"So they take one. That's why you have two. You get her pregnant before they do it, that's all. Or you . . . dunno. Freeze sperm, or whatever, and save it for after. And then you fight."

He heard what Dylan hadn't said. *What if I can't fight hard enough? What if I don't win?* And, as always, he stepped into the breach. "You're going to fight hard enough," he said. "You've got the blood of warriors. Time to prove it. I'll come home during the bye and go to the next appointment with you, talk to the doctors, find out what else we can do. You've got me behind you, and you've got Zora. You're going to fight, and you're going to win."

"Yeh," Dylan said, and drew in a long breath. "OK. That'd be good, if you came."

"How's Zora?" A question he never asked, but one he had to ask now.

"She . . ." Dylan said, then stopped.

"She what?" Never tell him Zora wasn't stepping up. Zora had steel underneath.

"She was talking about . . . leaving. Her and Isaiah. And I don't think I can do it without her." More shakiness, now.

"Wait. You got the diagnosis, and she told you she was leaving? Are you sure that's what she meant?"

"No. Before."

Rhys had a hand in his hair, was forcing the calm. "Bro. What did you do?"

A long silence. "She found a few texts. From a girl. And me. But I told her it was nothing," Dylan hurried on into the silence. "Just blowing off steam. You know it's nothing. She's in England anyway. She's not even here. Nothing for Zora to worry about."

*If it's nothing,* Rhys thought and didn't say, *why do you keep doing it?* He said, "I can't help you with that." He knew it was cold. He said it anyway.

"I need her," Dylan said. The words were halting. "I can't

do this without her. I can't do it if she leaves me."

"Then tell her so," Rhys said, "and hope she cares."

That was then. This was now. It couldn't be happening again. It wasn't possible. But why else would Zora sound like that? He tried to think of something else. Money, the house, her van, something with the kids at school, but none of that could be as bad as she'd sounded.

*Pregnancy.*

A leap at his heart, then a dive, like his heart had fallen into his belly. He knew the sound of "bad news coming."

He was going to make it better, though. He was going to make it as good as it could possibly be. That was his job.

♡♡♡

He knew bad news when he saw it, too, so he reckoned he'd know straight away, once he saw her. He couldn't even have told you how, except that it was the difference between the team in the sheds after the game, these last two weeks, and how they'd looked the week before. He could have watched a video of any one of his players unlacing his boots and unwinding the tape and have said whether he'd won or lost.

He held the anxiety at bay on match day, compartmentalized with all the skill of twenty-three years in the professional game, and punched his way through it. When everybody else was sleeping their way across the Pacific, though, exhausted by the battle in a way he didn't get to be anymore, he watched the game film once, then watched it again, making his notes and letting the strategies form, on his third beer now and feeling nothing, and knew sleep was still off in the distance, refusing to come close. *Peace is for other people,* it taunted him. *Not for you.*

Finally, when the images blurred on the screen and his pen faltered on the notebook page, he put his computer away, pushed the button to make his seat into a bed, and pulled the duvet over himself. He lay in the dark, opened his phone, and forced his eyes to work a few minutes longer, to read the thing he'd downloaded weeks earlier. The Song of Solomon. He read the words, then repeated them in his mind, the fatigue robbing him of his defences and his distance. The cadence and the imagery flowed through him like a Maori waiata sung in the marae, when your voice blended with all the others until they were one, your greenstone lay warm against your skin, and the blood of your ancestors coursed through your veins like you were the mountain and the river, and the mountain and the river were you.

*Set me as a seal upon thine heart, as a seal upon thine arm: for love is strong as death; jealousy is cruel as the grave: the coals thereof are coals of fire.*

*Many waters cannot quench love, neither can the floods drown it.*

He read it through once, then again, and thought, *You may drown trying to swim across, but you can't feel the water when you're standing on the riverbank. You're going to be there with her all the way to the other side this time, even if all you can be is her strong arm.*

The chevrons and whorls of his moko seemed to pulse against his skin. Whatever this was, however bad it got, she was going to know he was there.

He came past the barrier with Finn, both of them pushing their trolleys toward the group of wives, girlfriends, and kids, the same way they'd done thousands of times. This time, though, one of the little figures was for him. Somebody in a unicorn T-shirt and sparkly shoes who charged straight for him. His heart lifted and soared, and he scooped her up into his arms, felt her own monkey arms wrap around him, and thought, *This part's all right. This one, I can hold safe.*

"I missed you very, very much," Casey said. "You were gone for *forever.* And Zora has a new roof on her house. It looks the same as the old roof, but she doesn't have to have a bucket anymore."

"Good news," he said. "I missed you, too, monkey. How are the bunnies? Getting bigger?"

"They're grown *up,*" she said with a sigh. "I *told* you. They're *little,* that's all."

"Oh. I forgot."

"They hardly ever poop on the rug," she said, and he thought, *Wonderful.*

They got to the others, and he set Casey down and put his hand on Isaiah's head, then thought, *What the hell, mate,* crouched down, and gave him a one-armed cuddle instead. Baby steps. Isaiah stiffened for a second, then cuddled back, tentative as you can imagine, and Rhys's heart grew another size. *Progress,* he thought. And then, finally, he stood up and looked at Zora.

Nothing there. Blank.

She said, "Ready to go?"

"Yeh. Back to my place?"

"Isaiah and I already moved our things home. You can drop us."

He'd planned to go to the gym, as usual, when he got home, to get himself right. Instead, he pulled out his phone. "What's Hayden's number?"

"Pardon?"

"Hayden. What's his number?"

She gave it to him, and he dialed. "Hey, mate," he said when Hayden answered. "Rhys here. Could I get you to do some emergency child-minding? My place?"

"First," Hayden said, "you'd need to tell me where your place is. Zora hasn't clued me in yet."

"Rhys," Zora was saying. "No."

He told Hayden, "Hang on," put the phone against his chest, and told Zora, "I need to talk to you." He checked out her feet. "We could go by your place so you could change into some trainers and grab a jacket. A walk sounds good. A run sounds better."

"I am not going for a run." She was looking cross now, at least, instead of shut down, which was better. He could handle trouble. He couldn't handle silence, and not knowing.

"No," he said, "but I have a feeling I may need one. We'll walk first. Then I'll run." He got on the phone again. "Change of plans. Come to Zora's instead. If you'll bring some takeaway for you and the kids, I'll owe you."

He may not have been a natural as a dad, but he was learning. You always had to think about dinner.

$$\heartsuit \heartsuit \heartsuit$$

Zora drove on the way home, and she didn't talk, so he did.

"Did you ride in any subway cars in Japan?" Isaiah asked. "They push you in like sardines, because they're so crowded."

"Yeh," Rhys said. "We did. People stared at us on there, especially the big boys. You could say we didn't blend. Asked us if we were the All Blacks, and were a bit disappointed when we said no. Humbling, eh."

"You *are* an All Black, though," Isaiah said.

"That's not how they meant it. I don't think they'd have been impressed. We rode the train to Harajuku and visited a famous place called the Meiji Shrine. Very peaceful."

"Oh," Isaiah said, sounding disappointed.

"And then I went to the shops," Rhys said. "Biggest shopping area you've ever seen. They've got one called Kiddy Land that's a toy store."

"Did you go inside?" Casey asked.

"I may have done," he said. In fact, he'd had to buy another duffel. He may have got carried away, but then, he was new at this. "I can't remember. It was a long flight. Maybe when we get to Auntie Zora's house, I'll remember."

"Auntie Zora," Casey said, "can you please drive very fast?"

When they got to Zora's and he pulled out the first box and set it on the coffee table, Isaiah lost his words. He stared at it, then at Rhys, and Rhys crouched down again and said, "Yeh, mate. That's for you. Because I missed you, too."

Isaiah said, "It's LEGO Boost Creative Toolbox! I can make robots. *Cool.*" After that, he seemed to run out of things to say.

"Nearly forgot this." Rhys added the other thing, a kids'

tablet computer. "Controller, eh. Your mum will probably have some rules about using this thing, so I'll leave that to her."

Isaiah threw his arms around him. First time that had happened. Rhys held him tight for long seconds, then said, some gruffness in his voice that he couldn't help, "I'm your uncle, you know. Maybe I wasn't around much before, but I'm here now."

"Thank you," Isaiah said. "It's very exciting. It costs two hundred ninety-nine dollars and ninety-nine cents, though." He looked at Zora. "Can I play with it now, Mum?"

"Yeh," she said. "You can. There are probably instructions."

"I can read instructions," Isaiah said, then sat himself down and started opening the box. Rhys considered offering up some advice, like, "Take care how you go there," but Isaiah didn't need it. Besides, Casey was standing beside him, wriggling, moving from foot to foot.

Rhys asked, "Do you need to use the toilet?"

"No," she said. "I'm just very excited. Because I think you have a present for me, too."

"Do you?" He rummaged in his bag. "Not sure."

Casey was nearly jumping up and down now, and Rhys felt like Father Christmas. It wasn't a bad feeling at all. He said, "Oh, here's one," and drew out a squashy parcel. "You have to roll it out."

She did, then lay on top of it and hugged it, because it was a sleeping bag in the form of a teddy bear. It had been ridiculously expensive, it was silly, and when he'd seen it, he'd known he needed to buy it for her.

"This way," he told her, "when I'm not here, if you need a cuddle, your bear can cuddle you."

"I *love* it." She was already crawling inside and reaching down to rub the bear's fuzzy white tummy. "It's the best sleeping bag *ever*. I never had one before."

"A few more things," he said. "I think so, at least. Where did they go?" He felt around in his duffel, and Casey was scrambling out of her bag and right there with him, pulling out the packages.

*"Oh."* It was a sigh. "It's Moana clothes. Three *kinds."*

"Yeh. I got some modern ones as well, so she could dress like you. Now you can change her clothes and play with her on your special rug, with your bunnies."

"And there can be magic."

"There can definitely be magic."

She had her arms around his neck again, and he was picking her up, smoothing back her hair, kissing her cheek, saying, "I'm glad to be home." And meaning it.

"And you came back."

"I told you. I'll always come back."

When he set her down again, Zora wasn't there, but Hayden was.

"Uncle Hayden!" Isaiah said. "Uncle Rhys bought me LEGO Boost! It's almost three hundred dollars." Casey didn't say anything. She was sitting in her sleeping bag, changing Moana's clothes.

"Raising the bar," Hayden told Rhys, and he shrugged and said, "Yeh, nah. Can't be helped."

Hayden raised his brows in the direction Zora had gone and asked, "What's going on?"

"Dunno." Rhys stepped away from the kids. "I was hoping you could tell me. She wouldn't take my roof. Paid for it herself and told me afterwards."

That seemed to take Hayden as much by surprise as it had Rhys. "She wouldn't?"

Zora came out of the back of the house, looked from one of them to the other, and said, "If you're ready, Rhys, let's go," with all the excited anticipation of a woman on the way to her colonoscopy.

Hayden said, "Oh . . . kay," and Rhys thought, *You could say that, mate,* and did his level best to stay focused, to stay right here.

Whatever it was, he could make it better. That was his job.

# a rubbish liar

♡

Rhys changed into a track suit and trainers out of his bag in Zora's bathroom and thought about how she hadn't worn any makeup to come meet him, and about the shadows under her eyes. And this time, he drove.

It was less than ten minutes to the Arataki Visitor Centre. When they got there, she said, "I'm still not running," sounding a whole lot more narky than fearful, and climbed out of the car.

She wasn't ill. She was furious. She was *filthy*. He tried to think what he'd done, and couldn't come up with anything. "I never said you were running," he said, and led the way to the track that started behind the building. "Good to be out in the open, though. That way, you can yell as loud as you like, and say anything you need to. Go on. Fire away."

"You say that like you want to hear it," she said.

"Because I do." He headed down the track. "I've got a thick skin, and I get up from the tackle every time. So go on. Give me the bad news. I can handle it."

Silence, and finally, from behind him, "How much did you know? And when? Did you two . . ." Her voice trembled. *"Laugh* at me? Was it all a joke, then? Was it a deal you made? I'd stay with Dylan, take care of him, and you'd handle the rest of it? Except that the plan went wrong, didn't it? And you *still* didn't tell me. All this time. All these *years.*"

"Wait." His feet slowed on the packed earth. "What? Explain."

"I thought you said you could take it."

He turned around. Whose stupid idea had it been to take a walk? He needed to see her face. "I can take it. I just have to know what it is. Are you all right, then? Not ill?"

"What? Me?" She stared at him, then laughed, an angry huff, and shoved her hair back from her face. "I'm never ill. Don't you get it? It's never me." Her voice trembled. "I never get to . . ." Her hands rose, then fell. "To fall apart. I . . . I can't do this, though. I *can't*. I've been waiting, because I couldn't fly to Japan like I wanted to, not with two kids, and fourteen deliveries, and a wedding, and I've just had to wait, and . . ."

He had his arms around her, but there was nowhere to sit. He said, "Hang on. This was a stupid idea. We're going back."

By the time they were on a bench, with the few visitors around at five-thirty on a March evening giving them a wide berth, because clearly, they looked like two people on the verge of an explosion, Zora had a hand over her nose and mouth, either trying to breathe, or trying to hold back. He kept an arm around her, wished she was in his lap, because he needed to hold her more, and better, and completely, and said, "First—no. I didn't know. Whatever you found out—I didn't know, other than that Dylan cheated and lied about it. That, I knew. But you knew it, too."

She looked at him, then. Finally. "Is that true? Even though he was using your name?"

"I'm a rubbish liar."

Her face twisted. "I don't know what to . . . believe anymore. Everything's just a . . ." She waved a helpless arm. "A lie, you know? Everything's a *lie*."

"I'm not," he said. Fiercely, because that was how he felt. "I'm not a lie."

Another heave of her chest, and the tears came. He wrapped her up, held her close, rocked her back and forth, and let her cry. Just like he'd done before, except that this time, he got to kiss the top of her head, run his hand down her back, and say, "Shh, baby. Shh. It's all right. It's going to be all right." And he thought, *She's OK, then. She's OK. Thank you, God.*

He'd said he could take anything. It wasn't true.

She sat up, finally, wiped her face on her shirt, and tried to laugh, and he said, "The toilets aren't even open anymore. After hours, eh."

"Never mind. I'll just be disgusting."

"Tell me. What happened?"

She looked at him, then. Soberly. Straight on. Pink nose, blotchy cheeks. Honest as the day. "Casey's not yours. She's Dylan's."

It was a kick in the gut. "No. She's mine."

"No, Rhys. She's not. I found his emails with her mum. With India Hawk. And with other women, too. With . . ." She stopped, breathed, and went on. "Heni Johnson, in Nelson. I've *met* her. She cried, at Dylan's tangi, and I thought, that's sweet. But every time the Blues played the Crusaders, she came to see Dylan. Not to *see* him. To 'bring him luck.' Are you going to tell me you didn't know that?"

Heni Johnson. Their cousin Franklin's partner. Tall and beautiful in a lush Maori way that wasn't anything like Zora. "That particularly?" he said. "No. I didn't."

"And how many others? How many, Rhys? And all that time, he was paying for Casey. The payments stopped when he got ill. When did you take over? And why didn't you tell me?"

"I didn't. I didn't take over."

She stood up like a Jack-in-the-box. "Don't *lie* to me. I know you did. You must have, eventually, once he couldn't, because you were there as soon as her mum died, weren't you? I saw the email where she told him she was pregnant. I saw all of it, and I saw when she stopped asking. I found the email address he was using. He used the same password every time, did you know that? My name, and his All Blacks number. He used my *name* on the password he used to cheat. Who does that? How could he do that to me?"

He wanted to say, *He used it because he loved you,* but he

couldn't say that. It would be a slap in the face. Instead, he said, "I don't know. I never knew. If I'd had you and Isaiah, I'd never have let you go."

$$\heartsuit\heartsuit\heartsuit$$

She was barely listening to him. She couldn't. She had to get this out. "I found the account, too," she said. "I know you must have known about that."

"What account?"

"The one with a hundred twenty-seven thousand *dollars* in it. The *secret* one. Why didn't you tell me?" She was tearing up again. Too bad. He was just going to have to put up with it. "Why did you let me make a fool of myself? Do you know how *hard* it's been? Do you have any idea how I've worried?"

"Wait. Back up. Dylan left an account with money in it?"

"*Yes.* He was hiding money from me for years. For all . . ." Another breath. "All the years we were married. At least once I was pregnant with Isaiah." Her voice was shaking. "Do you know how that feels? Do you know how it *hurts?* I know I'm not glamorous. I've always known. I thought I wasn't . . . that it was me."

"No. It wasn't you. It was Dylan. And no, I don't know how it feels, but I can guess."

"And when Isaiah was born with a hole in his heart. When I was spending my time in hospital with him. That was when the emails started for real." She put a hand up and dashed away the tears. Stupid tears. "Like life was too much, and we weren't what he wanted after all, and he was just waiting to run away from it. From us. He was waiting for his chance, but his chance was *there.* Why didn't he take it? What, I couldn't have handled it? I could have handled it. I *did.* I *am.* I handled his *dying.* Why couldn't he have just left me, if he didn't want Isaiah, if he didn't want . . ." Her chin wobbled, and she hated that, too. "Me? Why couldn't he have left, so I didn't have to handle it anymore?"

"You could've handled it. But he couldn't. And so you know? I want to punch a wall right now. If Dylan were here, I'd punch him, except that I told myself I'd never do that again. D'you want to know how many times I've thought that since he died? I couldn't even tell you."

"What do you mean, he couldn't?"

This conversation was all over the place. Rhys's face had flushed dark, but that was good. That was what needed to happen. She needed this out, and she needed it over. "He couldn't take you leaving him," he said. "It was his biggest fear, when he fell ill, that you'd leave him alone. If he was saving money? He was saving it because he thought he was the one who'd be alone. He was so afraid of it, he made it happen. He was a brilliant rugby player, with heaps more talent than I ever had. Better looking, that's certain, and he lit up the room. Everybody wanted to be around him. Always. And he was a bloody fool and his own worst enemy, too. Also always."

"That makes no sense. None of it does. He didn't have to hide money away. He was the one *earning*. He took Isaiah's living from him. We ate eggs and brown rice for dinner twice a week after he died. We ate beans and kumara and . . . and . . ." She was running out of breath. "I lay awake at night and thought about losing the house."

"I didn't say it was right. I just said it was true. And you should've told me. Or I should've asked you. I should've known."

She bounced up, wound to her limit, and walked a circle, because she couldn't keep sitting. "What about Casey? Tell the truth, Rhys. I have to know now. I can't take any more lies."

He stood up, too, and stood solid, like you wouldn't move him with a crane. "First I heard of her was after her mum died. That's when I found out he'd put my name on the birth certificate."

"But you had to know she wasn't yours." She looked into his mountain-stream eyes, and the blood left her head. "Wait. No."

"No what?"

She was backing up. "You didn't know whose she was, because you knew she could've been yours just as easily. Tell me you both didn't sleep with her. That that wasn't a . . . thing between you." She was rocking again. "No." She had her hands over her ears, she realized, like she didn't want to hear. She took them away. "Or tell me if it's true. If I'm . . . part of it. If it was some kind of competition, some sick agreement. Tell me. I have to know."

"*No.*" It came out as a roar, and she jumped. "No. I was engaged to Victoria."

"And you didn't cheat? Come *on,* Rhys."

He was glowering now. Dylan had been wonderful at reassurance. Wonderful at talking. Wonderful at apology. Rhys wasn't wonderful at any of them. "No. Are you through insulting me? I never had a threesome with my brother. And, yeh, I cheated on girlfriends when I was younger. More than once. In Aussie. I got called out for it. I still hear about it. Couple of incidents there where somebody took a photo. You probably saw. I did everything wrong, I felt like shit, and I stopped doing it."

"That's your life lesson?" She was going to laugh. It was mad. It was impossible. But still, she was going to laugh.

"Yes, it's my life lesson. Don't do shit things that will make you feel like shit."

She did laugh, and she sat down again, too. "Noted."

He sat down beside her, looking like he was either going to growl, or he was going to smile. He smiled. Clearly reluctantly. She sobered and asked, "So if it wasn't you, couldn't have been you . . . why did you say she was yours?"

"What else could I do?"

"Well, let's see . . . take a DNA test?"

"Have you seen Casey's eyes?'

Her *eyes?* "That her eyes are like yours?" she hazarded.

It took him a minute, and when the words came out, they were jerky. "We weren't wanted kids. I wonder if you know what that means. I waited three days in the cold one winter, in Invercargill, for our Nan, wondering if she'd come. In the school holidays, that was, and our mum was gone, off with some fella. There's no school breakfast and lunch in the school holidays. We ate a packet of bologna out of the fridge, and five eggs, two every day until the last day, when there was only one to share between us. I took the blue bits off the bread and spread Marmite on the toast so you couldn't taste the mold. The heat was off, because she hadn't paid the bill. Dylan was supposed to go in the toilet every time. He was three. He kept forgetting. I'd shout at him. Hit him. When our Nan came at last, he had bruises on his arms." His eyes, when he looked at her again, were bleak. "She asked if our mum had done it. I said yes. Our mum didn't do it. I did. I hit him, and I lied about it. I know what it's like when nobody wants you, and you can only count on yourself, because somebody else will only take their anger and frustration out on you. I knew what Dylan felt, because I did it to him. I don't want that for Casey."

Her throat had closed, and she had a hand on his arm. "Rhys—you were *eight.*"

"Isaiah's eight."

"Isaiah knows how to care for somebody. He learned it from me. And he knows he doesn't have to be in charge. He's not alone in the dark and the cold, feeling the panic of knowing it's all on him. Maybe you could look at it this way. That you never left Dylan, whatever you think, anytime you had a choice. That you did your best, even if that was never going to be good enough, because you were eight, or nine, or ten, and you didn't know how to do it better. And that you *did* take Casey."

"Yeh, I took her. She's my whanau."

"But you didn't tell me about her."

"She's my blood. She's not yours."

She reared back at that, and he shook his head like a frustrated bull and said, "That's not what I mean. I couldn't tell you. You were on your feet again. I wanted to make it better, not worse."

They sat for a minute in silence. It was getting cold, and she shivered. Rhys put an arm around her, sighed, and said, "It was a mess, eh. I'm sorry I wasn't here when you found out. I wish you'd told me on the phone. It's been a bad couple of days. I thought something was wrong with you, or Isaiah. But I thought it was something wrong with you." He wasn't looking at her. He was staring into the bush instead.

"I'm sorry," she said. "I guess that's happened a lot."

His throat moved convulsively, and the rest of him didn't. "Yeh."

She found his hand and took it in hers. She'd never thought, somehow, of what he'd lost. "I'm here now. We're both here now."

He turned his head to look at her. "And you still have more to say. Go on and say it."

She hesitated, but he was right. She said, "What I want to know, what I keep coming back to, is—why didn't he tell you about Casey before, when he knew he was dying? Why didn't he tell me? About the money, either? I was frantic, some days. Some *months*. He left insurance, but it wasn't nearly enough. What must Casey's mum have gone through? She didn't have any insurance, and then she didn't have any child support, either. I read her emails. And that money was just *sitting* there." She beat the heel of her hand against her thigh, then did it again. She knew what Rhys had meant, because she was the one who wanted to put her fist through the wall now. "I hate that she felt that. I hate that she cried, and she worried. I hate that I didn't know."

"He'd have had to tell you, or he'd have had to tell me, which would've been even worse. He didn't want to be a disappointment again. He didn't want me telling him he was useless, feeling like I was smacking him again. He didn't want anybody looking deeper, because he couldn't stand to look there himself. And I love you."

She stopped beating on her thigh. "P-pardon?"

"I keep thinking—what is it? And I think it's that." He laced his fingers slowly through hers, then lifted her hand to his mouth and, his eyes still on hers, brushed his lips over her knuckles, and she could swear her heart melted. "I think it's your courage. I think it's your heart. I'm not happy I had to say all of that, but you're the only one I could have said it to."

She rested her head against his shoulder, finally, he put his arm around her, and it felt like coming home. "What are we going to do?" she asked. "Everybody's going to know about us."

"Yeh. Everybody's going to know. Except about Casey. I think we keep Casey to ourselves. She doesn't need to worry that she doesn't belong to anybody, and that one more person will leave, and she'll be alone again. She's my daughter in every way that counts anyway. She's my chance to get it right. And everything else? You and me? We're going to say—" He grinned. Like a pirate. Or a dragon. "Fuck 'em."

# the secret places

She didn't tell him she loved him, too, like another woman would have. Instead, she turned to him, put her hand against his face, and said, "Then—could you kiss me?"

They were on a bench beside the visitors' center. Only a few people around, but some of those few were watching. He didn't care. He brushed a thumb slowly under one eye, then the other, catching the last of the tears, then moved his hand slowly around until his palm was on her nape and his fingers in her hair. And then he tipped her head up, bent his head, and kissed her.

She tasted like ginger, spicy and sweet. She tasted like Christmas morning, and she felt like that, too. Her soft mouth opening under his, her eyes drifting shut. He kissed a slow, sweet path across her cheek, touched his lips to her temple, where her pulse beat, and thought of the words he'd read again and again in the dark hours on the plane, while exhausted men slept all around him, and he and the flight crew seemed to be the only ones awake on the black plane painted with a silver fern as it flew through the endless, lonely night.

"O my dove," he said, "that art in the clefts of the rock, in the secret places of the stairs, let me see thy countenance, let me hear thy voice." He kissed her temple again. "I read that, sometime in the wee hours, in the dark, and I wanted to be with you. In the secret places."

She had both hands on his shoulders, and this time, she

was the one finding his mouth. Gentle, and slow, and sweet, but the heat was burning anyway. She buried her face in his neck and kissed him there, and he shuddered.

"Take me home," she said. "Please, Rhys."

He pulled his phone out of the pocket of his trousers, and she said, "I don't want to wait. I want to be with you now. I need your hands on me. I need you inside me. Please."

Surely, there was a limit to what a man could take before he actually went up in flames. He said, "One second," and texted Hayden, *I will pay you five hundred dollars to stay with the kids until eight.* Then waited, not quite holding his breath, while the screen said a response was being typed, tantalizing him, and didn't form into words.

Finally, the bubble popped up. *No worries. Just be good to my sister.*

There was a blockage in his throat. He typed, *Always.* Then he put the phone back in his pocket, took her hand, and said, "Let's go."

♡♡♡

It wasn't even ten minutes to his house, and once again, they didn't talk. He drove, and she put her hand on his hard thigh, felt the muscle bunch under her palm, and didn't think at all. It wasn't even sunset yet, and all she wanted to do was to fall across his big white bed and feel his hand in her hair and his mouth on hers.

They didn't make it.

He pulled off the road, rolled down the curved drive to his house, pushed the button for the garage, then drove inside, turned the car off, and pushed the button again.

The rattle and crash behind them of the garage door closing, the faint light illuminating his hard face, and she leaned across the seat, pulled his head down, and kissed his mouth, letting her hunger free, and her hand, too, as she tugged his T-shirt up, found warm skin beneath, and ran her palm up his hard torso. He made a low noise in his throat, and she had her tongue in his mouth and both hands on his body, greedy to touch all of him, yanking at his shirt. She couldn't get it over his head, because his hands were wrapped around her head, pulling her into him.

She needed to feel more. She needed to see all of him, and to feel him, too. She dragged her mouth away from his and said, "Take your shirt off," even as she tugged some more, and he pulled it over his head impatiently and dropped it over the back of the seat. Which meant her hands were free to roam.

Above them, the garage light winked out. The darkness was heavy, absolutely complete, but she stroked her hands over the bunched muscle of Rhys's shoulders, down the planes of his heavy chest, over his solid sides, the ridges of his abs, feeling her way. Silken skin, the roughness of hair, and the hard muscle beneath. She could hear his harsh breathing, feel his hands on her, now, yanking her own shirt up.

"Get it off," he said through his teeth, so she did. Then he was reaching around, unfastening her bra with one hand, pulling it down her arms. His hand was on her breast, cupping it, teasing a nipple with his thumb, and she was shifting in the seat, forgetting that she was meant to be exploring him. That would be because he was dragging her halfway across the leather console between them, turning her face-up, lifting her for him, and sucking her nipple into his mouth while his other hand found the snap of her jeans and pulled down the zip.

She shifted, trying to get her balance, but he had his hand inside her bikinis now, and his mouth was still at her breast. She tried to say something, but all that came out was a moan. His finger was inside her, plunging and retreating, while his palm ground against her. A big hand, and the long middle finger was pressing on that perfect spot, the one that made you twist and turn. She cried out, and his mouth shifted until he was kissing her again, his tongue plunging to the rhythm of his hand. She had one foot against the door, was trying to get him further inside her, opening her mouth wider, taking him deeper, and now, he was swallowing up her cries. The blood pounded in her head, and the hand that held her up was hard as iron, but his other hand never stopped moving inside her.

She wanted to say, *"Rhys."* She wanted to say, *"Wait."* She couldn't say anything, because he had her mouth, and her words. Then he set her head on his thigh, got his other hand on her breast, began to pinch the nipple, and kept on doing it. Now, she could call out, and she did. Her hips were pumping, and she was keening.

His hands stopped, his finger slid out of her, and she uttered a sound of protest and said, "Rhys. No. Don't stop."

"Get your shoes and jeans off." His voice was harsh, but his hands were gentle, lifting her back over to her side of the car again. She could barely see a silhouette of his body, but she could hear his breathing, and the rustle of fabric as he took off his own clothes. She had her shoes and socks off, was tugging her jeans down, trying to get them down her calves, over her feet, when the flash of light, bright as neon, announced the opening of his door. She cried out and flung a hand up, the door slammed shut, and she could see him coming around the front of the car. Naked and huge, a warrior advancing. Her door opened, and he pulled her up with one hand, wrenched her clothes the rest of the way off with the other, and pulled her out of the car, slamming the door behind him.

Her legs went around him, and so did her arms, and he turned her against the car and held her there. She gasped, yelped, and said, "Cold," and he said, "Yeh," as the light in the car winked out and plunged them into blackness again.

She'd forgotten, surely, how big he was. He stood stock-still a moment, sucking the air in between his teeth. She kissed his mouth, moved her teeth over his neck, and said, "Come on. Please."

"Condom."

"I can't wait. I *can't*. Now."

He swore, carried her around the car as the light vanished, and they were in the blackness again. He set her down on the bonnet, the metal hard under her bottom, and said, "Put your feet on the bumper. I'm going to lay you down."

A surge of excitement, and she found the bumper in the dark, felt his hands on her shoulders, and went down onto her back.

He said, "Grab behind your knees. Pull them in," and she whimpered, unable to stop herself, and did it.

His hands, in the darkness, stroking down the backs of her thighs, over her bum, then spreading her wide, opening her up. A shift of his weight, and something else touching her. His tongue, and he was shoving her legs higher again, holding her thighs in hard hands.

"You like that?" he asked.

"Rhys." It was a moan.

The hard surface was still warm under her back, the sound of cooling metal ticking in her ears, the darkness around them complete, and Rhys was going so slowly, not letting her climb the way she needed to. She was trying to move, and she couldn't do it, because he was holding her too tightly. Her hands slid across the surface of the bonnet, trying to find something to hold onto, and failing.

She said, "Hurry. Please. Please." And he slowed down, his mouth lazy, like he had all day.

She was trying to climb, and he wasn't letting her. She said, "Please."

"I'm putting your feet on my shoulders," he said. "Keep them there. Hold still for me."

She reached behind her, found the indentation where the bonnet met the windscreen, and held on tight. And he got that finger inside her, spread her wide with the other hand, and ate her up by slow degrees. And when his little finger slid back to circle her, she sucked in a breath and moaned.

He held her there, breathless, trembling, for aching minutes, until her cries were bouncing off the hard walls of the garage, until she was burning. Until she was shaking. Then he sat back, pulled her feet off his shoulders, and said, "Not yet."

"Not . . . yet?"

"Spin around, baby. Put your feet on the windscreen."

Her entire body was throbbing. She had to come so badly, she was almost sobbing with it. He was helping her, though, repositioning her in the dark, when she was disoriented, pulling her down by the shoulders so her head hung off the edge of the bonnet and her legs were up high. He stroked her face, pulled her hair back, ran his hand down her neck, over her breasts, played there, and said, "Do you want to take me deep?"

"Yes."

His fingers were on her chin, tilting it up. "Open up," he said. And, slowly, slid inside.

♡♡♡

She was frustrated as hell, and he knew it. She was burning, and she was about a centimeter away from exploding. And he pushed his way slowly into her mouth, testing her limits, tried not to groan, and failed.

He still had his hands on her face, tipping her head back, and he wanted to shove all the way inside. Instead he said, "Put a . . . hand around my thigh and hold on, so you can control how deep you take me. If it's too much, if you want me to ease off . . . punch me. If you don't want me to . . . come in your mouth . . ." It was hard to get the words out. Her mouth was so hot, and his eyes had adjusted to the darkness enough that he could see her pale body spread out on the car, one foot flat on the bonnet, the other one stretching up onto the windscreen. He said, "Take your other hand and . . . let yourself come. Suck me hard. Show me how much you . . . missed me."

Her mouth. Her *mouth*. She started to shift, to rock as the orgasm built, hard and fast, and with every centimeter she went higher, she took him deeper. He wrapped his hand in her hair, held on, held still, and thought, *Let her do it, mate. You'll be too much otherwise.*

It was torture. It was going to kill him. She was making some sounds deep in her throat, where he was lodged, was gripping his thigh tighter, her own hand moving faster, and then, between one breath and the next, she was coming. He could hear her hips slamming against the metal, could feel the suction increasing as the sound of her breathing through her nose reached a frantic pace, and he had both hands in her hair and was yanking her head back and emptying himself down her throat. Like she was his, and he was her king.

Groaning. Cursing. Shaking. Gone.

♡♡♡

Her legs were trembling so hard, she couldn't control them. The blood had rushed to her head, because she was tipped nearly upside-down, and Rhys was salty-sweet in her mouth. He pulled out of her, and she kept her hand around his thigh and tried to get her breath. And still, her legs shook. He said, *"Fuck,"* which pretty much summed it up, leaned over, pulled her into his arms, carried her into the house, down the stairs, and into the bedroom the same way he had the first night, came down over her, and kissed her mouth.

"You were ..." she said. "That was ..." She couldn't think how to go on.

"Mm." He had her arms up over her head, was running his hands from her wrists to her shoulders, slowly, then back again, as he kissed her again. Still. "You're beautiful. Taku toi kahurangi."

"I don't know what that ... means," she said, glad that she didn't. Glad that this was just for her, just between the two of them.

"My precious jewel. I mean to be gentle, every time. I mean to be ... sweet."

She laughed softly against him and ran her own hand over the swell of biceps and rock-hardness of triceps. "You were a lot of things, but I don't think 'sweet' was one of them."

"Mm." He kissed her mouth again, twined his fingers in her hair, and asked, "Anything I did that you didn't like?"

"No. I love the way you surprise me."

He stilled over her. "Shit."

"What?"

He laughed, now, and pressed his forehead to hers. "You never asked if I brought you a present, too."

"Oh." She was laughing some more. "Never mind. I wasn't expecting a present. You offered me a roof. How would you do better than a roof?"

"And you wouldn't take my roof. Wait here. Don't move. Or—wait. You can move. Sorry. Bossy fella. But stay here."

He left, and she sat up in the dark, found the top edge of the duvet, and climbed inside. She should be going into the bathroom and washing up, but she wanted to wallow in this for a few minutes more. And after that, she wanted to take him into the bath with her, to lie over him, feel him reach around to kiss her, and to let his hands stroke over her and wash her clean, the way he'd wanted to do that night on the phone.

He came back into the room bare-chested, but in his track pants, and she said, "Clothes aren't fair."

"I told you. It's hotter if you're naked and I'm not." He rested a hand on the light switch and said, "Put a hand over your eyes."

"I'm OK."

"No. Seriously. Put a hand over your eyes, and close them."

She did it, but saw the darkness decrease anyway, then heard his footsteps retreat and come back. He said, "You can open them now."

She did, to find him standing over her, frowning, running a hand through his dark hair, and a dark-blue paper bag on the bed in front of him.

She looked at it, then at him, and said, "Uh . . . is this a good thing, or a bad thing?"

"Good thing. I hope."

"Then . . ." She scooted over. "How about coming and sitting with me? And not looking like you're about to breathe fire?"

"Oh." A smile, a slow one, and he climbed onto the bed, got an arm around her, and said, "Open it."

She did, and pulled out a square, flat velvet case in royal blue. Not a small one. She said, *"Rhys,"* and he said, again, "Open it." Like he was holding his breath. Like he wasn't sure.

She thought, *Three two one go,* flipped the case open, and stared at what was inside, then at Rhys, then back at the thing in the case.

He said, "Can I put it on you?" and she raised a hand, let it fall, and said, "Yes." It came out on a breath, because she couldn't *get* her breath.

The touch of the nearly luminescent, pinkish-white pearls was cool against her skin as Rhys draped the rope around her neck and fastened them. He pushed her hair aside with one hand, kissed her softly on the side of her neck, and said, "I've wanted to do this for so many years. You can put the clasp anyplace you like, all down the strand. It's a lariat. And it's exactly as beautiful on you, and exactly as sexy, as I knew it would be. I bought it, and I wanted to see you naked in it. I want to keep you in it for days, and take away all your clothes. Come into the bath and look."

She got out of bed, still feeling like somebody had stolen all the air out of her lungs, and followed him into the bathroom, where he turned the dimmer switch on low, put both hands on her shoulders, and turned her to face the mirror above the sinks.

She ran a hand over the rope of pearls, then touched the diamond clasp. Lightly. He'd fastened it so it caught at her collarbones, leaving a single line of pearls draped to her breastbone.

"This is what I've always thought," he said. He picked the necklace up off her breast with light fingers, then turned it around and laid it gently down her back, where its coolness made her shiver.

"Turn around," he said, "and see."

She did, and he handed her a shaving mirror.

It wasn't what you'd wear for dinner with your parents. The pearls formed a choker over her throat and dipped down her back, lying white, shimmering, and sensual against her skin, and Rhys was stroking his hand down every single lustrous bead, then all the way down to the small of her back. He said, "You have the most gorgeous back. Like a cello. Like something from another age. I want to buy you a dress. Black velvet, dark blue, something like that, cut low here. When you turn around, every man's breath will catch."

"It will?"

His smile was slow, and when he bent to kiss her, just below the nape of her neck, his lips were soft. "Yeh, baby. It will. Because you're beautiful."

He did take a bath with her, once she took her necklace off and stowed it carefully back in its velvet box, and they watched their reflection in the black windows as Rhys stroked a facecloth over her breast and belly, down her thighs, and back up again.

She said, "I should hate that you bought me a present like that. I should say it's too soon. Where am I going to . . ." She had to stop and breathe, because he had the facecloth dipping into those secret spaces. "Wear it?"

"Or you could say," he said, dripping some bath gel onto the facecloth, getting his hand under her thigh, and beginning to wash it, "that I've been waiting forever to do it. And that I'll make sure you have a place to wear it."

She hummed, then said sleepily, "The first night I met you . . . you made me shiver. I didn't know what it was. I thought you hated me. And then you never came around, and I was sure of it." It was easier to say when she could only see his reflection.

He said, "I didn't hate you. I wanted to take you to bed. Or on the car. Or anywhere else I could get you. It was too hard to control my thoughts, if I was with you. And you know . . . if this is going to come out anyway, we should practice. Friday night."

"Friday night isn't a . . . rugby date night."

"It is if you're not playing. And I'm going to buy you a dress. Maybe shoes as well."

"If I wear high heels, that means it's a hot date. With kissing."

His mouth brushed over the side of her neck, and he said, "Then I'd better buy you some very high heels."

# evaluation

It wasn't even nine o'clock on Monday night, and Rhys's eyes were closing. Too many time zones, and too much emotion. After the third time he'd started awake, he put down the book he was reading, headed for bed, and fell fathoms deep almost instantly.

He sat up in the dark, not knowing whether it had been minutes or hours, or what had woken him, and was rolling out of bed in almost the same motion. Whatever it was, he needed to be standing up to deal with it. Outside, the wind had risen, and he couldn't hear anything over the ever-shifting rustle and moan that was palm fronds clacking against each other, tree branches rubbing together, and a hundred thousand leaves trembling and shaking.

He was at the doorway, then beyond it. Still nothing to see, and no change in the faint glow of the night light in the kitchen, but *something* had woken him.

*Casey.*

He was across the room and up the stairs on the thought. And there was that noise again, barely audible above the wind. Something wrong.

Into Casey's room, and he heard it again. A hitch of breath. A whimper. A rustle that was the bunnies in their cage, and the glow of her pink crystal casting a dim pool of light near the door.

"Casey?" he asked. "What's wrong? Feeling ill?"

"Th-there was a . . ." He couldn't hear the rest, so he made his way across the castle rug to her bed, wincing when he stepped on one of the eighty-five surprises in the L.O.L. Surprise House with a bare foot. He was only wearing a pair of sleep pants, but that was OK, surely. She'd seen his chest before.

She was sitting up against the headboard of the white iron princess bed they'd picked out a few days before he'd left on the latest trip. It had a canopy top wrought in the shape of a pumpkin coach, and the iron of the headboard formed a butterfly. She'd loved it, it had cost too much, and he'd bought it for her anyway, along with white net curtains to hang at the head and foot, and a bedside table whose legs were more twists of butterflies. Zora would have said that it was important to match, and it all looked much better now. Like the bedroom of a little girl who was loved.

He sat down beside her on the ruffled white duvet, got his arm around her, and said, "Eh, monkey. What is it?"

"There was a . . ." Another hitch of her breath. "A very mean wolf."

"Nah. Really? What did it do?"

"I can't tell you. Or he might come back."

"If you tell, he won't come back. Telling takes away his power."

He couldn't see her expression that well, but he could see enough to know it was skeptical. "It does?"

"I promise. Tell me what happened."

She was still crying some, and he lifted the edge of the sheet and wiped her face with it. Probably not what a mum would've done, because mums probably remembered to buy tissues. He wasn't a mum, though, so there you were.

"I was in your car," she finally said, "and you said to wait inside, and then you went away, and I didn't want to wait anymore, because I was getting scared. And it was a very long time."

"Which I wouldn't have done. What, leave you in there alone? Nah. I'd take you with me."

"Maybe it wasn't a kid place, though. Maybe it was a grownup place."

303

"I'm in the casino, gambling away my pay packet? Not happening."

"Oh."

"So where does the wolf come in?" he asked.

"I was waiting in the car, and then the car was driving, and you looked in the mirror and I saw your face, but it wasn't you. It was a wolf, and he had gray hair and big teeth that were pointed. And he smiled really big, but it was a mean smile, and he was driving very fast."

She was shaking some now, and he wrapped her up tighter in his arm and said, "Good thing I'm Maui, then, and I can ride on the wind and the waves and come through the car window and get him."

"No, you can't. Because you said you weren't Maui, and anyway, Isaiah says Maui is only a story. He's not really real."

"He's real in a dream. And I'd come anyway, even if I wasn't Maui."

She'd stopped crying, at least. "You would?"

"Course I would. Just like the Runaway Bunny story says. Because you are my little bunny." It was easier to say in the dark.

"Except you always say monkey."

"You're both. Bunny and monkey. Depending."

She had both hands wrapped around his arm, like she needed to feel its strength. He might not remember to buy tissues, but strength was one thing he did have on offer. She said, "And you have a tattoo like Maui, and a fish hook like Maui, so maybe you could come."

"I could definitely come. And I would. Plus, there's you. You could fight the wolf."

"I can't fight a *wolf*. I'm a *kid*."

"My daughter, though, aren't you? Casey Moana. Fierce and strong. Yeh, that's it." He sighed. "I'm afraid that wolf's going to be wolf meat. He'll be lucky if you don't eat him for dinner."

She giggled, which was much better. "I don't think wolves taste good."

"How do you know? Have you ever tasted one?"

She was the one sighing now. "That's silly. And I don't think that's the right way to say it, when you have a bad dream. You're s'posed to hug me and say that there are no bad wolves, and it won't get me, and go to sleep now. That's what my mommy would say."

"I call that unfair. Here I am, hugging for all I'm worth, giving you a better alternative, and this is what I cop?" He gave her hair a stroke and pulled her in a little tighter. "You're missing your mum, maybe."

"She used to smell very nice." Casey might sound a wee bit drowsy, which meant he was doing it right. "Like flowers. Zora smells kind of like my mommy, and she's got a nice voice like my mommy, too. You have a big voice, like Maui, and you aren't soft like Zora, but you're kind of like my mommy anyway."

"That's because I'm your dad." He kissed the top of her head. "Dads don't smell as nice, maybe, but we have our good points. I can teach you how to fight the wolf, for one. Could teach you to use the taiaha, when you're a bit older. That's a fighting staff. Maori are fierce warriors, you know. That was the first thing I thought when I saw you in Chicago, sitting on that lady's couch. Thought you were fierce, and you were strong."

"You did? I was scared, though, because I didn't know who you were, and I missed my mommy very much."

"That's when you need to be fierce most, is when you're scared. You can run away, or you can fight back. You and I fight back, and we don't give up. That's how I recognized you, even though I'd never met you before. It's how I know you'll be eating wolf meat, too. I'll get there, riding on the wind, and you'll have dealt to him already and won't have left anything for me to do. Won't I be disappointed then."

She snuggled in closer. "You aren't really like a mom," she said, "but you're kind of like a dad, I guess."

"I'm exactly like a dad. Because I am one."

Ten hours later, and he was stuck into his work again, watching the training, going down his checklist from the Tokyo game.

"Hugh," he said, pulling the captain aside after one of the endless series of drills that were the reason New Zealand played the best rugby on the planet. "You got beat three times on Saturday getting to the breakdown, which is why their No. 8 could get in under you and snaffle the ball. What I'm seeing is you hanging in there at the last one a second too long. If the ball isn't there, let it go. Focus on getting in and out."

Hugh nodded, his dark, bearded face intense, and said, "Right," and Rhys flipped a page on his clipboard and headed over to where the tight forwards were working on their tackling, each man holding up a pad for his mate, who hit it hard, over and over again.

Tom Koru-Mansworth, the young lock who'd come off the bench in Tokyo and earned a yellow card in the seventy-first minute for a high tackle, was going at it *too* hard, he thought. Not methodical. Nearly frantic.

It mattered too much, maybe.

*You can't coach hunger,* he'd told Finn, but what he was seeing *was* hunger. It was more than that. It was desperation.

His push on the kid had hurt as much as it had helped, surely. He didn't usually stuff up with his players. Why had he done it this time? Because Kors was good-looking, Maori, and quick with a laugh? Reminding Rhys of Dylan, possibly, and frustrating him into too-hasty judgment?

What was it Casey had said? *I think it's very hard when you can't yell at people, so maybe you should just say, 'Good job,' or something. Or give them a sticker.*

He headed over and pulled Kors aside. The kid looked nothing but apprehensive. Rhys said, "Your first yellow card, eh."

"Yeh," Kors said, and looked even more nervous. Which wasn't how anybody learned, was it? It was good to care. It was bad to obsess. The line was fine.

"High tackle," Rhys said. "How long ago did you finish growing?"

"About a year," Kors said. He was all arms and legs, the way young locks tended to be. Six foot six could take you by surprise, and so could that extra fifteen Kg's of muscle you'd put on. Power and height and athleticism were all well and good, but judgment took time and focus.

Rhys said, "You had seven inches on Izu. Didn't get down low enough, that's all. Didn't know what *was* low enough, maybe." He pulled a roll of athletic tape from his pocket and called to Iain McCormick, "Bring that pad over, mate. "Iain obliged, and Rhys attached a strip of tape halfway up. "Nipple height," he told Kors. "That's what you're visualizing. Go through and switch off partners. Practice adjusting to that height difference." He put a hand on Kors's shoulder. "You went well for twenty minutes beforehand, got through a load of work, though you're hesitating out there at times, like you don't trust what you're seeing, which makes you a fraction of a second slower to the tackle and makes it harder to get it right. Your judgment's good. Commit to it. As for the yellow card—take that one and move on. I saw a mistake. When I see a pattern, I'll let you know."

"OK," Kors said, and something crossed his face very much like relief.

Rhys said, "Right there. Your shoulders relaxed and dropped down. That's the space you want to be in. You're overthinking it. You don't have to be four steps ahead, not now. Focus on doing your role, and trust your mate to do his. The rest of it will come."

Kors nodded, trotted off with Iain, and started in, and Rhys stuck his hands in his pockets and thought, *Thanks, monkey.*

He'd have given Kors the same feedback a season ago, but he would've given it differently. It wasn't a sticker, but it may have worked.

Also, Kors may not have been the only person who'd been getting too intense.

Another hour, and the group trotted off for lunch. Rhys picked up rugby balls along with Finn, tossed them into the bin, and headed in after them. His phone dinged, and he pulled it out of his pocket.

That was another change. He checked, now, during the day, in case it was something he needed to know. Zora was there to get any calls from the school about Casey, but still—he checked.

It *was* Zora. First time she'd texted him during the day. One photo, and then another. Dresses. Not on her, unfortunately.

*Pink with black flowers?* she asked. *Or black with pink flowers?*

*Black with pink,* he answered. The dress had little spaghetti straps. He loved straps like that, the kind you could push right off her shoulder. He hoped the dress wasn't too long. He couldn't tell.

*Black shoes or nude? Good news for me. They're having a sale.*

*Black,* he answered. *Don't show your toes. Save them for me. And I'm buying this. All of it.*

*You forget,* she texted back. *I'm not broke anymore.*

*Don't care. I'm buying it.*

*Why?*

That one had him stumped. Finn had gone on ahead, through the tunnel, and nobody was out here but Wally, the equipment manager, collecting gear. It was going to rain later, Rhys judged. Good. They needed the practice.

Finally, he texted, *Because it's hot. I want to buy everything you wear for this, all the way down to the skin. I want you to think about me when you buy it, and I want to walk in behind you and know it's all mine.*

A long pause, then her answer.

*That's primitive, boy.*

One last text, and he would put the phone away.

*I know.*

Once again, Zora was in her bathroom, and once again, she wasn't quite ready, because she'd had to feed the kids and help

Casey with her bath. She could hear Adele Simpson, the older lady who minded Isaiah from time to time, out there talking to Casey. And then she heard the doorbell.

She wished Hayden had been available to babysit. Going out there like this felt too revealing. Too momentous. Nobody would look at her tonight and think, *Out for a nice dinner with her brother-in-law. Probably talking about the kids.*

She blotted her deep-pink lips, set the color with a little powder, dropped the lipstick into her evening bag, and thought, *That's good enough.* She'd reapply it at the table, make a bit of a fuss over it, and drive Rhys crazy.

One last look in the mirror, then another deep breath, and she bent from the waist, got a hand in her hair, straightened, and checked it out.

That was it. With her hair like this, *absolutely* nobody would think this was anything but romance. She wasn't dressing for them, though. She was dressing for Rhys. She opened the bathroom door.

Rhys was standing by the couch, one casual hand in his pocket, talking to Casey. When she walked in, he looked up.

"Holy . . ." she breathed.

Black suit. Black shirt. Dark hair falling to chin length, and he hadn't shaved this time. He looked like . . . he looked . . . she couldn't even say. Like somebody who'd never been tamed. His eyes were even more gold than usual and fixed on her, and her legs didn't want to hold her up. That could have been the black suede stilettos. It could also have been too much dragon.

"Hi," he said, with no smile at all, like he'd forgotten to do it, or like his barely-there veneer of civilization was gone. "Ready to go?"

"Yes," she said. "One second." She bent down and gave Isaiah a kiss, then offered Casey a lengthier cuddle.

Casey said, "You smell very fancy, and you look very fancy, too. And you're wearing high heels, so that means it's a hot date."

"It is," Rhys said. He was jumping straight in there, then.

"Men generally think it's a hot date when the woman's looking very beautiful, like Auntie Zora is tonight."

"A hot date is with kissing," Isaiah said. "Like you kissed Uncle Rhys before, Mum, in the bathroom at his house."

A moment of frozen silence, and Adele said, on a flustered little laugh, "You look lovely, Zora. What a gorgeous dress," while her eyes went from Zora to Rhys and back again.

Zora quailed for a moment, then thought, *That's the point.* She was tired of waiting for the other shoe to drop. She wanted it to *drop.* "Did you meet Rhys?" she asked.

"Yes," Adele said. "He introduced himself, though I would have recognized him, of course. You do look like your brother, don't you?" she asked Rhys.

"Not as good-looking," he said, and Zora could see the moment when Adele realized, *Whoops. That's an awkward comparison for Zora,* and also when she thought but didn't say, *Oh, no. I think you're even better looking. Tougher. Harder.*

Not what you wanted when you were twenty, maybe. Intimidating. Overwhelming. What you oh-hell-yeah wanted when you were thirty, though. She said, "We'll be home by midnight."

"It's a very busy day tomorrow," Isaiah said. "You have to get up really early to do two weddings, plus it was a busy day today. You always say you need to go to sleep early on Fridays."

"That's right," she said. "Except that tonight, I have someplace special to go. Lucky I have you and Casey to get up early with me and help."

"Dinnertime doesn't take five hours," Isaiah said. "And dinner isn't until midnight. Dinnertime takes about a half an hour."

"Uncle Rhys and I need time to talk, too," Zora said. "That's why you go out. It's not just about eating dinner. It's a chance to spend time together."

"You could spend time here," Isaiah said. "Then we could have dinner all together."

"Except that I want to take your mum out somewhere

nice," Rhys said, "and let her dress up and be pretty. I want to spend some money on her. That's one way you show a woman you care about her."

Well, that was blunt. Maybe the floor could open up now. Rhys took the pale-pink sweater from her hand and helped her on with it. "Time to go," he told her. Still no smile. He dropped to his haunches, put an arm around Casey, kissed the top of her head, and said, "Good night, monkey. I'll see you in the morning."

"Did you feed the bunnies?" she asked.

"Yeh. I did. Didn't give them treats, though. You can do that tomorrow." He ruffled Isaiah's hair, did the one-armed cuddle that was the maximum Isaiah permitted from anybody but his mum, and said, "Kicking practice tomorrow morning, eh."

"OK," Isaiah said, "but I'm concentrating on my robot now, please."

Rhys said, "Good point."

He stood up, and Zora said, "Well—good night," and headed out feeling like she had a scarlet letter on her chest.

At least Adele hadn't mentioned the necklace.

♡♡♡

Rhys had got a driver again, which was good, because he could have a glass of wine with Zora, and bad, because he couldn't kiss her, or tell her how smoking hot she looked.

The dress was black with a print of pink roses that made it look like lace. It was form-fitting enough to show you the party she had going on under there, it had those spaghetti straps and dipped into a vee in front and a deeper one in back, and it hit a few fortunate centimeters above her knees. Her heels were high and whisper-thin, they were black suede, and they were killing him.

He wondered if she was, just possibly, wearing a black lace thong. Then he wondered how she'd look wearing only that, those heels, and that necklace down her back, and got a rush so hard, it nearly hurt.

He couldn't kiss her, but he could pick up her hand, and he did. He set it on his thigh, stroked his thumb over her knuckles and down to her wrist, then did it again, and she turned toward him.

He was already half-drunk on the smell of her. Three beers didn't make an impression, but Zora in the dark—she did him in. She tucked one high-heeled foot under her seat and stretched out the other leg so her foot was nearly brushing his, and he *didn't* put his hand on her thigh, under her dress.

He said, "I like your scent."

"It's Black Opium. Black coffee, white orchids, and vanilla." She leaned a tiny bit closer and mouthed something. It may have been, *You bought it,* but he was distracted. Mainly, he was looking at her mouth.

He realized, finally, that he should say something. "Sounds like something you'd do in flowers." There, that was neutral.

"Mm. You could. Vanilla's a kind of orchid, actually. That would be gorgeous, if you could get hold of it. White berries, though, not coffee. Good for a wedding bouquet."

"A bit like pearls." He reached a hand behind her, edged his fingers under the hem of her cropped sweater, and touched the necklace that lay against her spine. When he drew his hand down, he felt her shift under his touch.

"Yeh," she said, on a breath. "You said that about pearls. That they could look like your grandmother, or not."

His thumb was rubbing up and down her spine, his knuckles brushing against her skin. Not enough that the driver would be able to tell, but enough that Zora would. "In your case," he said, "not."

After that, she didn't say anything, and he couldn't think of what to say, either. Why had he picked a place all the way in Herne Bay? Twenty-five minutes was about twenty-four too long. And at the end of it, he'd have to sit in a restaurant with her for at least an hour. Probably two.

Never mind. It was what he'd told Isaiah: A chance for

Zora to dress up and be pretty, to remind herself that she was desirable, and that she was beautiful. A chance, too, to let that bombshell drop. He hadn't heard any rumblings after their earlier outing, but the restaurant had seated them discreetly, which he'd been grateful for at the time. At Jervois Steak House, though, on Friday night before a Blues game? Bound to be somebody there from the rugby world. Somebody who'd talk, he hoped.

The journey ended at last, as journeys always did, and he got to hold the door, take Zora's hand, and watch her slide out of the car. Black suede heel, slim ankle, pretty calf made even more shapely by the height of that heel, and a knee that you could hold while you kissed your way higher. Her dress rode up a little, and she laughed in a flustered way, tugged it down, and let him help balance her once she stood. He smelled that flowers-and-vanilla scent again, looked down at the most gorgeous cloud of bedhead you could ever hope to see, told the driver, "Thanks," and held the restaurant door. Her shoulder brushed against his chest as she walked past, and she turned, a step inside, and gave him a look over her shoulder.

Mussed hair, pink lips, secret smile, black heels.

It was going to be a long night.

# revelation

All they'd done was ride in the car. She'd barely even talked to him, he'd barely even touched her, and even so, her new black lace thong was already not up to its work. She considered telling him so. Delicately. Once she'd had a glass of wine, maybe. She'd lean across the table and whisper it, and watch him try to keep his composure.

He was a black-lace man all the way. Nothing subtle about Rhys. He was pure fire.

He still hadn't said anything, and he still hadn't smiled, either. He stopped at the host stand, his hand barely touching the small of her back, practically burning through the fabric, and said, "Evening. It's Fletcher."

"Evening," the young fella said. "We have a table for you upstairs. More private."

Zora thought, *I should want to be down here. Get it over with.* Pity that all she wanted was some more slow, sweet flirtation at a dimly lit corner table, while she wondered what was coming next and exactly how good it might be. And to touch his trouser leg with her toe, maybe. Almost accidentally.

She hadn't even kissed him since Sunday night, and it was Friday. They'd made dinner together all week at her place, and then Rhys and Casey had headed home. Better, they'd thought, not to spring too much physical intimacy on the kids. She hadn't imagined how hard that would be. A brush of hands, a long look, the touch of his hand on her waist as he stepped around her in the tiny kitchen, and that was all.

If he was feeling anything close to what she was, they wouldn't even make it out of his foyer, except that they would. He'd have planned for it. There were benefits, she thought hazily, following the server up the stairs and knowing that Rhys was watching her hips sway in high heels and enjoying the view, of being with a prepared man.

Unfortunately, when she got to the top of the central staircase around which the tables were placed for maximum viewing potential, she didn't just see exposed brickwork, low lighting, and one unoccupied table set with white linen. She also saw her parents.

♡♡♡

The host led them to a spot along the wall and held the chair facing the windows for Zora, and she thought, for one wild minute, *Maybe they won't see us.* Despite the fact that her mother was diagonally across from her, at a table for four. Zora didn't know who the other couple was. She wasn't looking.

Rhys said, "What?"

"Nothing. Well, something. My parents are here. They live about ten minutes' walk away. It's their local."

"Oh." He appeared to consider that while he put his serviette in his lap, then returned his hand to the table, and she looked at the diagonal scar on his forehead, the thickness of his broken nose, the black scruff on his jaw, and the dimple in his chin, and wondered how absolutely masculine it was possible for a man to be. He made the blood leave her head.

"You're worrying," he said, and took her hand across the table. His hand was big, hard, and scarred, too, and she had a discombobulating double thought. First, that just the sight of her hand in his was making her go a little more liquid inside, and second, that when she'd thought tonight could be a showdown, she hadn't planned for it to be this much of one. "Maybe you could remember that whatever happens, I'm here with you for it."

"I hope so, because my dad's coming over."

Rhys turned, and there was nothing in his expression as he rose but calm. He put out a hand. "Dr. Allen."

"Oh, please," her dad said, shaking it, "call me Craig. We've known each other too long for anything else. What's it been, ten years since we met you at Zora and Dylan's engagement dinner? This is a surprise. Come join us."

"No room," Zora said. "And you've already started on your dinner, surely. Always awkward." She laughed, wishing it sounded less tentative. More adult, you could say. *You're a grown woman with her own house, her own business, and her own child,* she reminded herself. *You're a widow, and your parents have nothing to say about anybody you date. Anybody you date.* This was the very good thing, she realized, about them not paying for her roof, her mortgage, or anything else. They didn't get a say.

"Oh," her dad said, "I'm sure the waiter will switch you out with the couple next to us. They've only just arrived, and your table's better than theirs." He raised a hand for the server, then beckoned him over in a way Rhys would never have done in a hundred years. All Blacks were required to be unassuming blokes, even if they actually weren't. Part of the job. Surgeons, not so much.

Rhys said, "Pleasure," but when they eventually got over to the other table, he asked Zora, "Can I help you off with your sweater?" Which is how she ended up surrendering it to him, then turning to sit and feeling the cool touch of the pearls on her back like they were tattooed there.

"Mum," she said, calling on every bit of poise she possessed, which had never been all that much, "you remember Rhys Fletcher. My mum, Tania. And this is Nils Larsen and his wife, Candy, Rhys. Dr. Larsen does neurosurgery. Rhys is coaching at the Blues now." She'd had a moment of blankness when she hadn't remembered their names. Good thing they'd come to her, or she'd be even more off-balance right now.

Candy pressed her cheek to Zora's in an air kiss, then sat back and said, her blue eyes widening, "Oh, my goodness. I just got the oddest feeling, a goose walking over my grave. I had the idea in my head that your husband had passed away. A rugby player was right, surely, but where did I get the rest of it? It must have been somebody else's husband. And I'm sorry. I shouldn't have said that. A goose walking over *your* grave, now."

"No," Zora said, feeling like her smile was pasted on, "you were right. My husband was Dylan Fletcher, and he did pass away a couple years ago. This is his brother, Rhys."

"Oh." Zora would call that "stunned silence."

The server came back, and Rhys asked Zora, not a flicker of his expression suggesting embarrassment, "Would you like a drink? They do pretty good cocktails." He looked around. "Anybody else? Cognac?"

"Sounds like you're familiar," her dad said.

"I've heard," Rhys said evenly. "Been here for the steak before, but I'm not much of a drinker, at least not before the game."

"A Mai Tai, please," Zora said, absolutely recklessly. She was wearing a black dress, as well as the highest, thinnest heels she'd ever owned. She wanted the whole fantasy, and never mind that she'd be having it in front of her parents. "I'll pretend we're on a tropical holiday. Rhys and I both have our busiest days tomorrow, but we're indulging tonight. How have you been, Candy? Are you still . . ." She struggled to remember anything about the other woman. "Doing your volunteer work?" she hazarded.

"With St. John," Candy said, and Zora passed a mental hand over her forehead in relief. "What a gorgeous necklace. I've never seen it worn that way. How unusual. It's almost . . . savage, isn't it?"

All right. The not-your-dead-husband had been one thing. Zora was remembering something about Candy after all. That she was Nils's second wife, for one, and that she'd been his nurse. "Yes," she said. "That's what's so appealing about it." Candy was between her and her mother, so she couldn't actually see her mum go rigid. She could imagine it, though.

"They look absolutely real," Candy said. "So much luster. And so does the clasp, although diamonds are easier that way. Where did you get them, can I ask?"

Zora's mother said, "I was thinking I didn't want a sweet, but I'm changing my mind. Passionfruit sorbet. Doesn't that sound good? Or Earl Grey crème caramel, maybe, though it's naughty."

Zora was thinking, *Not as naughty as chocolate torte. What is it with all the unsatisfying desserts?* And also, *Could Candy possibly have thought of anything more insulting to say?* Then Rhys said, "She got them from me. The pearls, that is. I brought them home for her from Tokyo last week."

Candy said, "Oh. Beautiful."

"M something," Zora said. "The jeweler."

"Mikimoto, possibly?" her mother asked.

"That was the one," Rhys said. "Busy place. In the Ginza." The waiter arrived with drinks, and Zora took a sip, and then another one. The tartness of lime and the sweet sting of rum, with the orange lingering behind. That was nice. In alcohol, fruit suited her fine.

Rhys reached across and took the glass from her, tried a sip of his own, and said, "That's good. I could make you share." A not-quite smile, and Zora thought, *Don't do that,* even as she thought, *Oh, yeh, boy. Do that.* It was turning out to be such a confusing dinner, and they hadn't even started yet.

Her mother may have been down, but she wasn't out. "The pearls are lovely," she said, and set her serviette on the table. "I'll be right back. Come with me, darling. Keep me company."

"Better to order first, probably." That was Rhys. Who else? He said it without emphasis, but with absolute assurance. She wasn't sure how he did that, but it was so bloody sexy.

Her mother sat down. "You're right, of course. What are you going to have, Zora? I did the fish. A grilled lemon sole that was so light, it was barely there. Lovely."

Rhys said, "Surely, the point of going to a steakhouse is to eat some good steak." He looked across the top of his menu and told Zora, "If that's what you want."

"I do," she said. "I'd like an eye fillet, in fact, or something else boneless and tender and easy. And Yorkshire pudding, and maybe some kind of veg."

"Salad?" he asked.

"No, thanks. I don't want a salad. Call that a declaration." She could practically hear her mother moan.

"Oysters to start?" Rhys asked. "I know you love oysters. And whitebait fritters as well, maybe. My own favorite. We can share some more. What kind of wine would you like?"

Her mother would be pressing her fingertips to her forehead now, doing a desperate calorie count in her head. *Whitebait fritter: four hundred fifty calories. Eye fillet: four hundred. Mai Tai: inconceivable.*

"I'd like," Zora said, "to let you choose. I love not deciding. That's either the ultimate luxury, or the ultimate danger, don't you think, Mum? And there are too many choices of steak on there. Japan. Australia. New Zealand. Mind-boggling. Could you order that for me as well, Rhys? I'm sure you know them all."

"Yeh," he said. "I could."

"You can share my rum," she said, and he smiled a little more and said, "I'll take that invitation."

"While the girls are gone," Nils Larsen said, "you could tell me what you're planning, Rhys, there at the Blues, and how you expect to go about winning tomorrow. You'll have a battle on your hands, won't you, against the Crusaders?"

"We're planning to play better than they do," Rhys said. "That's about the size of it."

"Oh, come on. You can share more than that," Nils said with a sort of pale Norwegian version of joviality, like pickled herring and crispbread that somebody had warmed in the microwave. "Kicking off the turnover, now—I'm guessing you've addressed that."

"Interesting point," Rhys said. "I have a question of my own about concussion, since we're all here, and you're the expert. I'd like to know what you think of our protocols. I'm interested, for obvious reasons, but I don't know the details. As I'm not a neurosurgeon."

"Come on, then, darling," her mother said, and stood up again. Candy rose, too, and Zora's mum said, "You don't mind if Zora and I have a mother-daughter chat, do you?"

Candy looked like a kitten who'd found the cream bowl empty, and Zora's mum headed toward the toilets with every line of her determinedly slim back offering up an absolutely prison-matron-level promise of delights to come.

Zora followed her. Nothing else to do.

♡♡♡

It didn't take long. Her mum didn't even go into the stalls. She reached for Zora's necklace, turned it around, and said, "I've been itching to do that since you took off your cardigan. I know it may be in a magazine somewhere, but wearing it like that makes you look like you're expecting cash on the bureau later."

Zora turned the necklace around to the back again, then took her lipstick out of her bag, leaned forward, and applied a little more pink to her mouth while her mother's hand rose, then fell, like she couldn't believe this atrocity could be happening. "Rhys asked me to wear it this way," she told her mother, "and since he bought it . . ."

Her mum *did* have her fingertips on her forehead. It was fascinating to be so right. She'd have to tell Hayden.

"The dress is almost too much on its own," her mother said. "A pale pink or cream would've been a better choice than black, with those spaghetti straps and that neckline. A little discretion, please, darling."

"Rhys bought that, too," Zora said. "And my shoes. He liked the black ones best. So you see . . ."

"You *are* sleeping with him," her mother said.

"I imagine it's pretty obvious. And because it's what you're wondering—yeh, that's because he's exactly as good as he looks. His rugby nickname's 'Drago,' did you know that? Means 'Dragon.' Like 'Rhys' does. Rhys ap Gruffydd, most powerful prince of Wales ever. That wasn't always a chinless bloke in a suit. Once, it was a warrior."

She'd looked it up. She didn't know how a man's name could excite you, except that it did.

Her mother had her mouth open to say something. Zora couldn't wait to hear what. A toilet flushed behind them, and her mother's mouth snapped shut. After a minute, a blonde came out of the stall, washed her hands, and cast a quick look at Zora, then another at the necklace, and Zora knew that sometime after tonight, she'd be news. She told her mother, not bothering to wait for the woman to leave, "I'm pretty far gone, Mum, and so is he, so you may want to think about what you say next."

Her mother said exactly nothing until the blonde had left, and then said, "You don't let a man buy you clothes. It's so inappropriate, I have no words. Nobody needs new clothes that badly."

Zora had turned her back against the benchtop. Now, her hands clutched the black-and-gold quartz for stability. "As it happens, I don't need to resort to prostitution. Dylan had money hidden away. Quite a lot of it. I found it last week."

"What? You mean, he had an account you didn't know about? That's wonderful news." Some of her mother's tension relaxed. "So why are you letting Rhys buy your clothes?"

"No," Zora said. "I mean he had an account he *hid* from me. An account he used to spend money he didn't have to tell me about."

"And your answer is to go out and find somebody with a secret child. One with even less polish than Dylan. One who wants you to wear his jewelry like you're advertising. We won't even *discuss* the fact that he's Dylan's brother, and everyone's going to wonder when that started."

"Yes," Zora said. "That's my answer. Do you know why?

Because I'm so mad for him, I can barely see straight. And maybe because . . . because being allowed to be everything I am again feels like coming out of a cocoon. It doesn't matter what happened before, or why. I've been in there long enough, I'm out here now, and I want to *fly*. And because of something Rhys said to me. 'Judge me for the man I am, not the man I used to be.' I know the man he is. I *want* the man he is, because he's pretty bloody wonderful."

Her mother's nostrils were flaring in what Hayden called her "wild brumby" look. That look could stop you in your tracks. "When he subjects you to this kind of scrutiny. That's your idea of 'wonderful.'" Her voice hadn't even risen. That was another scary thing about her. "When he's willing to have sex with his brother's wife, and flaunt it like this to her parents, not to mention exposing her to the world. What kind of loyalty is that? What kind of care does it show for you and your reputation, or for his own wife, for that matter? How about Isaiah? How's he going to feel when the boys at school find out? Does Rhys care about that? Consider this. If you do get him, in the end, what exactly will you have?"

For once, Zora wasn't waiting for that hoof to strike. Her perfume was dark, rich, and sensual, and that was how she felt. Like a woman who knew what she wanted, and was taking it. "His brother's *widow*. And Isaiah's oblivious to what the other kids think, if they care at all, which they won't—or they will, but not in the way you think. Do you know who Rhys *is?* He earned seventy-two test caps as a loose forward. I know you don't know what that means, or the kind of discipline and commitment it takes, but I do, and so do heaps of other people. He's the coach of the Blues. He won a Grand Final when he played rugby league, and a World Cup with the All Blacks. He's a legend, I'm pretty sure he's mine, and that gives me a thrill like you wouldn't believe. And as for Isaiah? He cares about his family, his friends, and the ideas in his head, and he's got all of those. I told you, you don't need to worry about Isaiah."

"He's odd, and you know it. He doesn't need to feel odder."

Zora had a wild brumby of her own inside, maybe, because here it was in all its fury. "I know who he is. He's Isaiah. He's brilliant, he's the hardest worker, and he's so sweet to Casey, it melts your heart. He has all sorts of people in his life who love him as he is, and he loves us back. And that includes Rhys. I know who Rhys is, too, and he's everything I want. I wish I could tell you all the ways that's true. I also know who I am. I'm reckless. I could even be wild. That should be obvious by now. I know you care about respectability, and I know why. It's because Nana wasn't respectable. I loved her anyway, and I think I've got her in me. I think I always have had."

Her grandmother, whose hair had been too improbably dark, who'd smoked too much and laughed too loud and probably drunk too much, who'd hugged hard and shared secrets and had a special play room under the stairs. Who'd been a single mum with no husband and too many boyfriends in her past, at a time when that mattered. Who'd made her daughter cringe.

"You could love her." Her mother's voice was tight, bouncing off the hard surfaces of benchtop and mirror. "You didn't have to grow up with her. I protected you from that."

Zora had been feeling exactly as wild and reckless as she'd said. Mai Tai, Rhys, necklace, dress, and all. Now, her heart did some kind of twist instead. The pit of emotion inside her that had been locked down for so long was opening up, and it was letting her see her mum's rigidity for what it was. The fear of a girl who'd grown up feeling laughed at, feeling alone and trapped and embarrassed, and was so terrified to end up back there again that she'd do anything to maintain the façade, even pretend not to know what her husband was doing on those long golf dates and late nights at the hospital.

Zora and Hayden had grown up with too many lies and too much unhappiness beneath the smooth surface, and she didn't want that for Isaiah. She didn't want it for *her*. And she'd been so afraid, when she'd realized the truth about Dylan, that she was falling into the exact same trap.

Except that she wasn't the one who was like her mother. Dylan was. Exactly as scared that somehow, everyone would know who he really was, because if they saw, he knew he wouldn't measure up. That he *couldn't* measure up, ever.

The balance shifted like the ions in the air had changed their polarity, and she felt a rush of compassion for her mum so strong, it rocked her in her heels. She said, her voice not one bit steady, "I know you protected me, Mum. I know you think that unless I follow the rules, I'll end up humiliated and ashamed. But don't you see how humiliated and ashamed I've been already? I got married, I was a good wife and a good mother, and it happened anyway. I can't go down that road anymore. It seems like the only safe option to you, but I can't do it. I have to go . . . off the road instead. I have to drive down the beach, knowing I may get stuck out there, and the tide may come in and sweep me away. Maybe Hayden and I both have too much of Nana in us to be careful, or maybe you just can't change who you are."

Her mother stood rigid, breathing shallowly, like if she moved, she'd crack into pieces. "I just want you to be happy," she finally said. "With a career and a family you can be proud of, not another thing you have to hide. There's a photo out there of Rhys having sex with somebody else's wife in the *toilets,* and it's going to come out over and over again for the rest of his life, because that's exactly how people are."

In other words, Zora should have a career her *mum* could be proud of, not a struggling florist's business, and she should have a husband who spent his weekends sailing and his weekdays in an office, not a Maori rugby player who'd never set foot inside a university and had been abandoned by his drug-addicted mother. Let alone that rugby player's notorious hard-man brother.

Zora still wanted to slap her, but another part of her wanted to hug her. Her mum, though, like Isaiah, didn't hug easily, so instead, she searched for the right words, gave up, and said, "I know you love me. That's why I'm going to explain it to you. I can only be happy with the wind in my hair. I can't help it. It's how I'm made. And as for Rhys and me? Maybe we'll be the scandal of the decade. Maybe we'll burn up and burn out, and we'll both go down in flames. Another vice. Another regret. But I can't think about that now. I've got no choice. He's everything I want, I admire him more than any man I've ever known, I need him like a drug, and I . . . I love him. I do. I love him, and I'm not ashamed. I've wanted him for ten years, he's wanted me just as long, and neither of us has ever done anything about it. We've done what's right. We've waited. Rhys's marriage is over, though, and Dylan is dead. We can't wait any longer."

Her mum was stepping forward, then turning, a jerky movement, and checking her makeup in the mirror. Patting her hair. Breathing hard.

You couldn't change who you were. Your fears went too deep for that, and so did your desires. Zora picked up her purse, and she didn't check her own hair, or the state of her cheeks. She probably looked wild. That was fine. That was brilliant, because that was how she felt. She told her mother, "'The heart wants what it wants, or else it does not care.' That's in a poem. My heart doesn't care what's easy, and it doesn't care what people will think. It wants what it wants, and that's all."

# opportunity cost

Rhys wanted to turn around and watch Zora walk away. And once she did, he wanted her back. Instead, he took another sip of her Mai Tai. It was like her, spicy and sweet, with a kick you didn't expect. After that, he got himself centered and waited for what would come next.

He'd done a couple hundred press conferences in his career. No difference. You told the truth with composure and respect, you said as little as possible, and you kept the upper hand. Subtly, if possible. Genial was always good, too, if you could manage it.

He gave their food orders to the server when he turned up, and asked, "Best New Zealand red you've got to pair with that?"

"You'll want an Australian shiraz instead," Craig said, "to stand up to the marbling in a Scotch fillet. That would be your best choice, based on what I've found with my own cellar. I'm guessing you're more of a beer man."

Rhys considered asking if Craig was actually planning a dick-measuring contest, but he didn't, partly because he was required to be polite in public and partly because Craig was Zora's dad. Instead, he said, turning his Maori accent up to 10, "I reckon there'll be a New Zealand wine that'll do the business."

"Supporting the homeland's always good," the server, a thirtyish bloke with spiky black hair, said. "And a pinot noir with some body will be beautiful with the lady's eye fillet. I'd suggest the Te Kairanga John Martin Martinborough Pinot Noir 2015. I don't think you'll be disappointed with your own pairing, either. There's enough fullness and richness there for it. And if the lady likes chocolate, the chocolate fondant with bourbon sauce would be a perfect match for that final glass."

"I think it's safe to say," Rhys said, "that the lady likes chocolate. Sounds good. Bring us a bottle of that." He handed over the menus. "Thanks."

"Can I just say," the waiter said, "that it's an honor."

"Cheers, mate," Rhys said.

The fella took the others' dessert orders, then headed off, and Rhys took another sip of Zora's Mai Tai and bided his time.

"We so rarely get that, in our line of work," Nils said. "Pity."

"Oh, I dunno," Rhys said. "It has its downside."

"Like clueless members of the public giving you helpful advice, possibly," Nils said, with a glint of humor.

Rhys had to smile. "It happens."

"I wish I thought *I* could have chocolate fondant," Candy said with a sigh. "I'm afraid it's a minute on the lips, a lifetime on the hips."

"And I appreciate your restraint," her husband said, and Rhys thought about Zora saying, "I am drowning in food lust." He also thought about her gorgeous arse in a black thong, the perfect roundness of her thighs and breasts, and what Nils was missing.

Chocolate fondant, definitely. They could share it. Nothing like something rich enough to make Zora moan, two spoons, and watching the way her eyes glazed over when she was feeling too much pleasure. Once they got rid of the doctors.

He said, "About those concussion protocols." Safer subject.

"What are you doing now?" Nils asked. "Three-week minimum suspension from contact?"

"Yeh."

"The danger, as I'm sure you know," Nils said, "is repeated

events, particularly when the brain hasn't recovered, and the answer is, we just don't know enough yet. You've got what we call the neurometabolic cascade with each event, which is fairly short-lived, a few days, but there are other physiological effects as well. I can send you some links to studies I've found particularly credible, if you're interested. The methodology can sometimes be suspect."

"I *am* interested," Rhys said. "Cheers." *Points for not being condescending,* he thought.

"They'll be fairly technical," Craig said. "Your team doctor would probably be the best person to interpret them. Of course, he's probably already read them."

"Could be good to have an idea what the experts are talking about," Rhys said. "That way, when the discussion happens, I'll have a base to start from. Assuming I can read the tricky words."

"That's true," Candy said, perfectly unexpectedly. "I was a nurse before I married Nils. Doctors can get frustrated when patients try to educate themselves, but I've always thought it was a good idea. How can you make the right choices if you don't understand your condition?"

"Licensed by internet," Craig said. "Spare me. Sorry, Candy, but you know I don't agree."

"How many times would you say you've been concussed yourself?" Nils asked Rhys, ignoring Craig's comment and the surprising flash from Candy's round blue eyes. Dr. Nils might be looking at an explosion later on, at home. But then, explosions could be exciting.

"I couldn't even tell you," Rhys said. "We weren't as careful then."

"Do you feel you've experienced behavioral changes?" Nils asked. "Any lessening of impulse control? Or cognitive changes, over time?"

"No," Rhys said. "Pretty much the same fella I've always been. More impulse control these days, actually, I'd say." His previous lack of impulse control wasn't news, after all.

"Risk isn't certainty, of course," Nils said. "It's only risk."

"All the same," Craig said, "I'd discourage my own kids from a career in professional rugby. Not worth the risk, I'd say, in all sorts of ways, not to mention the opportunity cost. What you give up doing instead when you make that choice, assuming you *have* a choice." *Assuming you aren't a farm kid from the back of beyond,* he didn't say, *or, worse, a poor Maori kid with no education, no brains, and no skills beyond running barefoot, catching a ball, and throwing people to the ground.*

You didn't run into that attitude often, not in New Zealand. Just sometimes.

Rhys said, "Could be fortunate, then, that so few people *are* forced to make the choice."

Nils's pale-blue eyes lit up with interest, and possibly surprise, and Craig asked, "How's that?"

Rhys thought, *You may be good at messing about with people's knees, mate, but you don't win any prizes for emotional intelligence. I know what "opportunity cost" means, too.* He asked, "How many doctors in New Zealand? Heaps, is it?"

"Fifteen thousand?" Craig said. "Somewhere around there. Why?"

Rhys passed a hand through his hair, doing his best to look like he was trying to puzzle it out. "What do you need to get started with it? A University diploma?"

"Of course," Craig said, sounding stiff. "Ten years of training in all. More like fourteen, for a surgeon."

"That's work," Rhys agreed. "Reward, too, though, I reckon. What's the percentage of Uni diplomas? In adults, that is?"

"About twenty percent," Nils said, starting to look interested.

"And three million adults in the country, or thereabouts? So you'd have six hundred thousand of them with some kind of diploma?"

"I'm guessing your own diploma's in maths," Nils said, with some more amusement. "Or statistics, maybe."

"I don't have one. I was one of those fellas who started getting professional concussions at eighteen. I can compute twenty percent, though. Maybe you can help me with the percentage of diploma holders who are doctors. What did we say? Fifteen thousand out of six hundred thousand?"

"Nothing wrong with your memory," Nils said.

"I'm feeling lost," Candy said, which at least gave her points for honesty.

Rhys told her, "If ten percent of diploma holders were doctors, that would be sixty thousand. It's fifteen thousand, though, so it's about two-point-five percent. Fair enough?"

"That would be about right." Craig sounded more than stiff now. "I'm sure there's a point to this."

"Nah," Rhys said. "I'm just running a couple of drills, making sure my cognitive function's still hitting minimum standard."

"Interesting," Nils said. "Let's have the second half of it, then. You can't judge the match by the first forty minutes. Two-point-five percent of diploma holders are doctors, we've got that established. Give me the statistics on the percentage of rugby players who become professionals."

"Maybe five hundred of them at any one time," Rhys said. "Out of a hundred fifty thousand registered players. You could say it's fortunate that only about a third of a percent of the people who give rugby a go will end up beating out the competition and facing that major concussion risk. Of course, there's still the opportunity cost, that missed Uni and all, but every profession's got its downside, eh."

Nils laughed out loud, sat back, and gave him a slow clap. "He's got you there," he told Craig. "You got *me* there, for a minute," he told Rhys. "Well done."

Which was when the server came back with the wine and the others' desserts, and also when Rhys felt a disturbance in the force, and looked around to see Zora charging back across the room.

Nils wasn't the only one who was going to be dealing with an explosion tonight. Also, Rhys may have failed to score in the "suck up to the girl's dad" department. He'd done all right on the composure, but not so much on the respect, probably.

But then, he was a competitive bloke. He may have had a few scores to settle for Dylan, too.

# always

Zora got back to the table and slid in opposite Rhys. Her dress rode up more than a few centimeters, and she wished she were alone with him so he could have watched it happen. She took a sip of her Mai Tai, and then another, and felt the rum burning its way down her throat, followed by the cooling touch of lime.

She needed cooling off, and Rhys . . . maybe didn't. The fire inside him was turned up to the max, he'd damped it ruthlessly down, and nobody did "controlled intensity" like Rhys.

Her own fire, unfortunately, wasn't controlled at all. Her mum's wasn't, either, and her dad, she realized, was looking seriously rattled, or seriously narky.

You could call that "unexpected." You could call it "unprecedented," in fact. Candy looked expectant, and Nils looked coolly amused. What had been going on here?

Rhys plucked her drink from her hand, took a sip, then said, "What the hell," and finished it off, and she laughed. He smiled at her in that slow, sweet way that melted her bones, like there were only the two of them here, and asked, "Good chat? You look a little flustered, baby. But so good." Which made everybody at the table sit up a little straighter.

The waiter came over with the wine and went through his presentation, which fortunately gave her Zora a chance to gather her wits. "Oysters and sweets in two seconds," the server said. "Not together, of course."

Thank goodness. They were moving this thing on.

"Can I offer anybody else a glass?" Rhys asked, holding the wine bottle aloft.

"I'd love to try some," Candy said. "But you won't want us drinking it up."

There was amusement lurking in Rhys's hazel eyes now. "I reckon I can run to another bottle, if I need to." The waiter came over with a tray and distributed tiny dishes, and Rhys asked, "Could you bring us four more wine glasses, please?"

Zora wanted to say, *What are you* doing? *They'll be here all night, and all I want is for them to leave.* Rhys looked back at her, and something about that look said, *Anticipation is a beautiful thing. I'd like to make you feel it.* And despite everything, despite her parents, despite her *mum,* she felt the shiver start low and move all the way up her body, and she thought he saw it.

The glasses came, Rhys poured wine for Nils and Candy, Zora's parents both refused it, and Zora's mum took a tiny spoonful of her already-minuscule serving of sorbet as if it contained more calories than a celery stick and asked, "Who's minding the kids while you're out?"

"I got a babysitter," Zora said. This was the oddest dinner she'd ever attended. She tipped up an oyster shell, swallowed down the salty freshness, sighed, touched her mouth with her serviette, and told Rhys, "Delicious."

He wanted her to anticipate? Maybe she wanted him to as well. He tipped his head back, drank down his own oyster, and said, "Nothing like the taste of the sea," while Zora's dad's face got, if possible, even tighter.

"I didn't realize you had more than one child," Candy told Zora. "I thought there was only one, somehow. They must be a comfort to you."

"One of them is mine," Rhys said, not a bit like somebody who was dropping a fifteen-kiloton bomb into the middle of the table. "My daughter, Casey Moana. I brought her back from Chicago recently, after her mum died."

"Oh," Candy said faintly. "That sounds like a . . . change."

"It was," Rhys said, "but a good one. I thought a move to

Auckland, my first real house, my first Super Rugby team, and my divorce were pushing the limits. I've ended up with a little girl to come home to, and some rabbits as well. And then I fell in love with my sister-in-law. Life can surprise you, eh."

Bomb detonated.

While everybody was still frozen in the fallout, Rhys pulled out his phone, clicked around, and handed it across the table to Candy. "That's my little girl, Casey, along with Zora's son, Isaiah, with the bunnies in my back garden."

"Oh," Candy said, not looking witchy at all. Looking like her heart was melted all the way into a puddle. By Rhys, by Casey, or by both, who knew. "She's adorable. What a look she has of you. Isaiah, too. They could be brother and sister. And the tiny bunnies with their ears hanging down. How old is she?"

"Six," Rhys said. "Year Two at school. She's had some catching up to do, as they do their schooling differently in the States, but she's getting on by leaps and bounds. Learning to play rugby, too. She's good, and so is Isaiah, and they're getting better."

"She is," Zora said. "To all of it."

"She's had to start again all over the shop," Rhys told Candy, "losing her mum and meeting me for the first time, not to mention a new country, a new school, and a new auntie and cousin. Fortunately, she does have that auntie and cousin, she's got courage to burn, and possibly a will of iron, too. I wouldn't have said that rabbits were on my list before, and now, somehow, I have four."

"Got you wrapped around her finger, is what it is," Zora teased.

"Probably so," Rhys said, his smile making it almost all the way out. "I have my own weaknesses, maybe. Seems I've just laid them on the table."

Candy showed the photo to Zora's mum, and she started to say something, stopped, started again, and stopped again, then handed the phone back to Candy. "Beautiful little girl," she finally said, then set her serviette on the table and asked

Zora's dad, "Are you nearly ready to go?"

Nils and Candy exchanged a glance, and Nils said, "You're right. We should leave Rhys and Zora to their evening," and finished off his glass of wine. "Excellent choice," he told Rhys. "Very nice."

Credit cards, then, and finally, good-byes. Nils shook Rhys's hand and said, "It's been illuminating. Good luck tomorrow."

"Cheers," Rhys said.

He bent and kissed Candy's cheek, and she put her hand to it once he'd stepped back, laughed in a flustered way, and said, "Lovely to meet you." After that, she kissed Zora and whispered in her ear, "Grab him," then tucked her arm through Zora's mum's and said, "What a lovely dinner. I'm so glad you asked us."

At least one of them was enthusiastic.

$$\heartsuit\heartsuit\heartsuit$$

Rhys waited until the waiter had moved their table back over, until Zora had tucked her skirt under herself and sat down again, crossing her legs, one hand going to her hair, as if she could tame it. As if that were possible. Her cheeks were still wonderfully flushed, and she wasn't quite looking at him. Instead, she was taking a bite of whitebait fritter, as if that were easier than the rest of it. Which was true.

"I love these," she said with a sigh. "My mum's horrified."

"By whitebait?"

She smiled, finally, reluctantly, and lost a bit of her tension. "By everything. My slutty dress. My undisciplined body. My unrestrained dining choices. Your pearls, and the way I'm wearing them, like I'm advertising to the entire world exactly how much I want you."

He was still reacting to that when she said, "And most of all . . . by you. The way you look tonight, so hard and so dark. The way you look at me. That you and I are out here for everyone to see. And you know what? I don't care. Told her so, too."

"Well," he said, his tongue feeling too big for his mouth, "that's good."

She was starting to smile now. Getting her confidence back, maybe. The sway in her step, the fierce in her curvy body. "You know what I call unfair, though?" she asked him, and he thought, *No, but I know what I do.* She said, "How easily men get off the hook. All you had to do was show Candy that photo of Casey and the bunnies, be that sweet about her, and she was melting. She didn't care about anything she'd heard about you, or that you're sleeping with your brother's widow. She cared about those muscles of yours, how you look in all that black, the dimple in your chin and the look in your eyes, and how you talked about your little girl."

He said, "I know what *I* call unfair. Having to watch you eat oysters in front of your parents. Having to waste all this time when I was planning to make you feel beautiful, and to show off how much I want *you*. Have I mentioned that you knock me out?" He had hold of her hand, somehow, and was running his thumb over her knuckles. "I don't give a damn what your mum thinks of your food choices. I know that I love the way you look in that dress, the way you wore my pearls down your back, and the way you bought the shoes I wanted. I love how soft and mussed your hair is right now, I love your gorgeous mouth, and I love your sweet body and every single thing it can do. And I want to take off your clothes right now."

She shuddered, because she couldn't do anything else. Long, slow, and rolling all the way through her, like a wave tumbling her, helpless, in the sea. His voice would never be smooth, and the edge of roughness only added to the thrill. He wasn't smiling anymore, and now, the fires weren't banked. He said, "Yeh. That's it. That's what I want. Tell me what you're wearing under that. Whisper it in my ear. Get me through this dinner."

She'd never been a woman who made a man's breath

catch, but she was that woman tonight. She said, "I've been wanting to tell you that all night. It's all I want. But first, I need to tell you something else. Something I told my mum."

"Did I mention," he said, "that I'm feeling a bit tired of your parents?"

She had to laugh, and to drink some more wine, which made her realize exactly how good it was, bursting with dark fruit and exotic spices, with veins of chocolate, tobacco, and smoke running through all of it. She took another bite of fritter, too, savoring its richness and the lemony sauce, and Rhys said, "And now I'd say you're stalling. If you need to tell me—tell me. Just don't tell me that thing again about how it's once, and then we're done. It's not once. It's never going to be once."

She had a hand on her heart, because it was racing. She waited to be able to breathe again, but it wasn't getting better, so she just said it. "Right. Here I go, then, because I need to say it. I hated that I couldn't tell my parents the truth about you. That I couldn't explain that you didn't cheat on Victoria, and exactly why and how you lied, and who you were protecting when you did it. I wanted to tell my mum that you took Casey when you didn't have to, and I wanted to tell her all about the man you are underneath that scary surface. And it hit me so hard to realize. It knocked me flat. I keep thinking about how you make my knees weak, how much I want to feel you kiss me, but it's so much more than that. It's how much I admire the man you are. How far you've brought yourself, how hard you've worked, and then how much harder, every time you think you've fallen short. How hard you are on yourself, and what that says about you. And maybe I realized how much trouble I'm in, too. The way I nearly stumble when I'm around you, because my feet stop working and I lose my train of thought. The way I feel when you look at me in the kitchen, when all I want is for you to put your hand on my waist and lean over and kiss me, and dance me around the room, just because you want to hold me. The way I need you, like it's an addiction. The way I . . . love you.

That's the main thing I realized, and it's the scariest thing of all."

The words fell out, and they took her breath with them. Across from her, Rhys was frozen, his eyes locked on her. She said, "Maybe this is an . . ." Her voice trembled, and she could no more help it than she could help going on. "An affair, and I don't know how to do an affair. If it's that, if it's a . . . a hookup, or—a series of hookups, whatever you call that, because I don't even know—I don't have any ammunition for that. I don't have any armor. So if it's that? Could you . . . could you tell me, so I can try to stop? Because right now, I'm so far gone, it scares me."

"Zora. Stop." He'd put his hand over her mouth, straight across the table. The couple next to them was looking over. Zora could see it, and she couldn't care. Rhys took his hand away, brushed the back of it over her cheek, and said, that edge of roughness still there in his voice, but so much warmth in his eyes, "Don't you remember, baby, that I already said it? I've already jumped in. I'm right here, ready to catch you, and I'm one hell of a swimmer. I'm not going to let you go."

"I . . ." Her hand was shaking on her fork. Too many emotions tonight, and no defenses left. Her heart was laid bare, and her blood felt too hot in her head, like she could actually feel it pulsing at her throat, her temples. She had nothing to cover herself with, not anymore. "I didn't know if you . . . if you meant it that way."

"I meant it that way. You're my Bathsheba, you always have been, and I need you like a needle in my vein. I don't care about right or wrong, or maybe that's not it. It's that I can't see how my feelings for you could possibly be wrong."

It was so hard to believe in him, but he was asking her to believe anyway. "This scares me so much." She tried to laugh, and couldn't. "I'd run away, but I can't."

"You don't need to be scared. Not while I'm here."

Surely, no man's voice had ever carried such assurance, or such tenderness. "And you won't lie to me?" she asked. "Please, Rhys. Promise me. I can hear the truth. I can *take* the truth, no matter how hard it is. I've done it so many times. I can't take any more lies, though. I can't."

She didn't cry in front of people, but she was holding Rhys's hand across a table in front of too many curious eyes, and the tears were right there on the edge of her lashes. One of them trembled there, a drop of silver at the edge of her vision, and she felt it travel slowly down her cheek, warm and wet, and more of them came after it. She sobbed once, pressed her serviette to her mouth, and tried to stop.

Rhys's thumbs came up and wiped the tears away, and his voice was gentle when he said, "I'll never lie to you. You have my word."

"And your word's . . ." She tried to get herself steady again, and failed. "Good."

She asked him with her eyes, and he answered.

"Always."

# belly deep

♡

He asked the server to put their steaks and sides in a box. He asked for the chocolate fondant, too, and he took the rest of the wine. And then he took Zora home.

Twenty-five minutes once again. The middle-aged woman behind the wheel was Maori, cheerful, and not chatty. Of course, maybe that was because she'd seen his face. She asked him, when she'd swung the car around a corner and onto the quiet, dark streets of Herne Bay, "Would you like music?"

"Yeh," he said. "Thanks."

Her hand hesitated on the dashboard knob. "Sounds of the heartland OK? Relaxing, eh. Good for driving at night."

"Uh . . . sure." He didn't care. He needed some cover while he got his equilibrium back, that was all. He had Zora's hand in his again. Her left hand. She was wearing no jewelry but his pearls, and he laced her bare fingers through his, thought how much better it would be if she were wearing a ring there, and touched the pulse at her wrist with his thumb as the haunting melody of the bone flute wove its way through his body, its only punctuation the breath of the musician. The car picked up speed, and the flute mingled with the resonant click of percussion instruments, all of it sounding, somehow, exactly like a waka full of warriors rowing in perfect unison down a nighttime river. The fern trees and vines hanging low on either side, the water rushing beneath them, hiding the sounds of their passage. The harshness of their breath, the muscles of shoulders and arms

339

standing out in fierce relief with their effort.

With every beat of wood on whalebone, the jade whale tail at his throat resonated all the way down his body, through his arm, his hand, and into Zora's. Her pulse, he could swear, was beating with his, and with the music, like they were somewhere out of time. Or in another one.

He'd competed with his brother for her. He'd fought her parents for her. And he'd won. She'd turned toward him on the seat again, and he see the rise and fall of her breasts, the luminous skin above her neckline, and the shine that was the choker of his pearls at the base of her throat. The music kept on, rising, falling, fading out and returning, all he was touching was Zora's hand, and he knew that all she could see was him.

In his driveway at last, the white lights reversing, a glow of red flashing briefly, then retreating as he walked with Zora to his front door, got it open, set the bag with the food on the narrow table under the mirror and his shoes on the low shelf on the opposite wall, and tried to think of something to say.

♡♡♡

She'd never got the chance to tell him what she was wearing under her dress, or how he'd made her feel from the moment he'd first looked at her tonight, and had let her know that he liked what he was seeing. The strength of his hand around hers, too, in the car, and what she'd felt from him then, like he needed her in his arms, and he was barely holding back.

Finally, though, the door had swung shut behind him in the tiled entryway with its single light shining on the two of them. The pale curve of the staircase floated down beyond it into the darkness, like they were on a raft floating on the sea, the only two people in their world. He was breathing hard, she could see it in the rise and fall of his chest under the black shirt, but he hadn't grabbed her. He'd taken off his shoes, and she hadn't.

They hung there, alone on their raft, for a long moment, and then she reached up, put a hand behind his neck, pulled his head down, and kissed his mouth.

She kept it gentle, trying to say with the touch of her lips everything that had been so hard to explain. She had her fingers splayed over his jaw, exploring the roughness of stubble, the indentation that was the dimple in his chin. He had an arm around her at last, his hand going not to her waist, but straight to her backside, tracing over the curve of it like he couldn't get enough, and then his hand was under the hem of her dress, moving up the back of her thigh, sending shocks all the way up her body as he traced his way over the sensitive flesh. The insistent throb she'd been feeling for hours now gave a hard pulse, and her hand was in his hair, pulling him down to her. And somehow, she was kissing him deeper.

His hand on her thigh, and the other one on her bare back, tracing down the vee of her dress and dipping beneath it, and still, he hadn't said anything. He found the zip, lowered it a centimeter at a time, and when he'd done it, brushed one spaghetti strap off her shoulder, then the other, and the dress fell to a floor with a whisper of fabric.

He said, "Step out." Low and nearly rough, the first words he'd spoken to her in half an hour. She did it, one heel, then another, and he kept his arm around her and steadied her through it. Her eyes weren't closed, and neither were his. He was drinking her in like she was all he wanted to see, and his hand was at the back clasp of her black satin strapless bra, the bottom curve of the cups outlined with tiny dots of pearl. The bottom hook opened, and then the top one, under his deft fingers, and the bra joined the dress on the floor.

All she was wearing was his pearls, her black heels, and a black lace thong that was more like a G-string. She wanted him to touch her there, and he didn't. His hands were on her breasts, his thumbs tracing over nipples that had long since gone hard. He said, "I want to suck these," she got another of those hard, fierce shudders, and he stood there and watched her do it.

She should be doing something, she realized fuzzily. Her hands went to his jacket, and he took a wrist in each hand and said, "No. Not right now," and then turned her around. Slowly. She stumbled a little in her heels, and he held her upright, then ran his hands up her arms, and then, slowly, over her sides, until he was holding her breasts again, her nipples caught between his big fingers. And he hauled in his breath.

♡♡♡

He'd meant to be romantic. But when she'd pulled his head down and kissed him like she couldn't wait another second, when he'd got his hand under her dress—how could he have done anything but take it off? And when she'd been heaving her breath from all the way up her body, he'd needed her bra gone, too.

Now, he was looking at exactly what he'd imagined for so long, and it was everything he'd dreamed of. Dark hair falling in a tangled cloud to just above her shoulders. A back like the gorgeously smooth, generous curves of a cello, flaring out again into rounded hips and thighs. A lush bottom covered by a single strip of black lace down the center, and that was all.

He ran his hand down the string of pearls once, then again, and she shuddered all the way down, swayed toward the wall, and put her palms flat against it.

Holy *shit*.

He could hear his breath in his ears, and he could see the tremble in her as he ran his hand down her spine, pulled the hair up from her neck with the other, bent down, and kissed her there, at her nape, then moved on to the side of her neck, his lips gentle, exploring.

"Rhys." It was barely an exhalation.

He kissed his way to her ear, explored it with his tongue, then took the lobe in his teeth. No earring there. Nothing but

342

nakedness. He bit gently, rested his elbow against the wall, shoving her a little farther forward, and got his other hand around her breast again. Round and full, the nipple hardening under his fingers the same way, he suspected, that it had all night.

"I need to be . . . soft," he said into her ear. "I know I do. And all I want is to fuck you against the wall." Not exactly the kind of declaration he'd been planning, and he couldn't help it. He squeezed her nipple some more, getting some rhythm into it, and she started breathing harder, rocking in the heels.

"I'm . . . not . . . tall enough," she got out. "Oh, that feels good. I'm going to . . . come. Please. Touch me."

He laughed, a huff of breath. "I told you, I'm here to take care of you." His lips were still at her neck, his hand still at her breast, but finally, his other hand was tracing down her side, moving on down, and he'd swear she was holding her breath.

He didn't go straight inside her thong. He touched her outside it, because he'd been exactly right. It was the tiniest vee of black lace, and it was soaked.

He said, "You were practically coming in front of your parents," then rubbed the rough-edged fabric into her, and she squirmed under his hand, called out, and rested her forehead against the wall.

The flames licked all the way up his body. And they burned.

"Y-yes," she managed to say. She was rocking now. "Oh. Do that. Do that. Please."

He kept it up, drove her up a little higher, and then, when she was making some noises that she couldn't help a bit, he slipped his hand under there, painted her with her own slickness while she shifted and moaned, got his fingers on either side of that nub, and started to squeeze in time with his other hand, the one that was on her nipple.

She was twisting. Trying to turn. Making some more noise. The pearls down her back swayed from side to side, her head was buried against her hands, and her entire body went taut.

And just like that, she went off like a firecracker, jerking against his hand, crying out as the shudders took her and rolled her hard.

He worked her through it while she shook and gasped, tried to say his name, and couldn't get the word out. Then he picked her up by the hips, lifted her, knocked the shoes off the top of the low shelf against the wall with a single kick, yanked it out with his heel, and put her on top of it. And she bent over, put her palms on the white wall, her legs shaking, and waited.

He didn't even have to take off the thong, so he didn't. He undid his zip, shoved the lace fabric of the thong aside, then had to put a finger inside her, just because there she was, so warm and wet, needing him so much. She closed around him, put the crown of her head against the wall, writhed some, and said, *"Rhys."*

He wasn't going to last nearly as long as he wanted to, once he was inside her. And he froze a second away from heaven. "Condom."

"I don't care. Do it now."

He groaned. He'd been hard for so long, he ached, and all he wanted was to bury himself to the hilt in her. What he wanted from her was something savage, and he couldn't care. "Birth control," he got out. "I'm clean. I'm . . . I've been waiting. But . . ."

"I want you to get me pregnant," she said, and his breath caught in his throat, the darkness surged, and he was holding her hips, parting her, shoving his way slowly inside. "I want you to fill me up," she said, and it was nearly a sob. "Come inside me. Do it now."

He did it. He couldn't have done anything else. And she stood there in her heels and her pearls, braced herself against the wall, and took it.

And when the sound of his breath was ragged in his ears, when he had one hand pulling her hips back into him, the other one inside the front of her thong again, and felt her going up with him? He said, "Say my name. Tell me who I am." His voice was ragged, torn to pieces, and so was everything inside him.

"Rhys." It was barely a breath. "Rhys. I love you. I need you so much. Please. Do it now."

After that, she didn't say anything at all. She shook, she shuddered, and she took him in, so deep and so hard, until he was piercing to the heart of her.

A shade of red so dark, it was nearly black. Pleasure so sharp, it was nearly pain. An explosion so strong, he could hardly stand. And Zora underneath him, twisting, calling out with the force of it.

Nothing but sin.

♡♡♡

They made it to bed eventually, but only because he carried her. He'd stripped off his clothes, finally, in the foyer, and when he put her on the bed, she was still in her shoes, her thong, and her pearls. She had her hand at the back of his neck, though, was pulling him down again, opening her mouth and welcoming the invasion of his tongue, the press of his big body over hers.

He levered himself off her at last, dropped a gentle kiss between her breasts, then was all the way down her body, slipping off first one black heel, then the other, and holding her feet in his hands.

"Red nail varnish," he said, tracing his thumbs over her toes, making her shiver. "My favorite, but even darker. Even better."

"Crimson," she said. "I saw at the Chanel counter when I was buying my dress. I bought it for you. It's called 'Dragon.'"

His hands stilled. "You're joking."

"No. It cost too much. I bought it anyway."

He grasped her left foot in one hand and pulled gently on each toe in turn. "Could hurt here. You aren't used to a heel that high. Calves, too. Could have some cramp, eh."

"Mm." She sighed. "Feels so good. Do that some more."

She could hear the smile in his voice, and his thumb was digging into the arch, making her moan with pleasure. "Seems to me you've said that to me before. I had a plan for tonight. I forgot it."

"And you don't do that." She had her other foot on his shoulder, pushing off there, arching her back with the relief of it as he rubbed his way up her calf and set in to massage the tight muscle.

"No," he said. "As soon as you kissed me, all I wanted was to be inside you." He leaned forward, taking her leg with him, kissed her belly, then headed slowly on down, and she shuddered again. "I think you could come again right now."

"Depends how good the . . . massage is," she said. "Do the other foot. Please."

Now, the amusement was right there on his dragon's face. "Just because I love to please you," he said, and set to work. Her toes, her arch, and her calf, taking his slow, sweet time, before he got his fingers under the skinny strap of the black lace thong and drew it down. He sighed, stroked his way down her thighs along with it, and said, "This was nice. This was what I wanted to see. I didn't use a condom, though. I'm trying to be upset about that, and I can't manage it. I don't do that anymore, either. I reckon you're going to have to take care of it, because I don't seem to have enough control."

"You think I didn't mean it," she said. He was kissing her inner thighs, the rasp of stubble on his jaw and the dark silk of his hair thrillingly alien against her skin. "But I did. I meant it."

He came up on his elbows and stared at her, all his intensity back, before he pushed his way up her body, took her head in his hands, and said, "Tell me."

"I can't . . ." She tried to look away, but he was still holding her head. "I wanted everything. I can't even explain." She tried to laugh, and couldn't do that, either. "You're not even just in my heart. You're in my belly." She put a hand over it. "Like a Maori, eh. My feelings for you are all the way inside my body. Belly deep. And I want all of you in me. I know it's too reckless. I know it would be all wrong, make everything too complicated again, and too hard. It's mad, and I can't help it. I want it anyway."

He kissed her, slow and deep, then brushed his lips over one cheek, then the other, and said, "First time we made love, here in this bed, and I was still inside you, afterwards, I thought, *You need to get out of her, mate, or you'll get her pregnant,* and I got this . . ." He sighed, then gave her one more gentle kiss. "This rush. Nearly out of control."

"And you don't do that anymore." Her hands were stroking over his shoulders, down his arms, wanting to touch all of him.

"No. Nothing close. I thought it could be about Dylan." His green-gold eyes looked into hers, troubled as the mountain air before the storm. "That it could be competition again. Some kind of claim I wanted to put on you. Some kind of stamp. That I want to put my baby in your belly for everybody to see. For *you* to see. For you to know. Like you said. Belly deep."

The thrill she got from that resonated all the way through her, exactly the way she'd told him. "Maybe it is," she said, "and maybe it's more than that. Maybe it's got nothing to do with Dylan. Maybe it has to do with you and me. Maybe it has to do with riding your bike down that longest hill, lifting your hands into the air, and letting gravity take you over."

"Roller coaster."

"No," she said. "That was how I felt with Dylan. Like I was carried away, almost . . . despite myself. This is different. This is *right*. This is us. I've got my hands in the air, but my legs and my belly are still working, and they've got me balanced. It's too much of a thrill, it's almost too much to take, but it's right. It's . . . inevitable. That's how I feel."

He stared at her for a long moment, then kissed her again and said, "Yeh. That's it. Bathsheba. Like there's no choice. But all the same . . ."

"Birth control," she said, and sighed. "I know you're right."

"I was going to say," he said, with the faintest of smiles showing around his eyes, "that I want to marry you first. Or during. Or now."

# heart and hand

What did you say to that? He was still over her, his hands in her hair, the energy all but pulsing out of his big frame.

And the tension, too. Just because you were used to putting your body and your heart on the line, digging deep for every bit of strength you possessed when everything inside you wanted to shut down—that didn't make it easy.

If it were easy, everybody would have this kind of mana.

She said, "I love you." It seemed like a pretty good starting place. It also seemed like what he most needed to hear right now. What he most needed to *know*.

She was right. Some of the tension left him, and he lowered his head, gently touched his forehead and nose to hers, and left it there for a long couple seconds, both of them inhaling together in a hongi.

There was nothing he could have done, nothing he could have said, that could have made her feel more seen, or more respected. When he pulled back, she said, knowing her voice wasn't steady and deciding it didn't matter, "Thank you."

"Not an answer." He wasn't going anywhere, either.

"I should say it's mad," she said. "I can see . . . issues. To say the least."

"Maybe one of them is that the fella's meant to do it better than that, and it doesn't suggest that I'll be brilliant going forward. It came out because I've had it there in my mind for weeks now, though that's not much of an excuse. When I bought you these . . ." His hand traced over the pearls at her

349

throat. "They were what I wanted to buy you, and they weren't it at all. This feels sudden to you, maybe, but to me, it feels like a mountain I've been climbing forever. I've been going downhill almost as much as I've been going up, with no idea if I'd ever make it. Now, I've got to the top, and I want to do something about it. I'm hoping you'll forgive me that I didn't do it right. You've forgiven more than that."

She said, "I don't care whether you do it right." And she didn't. She'd had the big gesture. She wanted the small ones.

It was like he hadn't heard her, because he was definitely looking worried. "I'll give you everything. I promise. And I realize you've heard promises before, too. And I . . ." He rolled off her, onto his back. "I know my track record for keeping them isn't what it should have been."

Now, she was the one propped on her elbow, running a hand over his tattooed shoulder, down his arm, bending down to drop a soft kiss on his chest. "Lately, would you say?"

She felt him still. "No," he said, and eased a little more. "Not so much lately. But I wasn't the best husband. May as well say it now." He turned his face to her, and his expression was sober. Nearly weary. "I didn't cheat, I didn't lie, and I brought my paycheck home. There's more to marriage than not doing the wrong things, though. There's doing the right things. I didn't give Victoria enough attention, and I definitely didn't give her enough sweetness. I could say I didn't know about that. It's probably more that I didn't try."

"Or," she said, her heart filling up a little more, "that you didn't know what that looked like."

"No. It was that I focused on one thing, and it wasn't her. I had examples around me of how to do it better. I'm not a stupid fella."

"Despite what my parents seem to think," she said, to tease him out of it.

He smiled. Reluctantly. "I'm going to be gone too much. And when I'm home, I'm going to work too much."

"Yes. You are."

His hand, which had been stroking her back, stilled.

"I'm going to miss you," she said. "I already do. But I'd rather miss somebody I love than not love him at all."

♡♡♡

Rhys had her hand in his again, was running his thumb over that bare ring finger, thinking that he wanted to put a diamond on it almost as much as he wanted to put a baby in her belly. He knew what she looked like pregnant, and he wanted to be the one making it happen. Call him whatever you like. He wanted it.

She sighed, then asked, "What time is it?"

He had to laugh. "Sweetheart. Not the most romantic thing I've ever heard."

She smiled, but said, "Kids. Babysitter. You may not realize how important that is. And that's the other thing we need to talk about."

"The babysitter? I'm paying her. Driving her home, too. Driving *you* home, but not yet. It can't be much past ten. We have time."

"You didn't get your steak yet. We should heat it up."

She sat up, and not like a languid woman stretching out. More like a Jack-in-the-box. Was there a reason she was dragging the conversation away?

He hadn't paid enough attention before? He was paying it now. "And the reason you're talking about that, instead of talking about rings and dates and moving in with me, is . . ."

She dragged a hand through her hair, mussing it some more. "It's not what people will say, whatever you're thinking. It's the kids, and maybe . . ."

"It's you," he said. His heart, which had been somewhere up there in the stands, took a dive that nearly gave him vertigo. "I did speak too soon."

"Yes. No." She sighed. "I feel it, too. I don't have your courage. I never have. I don't have your mana."

"Don't say that." It came out rough, and she jumped. "It's not true."

"I'm scared right now," she said. "By the thought of making the move. Of telling the kids. Of taking the leap."

"Of believing."

She didn't answer, and that told him everything. "I don't know how to answer that," he said, after searching around inside himself for a while. "And if you don't know the right answer, you don't answer at all. But I know one thing. It's a rugby thing, though, like most bits of wisdom I've got." He was sitting up, too, and had her hand again, because maybe it would help.

She was scared? He was here.

"I'll take rugby wisdom," she said.

"There's more than one way of being strong, then," he said. "There's being the player who has the magic moments that can turn your momentum around in a heartbeat, yeh, or the one who comes off the bench and finishes up with so much flash, the public asks why he isn't starting every time. And there's the bloke who doesn't do any of that, the one who does his role every single game and never has a bad one, and makes the team better. The one who's as strong in Minute Eighty as he was in Minute One. It's not because he's not tired. It's because he trained harder and he cared enough to do the boring parts of that, but it's also because he's got the kind of will that pulls his body along with him, and that when somebody else would say the tank is empty, he finds more in there, and he gives it. And because he won't let his mates down."

"Which is you," she said.

"It's who I tried to be in rugby. It's not who I've been in the rest of my life. It's who I want to be with you, though. I want to be that man who's as steady during the hard parts, when the tank's empty, as he was at the beginning. And none of that is my point. I didn't do it for the money, or for the glory, but the money and the glory were there. You haven't done it for either. You've done it because it's who you are, and because it had to be done. You're still doing it. Do you know what I see when I look at you?"

"No," she said. She wanted to hear, though, and he needed to tell her.

So he did. "I see the player you can trust to give until his heart bursts. The one who plants his feet, puts his head down, and gets stuck in. I see that fella in the front row who'll never win Player of the Year and never be the one scoring the try, whose nose will be broken too many times, and who'll play on through every one of them. A woman whose van breaks down on the side of the motorway, and who gets up the next day at five to start again. The teammate I can trust to be there with me in Minute Eighty, the one who'll empty the tank. I see the one with mana. And that's the one I want beside me."

She was crying. Silently this time, silver streaks down her face, her expression twisting with it. Not trying to be beautiful, and beautiful anyway. Belly deep. He said, "People are going to say you're lucky, because people can be bloody stupid. You're not going to be the one who's lucky. That's going to be me." He grabbed for a box of tissues from the drawer and handed it to her. "So if that one's solved, tell me the next one."

She wiped her eyes, blew her nose, tried to laugh, and said, "My mum would be so horrified. I'm sitting up in the most unflattering way possible, showing you my stretch marks and my tummy, I'm blowing my nose, and my eye makeup's streaking all over the shop. And you've just told me I'm not flash. Doubly horrified."

He smiled. "I'm not the most polished fella myself, in case you didn't notice. I told you I wouldn't say it right, didn't I. Tell me the next thing, though. I feel I'm on a roll here."

This time, she *did* laugh, but said, "Isaiah. I was a bit preoccupied earlier this evening, but you must have heard that, too. We need to go slowly. He's not like Casey. He's not a fast adapter. He needs stability."

He lay down again and sighed. "OK. I can't argue with that one. So what do you want to do?"

She came down over him, to his surprise, kissed his

mouth, and smiled into his eyes. "Do you know—that could be my favorite thing you've ever said to me. Thanks."

He tried to manufacture some outrage. "After all that? Minus the rugby part, comparing you to a front-rower, I've said more beautiful things in one night than I have in forty years."

Now, they were both laughing. "Nah, boy," she said, "I loved it all. But 'What do you want to do?' ranks right up there. You're still married, for one thing, and an engagement wouldn't look good for you anyway, never mind the part with Dylan, which is a pretty big part. But what I want to do? I want to hold your hand at home, to cuddle with you on the couch when we're watching a movie with the kids, and to give you a kiss when I see you. To tell Casey and Isaiah we're going on a date and let them get used to it, but hold off on the ring and the date and the moving-in part of it."

"What about the 'getting you pregnant' part of it?"

"Zoomed straight there, didn't you. Maybe we could think . . ." She considered. Another thing he appreciated about her. Normally. When he was getting his way, at least. "That pregnancy takes nine months. Worst case? We've got nine months to get Isaiah used to the idea."

"No," he said, and her head whipped around again. "That would be the best case." He smiled at her, then put a hand down low on her belly, where a few stripes showed the effort it had taken her body to carry Isaiah. Like his much-broken nose, the knuckles that didn't look anything like they had twenty years ago, the scar on his forehead, and all the rest of the trophies he carried on his body. The price you'd been willing to pay, because nothing that good came easy. Women could be warriors, too. He rolled over with her, pressed his lips to one of those lines, and said, "Good things come to those who wait, eh. I reckon we'll wait, then, and I'll do my best to settle for feeling engaged. And possibly buy you a ring and try to think of a more memorable way to offer you my heart and hand than blurting it out in bed. Meanwhile, let's heat up those steaks. If I'm going to keep you interested in our quasi-engagement, I could need my strength."

# kicking into space

The next morning, everything got more complicated.

The first part went fine. Rhys got up at six, pulled on a T-shirt, shorts, and trainers, and headed up the road a few kilometers for a dawn run on a track in the Waitakeres, the one he hadn't taken on that evening when he'd come back from Japan. When he'd sat on a bench instead, held Zora, and told her he loved her for the first time.

Six o'clock had come early after finally getting to bed at one, but as always, pushing his way up the first incline through his muscles' initial resistance, feeling his breath and his legs settling into their rhythm, then picking up the pace, did the business. No sound but birdsong, the pounding of his feet on earth and of the blood in his ears, and the snaking thoughts in his head had begun untwisting themselves.

He was a one-track man who was on about four tracks just now, between rugby and Casey and Isaiah and Zora, and Finn was right. A sportsman needed his workouts to make that kind of adjustment. You needed emotional balance to do his job, and more for the rest of this, but it came from the same place as physical balance. From knowing what tools to use and working to use them better. Which he knew how to do.

By the time he'd left the first few kilometers of bush behind and was headed across a windswept stretch at the top of the bluffs, with the wild waters of the Tasman foaming against the rocks below, the pink light of dawn had turned to glowing blue, a fresh breeze was blowing the mists away, and was stretching out and finding his stride, things were settling into place.

The air was chilly, but it was clean. You could breathe it deep into your lungs and collect your thoughts. That was the reason he'd come home. The connection to this place, to his mountain and his river and the spirit of his ancestors, was like no other.

He might not be an All Black anymore, except that you always were. That never left you from the minute you pulled on the black jersey, the first time your feet stamped the ground in the haka, connecting you to the earth beneath you and the mates around you.

Everyone he loved was here, and everything he loved, too, and he was going to make it work. Zora loved him, he was learning to be a dad, and surely he could learn to be a good husband, too. There was nothing like practice and determination to make you better at something. You made a plan, and you executed. It was trickier when somebody else was making the plan with you, but by the time a man was forty, he ought to have learned something. Maybe even to work on four tracks at once.

So that was good, and so was sluicing his body down in a shower that was too big for one, thinking that pretty soon, Zora's bottles of nail varnish would be lined up in the empty drawers under the sink, in a pretty basket, maybe, her perfume and shoes would be on the dressing-room shelves, and his house would smell like flowers.

He could need some better towels. The big, fluffy white kind. Another warmed towel rack, too, on the wall by the bath, so all she'd have to do was reach out for it afterwards. She'd enjoy that.

When he got to her house at nine-thirty, though, it was all a bit different than he'd expected. Zora was in the flower shed, dressed in stretchy black leggings, a long T-shirt, an apron, and jandals, her hair pulled back into a ponytail, her hands deft and quick as she put together an arrangement about the size of a bus. Isaiah and Casey were sitting on the floor at her feet, picking leaves off flowers and sticking them into buckets. Pop music was playing on a portable speaker, but Zora didn't look relaxed.

"Hi," he said, leaning against the open door.

Casey stuffed a pink rose into a bucket and ran to him, and he swung her up, gave her a cuddle, and said, "Morning, monkey. Did you have a good time last night?"

"Yes," she said, "except not really, because Isaiah said I couldn't do his robot, so I had to do a puzzle instead by myself. And I wanted to read a story with you, but you weren't there, and Auntie Zora wasn't there, either, and you won't be there tonight, because you have to do your job."

"Because I was at the hard part, and you don't know how," Isaiah said, still taking leaves off flowers. "Hi, Uncle Rhys. Mum's very busy."

"What can I do?" Rhys asked Zora. They weren't going to be having a talk with the kids this morning, clearly.

"Get me a very large coffee at the shop," Zora said, "and cook a better breakfast for the kids. Bring me a couple eggs on toast out here, and I'll be your slave."

He laughed out loud, then set Casey down, came over to give Zora a kiss on her smiling mouth, and said, "Done. What is that?"

"Wedding bouquet."

"Looks as big as the bride, eh."

"Trailing bouquet. It's a thing. Big's a thing, too. Dahlias, hydrangeas, roses, hypericum berries, calla lilies, greenery. The bride wanted an cottage garden effect."

He inspected it doubtfully. Well over a meter long, and, geez, almost that wide, too. The feathery greenery would nearly reach the floor. He said, "She's got the garden, anyway. Maybe if it was all one color." Peach, white, pink, lavender. It was all pale, which he guessed was good, but . . .

"You're not supposed to tell her it's not nice," Isaiah said. "That's not helpful."

"You're right, mate," he said. "No excuse."

Zora said, "Not my favorite, either, but she wants what

she wants, and she saw a picture. I shouldn't complain. She's got six bridesmaids and six groomsmen, and the bride and groom each have a mum and stepmum. Flower bonanza."

"It's three thousand seven hundred dollars," Isaiah informed him. "Because there's an arbor, too. Arbors cost heaps of money. Mum did that yesterday, though. The other wedding is only six hundred dollars, because it's just little."

Those would be the deep-purple and white bouquets on the other table, Rhys guessed. And she'd done an arbor yesterday besides all her deliveries? *And* gone out with him? "I like those other ones," he said. "The six-hundred-dollar ones. What are they?"

"Eggplant calla lilies, white roses, dusty miller leaves," Zora said. "Elegant. Striking, but soft. Nice, eh. And you say 'little' like it's a bad thing, Isaiah. I'm glad to have the big orders, but I've delivered too many flowers on wedding days to think those huge events are much fun. Too stressful, I'd say. Nothing like the view from the inside." She sounded weary, and she looked it, too.

"Right," Rhys said. "Very large latte, coming up." He told Casey, "Come with me to get Auntie Zora's coffee."

"OK," she said. She was wearing her *Girls Can* T-shirt with leggings, and she looked as cute as a bug. "I'm very hungry, too. We went to the flower market before it was even *light*. We had to get up in the nighttime. If we went to Café Vevo, we could get those kinds of special muffins that have chocolate inside. Muffins are breakfast. That would give Isaiah and me energy."

"Brioche," Zora said. "More dessert than breakfast, really."

"If you ask them to," Casey said, "they will put them in a little box and put whipped cream in the box."

Rhys was about to say, "Eggs on toast. Tomato. Mushrooms." Instead, he asked Zora, "D'you want a brioche? Breakfast, then dessert?"

"Possibly," she said. "Or possibly, I'd kill for one."

He laughed again. He had one of the toughest matches of the season coming up tonight, so why was being here better than being home alone, where he could think about it?

Because he'd made his preparations, and until things started unfolding tonight, it was out of his hands. He didn't even give the motivational speech anymore. He left that to the skipper. The players were the ones out there on the field, and they needed the confidence of knowing the game was in their hands, and that they could seize it. Leadership wasn't always telling people what to do. Sometimes, it was finding the right people to do the telling.

What he'd said to Zora was true. The way you'd always done things might not be the best way in the world. He said, "Sounds like I'd better provide, then."

He did, and then he cooked breakfast, did the washing-up, and took the kids to the park for some rugby practice while Zora did her deliveries, which would help, too.

When he'd taken them through their warmups and passing drills and was going through some kicking with Casey, Isaiah said, "You kissed Mum on the lips again today."

"I did." Rhys kicked the ball back to Casey, watched as she jumped for it and brought it down, thought, *Not bad, monkey,* then turned his attention back to the boy.

What did you say? Something simple, he guessed, and true. He decided on, "That's because I love her."

"You're my uncle, though," Isaiah said. "Your uncle isn't supposed to kiss your mum. I asked my friend Aiden. He said, your mum can *say* he's your uncle, but he isn't really. That just means he sleeps in your mum's bed and they have sex, but he's not your stepdad. But you really *are* my uncle. Uncle Hayden only kisses Mum on the cheek, and only sometimes. Usually, he just kind of hugs her."

"Because he's her brother," Rhys said. He kicked another ball back to Casey and tried not to sweat. Was he meant to get into a discussion of incest taboos here? He'd better not be supposed to explain sex. Did you do that at eight years old? He'd known by then, but he'd learned from his cousins. Also, their information may not have been precisely accurate.

"But *you're* kind of her brother too," Isaiah said. "You're my dad's brother. That's almost the same."

"But not," Rhys said. "We don't share blood." Seemed he *was* talking about incest taboos.

"Yuck. People don't share *blood*. Except if they're vampires, and that's not sharing, either. That's *drinking.*"

Rhys had to laugh, but rearranged his face when Isaiah looked affronted. "Means we're not in the same family," he explained. "We don't have the same mum and dad, and we're not cousins, either, whose parents—or their grandparents or aunties or uncles, if you're Maori, which you are—had the same mum and dad."

"Oh." Isaiah considered that. "Like Casey."

"Exactly like Casey." *More than you know, mate.*

"Aiden still says it's gross, though," Isaiah persisted. "If you're kissing Mum, I mean, even though he says it's probably good, because you're famous, and because you're richer than her, and boyfriends sometimes buy things. But Mum is very busy. She always says she doesn't have time to do fun things at the weekend. She has to go to bed early, and then she has to clean the house and go grocery shopping and do paperwork and lots of other things when she's done with the flowers. I don't think she has time to have a boyfriend."

Zora might know what to say about that, but she wasn't here. Rhys was, so he took his best shot. "Could be you're the one missing some time with her," he said. "Sharing her with Casey, and with me. Could be that your Saturday isn't looking like you think it should."

"Yes. Because I wanted to ask Aiden to come over today and build robots with me, but Casey's still going to be there, and she can't go home, because of your game."

"Oh. Huh." Rhys considered that, then had to sprint for a wild ball from Casey. "Here," he told Isaiah, flicking the ball to him from behind his back. "Talking and training's better. Keep your head up and your eye on Casey while you're kicking it. She's your target. Your foot goes where your eye does."

Isaiah kicked. "Better," Rhys said. "Always think about

where you're sending it. You're never just booting it off into space. You always have a plan."

"OK."

"Here's another idea. Why don't you tell your mum that you need some time with your friend?"

"Because Casey will be lonesome if I say she can't come in my room, and she'll be more lonesome if Aiden's there. I have to be nice, because her mum died, and she's only six."

"It's hard to be nice when you're feeling narky," Rhys said. "And the narkier you feel, the harder it is to hide it, until you can't be nice at all anymore, and you explode, which is no good for anybody. At least that's what generally happens to me. Your mum's a pretty clever lady. If you tell her what you told me, I reckon she can think of something that will work for everybody."

Which was, yes, booting the ball into space without a plan. Fortunately, Zora was good at picking it up and running with it. He'd have a word with her when he dropped the kids off.

One step at a time.

♡♡♡

So all that wasn't bad. When he was in the glassed-in coach's box high above Eden Park about ten hours later, though, and the game clock had ticked down to seventy-six minutes? Things were a little more tense.

The score was thirteen to ten, and the Crusaders had the thirteen. A defensive battle, but his defense had mostly held. On attack, they hadn't gone quite so well.

Just now, though, he was sitting rigid, his pen forgotten in his hand, while they held again. The Crusaders were inside ten meters, their forwards smashing into the line time after time, and being met and driven back, over and over again. A surprise cutout pass, then, a long one, to one of the backs on the wing, and Finn was leaning forward beside Rhys, the tension all but quivering in him.

361

The wing took four steps toward the inside, his halfback running at his shoulder, pitched the dummy pass toward the tramlines at the edge of the field, making Kevin McNicholl move that way, then passed it back inside to a lock. To Kane Armstrong, all six foot eight of him, with a wingspan like an albatross, four meters from the line.

Tom Koru-Mansworth hadn't been fooled by that dummy pass, not this time. The second the ball was in the air to Kane, he'd started moving, and Kane hadn't pulled it in yet when Tom hit him hard.

Six foot six, fifteen Kg's of new muscle on him, and still growing. He smashed Kane straight in the chest, and you could practically hear the impact as he sent Kane backward. And released him, exactly like he should have done, before plunging back into the battle. Marko Sendoa was at the breakdown in a heartbeat, getting himself over the ball as the Crusaders did the same on the other side.

Finn had his hands on the table in front of him. Rhys didn't. He was just watching. Marko's feet were planted, supporting his body weight, and he was still wrestling for that ball as Hugh barreled in behind him and Kors did the same on the other side.

Marko pulled the ball out. Three meters from the line, but passed back hard to Nico, the fullback, in the time it took to blink, and it was off Nico's boot and sailing, not toward the touchline, where the Crusaders would get their chance again in a lineout, but in a short box kick, high into the air, where the Blues could compete for it.

*No risk, no reward.* Seventy-eight minutes on the clock, two minutes to go, and Nico was chasing his own kick, looking up, then leaping more than a meter into the air at the same time the Crusaders' No. 10 went for the ball.

A clash of bodies, and Nico went down hard onto the turf and stayed down as a Crusaders forward collected the spilled ball and Nico got to his feet, shook his head, worked his shoulder, and trotted back into position.

Seventy-nine minutes and thirty seconds, and the

Crusaders were the ones not giving up the ball.

Twenty seconds.

Ten seconds.

The hooter sounded, a Crusaders player kicked the ball into touch, and the referee blew his whistle.

Game over.

♡♡♡

Heading into the sheds after the game as the players sat on their benches, unwound tape from around wrists and thighs, and didn't meet each other's eyes. Nobody was going for the beer, which was good. Rhys shook hands, each in turn, spending a moment extra with Nico. "You collected a stinger there," he said, and Nico said, "Yeh. No worries."

Tomorrow was soon enough. Rhys moved down to Kors. The kid was taking off his boots, all of him mud- and grass-stained, his cheekbone already swelling red.

"That was switched on," Rhys said, clasping his hand. "And then it was switched higher. Well done."

Kors nodded, but he didn't look happy. Which was good, too. You weren't meant to look happy, or feel that way, after a loss.

A half hour later, he was saying the same thing from the coach's table, sitting beside Finn at the postgame press conference.

"What's the mood in the sheds?" a journo asked.

"What do you think?" Rhys asked. "They're gutted."

"A good effort, surely," the man persisted. "Especially from your bench."

"We made good progress on some things," Rhys said. "Our defense, for one, which is mainly down to Finn, and the leadership on the field. But if you don't hate to lose, you don't belong here."

"It was risky, surely, going for the box kick at the end," another man said. "Should you have kicked into touch instead and tried to steal the lineout, or held onto the ball, with that little time on the clock?"

"If it had come off," Rhys said, "you'd be telling me we were brilliant. I'm feeling pretty proud of the stand we made, down there at the end, and the turnover, too. Full credit to the Crusaders, though. They played a good game tonight."

"How would you rate your own performance?" somebody else had to ask. "Three wins and two losses put you fourth on the table, if the Hurricanes win against the Brumbies tomorrow as expected. Are you thinking about your job?"

*Cheers, mate,* Rhys didn't say. *I hadn't noticed.* "The season's got a ways to go yet," he said. "I'm not in charge of rating my performance, and I'll worry about my job when somebody gives me reason to. We'll take our learnings from this and get better from it. You can't change the past. All you can do is move ahead into the future."

They should put him on a fortune cookie. It was what he'd told Zora. All he had was rugby wisdom.

Part of that hadn't been true, though. He *was* in charge of rating his performance and, if it wasn't up to scratch, seeing what he needed to do to improve it. Which meant he had a couple things he needed to do tomorrow. Things he should have done weeks ago.

He needed to call Zora.

# unfinished business

Eleven o'clock on Sunday morning, and Rhys was descending the plane's staircase onto the tarmac of Christchurch Airport in the blowing rain, something he'd done about a thousand times before. This time, though, he wasn't collecting a bag, or carrying one, either. Today's was a day trip. Two day trips, actually. This was Step One.

A stop at the car-hire counter, where the young woman said, "Here you are," without a flicker of recognition, and handed over the keys, and he thought about fourteen years in this city, about not being able to go anywhere without posing for a photo on somebody's phone, and didn't mind the change a bit. Somebody else's turn, and it had never been his favorite thing anyway.

His favorite thing had been playing. Absolutely no contest. Playing was an ice cream at the beach on a summer day, or your first time out with the girl you wanted most, when she was smiling at you and letting you know that she wanted you, too. Playing was all the best things rolled into one.

Except that days weren't always sunny, and girls didn't always keep smiling.

He drove toward Sumner, his windscreen wipers struggling to keep up with the wind-driven deluge. The block of exclusive townhouses where he'd lived was still perched up there on a cliff, overlooking the sea. It hadn't been damaged too badly in the earthquakes, so that wasn't why Victoria wasn't living in it anymore. She'd wanted a fresh start, and she probably hadn't been able to manage the mortgage alone, even with alimony.

Everybody had to move on, he guessed.

He didn't drive all the way there, because most of Sumner's retail space was still missing. Instead, he headed to Ferry Road, and the new place where Vic had asked him to meet her. It was on the water, which was good. A sea view was always better for calming the mind, and she'd feel on home turf.

His hands tensed on the wheel, and he flexed his fingers and drew his shoulder blades down his back with a deliberate effort. It was that same old thing. You couldn't outrun trouble. Trouble had a way of catching up. If you were smart, you went to meet it.

He spotted the place through the rain. Evil Genius, it was called. New since his time, or rather, an old building made new again, weathered brick and wood. He shrugged his anorak on and headed in, moving fast and getting wet anyway.

It was a bit loud inside, and crowded, too, which was no surprise. Things were always crowded in Christchurch. Too many people wanting someplace to go on Sunday morning, and not enough places for them to be.

He found Victoria instantly, his eyes going to the right spot in the way they did when you knew somebody that well. She was sitting at the end of the bar, having a chat with the fella behind it, looking poised. Confident, and not a bit dressed up for this, in loose cotton trousers and a snug top that showed off her slim, strong figure and the muscle tone of her arms. Her blonde hair was loose, but in a casual way rather than a sexy one. Showing him she hadn't made a special effort for him. Fair enough.

She didn't look around. Not watching for him, then. He headed over there, waited until she noticed him, and said, "Hi, Vic."

"Hi, Rhys." She didn't stand, and he thought about kissing her cheek and decided, *Better not.* Instead, he sat down.

"Thanks for coming," he said. "How ya goin'? The personal training going well, is it?"

"Going fine," she said. "Going better once we're divorced."

All right, then. He saw wariness in the set of her shoulders, thought about the vibrant woman he'd married, and set the thought aside. She could be that woman again. She might be that woman already. Just not today.

She wouldn't be seeing the man she'd married, either. He hoped she was seeing a better one. He suspected she wouldn't care.

"If this is about the property settlement," she said, "I'm not discussing it with you. That's why you have attorneys." She took a sip of something that looked healthy. Green and thick, and he'd bet it had flaxseed in it. Victoria was disciplined. He'd liked that about her, and she'd liked it about him. Discipline gave you a place to go when everything else had failed to function, and that was comfort.

Sometimes, though, disciplined people had trouble with barriers. Letting them down, that is. Just now, Victoria's barriers were fully operational, which meant he needed to come out from behind his and take the flak, or there was no point to this.

Not easy.

"Can I get you something?" the fella behind the bar asked, and Rhys said, "Flat white, please. Single." He didn't need any more jitters.

"It's not about the settlement," he told Vic once the man moved off, "and it's not about the divorce. Two weeks, and it's done. I didn't come to talk about that. I came because there are a couple of issues in my life that are bound to come out pretty soon in the press, and I wanted you to hear about them from me first."

She'd been starting to take a drink of her smoothie. Now, she put the glass down, every line of her taut body saying she was holding it together with an effort.

He hated that he had to say all this. He needed to say it anyway. It was hard for him to do? It would be harder on her if he didn't, and he owed her this much.

"What issues?" she asked.

He'd assumed he'd get something to eat while they were here. Probably not happening. "First," he said, "that I have a daughter. Casey. She was living in Chicago, and now she's with me, because her mum's died. She's six years and nine months old."

He'd thought about which thing to discuss first. He'd decided it didn't matter. Neither of them was going to be any fun for her to hear.

Her fingers shook on the glass, and he wanted to grab her hand and hold it. He wanted to tell her it wasn't true, that he hadn't just swept the rug of her life out from under her and told her that nothing about the two of them had been real.

He had to keep this secret, though. Nothing else was going to work for Casey. What would Vic have said anyway, if he'd told her the truth? If he'd said, "It actually wasn't me. It was Dylan. He told her he was me, you see, and then he put my name on the birth certificate, and . . ." Who would believe that? Then he'd not only be a cheater and a liar, he'd be a coward, too. She didn't need to think she'd been married to a coward, and he couldn't stand to have her think it.

Which didn't matter, because he couldn't say it.

She grabbed the edge of the bar, and he said, "I'm sorry." Which wasn't nearly enough to say, but what else did he have?

She swallowed hard, and then her blue eyes met his. A world of pain in there. She took a breath, then asked, "What's the other thing?"

Nothing wrong with her courage, then or now.

He said, "I'm seeing Zora, and I plan to marry her as soon as we can."

It took her a moment. Shock, was what that was. "Your sister-in-law? Dylan's wife? *That* Zora?"

Now, he saw something else besides hurt. Anger. Fury, in fact. That was good, though. Better to think he was a son of a bitch than that something was wrong with her. That was how Zora had felt—that she wasn't desirable enough for Dylan to stick to, that she didn't mean enough to him to matter.

Anger was definitely better.

"Yeh," he said. "That Zora."

The fella behind the bar set his flat white down in front of him, probably considered whether to ask about ordering food, and prudently decided that the answer was "No," because he headed to the other side of the place instead. *Explosion imminent,* his posture said. Which was what Vic's said, too.

"Were you . . . sleeping with her?" Vic was barely getting the words out. "While we were married? Was that why it was so awkward? Why you went so odd while he was dying? Just waiting, were you? I thought it was me, but it was you, wasn't it?" Her fingers shook on the bar, and he knew that if he did grab them, they'd be ice. When she took too much emotion on board, her body went cold. Trying to shut down, or to send the blood to the parts that needed it. Her heart, and her brain. Trying to stay in control.

She couldn't stand to lose control, because it meant letting the hurt in. He knew how she felt. He'd had forty years to find out.

*Stay calm,* he told himself. *Show some maturity. Show some bloody compassion. Take what she has to dish out. She's going to need to know she said it.* "No," he said. "Not before we were married, and not while we were married, or while she was, either. I didn't sleep with anybody else while you and I were married. Not until I moved out, anyway. Didn't kiss anybody else, for that matter, from the time I married you." He could give her that, anyway. Maybe.

"And you expect me to believe that." She stood up, nearly stumbling over the stool in her haste, not a bit like cool, collected Victoria. "You were in love with her all along. You were holding *back* all along. That was what was wrong, not me. Do you know how much I thought it was me? You *bastard.*"

He stood up himself. "I don't expect you to believe anything. I'm telling you the truth anyway, because it matters to me that I do, and because whatever you think now, I care about you. I wasn't a good enough husband. I could say that was because I'd always been so focused on getting out, on moving up out of where I'd started, and that being single-minded about my career was the only way I knew how to do that. I could say that I thought I was doing the right thing for you, too, making a better future for both of us. The truth is that getting married at all was probably a mistake. You deserved better."

*She's not perfect, either,* he'd told himself at the time, pulling up the same old list of grievances. They didn't matter, not anymore.

"Yes," she said. "I did deserve better." She laughed, an angry huff of breath, shoved her hair out of her face, looked around like she wanted to be anywhere else, like all she wanted was to escape. He knew how she felt. "You were so . . . *unavailable.*" The tears were there, he could tell, but she wasn't letting them out. "I know the word now. I've learned it. And it doesn't help a bit. I want to slap you." Her voice had begun to tremble. "I want to scream at you. I want to . . . burn down your *house.* And I don't believe you." She blinked hard, forcing the tears back. Guts again, or too much control, because surely, she needed to let it go.

"I know you don't." His chest ached with a pain worse than any loss. There was no next game where you could redeem yourself. These mistakes, you had to live with forever. "I loved you. I just wasn't good at it."

She said, "I can't hear any more. I'm going."

He said, "Fine. I'll pay for your drink."

"Fuck you," she said. And left.

# carry that weight

Zora was running the vacuum in the lounge when she jumped at a touch on her arm.

"Sorry," Hayden said when she turned the machine off. "You didn't answer my knock."

"Don't *scare* me like that."

"You? I'm the one who was attacked in here. I could develop an aversion."

"You weren't attacked. It was a fend."

"Excuse me, were you here? Flew across the room, didn't I." He looked around. "Where's Isaiah?"

"Cleaning his room. Supposedly. Or playing with his robots with Casey, more likely. She's meant to be dusting."

"Coast is clear, then. Good."

He sat at the end of the couch, and she headed into the kitchen, came back with a bottle of cleanser and two sponges, and handed him one of them. "If you're going to talk to me, talk while we work. Bathroom. I have an hour to spend on this. Why are you here? I thought you had a date last night."

"I did. Out late, and yet I came anyway. Mum woke me with the phone at eight, thank you very much, and there was no getting back to sleep after twenty minutes of that."

He went into the bathroom with her, and she gave him the cleanser and said, "You can do the tub."

"Why do I get the hard part?"

"Because you're taller. D'you know how tricky it is to reach the far side when you're my height? And scrub well, please. Casey and Isaiah both came home from rugby with Rhys yesterday covered with dirt, and I'm not taking a bath again until that's sanitized."

He sighed. "'Talk to your sister,' Mum said. 'It's my duty as a brother,' I thought. 'I'm dying to hear more, because it sounds fraught, and maybe she'll give me breakfast.' Pancakes and caramelized bananas, I thought. I saw a thing where you did the bananas with toasted walnuts. Looked fab."

"Dream on." She squirted cleanser around the toilet bowl, then got to work on the floor behind it. "I don't make breakfast at ten in the morning. Also, I could have more appetite for cooking pancakes if boys aimed better. What do I have to do, put a floating target in here? But I can't wait to hear how Mum spun this. Let's have it."

"You should have him clean the floor instead of doing it yourself," Hayden said. "The message is more likely to get through if he's wiping up the dried pee."

She stopped wiping for a moment and sat back on her heels. "Huh. That's a surprisingly good idea. And it *was* fraught. I said things I've never said before. You could call it a scene. Dad didn't look too happy, either, thinking back. I don't know what happened, but I'm guessing he tried to condescend to Rhys, and that it didn't go well. Parental relationship blown to bits, or reestablished on more even footing, perhaps. Time will tell. What did Mum say? She hasn't rung me since."

She should go over there and have a chat, probably. Isaiah needed a relationship with his grandparents, and it was going to have to come from her. She needed to haul up some compassion and be the bigger person.

She was so very tired of being the bigger person.

Also, she had Casey today, and she didn't want to drag her into it. Her mum wouldn't actually make Casey feel unwelcome, though, would she? Or say something in front of her?

The truth was—she wasn't sure. Besides, how many emotional explosions could you take in one weekend, on how little sleep, before you broke? She was raw inside, the weepiness just under the surface, and she was having trouble shoving it back down.

Everything was *good,* though. Everything was brilliant. Rhys had said he loved her, and her worries about money had lifted like a cloud you'd had hanging over you for so long that you hadn't even known it was there. Suddenly, she could not only buy a van, she could buy a heat pump, too, and even replace the floor in her kitchen. She was still going to do the work herself, though. No need to go wild.

Except that Rhys wanted her to move in. That was a . . . complicated thought.

She should be ecstatic. Instead, all she wanted was a couple hours alone. She wanted to climb into bed and fall asleep watching a movie, and she couldn't. She *did* have both kids, Isaiah had been a bit intense himself yesterday, and she needed to pay attention. And then there was everything that had backed up on her this week. Laundry and cleaning and paperwork and grocery shopping and . . . everything. Tomorrow, she'd be up at five again, creating her business arrangements and making her deliveries, running all day. She didn't have time to fall apart, and she didn't want to cry in front of the kids. It scared Isaiah too much when she did, and it would scare Casey, too.

Tuesday. She'd get through all this, and on Tuesday, she'd take her break. Meanwhile, it was life, that was all. It was getting on with things. And if Rhys hadn't told her why he had to leave? She could tell him how that made her feel. Just not tonight.

"I believe," Hayden said, putting some muscle into his scrubbing, "that Mum's theme ran along the lines of you prostituting yourself. Which made me laugh, for the record. Does she even *know* you? Carried away by animal lust, now? *That,* I can imagine. There was something about a necklace, and you wearing it backward, which is apparently the new tramp stamp. I didn't quite get it, or maybe I zoned out. You could say she went on about it."

"Rhys brought me a pearl necklace home from Japan. Bought me a new dress and shoes, too, and took me to Jervois, which I'm sure Mum told you. I'm not sure if she thought I was just selling my body, or if I'd thrown my soul in there as well. Is she more upset that it's another rugby player with too much history, or that he's Dylan's brother? Since we're being crass anyway, I'm sure he's out-earned Dad for years. Also, if she thinks coaching is easy, she can think again."

"I'm not the one you have to convince," Hayden said. "Going back to this necklace . . . what are we talking about here?"

She sighed, finished brushing out the toilet, flushed, and didn't look at Hayden. "Oh, we're talking major league."

"Huh. Bit early for that, surely. And he bought your clothes? You didn't tell him about the money you found, then."

"Yeh. I did. The dress wasn't about the money." She hadn't told Hayden that Dylan was Casey's father, and she wasn't going to. Once enough people knew a secret, it didn't tend to stay secret.

"Ah," Hayden said. "Interesting. The man's got one hell of a power thing going on, doesn't he? Possessive, too, I'm guessing. It almost turns *me* on, and I bat for the other team. On the other hand, where does it put you? Also, what did he say about the account?"

"Not too much. That Dylan was a dickhead, basically."

"Of course," Hayden said, "Rhys hasn't covered himself with glory, either, in the personal-life department. Another thing Mum brought up. And on that note—why is Casey here? The game was last night. Surely he should have her today. Why are you letting him dump her on you? You know I never think Mum's right, but in this case? She could be right."

She wanted to leave the room. She didn't. "Rhys had to go to the South Island for the day. He'll be back tonight."

Hayden looked her over. "For what?"

"He didn't say. Just said he had to go, and could I take

Casey. And what's that look meant to be?"

"How do you spell 'unavailable'?"

"He's not. He's nothing like unavailable. You don't know." She was getting that thing again, like in the bank. In another minute, she'd have to put her head between her knees. "And I don't have any . . ." She had to blink. She had to *breathe.* "Any room left for any more of this. I can't. I love you, but I can't talk about it anymore."

Hayden looked at her for a long moment, and finally climbed out of the tub, put his arm around her, and held on, and she had to breathe those stupid tears back one more time. For once, there was no laughter in his voice when he said, "I'm torn here. On the one hand, we have Mum, telling me that Rhys is choosing your clothes and buying you inappropriate jewelry and making a fool of you. On the other hand, she's, well, Mum, and you're you. But Rhys has buggered off again and left you holding the bag, exactly like before. Do you think you may . . ." He hesitated. "Love too hard, maybe? Such a thing as asking for something yourself, you know. Such a thing as 'mutual.'" He smiled, but it looked a little pained. Something she should ask him about, probably. Just not today, because she had nothing left. "Or so I hear."

She wanted to tell him, and she didn't want to. That this morning, when she'd asked Rhys what was going on, he hadn't said nearly enough. "A couple things I need to do down there," he'd said instead.

A day earlier, she'd felt like they could see straight into each others' hearts, and now, his seemed all the way closed again. Hayden's questions were making the doubts rise, but if she didn't trust Rhys now, at the very first test, what was she doing here?

She didn't know. "I need a life," she finally said, "even if it's complicated. Even if it's scary. I need to live it anyway. And I love him."

It was raining in Nelson, too, the commuter jet rocking and rolling its way down, dropping out of the sky with a series of jolts that were causing outbursts from the passengers, and even the occasional shriek. Rhys had flown too often, himself, to worry much about a few bumps. He guessed a pilot would have more hours in the air, but that was about it. He figured if he didn't see flames and the oxygen masks didn't come down, he was all good. He looked outside and saw nothing but streaks like tearstains on the glass, thought again about how he could have done this part on the phone, and dismissed it.

*Harden up. It has to be done. Decide, do it, and move on. The deciding's done. It's time to do it, so you* can *move on.*

Another hired car, and this time, the kid behind the counter *did* recognize him. Hard to avoid, though, in Nelson. He posed for a photo with him, got the keys, and made the drive.

Thirty miles north. Past shops and businesses, quiet on a Sunday, the crossings in front of Auckland Point School empty instead of swarming with kids not looking where they were going.

His first day here, the start of the third term. Eight years old, wearing the same navy-blue shirt and shorts the kids would be wearing tomorrow, though his had been bought used from the school shop. Taking off his shoes the second he came out of the school gates, because he wasn't in Invercargill anymore.

He tried to remember how that day had felt starting out, if he'd been scared, and he couldn't. There had been no choice but to do it, so he'd done it. You could call that the theme of his childhood.

He hadn't gone home straight away most days, though, the way he was meant to, because as soon as he did, he'd be expected to mind Dylan and Te Rangi, and whatever other littlies were around. He'd headed with his mates down to the Maitai River Walkway instead, looking for treasures washed up on the rocks. Stripping off their uniforms and jumping off the bridge until somebody chased them off. Playing rugby barefoot in the park, running and tackling and passing and kicking until it got too dark to see, until mums would be putting their hands on their hips and getting loud. Not his mum, but some.

It hadn't all been bad, not a bit of it. Of course, when he'd got home at last, Nan would warm his backside with her jandal for being late, and Dylan would ask, "Can I go to school with you tomorrow, Rhys?"

"You aren't old enough to go to school. You're a baby," he'd snap. And feel exactly the same frustration every time at the hurt in his brother's face.

Eventually, Dylan had quit asking. He couldn't remember when that had happened.

The landscape changed, and there were rain-soaked orchards and vineyards outside the windows now, the apples and pears and grapes harvested and the workers gone on to other jobs for the winter. The fishermen would still be out, though. Rain and wind didn't matter to the fish.

Ten minutes more, and he was pulling up outside The Sprig & Fern in Motueka. At least he'd be able to eat this time. There was no situation where Te Rangi would think, *Nah, too tense to eat.* Not happening.

His cousin had said, when Rhys had rung up, "Come to the house instead, cuz. Everybody will want to see you, and nobody'll be out on the boats on a Sunday. Come for the afternoon, and we'll have a proper boil-up."

Rhys had said, "Not this time, bro. I'd rather talk to you alone. We'll do it at the pub."

Te Rangi had laughed, as usual. "Sounds ominous. But OK, if you're buying."

His cousin was already sitting at a wooden table by the wood stove, drinking beer from a pint glass, but at sight of Rhys, he got up, hongi'd him, then grasped him in a tight hug.

When he brought Casey down here, she'd change her mind that Rhys was Maui. Te Rangi's tattoo went down his arm all the way to the wrist and spilled over half his barrel chest, his hair curled below his shoulders, and he had a voice like thunder. A laugh like it, too.

"Good to see you," he said, clapping Rhys on the back. "You're looking good, bro. Fit, as usual."

Rhys had to grin. "And you're getting fatter."

"Nah." Te Rangi punched himself in the belly. "That's ballast. Good for cranking the nets up, eh." Another laugh. "Got you a beer already. That's a start for you."

Rhys considered declining it. He didn't. He had an hour and a half before he had to leave to catch the plane back to Auckland. He carefully *didn't* think, *I need a beer.* That way lay weakness. "Hang on," he said. "Let me order a burger. Want one?"

"I won't say no."

"Crispy potatoes?"

"You know me too well."

When he came back, Te Rangi said, "So. You flew down for an hour, during the season. I'm thinking that's because you've got something to say."

"Something to ask, more like." Rhys turned his pint glass in his hand and looked down at the foam, then back at his cousin. "And I'm thinking you know what."

"Nah, mate," Te Rangi said. "I never was much chop at guessing." Still genial, but awareness in the brown eyes. He wasn't a fool.

"Dylan," Rhys said. "And Casey."

"Casey," Te Rangi said slowly. "Don't know any Caseys."

"His daughter."

Around them, locals chatted and laughed, and the fire was warm on Rhys's back, but he barely noticed.

"Ah," Te Rangi finally said, no laughter in his eyes this time. "That Casey."

"Yeh." Rhys did take a pull at his beer, then. A long one. "Her mum died. She's got no whanau in the States."

"Oh. Huh. That's rough. I reckon we'd better find somebody to take her, then. Ari and Terina have been having some trouble having a second. Waited too long, maybe, but he's out on the boats every day now, earning all right. They've got a wee house out near Riwaka. Or there's me. I'd have to ask Nia. Not sure how keen she'll be at the start, since we've got the oldest nearly out of the house and the others not far behind, but whanau comes first, eh. You and I have some debt to pay along those lines, I reckon."

"We do," Rhys said. "But nobody has to take her. I already did. I've got her, and I'll be keeping her."

Silence for a long, long minute, and then Te Rangi said, "Dylan told you after all, then. That's good."

"No. He didn't. First I found out was my lawyer ringing me up, saying there was this girl in Chicago, and my name was on the acknowledgment of paternity. Witnessed by Te Rangi Walton."

Te Rangi sighed, took a swallow of beer, and raised a beefy shoulder. "Yeh, cuz. I did. Somebody needed to. Better than not having her provided for at all, I thought."

"And you didn't think," Rhys said, knowing his voice was too harsh but unable to make it be anything else, "that I ought to know. Even when Dylan fell ill. Even after he died."

Te Rangi's gaze sharpened. "He had her looked after, though."

"No. He didn't. Even less than he had Zora and Isaiah looked after. Why would you think anything else?"

"I asked him, though." Te Rangi's genial face was troubled at last. "When I went up to see him, when he fell ill. Asked him if she was set, and he told me he was going to see to it."

"When did he ever keep his promises?"

The words hung there between them, a young fella brought over the burgers and left again, and Te Rangi still didn't speak.

Rhys waited, and finally, his cousin said slowly, "He didn't leave anything for her, then."

"No. And you should've told me, so *I* could've seen to it. Her mum wasn't too well off. She died running across the street at night to get to work. They put Casey in foster care."

Te Rangi closed his eyes. "Shit," he said quietly. "Sorry, mate."

The rage that had boiled up started to settle, and Rhys breathed some, picked up his burger, and said, "Never mind. I've got her now. But I need to know who you told." He took a bite, and Te Rangi did the same. Sometimes, you needed a minute to regroup.

"I didn't tell anybody," his cousin said when he'd finished chewing. "Dylan didn't want you to know, and if I'd told anybody, you'd have known. Nobody's going to keep a secret like that."

"Nobody but you."

"Could be I owe you."

Rhys nearly winced. "You don't owe me." The words came out rough. He couldn't help it.

"Cuz." Te Rangi's hand came out to grip his shoulder. "Yeh, I do. Made the tea enough times, didn't you. Looked after us as well as you could. Set an example, too, you could say. My dad's worthless, and yours wasn't too flash. I've done better, and if you went to get Casey, seems to me that you have, too."

The burger was sticking in Rhys's throat. Something about the tightness in his chest, maybe. He nodded and focused on swallowing. On getting it together, because he was dangerously near the edge. He didn't go over that edge anymore, but he was very nearly doing it now.

"Does Zora know?" Te Rangi asked.

"Yeh. Isaiah doesn't, and neither does Casey. I needed to make sure nobody else did, because otherwise, I'd need to tell both of them. Better it comes from me, eh."

"No worries. You don't have to tell anybody, because I didn't."

Rhys nodded.

"You're wondering why he used your name in the first place," Te Rangi said. "Because of Zora, of course, even though you were about to be married yourself. I mentioned that, and he said, 'It's not going to come out. He's never going to know.' Hard to see how that could be true. I pointed that out. All the kid had to do was to look her dad's name up, then look *you* up, and, bang, you'd know, and so would Victoria. What he *didn't* say was that if you found out, you'd handle it, like you've handled everything else. Downside to being so bloody good at life, eh." His face changed. "Hang on. What about Victoria?"

"I saw her today," Rhys said. "I told her."

Te Rangi laughed, and it was so unexpected, Rhys jumped. "Nah, cuz. It's just—what a shit day, eh. You lose the game last night, and you've got to come down the next day in the pissing rain and tell your wife that you've got a kid you never mentioned? From a hookup you *also* never mentioned? Yeh, that's a shit day." He lifted the burger and saluted Rhys with it. "At least the kai's good."

Some of the tension inside loosened, and Rhys had to laugh himself. It was the first time he'd done that today, for sure. "That wasn't all I said. I also told her I was planning to marry Zora. That went over well."

# ka kite ano

The rain eased up some on the drive back to Nelson, at least.

Rhys had always had an engine that wouldn't quit. Now, though, it was sputtering. His arms and legs felt heavy, and his eyes strained against the grayness of the day.

Back to the airport. An hour and a half to Auckland, and another half an hour's drive when he got there. A few more hours, and nothing hard to do. Get home, that was all. Home to Zora's, first, and then taking Casey home and putting her to bed. Reading the dinosaur book.

Doing the job right.

Nearly there, now. Past the school again, and the shops, and the businesses. The left turn onto Quarantine Road was barely a kilometer ahead when he took a right instead, onto Songer Street.

*It'll take a few minutes,* he thought, taking the quick left onto Seaview Road. His heart was beating faster now, his hands tensing on the wheel again, and he relaxed them with an effort. *You can do a few minutes. One step at a time.*

The walk across the grass was wet, and the rain dampened his hair and ran in streaks down his face. He walked along a row and found the spot. Funny, he'd thought as a kid, that you had an address here. That you had neighbors.

Three headstones in a row.

*Manaia Louise Fletcher*

*Rest in peace*

His Nan. Gone too soon, probably from the stress of

raising three kids, then four of her mokopuna as well. Not enough money, and not enough time. Nothing but doing her best. It hadn't been as much as they'd all needed, maybe. It had still been her best.

He crouched down and ran his hand over the rough edge at the top of the polished granite stone, barely big enough for her name and the dates. He rubbed it gently and remembered the gentle kiss of the sun, the sparkle on the wave tips and the vibrant green of the grass on the day they'd laid her here. Like the earth and sea were welcoming her home.

He'd been eighteen that day, newly contracted to the Brisbane Broncos, thrown off whatever balance he'd had at the time by more money than he'd ever realized you could make. Drinking too much after every game, trying to run away from the gripping fear that all of this would vanish as suddenly as it had appeared, that he wouldn't be enough after all, that he would fail.

The next one, no bigger.

*Tane Hau Fletcher*

*Do not go gentle into that good night*

Six years later, back here again, burying his dad. Flying with his body from Brisbane, his heart no lighter than the coffin. Bringing his father home to the whanau.

Tane had brushed off the persistent cough with a "Nah, I'm fine," until his back had begun to ache. Until the day when he'd fallen at work, his legs refusing to hold him up anymore. Even then, he'd fought, refusing to go down until the bitter end.

He hadn't been the best dad, and he hadn't been a gentle one. But he'd been the hardest worker Rhys had ever seen.

After the third day of his dad's tangi, when the final haka had been performed and the sun had set, he'd gone to Mapua Wharf with Dylan and Te Rangi and some of the other cousins. They'd sat on the end of the pier, looking out over the dark water, and he'd tried to feel something. Anything. And hadn't managed it. His dad was the one who'd died, but Rhys was the one whose soul seemed to be sputtering out, unable to find a resting place. A sea bird who had flown too long, whose wings were battered by the storm, whose muscles ached with the effort of holding himself up, with no land in sight. Nothing out there but towering swells and angry troughs of gray water that wanted to pull you down into the depths and drown you.

"Never thought a tough old bugger like that could die that fast," Te Rangi finally said.

"Yeh," Rhys said, and drank down half of his third beer at a go.

"Good thing we don't smoke, eh, Drago," Dylan said. "Else we'd be worried. Course, nothing bad ever happens to you anyway. Probably be me. A charmed life, that's you. Getting lucky in the lucky country."

There'd been a feverish quality to his brother that night. Nineteen, moving up himself, but laughing too loud, drinking too much, with not enough to hold onto, like a rice-paper kite that had caught fire, going too high.

Rhys looked up at the stars above the dark water, listened to the voices, the laughter, and the lap of the waves against the pier, and thought, *Time to see if I can still play Union, maybe. Time to see if I can come back.* The Broncos had won the NRL Grand Final, the box was ticked, and Rhys's star was on the rise. Professionally, at least. Personally? Not so much. A fresh start sounded good. Better for Dylan, and better for him, too.

When the deal was signed and he rang his brother to tell him, Dylan was silent for so long, Rhys thought he'd lost the connection.

"Still there, bro?" he asked.

"Yeh," Dylan said. "You could've told me before I moved to the Blues."

*You didn't have much choice,* Rhys didn't say. Dylan had had too mixed a season with the Crusaders. Brilliant one week, strangely absent the next, unable to string together more than two good games in a row. "Could be we both needed a change," he decided to say. "Second chance can be good."

The third tombstone.

*Dylan Ihaka Fletcher*
*Into the sunshine*

Ihaka. "He will laugh." And Dylan had, always. Lighting up a room or a crowd as easily as turning on a lamp, like that rice-paper kite flying high. The skills that dazzled you, and the grin on his face when he'd scored a try. He'd inked Zora's name on his left wristband, closest to his heart, before every game, and after every one of those brilliant tries, he'd kissed it.

He'd fallen so frustratingly short so many times, or maybe it was something else. Maybe he'd never been able to grab hold of the best of himself for long enough, set it down firmly enough, to build on a solid foundation.

Rhys had never understood him, but he'd loved him, and he'd protected him as best he could. Imperfectly, always. But he'd tried.

This stone was larger, because it had finally dawned on Rhys that he could pay for better, and that it might be good for Zora and Isaiah if he did. Or maybe that wasn't it at all. Maybe he'd needed to know that he'd done his best for his brother, this one last time.

His hair was dripping with rain now, his trousers and shoes soaked, as he crouched at the head of the grave and traced the winding path of pebbles placed amidst the nearly white granite from the bottom on up to the top, Dylan's rocky journey through his too-short, blazingly-bright life. He touched the albatross carved into the V-shaped cutout in the top of the stone, where that path ended, running his fingers over the bird's body. It was soaring already, its great wings outstretched, held to the stone only by their tips. Leaving the stony path behind and flying free, where his feet wouldn't be caught up by obstacles, where he could sail across the tryline with a smile on his face, could kiss the name on his wrist and know that he was home.

Into the sunshine.

Rhys had left his brother alone, the thing Dylan had feared most. And then he'd come back.

Now, though? What was he doing now?

Was he taking Dylan's wife and son, or was he taking care of them? You could see it either way. A double-edged sword. Or like Tumatauenga, who was the god of war, but also the god of hunting, of fishing, of cooking. The provider, and the conquerer.

You could only be the best of who you were. You couldn't be somebody else.

*He hono tangata e kore e motu; ka pa he taura waka e motu.*

*One can cut a canoe rope, but the bond between two hearts can never be severed.*

"Haere ra, bro," he said, feeling the prick of tears behind his eyelids, then a few escaping, and not caring. Nobody to see, not out here. Nobody to know. "Ka kite ano."

*Goodbye, brother. I'll see you later.*

He was only ten minutes from the airport, but he wasn't going to catch that plane. He'd get the next one instead.

♡♡♡

It was well after eight, and Rhys still wasn't back. He'd said six-thirty, and then he'd texted that it would be later. Right now, Zora was reading *Horton Hatches the Egg* aloud on the couch. Casey was listening, and Isaiah was pretending he wasn't. Zora had already given Casey her bath, and in another ten minutes, she was going to put her into Isaiah's bottom bunk.

She finished the book, and Casey sighed and said, "I like this book very much, because Horton was always faithful, one hundred percent. He kept his promise and sat on the egg, even though the baby bird wasn't really his. And then at the end, it was, and he got to keep it."

Zora smoothed her hand over the girl's hair, bent to kiss her head, and said, "He did keep his promise. Elephants never forget, that's what they say. And elephant families stay together all their lives. A mother elephant stays with her daughters, and her daughters never forget her, even after she dies. If they go past another elephant's bones, they stop and touch them gently with their trunks to say goodbye."

"Only the females stay, though," Isaiah said. Not just playing with Legos, then. "The males go off on their own. That's because you can't mate with your family. Like, cousins can't. Or brothers and sisters. It's if you share blood. Which doesn't mean *real* blood. It means your family."

"What's 'mate'?" Casey asked.

"Having sex," Isaiah said. "To make babies. You can't make babies with your family. That's why the males have to leave."

Well, that had escalated quickly.

"True," Zora said. She was about to say, "Well! Bedtime!" But Casey's head had gone up, her entire body had gone still, and then she was running to the kitchen in her bare feet, flinging the door open.

A car engine turning off, the slam of a car door. And Rhys's deep voice.

Elephants "heard" things through their feet that their ears couldn't, and that was how Zora felt. Rhys's voice seemed to come all the way through the soles of her feet and up her legs to lodge inside her. Belly deep.

She was standing up when he came into the lounge. He had Casey wrapped around him, her head on his shoulder, and he looked . . .

Exhausted.

She'd never seen him look like that. It tilted her world on its axis, and she was having trouble catching her breath.

"Hey," she said softly, then went to him, wrapped her arms around him and Casey, and pressed her lips to the spot at the base of his throat where his pulse beat.

He bent his head, kissed her mouth, and said, "Good to be back. Thanks for taking her."

He was wet. His trousers were damp, and so was his shirt. The skin of his arms, which was normally turned up a degree or two hotter than hers, felt cool under her hands. She said,

"I think Casey should sleep here tonight."

"No," Casey protested. "Because we need to shut up the bunnies."

"I'll shut up the bunnies," Rhys said. "Could be that Auntie Zora's right. It's late. I'll come early in the morning, so you and Isaiah don't have to wake up in the dark, how's that? I'll cook the brekkie, and bring you your uniform."

"But—" Casey started to say.

"Your dad's very tired, I think," Zora said, keeping it calm. Nothing wrong with kids realizing that their parents had feelings, too. "Everybody needs to go to bed early tonight, including me, because I *do* have that five o'clock start tomorrow."

"I can get up and help you," Isaiah said. "I always get up. I'm used to it."

She was about to say, *No, love, sleep in this time.* But there was too much intensity in his face. She wasn't the only one who had too many emotions today. It was practically hanging in the air. She said, "You need some Mum time, maybe."

"Yes," Isaiah said. "And I'm good at picking out flowers."

"You are. All right. Rhys can come over to stay with Casey, but you and I will go to the flower market." She was going to have to carve out more one-on-one time with him, somehow. Another thing to juggle, but it had to be done, or they were going to have explosions.

Surely, though, explosions were better than resentments held inside. You could move on from explosions, once you'd picked up the pieces. Resentments were like poison in the water supply. She was too tired to deal with this one tonight, but in the morning, they'd work something out.

"Sounds like a plan," Rhys said. "There's one thing I need to do before bedtime, though." He sat on the couch like he needed to, set Casey down beside him, and told Isaiah, "Come over here, mate."

Isaiah had been hovering slightly out of frame, like he wasn't sure what his part was. Now, he came over to the couch and hesitated.

"Come sit by me," Rhys said. "You too, Zora. I've got something I need to say. Something I need to do."

She said, "Rhys. Maybe tomorrow."

"No," he said. "It needs to be tonight." He might be more tired than she'd ever seen him, but his eyes were steady. He reached into his pocket and pulled something out. Another flax kete, but this time, he was pressing it into Isaiah's hand. "I went to see your dad's grave today," he told him. "In Nelson, at Seaview Cemetery. Near the place he grew up, the place he went to school. It was peaceful. You can't really see the sea, but you can see the grass and the trees and the sky, and you can feel how close the sea is. Your dad loved Nelson. His favorite place."

"I remember the cemetery," Isaiah said. "We went last year, after they made his tombstone."

"That's right," Rhys said. "We both did. D'you remember what his tombstone has on it?"

"A bird," Isaiah said.

"An albatross." Another reach into his pocket, and Rhys was thumbing his phone, showing Isaiah the photo, and Zora, too. An image that still made her heart twist and the tears rise. The path of stones, and the white albatross spreading his wings. "A sea bird."

"I know," Isaiah said. "It has the largest wingspan of any bird. It's so big that it can fly for hours without even flapping its wings, and it hardly ever has to land."

"That's right," Rhys said. "I thought about that, about that bird flying forever, and about your dad, and then I went and found your pendant. Made of greenstone from Tasman Bay, like his was. Open it and see."

Isaiah worked the ties, and Zora helped him until he was tipping the thing into his hands.

A long, narrow shape like a rounded, extended adze, carved of a vibrant, translucent piece of jade that shone with light.

"Roimata," Rhys said. "Tears of the albatross."

Isaiah held it tentatively. Doubtfully. "That sounds sad."

"Not sad. Healing and comfort and positive energy. Brings you strength and centering, that's the idea, when things get noisy and it's hard to concentrate. That's what your dad will have called on when he ran out in a rugby game, because he knew that strength isn't enough. It's your focus that matters, and knowing where to put your strength. It's a meditation stone. Any time you need to quiet your mind, when the world gets too loud and too busy, you can put your hand on this and go inside. You can remember that an albatross can fly for hours on a single flap of its wings, and that you can do that, too. It's all in knowing how."

Isaiah was running his thumb along the smooth, cool surface, up and down. "I think I can feel it." He looked up at Zora and asked, "Can you feel it, Mum?"

She laid her thumb onto the narrow shape beside his, put her other arm around him, and said, "Yeh. I can. Feels strong."

"It's not magic," Isaiah said, "because there isn't really magic. There's only science, and the things we don't understand yet. It's just a symbol."

"You're right, mate," Rhys said. "But symbols have power."

$$\heartsuit\heartsuit\heartsuit$$

*Fifteen minutes,* Rhys thought. You could always do fifteen more minutes. If you couldn't, you could do one more minute, and then you could do another one, until the whistle blew.

He tucked Casey into bed and kissed her goodnight, and she wound her arms around his neck and said, "I'm very glad you came home."

"So am I," he said, and meant it. Then he stood up, put a hand on Isaiah's arm, and said, "Night, mate."

"Goodnight, Uncle Rhys," the boy said. "Thank you for my pendant. I feel like it's a little bit from my dad."

*One more minute.* He could do it, even with his throat closing up and the tears too close. "That's because it is."

Finally, he was shutting the door quietly behind him, going out to the lounge, and finding Zora. She was turning the gas stove on, which was still just pressing the rocker switch, and turning the overhead light off. Even though it wasn't really cold enough for that, it felt good.

"Did you get dinner?" she asked.

"Had a burger with my cousin. Te Rangi. I'll get some eggs at home."

"You went to Motueka."

"Yeh. I did." He checked her out. "You look tired."

She laughed and pushed her hair back with a weary hand. "So do you. Do you want a beer? Or want me to fix those eggs?"

"Already had a beer. With the burger. What I want is to sit on the couch with you."

"You're cold, though. When did you get wet?"

"When didn't I? Nah. I'm good."

She put a throw over them all the same, when she'd curled on the couch beside him. When he had his arm around her, and she had her hand on his chest, and it was what he'd told Isaiah. When you could fly for hours on a single flap of your wings, because the weight had shifted, and you were perfectly balanced again. He stroked a hand over her hair, then did it again, felt the softness between his fingers, and thought, *It's good to be home.*

"Do you want to know about it?" he asked.

"Yes. I do."

So he told her. About Victoria, first, about her anger, and her pain. "I hated it," he finished.

"But you did it."

"I had to."

A movement against his shoulder that was her laugh. "No, Rhys. You didn't. And you did it anyway. There was no good way to say that. No good way to hear it. You did the best you could."

His throat closed a little more tightly, and his chest ached.

"And then you went to Nelson," she said. "And to Motueka."

"I needed to know who else Te Rangi had told about Casey."

Tension in her shoulders, now. "And who had he told?"

"Nobody." He felt her relax, like it mattered as much to her as it did to him. "So that's good. He didn't know that Dylan hadn't taken care of Casey. He'd promised he would."

She sighed. "I wish I could be surprised. I wish he would have, except that if he had—would we ever have known about her?"

His hand stopped moving. "You're right. When the wheels finally lifted off tonight, I thought, *Thank God. Going home.* And I meant it. It was a . . ." He blew out a breath. "A hard day."

"Yeh. For me, too."

That took him a second. "Because I didn't tell you. *Shit.* I just thought . . . I wasn't sure . . ."

His hand was shaking on her shoulder. He tried to hold it still, and he couldn't. Not even close. It was a leaf hanging on a tree, long since turned brown, about to fall, and you could no more stop the leaves from falling than you could stop the tide from going out. Than you could stop death. He got a hand up to his eyes and squeezed them shut, and that didn't work, either. His chest was too tight, and the tears wouldn't stay inside.

An ugly, ragged sound that was a sob, painful, feeling like it was piercing his chest. Another one, and there the tears were, forcing their way past his eyelids, past his hand, and down his cheeks, like he had no control at all.

The dam burst. He wrenched his arm from around Zora's shoulders, got his elbows onto his knees and his hands over his face, and cried some more. Washed away in the flood, and not even able to swim. Going under.

Darkness. Panic. And something else. Zora's gentle hands on him. Zora's voice, calling to him.

"Rhys. You're OK. That's OK. You did so well." Her hands cradling his head, her lips on his forehead. Seeing his tears, and letting them fall. Nothing frantic in her. Nothing but peace. "I'm so proud of you," she said. "I love you so much, and I've got you. It's going to be OK."

Zora, weaving a net for him with her hands and her voice, her softness and her strength. Giving him a place to catch himself, a place to land.

Bringing him home.

# family ties

A couple weeks later, a few things had happened.

The Blues had drawn a game against the Hurricanes, then won one against the Rebels in Canberra, and were lying third on the New Zealand table, one point below the 'Canes. Not the spot you'd choose. On the other hand, Rhys had left Casey with Zora and Isaiah again, and they were all in his house, which made him feel about a hundred percent better.

Also, as of today, he was divorced.

You didn't have to be present for it to happen, which was fortunate, as he was in Brisbane, preparing for the game against the Reds in two days, and he couldn't afford to be distracted.

He wasn't thinking about either thing right now, because he was reading with Casey. On this trip, he'd come up with the somewhat brilliant idea to get himself an electronic copy of *The Runaway Bunny,* so he could read it to her last thing at night, and they could turn the pages together.

He finished the story, and she said, "I like the part where the mother bunny is the wind the best, because the little bunny's ears are the sails on a sailboat, but they're still pink, because they're the inside part." She was sitting cross-legged in her PJs on her princess bed with Marshmallow in her lap, and she lifted the bunny's ears gently to show him. "See?"

"Mm," he said. "The little bunny in the story looks like Marshmallow, a bit."

"Except Marshmallow's cuter."

He considered saying, "He ought to be. He cost a hundred dollars," but he didn't. Instead, he said, "Time to go to sleep, then, and you can imagine being the sailboat, with your bunny ears being blown across the harbor by the wind."

"Because you're the wind," she said. "But if I get a bad dream, you're very far away."

"Good thing I've got heaps of breath," he said. "Enough to reach all the way across the Tasman."

Yes, it was silly, but she'd like to hear it.

"And you have a very loud voice." She *did* want to hear it.

"I do. Right now, it's telling you to give the phone to Auntie Zora so you can go to sleep. I'll call you tomorrow."

She got off the bed and put Marshmallow back in his cage, her hands gentle, giving each of the bunnies a stroke, and then she headed out the door and down the stairs.

He needed to get that staircase replaced. If he and Zora had a baby, the open steps wouldn't be one bit safe. He didn't even like watching Casey on them.

A regular staircase, definitely. With carpet. Not just for the baby. What if Zora were pregnant, awkward with it, and she slipped?

Finn would know a builder. Sure to. That was how Rhys had found the roofer. He was going to get it done straight away, pulling strings if he had to. If you wanted your life to change? You changed it.

"Can you read the Horton book tomorrow?" Casey asked. "Not the one where he hears a Who. The one where he sits on the egg. Maybe you can get it on your phone, too, and we can read it together."

"I'll see what I can do. *If* you go to bed now."

"I *am,*" she said.

He had to smile. "Night, monkey."

"Night."

He lost the image of her, and saw Zora's face instead.

"Hey," she said. Just that one word, and the churned-up pieces of him were settling again. "I'll come kiss you goodnight in a minute," she told Casey, and he waited while Casey said something inaudible.

"OK," Zora said. "I'm back. Hi."

"Hi, sweetheart. Good day?"

"Not bad at all. I got another customer for tomorrow. Good news, eh."

"It is. What flowers are you doing?"

"Have to see what looks good at the market, but I'm thinking dahlias and roses in shades of apricot, maybe, with eucalyptus. Autumn colors."

"Send me a photo."

"I will."

She hesitated, and he said, "You want to ask me about the divorce, and you're wondering if it's sensitive. You don't have to be sensitive. It's me. And, yeh, it's done."

"Oh. Good. I don't know how you do that, and from a distance. It's very scary. I don't know why in the world you think you aren't sensitive, either. How are you feeling?"

"Honestly? Wondering how Vic's doing, I guess, mostly."

"Relieved, probably. Sad that it didn't work. Hating you. In proportions I can't guess. If it were me—eating ice cream from the carton or drinking wine, or quite possibly both at once. She's probably not doing either."

"Probably more along the 'hating' lines. And you're right about her with the wine and ice cream, though the night of your divorce could be an exception." It was odd that he could talk to Zora about this, but he was glad. "It's strange not to be able to ask her. To know I'm the last person who could make anything better. It's been two years, and I'm no part of her life anymore, other than the part she's leaving behind, but it's strange anyway."

"To go from sharing a name and a house," she said, "having your ring on her finger and hers on yours, sharing— whatever you did share with her, to her not wanting to hear your name at all."

"Yeh. It's odd. Seeing the document on my phone was . . . I guess I'll stay with 'odd.' Hollow, maybe that's the word. I was thinking that I can't afford to be distracted, but there you are. I'm distracted anyway."

"Rhys." She laughed, but it was gentle. "Of course you are. How could you not be? Maybe let yourself be sorry tonight. You can go back to not being distracted tomorrow."

Which wasn't exactly how it happened.

♡♡♡

It came from Finn, first.

Rhys was in the hotel gym, getting in a quick workout before breakfast, and Finn was suddenly standing over him as he lay on his back on the weight bench, doing triceps extensions.

"Hey," Rhys said, lifting the heavy dumbbells overhead, then lowering them behind him as slowly as he could, welcoming the effort.

"You may want to sit up," Finn said. "Here, I've got these." He disappeared behind Rhys and took the dumbbells from him.

Rhys sat up. You knew in a voice when it was bad. In a face.

"What happened?" he asked. This wasn't somebody's injury worsening overnight, or somebody coming down with the flu. This was bad news from home. Somebody's dad, or worse. Somebody's baby.

Finn held out a newspaper. Oh. That meant it was the other thing: A scandal. Nothing like the Aussie media for that, and Friday, the day before the game? Yeh, that was the timing.

Well, a scandal wasn't the worst. Nobody would have died. Somebody's marriage might take a turn for the worse, though.

He looked at the headline, and then at the photos.

*Not the worst,* he told his sinking heart. *The other shoe dropping, that's all. Sooner it's done, sooner we're moving past it.*

Four photos, laid out as a sort of "This is your life" in pictures. The first, cropped from a shot of the All Blacks lined up for the national anthem, showed Rhys beside Dylan, their arms around each other's backs. Rhys was looking unshaven and brutal, and Dylan was looking handsome and noble. Which was fine.

The second was Dylan and Zora with a two-year-old Isaiah. Isaiah sitting on Dylan's shoulders, Dylan with his arm around Zora, and Zora laughing, shoving her hair back with one hand, looking pretty and happy and extremely short.

Also fine. Except not.

The third was of Rhys with both kids at the Blues' Family Day, before the game with the Hurricanes. He was standing with a hand on Isaiah's head, and with Casey on his hip, her arms around his neck and both kids wearing Blues jerseys.

Newsworthy, maybe, but not in the Crisis Zone.

And the fourth? That was an image from seventeen years ago, the one they'd probably print with his obituary. Coming out of a door plainly marked *Ladies,* tucking his shirt into his trousers.

*Thou shalt not covet?* the headline said, and in smaller letters beneath, *Family ties: Rhys Fletcher comes home to the Blues, a long-lost daughter, and his brother's wife.*

Brilliant.

He read the first lines, wondering as always why anybody cared. Better than watching *Neighbours,* he guessed, because the people were real. More or less.

*Rhys "Drago" Fletcher, the 72-cap All Black newly appointed to coach the Auckland Blues after stints in Japan and France, comes to the job with baggage. Fletcher, who rocketed to early stardom and a Grand Final win with the Brisbane Broncos, saw his NRL career marred by numerous sex scandals, culminating in a drunken incident in a restaurant toilet with Poppy Harburton, then married to his teammate, Gerard Ailes. The ensuing drama saw Fletcher returning to New Zealand and the Crusaders the following year, where his storied career . . .*

"Blah blah," Rhys muttered. "And so forth." He scanned down the column to see what else they had. *Fletcher, whose divorce from Christchurch beauty Victoria Carrington was final yesterday, has long maintained that his drinking, and his exploits off the field, are in the past. When he returned to his New Zealand roots this year after the dissolution of his seven-year marriage, however, he brought with him a six-year-old daughter who had previously been living in the United States with her mother, a Chicago waitress whom Fletcher encountered during a brief stay in the city with the All Blacks.*

*In addition to his newly acquired family, Fletcher appears to have taken on yet another one, being seen in recent weeks at various Auckland eateries with his brother Dylan's widow, often holding hands across the table.*

*Dylan Fletcher, a Blues star and All Black himself, was often overshadowed in life by his elder brother. Even after his death, it would seem, the rivalry continues.*

And on in the same vein. "Right," Rhys said, and handed the paper back to Finn. "About what you'd expect." His heart was beating harder, but he'd been working out.

"Aiming for distraction before the game, that's all," Finn said.

"What else is in there?" Rhys asked. "I need to finish this workout and get a shower."

"Rubbish piece with a psychologist. Headline is *Sport, drink, sex, and poaching on your teammate's turf: When does cheating cross the line?* And another one called, *Role models? Why sportsmen aren't always the best choice.* Which either of us could have written. 'Because they're young, dumb, male, and paid too much,' is the answer. You need to add a few hundred more words to sell papers, though, I reckon."

"Has it been picked up in En Zed yet?" Rhys asked.

"Not yet, mate. Too early in the morning. It will be, though. You may want to ring Zora after breakfast."

"You think?" Rhys tried a smile.

"Better if it had come out while you were home," Finn said. "And not on the day before the game, as far as the team's concerned. It was always going to come out, though. I can't think it's news to Zora, either."

"No," Rhys said. "We've discussed it. Only a matter of time. Anyway, she knows about sport, drink, and sex."

"Except," Finn said, "that they're talking about the wrong brother. And that you can't tell them so."

# strength class 100

He faced the squad the only way he knew how. Head-on.

He waited until everybody had turned up to breakfast, then stood at the front of the room and said, "Right, then. Some of you will have seen the papers, and some won't. Short version: I have a daughter, Casey. You met her at Family Day. Her mum was American, and she wasn't my ex-wife. I'm also seeing my brother Dylan's widow, Zora. Some of you played with Dylan. I expect you'll be asked about him today, and about me. You can say whatever you like in response. I loved my brother, but he's been gone for two years. Zora and I are planning on getting married, though I'd rather you didn't mention that one to the press, as we've got a couple of kids to think about. Otherwise? Whatever you want to say—go on and say it. To whoever asks."

*About loyalty,* he didn't say. *Or betrayal.*

He'd slept with his teammate's wife. Well, not "slept" with. Hooked up in the toilets with. Not his proudest moment.

In fact, his lowest moment. When his dad had been dying, and he'd gone well and truly off the rails. The bad year. The reason he'd left the NRL, and Australia. The reason he'd changed his life. How did you look your teammates in the eye after something like that? Worse—how did you look in the mirror?

With difficulty, that was how. With shame. And the knowledge that your life had to change, because you couldn't stay where you were. The moment when you knew for sure

400

that all you wanted to be from here on out was a man to be respected. A man with some mana.

Not, for example, a man who cheated on his fiancée. Or a man who betrayed both his wife and his brother in one go. Call that a twofer.

A scrape of a chair, and Hugh stood up. "I've got something to say now," he said.

"Go ahead," Rhys said, and braced for it.

Hugh looked around the room and let it build for a minute. A good skipper, and a family man. Like Finn. Rhys had no idea what was going to come out of his mouth.

"The answer's the same, boys," Hugh said, "no matter what question they ask you. 'I stand behind the coach.' And as far as I'm concerned, here in this room? Drago's got a daughter, and he's raising her. He's in love with a woman, and he's marrying her. That's it. Full stop. If you haven't done anything in your life that you regret—congratulations, I guess. I know I have. We've all got a story, and the history of it doesn't matter. What matters is how we're living the story now. They've put this out in Brisbane because this is where it hits Drago hardest, and they've done it today to distract us. They know where we are on the table, and that we need a win. That's no secret. They're trying to keep us from getting it by getting in our heads. It's up to us whether they succeed. It's what Drago says. You're switched on, or you're switched higher. We go out there today and switch on, and we go out there tomorrow and switch higher. We play the bloody best game we've got in us. We go out there and win, and we shut them up. End of story."

$\heartsuit\heartsuit\heartsuit$

It was five-thirty in the morning and still dark when Zora's phone rang. She picked it up and said, "Hey. We're just having toast before we head out to the flower market. Aren't you on your way to training?"

"Yeh," Rhys said. "I have about ten minutes. Put the camera on and sit with the kids a minute, would you?"

"O . . . OK," she said, and switched over.

Something was off. She saw it in his face right away. Something was wrong. He'd been nothing but sweet last night, despite the divorce, or because of it. What could have happened in nine hours?

He said, "Normally, I'd tell Zora first, and she'd think of some clever way to talk to the two of you about it. She's good at explaining. We don't have time for that, though, and you may have questions for me, so I'll do my own explaining. There's going to be a story in the newspaper today, and your friends could say something at school."

"My friends don't read the newspaper," Isaiah said. "Well, my main friend is Ethan. He doesn't read the newspaper, though."

"My main friend is Esme," Casey said. "I don't think she *can* read the newspaper. It has a lot of really big words."

Rhys's face had lost some of its rigidity. "All right. Your friends won't read it in the newspaper, but they'll hear about it, because it'll be online."

"Ethan's mum doesn't let him go online," Isaiah said. "Except for a couple of games."

"Esme doesn't—" Casey started, but Zora said, "Wait, guys. Let's hear what it's about. It sounds like it could be gossip."

"Gossip is where people say mean things," Isaiah told Casey. "Sometimes they're true and sometimes they're not. It doesn't matter, not really. Mostly, they're just to be mean."

"Right," Rhys said. "This will be gossip, then. It's going to say Casey's my daughter, and that Zora is my girlfriend, and probably that I've had lots of girlfriends."

"Oh," Isaiah said. He and Casey looked at each other. "Except Mum *is* your girlfriend, because you kiss her all the time, and Casey *is* your daughter. So I don't see how that's mean."

"Not everybody knows it now," Rhys said. "And they

could say there's something wrong with your Mum being my girlfriend, because she was married to your Dad before."

"It isn't bad for your mum to be your uncle's girlfriend, though," Isaiah said, "if he's not your *real* uncle, like your mum's brother. Like elephants. You can't mate if you're the brother elephant, but if you came from a different elephant family, you can mate."

"This isn't about . . ." Rhys looked absolutely stumped. Zora should care about this—it sounded as if things were hitting the fan—but she had to laugh anyway.

"Uncle Rhys and I aren't elephants," she said, "and people *can* sometimes say mean things. I think Uncle Rhys is saying that if somebody asks you at school, you can just say, 'Yes, my mum is Uncle Rhys's girlfriend.'"

"And then we tell them he was a very famous All Black," Isaiah said. "Being an All Black is better than anything else, but being a famous one is the best. Like, if he was in a comic book, he would be strength class 100."

"It's not actually better than anything else," Rhys said. "It's more important to be a good person."

"But you *are* a good person," Casey said. "And so is Auntie Zora. You're both nice to animals and things. So I think if they say you're bad, I should punch them very hard."

"No punching," Rhys said. "Absolutely not."

"But if they say bad things about you," Casey argued, "I'll kind of *have* to punch them, because I'll be so mad that my brain will let go of my hand."

"No letting go." Rhys looked stern now, but at least he'd stopped looking tense. "Not an excuse. Tell your brain to keep hold of your hand. Here's what you do instead. You say that you already knew I was Auntie Zora's boyfriend, because we're in love."

"Eww," Isaiah said.

This time, Rhys was the one who laughed. "All right. You may not want to say that. Just say that you know we're going out, and it's OK with you. And then throw in whatever nice thing you want to say about me, if you like."

"But mostly the All Black part," Isaiah said.

"OK," Rhys said. "Mostly the All Black part. Whatever works. And Casey?"

"Yeah?"

"No punching."

♡♡♡

It was a truly lovely day.

Nothing like seeing your photo in the newspaper, reading a character assassination of the man you loved, and knowing every comments section would be full of discussion of his failings, without even having to look. Nothing like having five rugby WAGs, on opening their doors to you, giving you a hug and asking how you were doing. Nothing like having your mum call you, midway through your deliveries, to say, "I hate to say 'I told you so,' darling, but—I did tell you so. There's a chat show on TV right this minute talking about it. Whether you can date your late spouse's family member, and what effect it has on the kids. It can't be pleasant to be a conversational topic, especially when the topic is your morals."

"Which makes me wonder," Zora said, keeping her focus on navigating the streets of Mount Eden on a busy Friday afternoon, "why you're ringing me to tell me about it. What do you want me to do? Go into seclusion? Sorry, can't. I'm making deliveries. Break it off with Rhys? The damage is done, isn't it? Besides, I'm not doing it. Which would be because I'm in love with him." She didn't add, *And I'm marrying him,* because they had to tell the kids first, but she wanted to. She wanted the ring on her finger. She wanted to announce to the world that he was hers, and she was his, and to hell with what they thought of it. Casey wasn't the only fierce girl in the family.

"I'm just telling you—" her mum said, and then stopped, presumably because she couldn't work out a good version of what she was just telling her.

"Yeh," Zora said. "Exactly." She relaxed her legs, which were somehow gripping around the thigh area like that would help. "Rhys said weeks ago, when I said people would find out . . . uh . . ." She had to stop. What he'd actually said was, 'Fuck 'em.' She decided on, "He said, 'Bugger 'em.' That's more or less my planned approach. Want to help me do it?"

"Well, of course I'm doing it," her mum said, sounding cross. "What do you expect? And, really, Zora. That language isn't appropriate for him to be using with you."

"I'd better not tell you what he actually said, then." She had to laugh, it was all so ridiculous. "What do I care what people say, really? And I'm almost at my next stop. Listen, Mum. Want to come with Casey and me tomorrow to do some shopping? She needs winter clothes, and she's growing so fast. I've never shopped for a little girl before, and you were always so good at it. I need a few things for Isaiah, too, and you know he won't try on. He has a play date with his friend Ethan, though, and I don't have a wedding, so Casey and I are going to have a Girl's Day. Want to meet us in Newmarket at ten?"

It was flattery, maybe, but why not? Isaiah needed a relationship with his grandparents, Casey was part of her life now, and so was Rhys. You could stay stuck in the mire, or you could keep moving and get out of it.

She tried to explain it to Rhys that night, the first chance she'd had to talk to him alone. Of course, the first thing he said was, "You OK?"

"Yes. Of course."

"It was all over the news there, though," he said. "Can't have been pleasant."

"On the other hand," she said, "I'm not the one with a rugby game against fired-up opposition tomorrow, and it was probably good for business. I'm notorious, eh. I'll have to remember to thank my Mum for giving me such an unusual name. And thank myself for using my unusual name for the business."

"That can't really be how you feel." He sounded strong, as always, but tired, too. Rhys could stand up to anything. That didn't mean it was easy to do it. "Victoria said I was 'unavailable.' That's how you're sounding."

"Funny," she said, "Hayden said the same thing. You're not unavailable. You're the last thing from it. Look at you last night, and today. Look at you right now, for that matter."

"But you may be," he said. "I don't want to hear that you're fine, or that it's good for business. I want to hear the truth."

"Oh." That was a new thought. That *she* was unavailable? So intent on keeping up a good front that even he felt shut out? She blew out a breath, sat back against the pillows, and looked out at her glassy black reflection in the floor-to-ceiling glass of Rhys's bedroom. No help available there. It was going to have to come from inside.

"Right," she said. "It's this thing I thought today, then. That you and I have had this muddy spot in the road to get past on our way to the other side. We've stood there for a wee while now, staring at it, and now we're in it waist-deep, because there was no way around. If I have to be here, though, you're the man I want with me for it. If I lose my footing, you'll hold me up, and if I can't go any farther, you'll carry me. I know you'll haul me to safe ground if it takes your last breath to do it. Do you know how lucky I feel to know that?"

She'd thought that holding on today, getting through, was strength, and it was. But surely, it was also strength to admit that it hurt, to say that you could use some help. She said, "I want to keep on wading until we get to the other side, because it's beautiful over there. And I want to be with you. Even if it's muddy. Even if it's hard. I want to be with you."

It took him a few seconds, and when he finally answered, his voice wasn't much steadier than hers. "It *is* going to be beautiful. And you're right. That's what I'd do. I'm here to hold you, and I'm here to stay."

"It's not anybody else's life," she told him. "It's ours. I'd rather be with the right man and have people tell me he's the wrong one, than be with the wrong man and have everyone think he's the right one. I've done that. It was rubbish. You're the right man. It doesn't matter if nobody else knows it. *I* know it. I found out for sure that I don't need the flash house or the flash life to be happy. I don't need anybody to envy me, either. They can feel sorry for me if they like, or think I'm a tramp, or whatever the latest thought is. They don't know me, and they don't know you. I don't need them, but I do need Isaiah, and Casey, too. And I need you."

A long, long moment, and then he said, "I want to marry you."

"Well, she said, "ditto."

# trick play

♡

At ten o'clock Saturday morning, Zora arrived at Kid Republic in Newmarket with Casey to find her mum already inside, flipping through hangers on racks with the air of a woman on a mission. Which she probably was.

"Morning, darling," she said when she saw Zora, giving her a kiss like the confrontation in the toilets hadn't happened, or the news the day before, either. "And you must be Casey. Aren't you cute. I'm Zora's mum."

She held out her hand, and Casey shook it. She *did* look cute, Zora thought, in her black-and-white-striped top, the gray leggings with pink butterflies, and her sparkly silver trainers. Zora had pulled her hair back into twin French plaits fastened with pink bows, too. Leaving no stone unturned, she hoped. Her mum could criticize Zora's looks. Casey didn't need to hear it.

Casey, planted solidly as usual, said, "I like your pretty shoes and your shirt. You look very nice and very fancy." Zora's mum was, in fact, wearing black patent-leather ballerina flats studded around the edges with gold, a side-wrapped top in a purple print, and dark skinny jeans. Her patent-leather purse matched her shoes. Naturally. It also had a deep-purple scarf tied around the strap that coordinated with her top. Evidently, that was a thing.

Well, Zora was wearing jeans, too. It was a jeans occasion. You didn't dress up to buy kids' clothes. At least, she didn't.

"Thank you, darling," Zora's mum said. She glanced pointedly at Zora.

What? Oh. Introductions. Zora said, "My mum's name is Mrs. Allen, Casey."

"Oh, that sounds so formal," her mum said. "I think you should call me Nana Tania, don't you? That's more comfortable, surely."

"OK," Casey said.

"I'll tell you a secret." Her mum was still talking to Casey, probably because Zora was insufficiently nice and fancy. "I look nice because I make an effort with my appearance." Zora did *not* roll her eyes. "Spending twenty minutes on your face and a few minutes to get your hair right in the morning makes all the difference."

"Oh." Casey considered that. "What are you supposed to do to your face? I just wash it."

"You don't have to do it yet," her not-Nana said. "Not until you're in high school. For now, keeping your hair and clothes pretty and neat is enough. Zora's done a good job with that, anyway."

"My dad does my hair, usually," Casey said. "When he's home he does. He used to be very bad at it, and he made lumps when he did braids, except they're called plaits here. But now he doesn't. He says you just have to practice and be disciplined, and you get better. He thinks it's most important to practice and be disciplined at rugby, though, not hair. And maybe school, because he does reading with me, and he's helping me do the big words. He had to practice being a dad, too, because he didn't know how, but he did practice, and now he's good at being a dad. I never had a dad before. I only had a mommy, but she died, so now I have him instead."

"Oh, sweetheart," Zora's mum said, falling straight into Casey's big eyes and charm like the granddaughter-less sucker she was. "You're just precious, aren't you?"

"No," Casey said, "because precious is like jewels, and I'm not a jewel. My dad bought me a pink suitcase that's like a diamond, though. It's a princess suitcase. It's kind of precious."

Zora had never heard Casey call Rhys "Dad." She hadn't

thought the girl was there yet. Casey was like Rhys, though. She rose to the occasion.

"Well, he's right about one thing," her mum said. "About practice and discipline. That's what I tell Zora about her exercise regimen. Now, let's get shopping, shall we? Here." She held up navy track pants with a funky, faded sea-star print, and a pair of jeans embroidered with roses. "I found these before you came. What do you think? So fresh and comfy. Let's find you some more long-sleeved tops to go with them. An oversized hoodie, maybe. That's a cute look, and so practical. Look at this one, the baby fawn lying in the midst of the red mushrooms. It's perfect, wouldn't you say?"

Zora considered asking if she should just go for a coffee, since she was so clearly surplus to requirements. Oh, well. She needed to shop for Isaiah anyway.

"Oh," Casey breathed, "he's so, so aborable. He looks so happy and sleepy. I *love* him." In fact, she had hold of the sleeve and was hugging the hoodie to her. "I think you must be a very good shopper."

"I am," Tania said. "It's my gift." She waved to a clerk. "Could you put these in a fitting room, please? We'll be here a while."

They were. Eventually, though, they had lunch in a café, and Casey told Nana Tania about her bunnies and her school and the jungle trees at Rhys's house, and then they shopped some more, for an anorak and a fleece jacket and gumboots with flowers on.

They'd finished up and were headed to the carpark when Zora's mum said, "It's lovely to be able to buy really nice things, isn't it? You don't do this for yourself or Isaiah nearly enough."

Casey had dashed ahead of them, fortunately, and was looking in the window of a toy store, so Zora said, "That's because I haven't been able to afford it. I'm using Rhys's credit card for this, though, and he *can* afford it. Just like he can afford gorgeous pearls from Mikimoto. Do you still think he's a big mistake?"

"I never said he was a mistake," her mother said serenely, which just about made Zora drop her shopping bags. "Said it would be a challenge, didn't I."

*Well, no,* Zora thought, *I'm pretty sure you said he was a mistake.* She didn't say it, though. She said, "Actually, he's not even that. He's pretty wonderful, Mum."

"Well, he's doing a good job with that little girl," her mother said. "You can tell from the child, I always say." She caught up to Casey, who was checking out the baby doll display in the shop window, and asked, "Do you like dolls, then, love? I always liked them best. Dolls never go out of fashion, do they?"

"Yes," Casey said, "except I already have one, so I don't need another one. I just like to look at them."

"Having a doll collection can be lovely, though."

"No," Casey said, "because Moana would be sad if I had another doll. She wants to be special. Bunnies are nice because they're real, but you can't make them go where you want them to, the way you can do with dolls. You can pretend better with dolls, and I like pretending best."

"I think it's time for a hot chocolate," Zora's mum said, "and I have a very good idea. Let's have it at my house, and I'll show you something special."

♡♡♡

It was a blowing, rainy five o'clock in Brisbane, and early afternoon in Auckland. In five more minutes, Rhys would be getting on the bus with the team to go to the stadium, but at the moment, he was having a quick chat with Zora.

"And *then,*" she said, "Mum showed Casey her latest dollhouse. Don't be surprised if Casey decides she doesn't want to live with either of us anymore. She wants to magically shrink herself and live in the dollhouse, or possibly just move in with Mum and help her finish it. Fair warning."

Rhys was laughing. He shouldn't be. He should be switched on. He could switch on in five minutes, though.

411

Right now, he was laughing. "And here I'd have said your Mum was a hard nut."

"She wants a granddaughter. Hidden lusts are the hardest to control. Ask me how I know. On the other hand, that's how I got interested in architecture, doing dollhouses with my Mum, so there you are."

"What does she do with them?"

"You don't care about this. I just thought it might amuse you."

"Nah. Fascinating stuff. Go on. Tell me."

"Donates them to Starship, for the children's hospital. They get auctioned off every year at Christmas, furnished all the way down to the chandelier in the dining room and the food on the teeny-tiny table, and they bring in a surprising amount. They're collectors' items. She only does one a year, and she's very good."

"Somehow," Rhys said, "that doesn't surprise me."

"And Casey . . ." Zora stopped a moment, and Rhys waited. "It's like she's a mixture of you and Dylan," she finally said. "She looks like you, her eyes and her expression. She *stands* like you, and she's got all your toughness, somehow. But she's got so much charm, too. That's all Dylan. And something of her Mum, I'm sure. Also, I just realized I told you that you aren't charming. Whoops. Sorry."

"That's all right. I'm *not* charming. I'll settle for 'tough.' That'll do me."

"And you've got to go."

"Yeh, I do. See you tomorrow, baby. Love you."

He was in the lobby of the hotel with Finn. He didn't care. Finn already knew.

"I love you, too," she said. "Good luck tonight."

She rang off, and he thought about how she hadn't said, *I'll love you either way,* because it might jinx him.

You always assumed you'd win. No other attitude possible. That was how you came out fighting, and it was how you kept on fighting. All the way to the end.

412

Four hours later, the wind and the rain were still blowing at Suncorp Stadium, it *was* almost the end, and the Blues were still fighting. Down by three at 14 to 17, with seven minutes to go, which meant that a penalty would give the Blues a draw. Except that once again, they didn't have the ball. The Reds did, and they were hanging on to it. Catch and pass, then pick and go, into the breakdown and out of it again, the machinery turning over. Eight phases. Nine. Ten.

They weren't getting anywhere, though. In fact, they were going backward. A hundred-twenty-Kg lock driven back in a tackle by Marko Sendoa that you could practically hear in the coaches' box, then another player wrapped up by Iain McCormick, his long arms reaching farther than anybody's ought to have been able to as he wrestled the man to the ground.

The ball went back to the halfback, then to the No. 10, and this time, the Reds were going for the box kick. An acknowledgment of stalemate, and attempting the high-risk strategy, competing for the ball in the air and counting on winning it, or on being able to hold the Blues out from the tryline and preserve the win.

The No. 10 was chasing his own kick, and he knew where it would come down. Same as the game against the Crusaders, with Nic Wilkinson going up for it, and the Reds' No. 10 leaping with him. Two bodies going up impossibly high, seeming to hang in the air, both of their hands on the ball. Nico coming down with the other man, caring more about the ball than he did about how he hit the ground, still wrestling. The Reds player had it, though. He was going to take it. Until Nico's grip pried it loose, a split second before he landed on his back, and the ball came forward out of the 10's hands.

The referee's whistle, his hand out toward the Blues. Penalty.

They were forty meters out, close to the center of the field. Not a sure thing, not in the wind, but within Will Tawera's range and his skill, even as knackered as he was. A penalty kick, three points, and it would be a draw.

Hugh, talking to the referee, making the decision.

You trusted your skipper to make the hard calls, to know what he saw out there and what the team could do. That was why he was the skipper.

The team lined up, and the kicking tee didn't come out. Hugh was going for the corner. Going for the try, with three minutes to go. Will kicked it, conservative in the wind, making sure it went out, and they were eighteen meters from the tryline, and the win.

You didn't worry about the mistakes you could make out there, or the ones you already had. You didn't second-guess. You committed. No hesitation in Hugh at all, not tonight, or in anybody else. They were all in. They were believing.

The lineout, and the ball thrown in. Iain McCormick being lifted, rising high, snatching the ball out of the air, then coming down with it and passing it.

Except that he didn't. It even took Rhys a second. Iain had sold the dummy pass to the halfback on the openside, then handed it to the blind side, to Hugh. The trick play that the squad had been practicing, that other day in the rain, the day he'd found out about Casey. Hugh was going down in a tackle, but he offloaded it behind his back to Tom Koru-Mansworth as he went, a tricky pass that a forward shouldn't have been able to make.

A Reds player caught unawares, offside, and the ref blew the whistle again.

Another penalty to the Blues. Another choice for Hugh.

Thirteen meters out. Eighty minutes and thirty seconds gone on the clock. An easy penalty kick for Will this time. An easy draw.

The referee was talking to Hugh, who was standing, hands on hips, saying something to Will, then to the ref. Players on both sides had their hands on their heads, sucking in the big ones, their tanks on empty. Nothing left to give, unless it came from the heart.

The nearly certain draw, and two points to the team in the

Super Rugby race. Or going for it all, for four points and a move up on the table. For the win.

Once again, Will wasn't taking the kick. Instead, he kicked a perfectly weighted ball to inside the five-meter line. They were going for it.

Hugh was barking commands, his face set but not tense, his body language calm, the senior players running into place around him, spreading certainty and belief like oil on water, settling the younger boys down.

*Do your role, and trust your mate to do his.*

Another lineout, and nothing tricky about it this time. Iain taking it again, turning his back to the tryline, the rest of the forwards forming a rolling maul around him, and the ball passed back, hand to hand, to Hugh standing behind the rest of them, protecting the ball.

All eight forwards plowed onward, and one by one, the Reds forwards joined them, leaving their flanks exposed. The referee signaled advantage, which meant another penalty coming the Blues' way, but Rhys dismissed the thought.

*No guts, no glory.*

On the field, Iain, still going backward, had his arms over the chests of his opponents, his legs planted, his mouth open to get more air, driving centimeter by centimeter for the tryline, nothing but belief keeping him going. Legs would be stiffening up out there, cramping, shaking with effort, and still, nobody was letting up. Beside Iain, Kors had his head down and was pushing like a truck. The little halfback, meanwhile, danced beside the shoving mass of men, waving his arms and shouting, a sheepdog urging his charges on.

Two meters.

One.

Hugh was going to go across the line.

The Reds were stopping them.

*Penalty advantage. Penalty kick. Draw.* As soon as Rhys's brain formed the thought, in the split-second when the momentum shifted, Hugh had the ball off to the halfback, who didn't take the tempting route and dive for the line. Too many big bodies in the way. He sent a hard, fast ball off instead, spinning like a bullet, twenty meters across the field to Kevin McNicholl on the wing.

Kevvie, who wasn't a battering ram anymore. Who had a player coming straight at him.

He sidestepped, and the man grasped for his jersey and held on, trying to drag him into touch and end the game. Kevin kept his legs going even as another player closed in on him, and there the halfback was again, the sheepdog at his shoulder.

Centimeters from touch, and Kevvie flicking the ball behind him without looking. In and out of soft hands, and into Koti James's sure grasp. A red jersey there, too, and Koti stepping, diving, stretching.

Over the line.

Try.

Will made the conversion. Of course he did. The scoreboard flashed 21 to 17, the referee blew his whistle and raised his arm, and Rhys stood up like he was on springs, unable to feel his feet, and shook Finn's hand.

"That's belief," Finn said, standing, laughing, clapping him on the back. "That's heart. That's you, Drago. That's you."

# giving the signals

Sunday morning in Auckland, and it was another rainy and windy one, just as it had been all the way across the Tasman. Winter was coming and no mistake, and the ride on the 777 confirmed it. The plane was bucking up and down, but none of the players behind Rhys was saying much.

If you were a white-knuckled flyer, you either got over it or got out of rugby. You flew tens of thousands of kilometers a year, you lived on a group of islands in the middle of often-stormy seas, and Air New Zealand had one of the best safety records in the world.

He couldn't see anything out the window except streaks of rain and streamers of gray cloud, glowing red from the lights on the wings. His seatback screen, though, told him they were six minutes out. Nearly home.

He'd told Zora, before he'd got on the plane, when she still sounded sleepy in the sexiest possible way, "You don't need to come out in the storm, or take the kids. I'll get a lift. Be there soon, baby."

"Don't be ridiculous. Of course we're going to come. We can't *wait* to come. We could bring balloons and banners."

Now, he smiled, remembering. Another lurch of the plane that had him holding the armrest, then the *clunk* of the landing gear lowering. As soon as he was alone with her, he was going to talk to Zora about moving in again.

What kind of bedroom furniture would Isaiah like? How about if you painted one wall with the solar system, and another with a map of the world? Could be challenging, but you could probably get some sort of stick-on thing. Or hire an art student, maybe, and the kids could help . . .

Something had changed. His body realized it before his mind did, as usual. The plane wasn't descending anymore. They were going up, and turning to the right at the same time, heading south.

It wasn't *that* windy, not enough to close the airport, he thought at the exact moment a male voice came over the intercom. "Ladies and gentlemen, this is the captain speaking. We've got some sticky landing gear, and we're going to fly a pattern around the city for a few minutes until we get it sorted out."

Fair enough. He shot Zora a quick text, even though the players behind him would be doing the same, and word would spread quickly amongst the families and partners awaiting their arrival. Fifteen minutes, probably. No worries.

"Flight attendants," the captain said, "take your seats." It was as bumpy as ever, and the two Business Premier flight attendants held onto the backs of seats as they made their way forward and buckled themselves in a few meters from Rhys's Row 1.

Some more grinding and bumping underneath him. That was the gear down, then, because the plane was turning again, heading back west, toward the airport.

Except that they weren't descending.

"We're still working on getting that landing gear down," the captain said over the PA system. "Looks like we'll be circling for a while more. Please ensure that your seatbelt is securely fastened. It's a little rough out there."

Rhys couldn't see anybody from his pod except Finn. The other man looked at him and raised his eyebrows. Rhys considered texting him, because even he couldn't shout loud enough to be heard over the engines, and discarded the idea. Nothing to say, other than placing a bet on how long it took them to get down, which could very well be happening in the seats behind him. He wondered how long the Wi-Fi would hold up to the load being placed on it.

Five minutes passed, then ten, and they were still circling. Rhys would have placed his bet on twenty minutes. Too late to get into the action now. The two flight attendants appeared in the aisle again, and the captain said in a voice so calm, it was practically hypnotic, "Folks, our right landing gear isn't coming down, so we're going to be landing on the left gear only. There are a few things we need to do to prepare for that. I'll outline them now, and your flight attendants will be assisting us in carrying those out."

Rhys glanced at Finn again. The other man's eyebrows were higher this time. Well, *this* was a new one. The captain went on, "We're going to dump and burn as much fuel as possible before landing, so you could see some flame coming from the wings. That won't be a fire. It'll be a controlled dump and burn."

This was not good. They were dumping fuel in preparation for landing because they thought the engines were likely to catch fire. You didn't need to be an expert to realize that.

He was too far forward to see it happen, but he saw the reflection in the clouds, lit up like a log flaring in a fireplace, or Zora switching the gas fire on in the black stove that first night. Smiling at him, knowing that he'd wanted to do something competent, something for her.

The captain went on. "We're going to circle and hold for a wee while longer while we prepare for landing. The plane will be coming down on its belly on the right side, and we're likely to go off the runway into terrain, so I'll tell you to brace as we land in preparation for that. Flight attendants are demonstrating the brace position now, and there's a card in your seatback pocket to refer to. Once we're down and have stopped the engines, we'll be evacuating the plane. As soon as you hear the order from the cockpit, you'll head toward your nearest exit and get out. Don't wait, and don't take any belongings with you. Flight attendants are pointing out the exits now. Keep in mind that your nearest exit may be behind you. Those of you in exit rows will follow procedures to remove the window, which the flight attendants will remind you of in the next few minutes. Please do *not* open your window until instructed to do so by the flight attendant. Meanwhile, if the flight attendant asks you to change your seat, please comply immediately. Their only concern is your safety. I'll repeat these instructions again as we get closer."

Rhys could imagine the looks being exchanged, the tears starting for some, the shakes. He wasn't doing any shaking. He was motioning to the flight attendant nearest to him, and she was heading over. Constance McGill, a fiftyish redhead he'd flown with a hundred times. Competent and calm, and, he thought, probably the lead flight attendant on this one.

He said, shouting to be heard over the roar of the engines and the commotion behind him, three hundred souls trying not to panic, "Reseat some of us in the back, Connie. Put us at the exits. You'll need the first people down the slides to catch the rest of them, surely, especially if the plane's tilted, and if the engines catch fire, you'll need help getting everybody well away and keeping them together. Kids. Old people. Whatever you've got. Put us next to whoever needs help, and we'll get them out."

She said, "Can do."

He said, "Forwards at the exits. Go back and tell them—'Forwards, come with me.' Move them first, and then we'll do the backs. Put the backs with the passengers who need help." Easiest way to separate them, to make sure every man knew his role. He thought of something else. "We'll send the doctor down first, also. Are the engines likely to catch fire?"

"Yes," Connie said.

"Keep people from opening those overwing exits, then?" He was pretty sure the crew could land the plane, on its belly or not. Fire was the big danger. The flight crew would have only a couple minutes to evacuate three hundred people before the fuselage filled with smoke, and despite the dump and burn, the fuel could explode at any time. "Are we likely to end up in the Harbour?"

"Yes," Connie said. "Keep them off the overwing exits, and we could end up in the water."

"Finn and me over the wings, then. Our captain and vice-captain as well." If the engines caught fire, everybody would have to exit through the front and rear, and if the jet landed in the water, you'd have to keep them all out of it. A hundred fifty passengers in each direction, and those over the wings could be last in line. Frantic, maybe. "I need to talk to a few of them. Forty seconds out of my seat."

She said, "Right. Go. I'm moving the forwards."

He was up on the words, grabbing the seat back as a jolt tried to send him off his feet, crouching by Finn's ear, telling him the plan.

Finn said, "Got it," and Rhys stopped at the trainer's seat, then headed all the way to the back of the Business Premier compartment, where the senior players were sitting. The bus drove from the back, they said. At least they were all together. He stopped at a row and bellowed, "Hugh. Nico. Nines. Tens. Listen up. Forwards are going to the exits now, and they'll be first out. They'll catch the passengers as they come down the slides, help get them away from the plane. Also, if we're in the water, get everybody onto the slides if you can. Keep them out of the water. Once they're all out, if we're on land, everybody follows the nine and ten. Backs are with the passengers, anybody who needs help. Nines and tens, get everybody to a clear spot, well away from the plane, away from the engines especially. You'll go down the slides first, and take the trainer with you."

Nods, and he was in the other aisle, repeating the message, back in his seat, fastening his seatbelt, ready for Connie to move him. Passport and phone in his pocket. Ready to go.

You always assumed you'd win, all the way to the end. That was how you came out fighting, and how you kept fighting. You prepared, you kept your head, you did your role, and you trusted your mate to do his.

No difference.

When the murmur started, Zora barely noticed. She was standing with Jenna and her kids, trying to think of something to say, and only being able to think *five more minutes*.

"Delay," Jenna said at a *ding* from her phone, joggling Ethan on her hip. "Finn says twenty minutes or so. Good thing the kids are playing."

There was a whole group of kids, in fact, sitting on the floor. Zora checked out hers. Isaiah was reading on his tablet, and Casey was playing with Moana along with Jenna's little girl, Lily. Making up a story.

It wasn't twenty minutes, though, when the murmur got louder. Some gasps from around them, and then a new hubbub, the sound of dozens of cellphone speakers, and some activity over at the side. An airport employee, by the uniform, beckoning, shouting out the flight number. "Air New Zealand Flight 732 from Brisbane. Those meeting Flight 732, come with me." The words crackling over the PA system, and Zora was grabbing Isaiah and Casey, her heart knocking against her chest like a bass drum. *Boom. Boom. Boom.*

"Where are we going?" Casey asked. Isaiah didn't say anything. As usual when things got tense, he went inside himself and watched.

"I'm not sure," Zora said. "Hang on." The crowd streamed along behind the woman with her radio, through a white door marked *Authorized Personnel Only,* along a blank corridor, then into a big, bare room marked *International Hold*.

The explanation, then. The plane's gear hadn't descended on one side, and they'd be landing on one wheel. Not a crash, they said again and again. A hard landing, the plane off the runway, and an evacuation. A scenario the pilots had practiced and prepared for. The airline would keep them informed of developments, including when the plane was coming in on final approach. Ten minutes, probably. That was all the information there was to give. Please stand by for more.

The anxiety had risen in pitch now. The rugby families coalesced into a corner of the room by unspoken agreement, and most of the women had their phones out, their kids gathered close. Looking at news coverage, Zora guessed. She could see a graphic over Kate James's shoulder. A series of sketches of a plane coming down, rolling to the right, catching a wing tip, and somersaulting off the runway, breaking apart, before orange triangles of flame obliterated the pieces.

Or landing in the water. They weren't saying that, but it was obvious. If they went off the runway, surely they'd end up in the water.

She was going to be sick. She *couldn't* be sick. She crouched down with the kids, got an arm around each of them, and said, "There's a problem with the plane. They're going to land it anyway, but it'll take a little while to get everybody here. We're going to have to wait for them."

Isaiah said, "Somebody said the plane was crashing." His eyes were too big, searching her face.

"It's not crashing," she said, and made it firm. "It's making a hard landing, and then they'll get everybody out."

"Is my dad going to die?"

That was Casey. She was still standing square, but she was shaking.

"No," Zora said. Nothing else was thinkable. They couldn't go through everything they had, and have Rhys taken from them. It wasn't possible.

She knew it was possible. But it still wasn't thinkable. She told Casey, "You want to know one reason I love your dad?"

"Is he going to die?"

"Stop," Zora said. "Listen to me. Here, let's sit down." She dropped to the floor, ignoring the coldness of the tile under her bare legs. She'd worn a skirt despite the weather, because Rhys liked looking at her legs. Because she'd wanted him to enjoy looking at them.

*Oh, God. Please, no.*

She pulled Casey into her lap, wrapped her arm around her front to pull her in tight, held Isaiah's hand on her other side, and said, "I know that if we're in an emergency, he'll get us safe. He'll do that every time, and he'll get everybody else around him safe, too, no matter how hard it is to do. He's up there right now, helping to do that."

*Don't be a hero,* she wanted to say. She wanted to text it to him, but she didn't. He could no more keep from being a hero than he could keep from breathing. You couldn't love somebody for the man he was and then turn around and tell him not to be that man.

Isaiah had dropped her hand to take Casey's. He told her, "Uncle Rhys isn't going to die. He's not sick, and he's got Strength Class 100."

"My mommy died." Casey was losing the battle not to cry. "She got hit by a car, and she died. She wasn't sick. I don't want my dad to die."

"He's not going to die," Isaiah said. "He loves us. He's going to come back."

Zora's phone dinged, and it took her long seconds to get it out of her purse. Her fingers were fumbling and cold, and it was getting hard to see. Hard to focus.

*Don't worry,* Rhys had written. *I love you and Isaiah and Casey, and I'm coming home. Will you marry me?*

"It's your dad," she told Casey, and showed her and Isaiah the text, then read it aloud for Casey.

"See?" Isaiah said. "I told you so, Casey. You should say yes, Mum, about getting married. Uncle Rhys is very strong, and he's nice to Casey and me, and he has lots of money. If you marry him, he'll be your husband, and husbands are supposed to be strong and nice. So I think you should say yes."

Zora said, "I already did," and held up the phone to show them the screen.

*I love you,* she'd typed. *And yes.*

♡♡♡

The jet was descending again. Finn was at the left exit window, and Rhys was at the right one, the frame outlined in

424

red, the wing outside the only thing visible in the murk. That, and the bulge of the engine.

Hugh sat beside him, their shoulders touching back here in the narrow seats. The skipper had done his own texting five minutes before, and he'd got an answer. He had four kids at home, two of them babies, not walking yet. Across the aisle, Nico sat beside Finn. Two kids and four kids there. Amongst them, the four of them had twelve.

And every possible reason to make it home.

Random thoughts, and not really helpful. Rhys brought his mind back to the landing, and went over the procedure for getting the window out of the plane, sending the message to his hands, his feet, his body, rehearsing the movements, getting the sequence into his muscles.

They were dropping fast. You still couldn't see anything, but they'd been descending for minutes. Surely, they were almost down.

*"Brace brace brace."* The command came over the speaker, surprisingly loud, and hands went out to seat backs, heads bowed over them. Some sobs. Some prayers. A baby crying.

The flight attendants chanting in unison at the front of the cabin.

*"Emergency brace. Emergency brace. Emergency brace."*

His hands on the seat, and Hugh's big hands beside his, as scarred as his own. The hard jolt from underneath them, different from the wind gusts.

Impact.

The landing gear struck once on the left side, and the plane lifted up, wobbled, then came down hard again. The wing outside rose, then fell. Hugh's forearm pressing into his, the left wheel hitting again and again, then holding.

Tilted to the left. The side where the landing gear was. Going too fast.

His body jerked backward as the pilot rammed on the brakes, and the plane swiveled around, skidded, and tilted some more, to the right this time. Tilted far. The wing tip, out his window, was striking sparks on the runway.

425

*Too fast. Too fast.*

They skidded off the runway to the right, tail first, like a carnival ride, the green that was grass, not tarmac, coming closer and closer, until they were bumping, because they'd gone off. Like it was happening in slow motion. A series of jolts, and people were screaming. They were still tipped too far, the plane resting on one wheel on the left side, its belly on the right, the wing digging in, ripping through the earth like butter, and then a hard *crunch.*

They were canted so far over, Hugh was practically in his lap, but the plane was slowing. Stopping. Outside, a bloom of orange flame. Beyond it, nothing but gray.

*Engine fire. And water. We're in the Harbour.*

Not even a split second, and the voice on the speaker.

*"Evacuate evacuate evacuate."*

Ahead of him, and behind him, he was sure, the flight attendants were going to the door. Only on the left side, though, where the exit slides wouldn't reach the ground. Which was why he'd put the forwards there, able to fall correctly, and then to catch the others.

Why was nobody going out the right side, though? He forced the logic. They couldn't get the doors open on that side, maybe. There wouldn't be room for them to swing up and out, not with the plane tipped almost on top of them.

And—wait. Maybe there was land on their left. They couldn't be in the water. If they had been, people would've been putting on life vests. They were just close.

He told Hugh, "Everybody goes out the left exits," and Hugh nodded.

More chanting.

*"Unfasten seatbelts, come this way. Unfasten seatbelts, come this way. Unfasten seatbelts, come this way."* And passengers standing, hanging onto seat backs.

The man in the seat ahead of Rhys, his dark hair rumpled, turned around, shouting into his face. "Open the exit! Open the window! We need to get out!"

"Go forward," Rhys bellowed back. "Go forward. Go forward."

Hugh was turned around, shouting, "Go back. Go back. Go back," to the rows behind them. He was waving an arm, too. *Good idea,* Rhys thought, and added the arm motion.

He could see, in the aisles, the taller frames that were his players. Koti James with a toddler in his arms, heading steadily forward ahead of a mum with a baby so tiny, how was she going to get down the slide safely with it? Matt Grainger, the right winger, behind her, though. He'd be holding her and the baby on the way down. Kevin McNicholl, six or seven seats ahead, lifting a frail lady who looked ninety into his arms, saying something to her, smiling, carrying her out.

Outside his window, the fire was raging. Inside the fuselage, he smelled smoke. And still the rows emptied. So slowly. Too slowly. He told Hugh, "I'll go forward. You go back," and saw Finn and Nico splitting off in the same way opposite him. Waiting to make sure everybody was out. Waiting until the end. The smoke was thicker, a choking blanket of gray, and he was finally moving forward, touching seatbacks, counting his way to the exit, row by row.

*Ten. Eleven. Twelve.*

Emergency lighting, two ribbons of white, showing him the way. Nico pulled his shirt up over his nose and mouth, and Rhys thought, *Oh,* and did the same thing.

*Seventeen. Eighteen. Nineteen.*

Nico ahead of him, moving steadily onward. Rhys didn't look behind him. He couldn't have seen through the smoke anyway, and he didn't need to, because his players would have done their jobs. He knew it as surely as he knew they'd be running at their mate's shoulder when the pass came. Doing their part, and trusting their mate to do his. Playing what was in front of them. Keeping their heads.

Coughing, now, in the smoke, which smelled evil, like burning metal. The flight attendants at the exit, the last ones left, the only ones looking backward. Nico's head disappearing as he jumped onto the slide, and then Rhys was jumping after him, landing on the soft surface and feeling the rain begin to pelt him, like a ride at a water park. He slid down

427

fast and was caught in midair by arms he couldn't see, then moved off to the side, because there'd be two more after him. The last two. The flight attendants. Everybody on the ground.

He pivoted so he was beside the men at the left-hand side of the slide. Marko Sendoa, and Kors beside him. They caught a flight attendant between them, and Rhys shouted, "That's it! Go go go!" Marko pointed to the left and they headed off. Alongside the plane, staying clear of the wings, around the tail, and to the left, toward the runway, because on the other side, meters away, was the water.

Shouts ahead of them. Will Tawera, yelling the way you had to in order to be heard above eighty thousand screaming fans, directing his squad. *"Toward me! Toward me! Keep moving! Toward me!"*

Rhys could feel the heat of the fire on his back, but he didn't look. He followed Marko and Kors and headed toward that voice as the rain plastered his hair to his head and beat down on his body.

They were nearly at the runway—he could see the black tarmac, the whirling red lights of emergency vehicles reflected in the wet surface—when the plane exploded.

# believe

Zora only remembered a few things, afterwards, about that wait.

The hush amongst the group of people huddled in the bare room, punctuated by the wail of a baby, the soft sobbing of an older Asian lady, a scarf over her hair, and her husband's arm around her. A child on the plane, Zora guessed. Her grandchildren, maybe.

The pattern of the floor tiles, a curving gray shape like the neck of a dragon, and how she'd pointed it out to the kids. "Look," she told Casey, tracing the shape. "It's a dragon. It's an omen."

"There's no such thing as omens," Isaiah said.

"Yes, there are," Casey said.

"You don't even know what omens are," Isaiah said.

"They're good things," Casey said. "Like my pendant. My dad says it's him holding me, and the part at the inside is me being strong. That's like an omen. It says he's very strong. And yours is not being scared."

"No," Zora said, "it's not about not being scared. It's about being scared, and holding strong anyway. We're going to sit here, and we can feel scared, but we can hold hands anyway. We can believe."

"I believe," Casey said.

"Close your eyes," Zora said. There was too much crying around them, too many clasped hands at mouths. "Say it. *I believe. I believe.*"

"I believe," Casey said, scrunching her eyes shut. She was crying again, her skinny chest heaving, but she was saying it. Isaiah still had hold of her hand, and his mouth was moving silently.

Zora held both of them and thought the words.

*Rhys. Come on. You can do it. Come on.*

When the speaker crackled into life again, everybody jumped, and there were some screams.

"The plane is on the ground," the disembodied voice said. "Passengers have been evacuated."

A cheer went up all around them, and Zora looked at her hands, shaking like leaves where they clasped the kids, and said, "I told you so. I told you. He's coming home."

♡♡♡

The blast threw Rhys forward, and he hit the runway hard, tucking and rolling like he knew how, because he did. Scrape of palm and face on tarmac, a pain you wouldn't feel until later, and a bloom of heat on his back. Leaping to his feet and looking around. Nico, staggering up in front of him, and other shapes. Marko and Kors and Iain, Finn, and the final two flight attendants. All of them moving ahead without a word to join the crocodile of wet passengers, shivering with shock and cold, stumbling in bare feet, jandals lost in the scramble from the plane, into puddles and out of them again, directed by workers in fluorescent vests holding signal beacons. Heading toward the bright twin lights that pierced the gloom.

Buses. They'd sent buses, a whole fleet of them. Airport shuttles, their drivers standing outside, anoraks streaming with water, yellow vests on top, waving their arms, directing the final group onward. To the last bus.

Hand over hand again, clutching seat backs, nodding to familiar faces. All rugby players here, his forwards, his nines and tens, who'd got everybody away from the plane and onto the runway, doing their roles. Them, and the flight attendants. A commotion behind Rhys, and he turned to see the pilot and co-pilot, their hats gone, their faces muddy, a red graze on the older man's cheek oozing blood, mixing with the rainwater.

They'd made it, too, and nobody could have been left behind. Surely, nobody would have got past his team.

He found his seat beside Finn, shook his hand, lifted his jacket to wipe blood from his face, and tried not to let any of it out.

Nearly there. A few minutes more.

"Mate." Finn had a hand on his shoulder. "We made it." He was standing to shake hands with the pilots, and Rhys did the same, feeling the sting on his grazed palm and fingertips only vaguely, like they belonged to somebody else. At the front of the bus, the driver leaped up the stairs, put the vehicle in gear, and rumbled forward. Driving up the runway, then, following the other buses to the terminal.

Rhys looked behind him. A glow out the rear window that was a 777 burning to the metal, the fuselage filled with toxic smoke. He leaned forward, put his elbows on his knees, and tried not to shake. Adrenaline, bleeding off. Absolutely normal.

Out of the bus, ten minutes later, into a sea of flashing red lights. Back into the rain, then through a door, down a corridor, into a room. Official faces, official voices. A woman checking names against a manifest. A man assessing people for injury, elderly people being deposited in wheelchairs, putting an older bloke onto a gurney and wheeling him off fast. Heart, maybe. Kids crying, everybody shaking. Two women handing out blankets, and the damp chill trying to get through to your bones as shock set in.

Five more minutes. You could always do five more minutes. Rhys gave his name, collected his blanket, suffered the cut on his face to be cleaned and closed with butterfly bandages, and brushed off anything else with, "I'm all good. No worries." Then raised his voice, waved his arm, and called out, "Blues! Over here! Let's go!"

Time to get them together. Time to count heads, and make sure everybody was accounted for. Time to check everybody's mental and physical state and settle the nerves. Time to be the coach.

♡♡♡

When the first person jumped up and shouted the news out, holding the phone up in his hand, saying, "They're here! They made it! Being held while they do counts and process them, but they're here!" Zora closed her eyes and held the kids tighter. When the tenth and the twentieth and the fiftieth texts came, half the room was standing up. And still, she hadn't heard anything.

The first thing she got was buzz. Not the buzz of her cell phone. Buzz around her. "They're coming. They've let the team go. They're coming." Heads turning toward the door, bodies shifting. Everybody watching.

When the first player came through, raising his arms above his head in triumph, there was nearly a sob from the room, and then the doors were being rushed.

"They let us go first," Zora heard from somewhere. From Koti James, that was, who had a kid in each arm and was still, somehow, managing to kiss his wife. "Everyone had their passport, and the coaches could vouch for us. Still processing the rest." He raised his voice so the words reverberated off the walls. "Everybody's off. Everybody got off."

And then, to his wife, Kate, as his face sobered, "The plane exploded. That was too close."

Zora wasn't listening, not really. One after another, the men came through the door. Twenty of them. Thirty. And after them, the training staff, the team manager, the equipment manager.

Finn, ducking his head out of reflex, his eyes scanning the crowd, his body absorbing the impact of two bodies hurtling themselves against his legs, and another one following after.

Lily, not as fast as her brother and sister.

And, finally, the last one out. Rhys. Limping, his hair soaked, dried blood on his neck and shirt and a line of white covering his cheekbone, his eyes scanning the crowd. Looking for them. Looking for *her*.

The room was full of knots of people. Crying. Hugging. Men lifting babies, kissing toddlers, kissing wives, laughing, talking. And that last man in the door, the one who'd waited to make sure everybody else was in first. The one who always would.

Casey, running toward him, her arms stretched wide, saying the word for the very first time.

*"Dadddyyyyy."*

Rhys was picking her up, cuddling her close, kissing her cheek, but his eyes were sweeping the whole time. Looking for Isaiah. Looking for her.

The man you'd want with you at the very worst moments, because he'd do anything to haul you to safe ground, even if it took his last breath.

Full of mana.

Rhys.

# one hundred percent

It was funny, Rhys thought nearly two weeks later, how much difference a day could make. Winning a game was good. Helping with an evacuation was better, even if it had been nothing more than anybody would have done. The team had been in the right place at the right time, that was all.

He'd said that, but other people had said something else. He suspected that Hugh had had a hand in starting that, because when they'd held a press conference the day after their exciting landing, Hugh had said, "Wasn't us, really. It was Drago setting out our roles, making a plan, and communicating it, all in about two minutes. We executed, that was all." To Rhys's considerable embarrassment, Finn and the other players had all echoed that line of thought. Hugh had decided that Rhys needed the good PR, he guessed, and he'd made it happen. Hugh was going to end up as a coach one of these days, if he didn't watch out.

It was better for Zora and the kids, though, for Rhys to be a hero instead of the villain of the piece, so he was going to take advantage of his moment. The team had won their first game back on home soil, and after tomorrow night, they had a much-needed bye, during which Rhys was taking Zora and the kids to Nelson to visit the whanau. Past time to introduce Casey, to let the kids spend time with their cousins and to go out on the fishing boat, and to let everybody see him and Zora together. Heni Johnson, though, who'd been the person *actually* carrying on an affair under everybody's noses, would be making herself scarce. He'd see to that.

Just now, it was Friday afternoon, and he was at the park near his house, practicing kicking with Isaiah, having some one-on-one time while Casey was at her friend Esme's house. Zora, he very much hoped, was having a long, luxurious bath in front of the windows and painting her toenails on his bed. Her parents were minding the kids tonight, in another first, so he could take her out. His elevated status was working a treat for Zora's mum, even if her dad still wasn't sold.

Too bad. Her dad would come around, or he wouldn't. If he wanted to throw away his daughter and his mokopuna, it was his loss.

He collected Isaiah's latest kick, jogged over to him, and said, "Better, mate. Same technique every time, that's the idea. Have you thought about playing at fullback? You've got the steadiness for it, and the vision."

"I do?" Isaiah asked.

"From what I've seen? Yeh. A fullback has to have a cool head, and you've got that."

"You can't just change where you play, though," Isaiah said.

"You're right. You can tell the coach you're interested in giving it a go, though, and you can work on your running and your fitness and your kicking and passing with me. And for the rest? There's no secret to it, and no magic. Mostly, it's a bit of aptitude, and then heaps of hard work and discipline and paying attention. Being humble, eh. Being willing to listen."

Isaiah looked at him, then looked away. "You had spectacular on-field vision, though. That's what this one person said. I don't think I have spectacular on-field vision."

"Aw, mate," Rhys said, letting his hand rest on Isaiah's head, "people say all sorts of rubbish. I paid attention, that's all, and I wanted it more. You can pay attention too. Nobody better at that, I'd say. But I've got something to talk to you about. Something I need your help with. Let's sit, and I'll explain."

On Saturday night, Zora sat, rugged up with the kids in coats and boots against the autumn chill, and watched the Blues play. They'd moved steadily up the table these past four weeks, and were now lying second amongst the New Zealand teams, which had Auckland very much more excited about Rhys. Fickle bastards.

Right now, she watched the ball go from hand to hand, the forwards setting up a rock-solid platform for the backs to work their magic, and wondered what an experience like the one on the plane would do for a team.

The players hadn't talked about it much, and neither had the coaches, shrugging the incident off with the humility expected of them. The passengers, though, hadn't been so reticent. Stories of players carrying wheelchair-bound passengers in their arms, of Kevin McNicholl cradling a toddler, Nic Wilkinson holding a teenage girl's hand, Koti James charming a scared twelve-year-old flying alone . . . well, they warmed *her* heart, and she was used to it. It wasn't just a winning moment for the team with the public, though. Surely, coming together like that would strengthen the ties that bound the group.

Your teammates were your brothers, Dylan had always said, and that was what she was seeing on the field now. Will Tawera chipping a little grubber kick through, reading the bounce, reacting faster than you'd think possible, and picking it up himself, then pitching it back to Koti James without looking, five meters out, because he knew he'd be there, and because it wasn't about who scored the try, it was about the team. Koti stepping, fooling one South African, then going straight through another one, dotting down with a smile on his face and springing up again with his hands crossed over his heart as the crowd rose and cheered the effort.

That gesture would be for his wife. There was something else that kind of experience did, too. It let a man know exactly how much he wanted to go home to his family. And for his partner? It let her know how much she needed to see that one special person come through the door. The one who'd been made just for her.

Rhys had taken her out last night, had kissed her in the car, and had made love to her so slowly and with so much tender attention that her body had hummed all night long. But he hadn't said anything more, hadn't made any declarations or suggested any plans, and as she watched Will slot the kick between the posts, converting the try, she admitted that she was wondering why not.

She'd said, at first, that they should wait, but now, she couldn't bear to wait anymore. She knew how much she'd needed to see him come through that door, and she needed to know he always would.

She and Isaiah hadn't moved out of his house again, but they hadn't exactly moved in, either. And, yes, she knew that she could bring the subject up herself. It wasn't as if Rhys hadn't asked her to marry him. Three times. It also wasn't as if she hadn't answered, because she had.

It was just that—maybe she didn't want it to be a logistical discussion, a rational talk. She'd told him she didn't need the big gesture, and she'd meant it. At the time. How did you take that back?

Tomorrow, she decided, she'd say something. The Blues had a bye, which gave them the time to do it. They'd take a . . . a walk, or something. With the kids, but there'd be some period in there where the kids would run ahead, and she could say something. Bring it up.

Somehow.

Seventy-five minutes gone, and the Blues up by ten and still holding the ball, which meant she didn't have to watch that closely. Her toes were cold, and she curled them under in her boots and thought about possible openings.

*So, about that thing you said. About us getting married.* Or maybe, *Did you want to wait a while for the marriage bit? Or should we do it now?* Pity they both sounded like you were discussing replacing the washing machine.

Maybe she should ask him out to dinner herself and offer him a wedding band across the table. She had to laugh at that one.

"What's funny?" Isaiah asked.

"Nothing. Just a silly thought."

Isaiah said, "Oh," and fidgeted. He hadn't paid much attention tonight. Could he be feeling off-balance again? They'd talked about staying at Rhys's house before they'd done it, though, and she'd taken care that she did her early-morning flower-market runs alone with him, when Rhys was home, to give him his Mum time.

She'd talk to him tomorrow anyway. Get him to help her fold the washing, maybe, and have the discussion.

Seventy-nine minutes and thirty seconds, then, finally, eighty minutes. Will kicked the ball into touch, and the game was over. A win. She was standing, clapping with the others, her heart lifting, as always, when she saw Rhys on the field, shaking hands with the Stormers' head coach, having a word, then congratulating his players, his intense expression not giving much away. The same man after a win as after a loss. A good man, and a solid one. Her man.

People were standing, shuffling out of their rows, when the music suddenly swelled over the loudspeaker, a fanfare of trumpets, startling everybody, or at least her. The torches at the sides of the field belched out gouts of flame, and the scoreboard, which had been displaying the score, changed. A blue-and-gold dragon appeared on the screen, its tongue out, roaring. Or maybe that was a taniwha, the Maori version of the dragon. A new team symbol?

The departing crowd paused, people looking around, looking confused.

Words on the scoreboard now, and Isaiah beside her, bouncing up and down in his seat, pulling on her arm, saying, "Mum. *Mum.* It's you. He really did it. He *did* it."

*I love you, Zora Fletcher,* the scoreboard flashed in huge letters. *Will you marry me?*

The players weren't moving off. They'd come to stand behind Rhys, and they were clapping. Isaiah was pulling on her arm some more, saying, "Come on, Mum. You too, Casey. We have to go down there."

Rhys, in his blue suit, standing strong, looking up into the stands. Looking straight at her. Her hand was on her chest, and she was laughing, and then, as Isaiah continued to pull on her arm, going down the stairs to the field. Rhys was there, was lifting her over the barrier, setting her on her feet, then reaching for the kids.

Isaiah was practically jumping up and down. Casey was saying, "What's happening? What did it say?"

"He's doing a proposal," Isaiah told her. "Like to get married. It's a surprise. He's been planning it all week long."

Zora was wearing the following: Black leggings, a puffy jacket, not-very-stylish boots, a woolly cap, and a Blues scarf. She hadn't spent twenty minutes on her face, either. She hadn't spent *five*. Her mum would watch the footage of this and be mortified, and she didn't care. She was laughing, and Rhys's face had lost all its hardness. His jaw was black with scruff, the latest scar on his cheekbone still showing pink where he'd been stitched up after the plane, but there was nothing but tenderness on his face as he pulled the box out of his pocket.

She said, *"Rhys,"* then tried to think of something else to say. "I don't . . . I said I didn't need a . . . big thing."

"I heard you, baby," he said, "and I thought maybe you did. Maybe you needed to know you're special. Maybe you needed to hear that you're my light and my life. Taku toi kahurangi. My precious jewel. Maybe I need to say the words the right way, give you something to remember."

He knelt down, and she put a hand over her eyes, because she was going to cry, and then took it away again, because she needed to see him.

"I love you, Zora Fletcher," he said. "Will you marry me?"

She'd have said she didn't need much of a ring. She needed this one. An intricately carved Art Deco design, paved with diamonds on either side of the frankly enormous solitaire. It made her heart happy, and if he'd looked at every ring in the world, he couldn't have chosen anything more perfect.

"Yes," she said, because she couldn't manage anything

more. Her mouth was trembling, and she was crying in front of other people. She thought he might be, too, a little. He slid the ring onto her finger, then lifted her hand to his mouth and kissed her knuckles, not one bit embarrassed to do it in public.

Around them, the crowd was cheering, clapping, and so were the players. She didn't care about that. She was pulling Rhys to his feet, throwing herself into his arms, and laughing.

Which was when Koti James called out the words and the team formed up into rows. When Rhys pulled her into his side, and they turned and watched as twenty-three men in blue uniforms crouched low, then began to slap their thighs and stamp their feet like they could shake the very earth with their conviction.

Koti, pacing between the rows, issuing the commands in a voice that carried past the noise, and the team chanting, loud enough and low enough to be heard all the way up in the stands, or all the way through the soles of your feet. Hands slapping against forearms, feet coming down hard.

A celebration. A song of praise. And a launching. A haka for the coach, and for her. A haka to remember.

*"Hi aue hi!"* They yelled out the final words and stood there, sweating and spent, fierce, then came forward to shake Rhys's hand and give him a slap on the back. The crowd was making some noise around them, but Zora barely heard. She pulled Casey into her, crouched down, gave her a cuddle and a kiss, and told her, "Now we really get to be a family. Always."

Rhys had his arm around Isaiah, who'd clearly been in on the whole thing, and the team was surrounding them, shaking her hand, now. Overwhelming her. Putting a stamp on it forever.

You didn't need public approval, no, but if you got this moment? You took it.

Finn was there, too. He gave Zora a kiss and slapped Rhys one more time on the back, a blow that would have sent another man flying, beamed, and said, "Congrats, mate. When you get a haka like that to seal the deal, I reckon she knows you mean it."

"Uncle Rhys always means it," Isaiah said. "He's like Horton the elephant. He meant what he said, and he said what he meant."

Casey was very nearly jumping up and down. She said, "You are, Dad. You're igg-zackly like Horton!"

Rhys lifted her into his arms, and Zora's heart filled so much, it could have lifted her off the ground. Casey threw out a hand like the pint-sized drama queen she was and declared for the cameras, "He meant what he said, and he said what he meant. And he's always faithful. One hundred percent!"

# a kiwi glossary

A few notes about Maori pronunciation:

- The accent is normally on the first syllable.
- All vowels are pronounced separately.
- All vowels except u have a short vowel sound.
- "wh" is pronounced "f."
- "ng" is pronounced as in "singer," not as in "anger."

**ABs:** All Blacks

**across the Ditch:** in Australia (across the Tasman Sea). Or, if you're in Australia, in New Zealand!

**advert:** commercial

**agro:** aggravation

**air con:** air conditioning

**All Blacks:** National rugby team. Members are selected for every series from amongst the five NZ Super 15 teams. The All Blacks play similarly selected teams from other nations.

**ambo:** paramedic

**Aotearoa:** New Zealand (the other official name, meaning "The Land of the Long White Cloud" in Maori)

**arvo, this arvo:** afternoon

**Aussie, Oz:** Australia. (An Australian is also an Aussie. Pronounced "Ozzie.")

**bach:** holiday home (pronounced like "bachelor")

**backs:** rugby players who aren't in the scrum and do more running, kicking, and ball-carrying—though all players do all jobs and play both offense and defense. Backs tend to be faster and leaner than forwards.

**bangers and mash:** sausages and potatoes

**barrack for:** cheer for

**bench:** counter (kitchen bench)

**berko:** berserk

**Big Smoke:** the big city (usually Auckland)

**bikkies:** cookies

**billy-o, like billy-o:** like crazy. "I paddled like billy-o and just barely made it through that rapid."

**bin, rubbish bin:** trash can

**binned:** thrown in the trash

**bit of a dag:** a comedian, a funny guy

**bits and bobs:** stuff ("be sure you get all your bits and bobs")

**blood bin:** players leaving field for injury

**Blues:** Auckland's Super 15 team

**bollocks:** rubbish, nonsense

**boofhead:** fool, jerk

**booking:** reservation

**boots and all:** full tilt, no holding back

**bot, the bot:** flu, a bug

**Boxing Day:** December 26—a holiday

**brekkie:** breakfast

**brilliant:** fantastic

**bub:** baby, small child

**buggered:** messed up, exhausted

**bull's roar:** close. "They never came within a bull's roar of winning."

**bunk off:** duck out, skip (bunk off school)

**bust a gut:** do your utmost, make a supreme effort

**Cake Tin:** Wellington's rugby stadium (not the official name, but it looks exactly like a springform pan)

**caravan:** travel trailer

**cardie:** a cardigan sweater

**chat up:** flirt with

**chilly bin:** ice chest

**chips:** French fries. (potato chips are "crisps")

**chocolate bits:** chocolate chips

**chocolate fish:** pink or white marshmallow coated with milk chocolate, in the shape of a fish. A common treat/reward for kids (and for adults. You often get a chocolate fish on the saucer when you order a mochaccino—a mocha).

**choice:** fantastic

**chokka:** full

**chooks:** chickens

**Chrissy:** Christmas

**chuck out:** throw away

**chuffed:** pleased

**collywobbles:** nervous tummy, upset stomach

**come a greaser:** take a bad fall

**costume, cossie:** swimsuit (female only)

**cot:** crib (for a baby)

**crook:** ill

**cuddle:** hug (give a cuddle)

**cuppa:** a cup of tea (the universal remedy)

**CV:** resumé

**cyclone:** hurricane (Southern Hemisphere)

**dairy:** corner shop (not just for milk!)

**dead:** very; e.g., "dead sexy."

**dill:** fool

**do your block:** lose your temper

**dob in:** turn in; report to authorities. Frowned upon.

**doco:** documentary

**doddle:** easy. "That'll be a doddle."

**dodgy:** suspect, low-quality

**dogbox:** The doghouse—in trouble

**dole:** unemployment.

**dole bludger:** somebody who doesn't try to get work and lives off unemployment (which doesn't have a time limit in NZ)

**Domain:** a good-sized park; often the "official" park of the town.

**dressing gown:** bathrobe

**drongo:** fool (Australian, but used sometimes in NZ as well)

**drop your gear:** take off your clothes

**duvet:** comforter

**earbashing:** talking-to, one-sided chat

**electric jug:** electric teakettle to heat water. Every Kiwi kitchen has one.

**En Zed:** Pronunciation of NZ. ("Z" is pronounced "Zed.")

**ensuite:** master bath (a bath in the bedroom).

**eye fillet:** premium steak (filet mignon)

**fair go:** a fair chance. Kiwi ideology: everyone deserves a fair go.

**fair wound me up:** Got me very upset

**fantail:** small, friendly native bird

**farewelled, he'll be farewelled:** funeral; he'll have his funeral.

**feed, have a feed:** meal

**first five, first five-eighth:** rugby back—does most of the big kicking jobs and is the main director of the backs. Also called the No. 10.

**fixtures:** playing schedule

**fizz, fizzie:** soft drink

**fizzing:** fired up

**flaked out:** tired

**flash:** fancy

**flat to the boards:** at top speed

**flat white:** most popular NZ coffee. An espresso with milk but no foam.

**flattie:** roommate

**flicks:** movies

**flying fox:** zipline

**footpath:** sidewalk

**footy, football:** rugby

**forwards:** rugby players who make up the scrum and do the most physical battling for position. Tend to be bigger and more heavily muscled than backs.

**fossick about:** hunt around for something

**front up:** face the music, show your mettle

**garden:** yard

**get on the piss:** get drunk

**get stuck in:** commit to something

**give way:** yield

**giving him stick, give him some stick about it:** teasing, needling

**glowworms:** larvae of a fly found only in NZ. They shine a light to attract insects. Found in caves or other dark, moist places.

**go crook, be crook:** go wrong, be ill

**go on the turps:** get drunk

**gobsmacked:** astounded

**good hiding:** beating ("They gave us a good hiding in Dunedin.")

**grotty:** grungy, badly done up

**ground floor:** what the U.S. calls the first floor. The "first floor" is one floor up.

**gumboots, gummies:** knee-high rubber boots. It rains a lot in New Zealand.

**gutted:** thoroughly upset

**Haast's Eagle:** (extinct). Huge native NZ eagle. Ate moa.

**haere mai:** welcome (Maori; but used commonly)

**haka:** ceremonial Maori challenge—done before every All Blacks game

**halfback:** rugby back (No. 9). With the first-five, directs the game. Also feeds the scrum and generally collects the ball from the ball carrier at the breakdown and distributes it.

**hang on a tick:** wait a minute

**hard man:** the tough guy, the enforcer

**hard yakka:** hard work (from Australian)

**harden up:** toughen up. Standard NZ (male) response to (male) complaints: "Harden the f*** up!"

**have a bit on:** I have placed a bet on [whatever]. Sports gambling and prostitution are both legal in New Zealand.

**have a go:** try

**have a nosy for... :** look around for

**head:** principal (headmaster)

**head down:** or head down, bum up. Put your head down. Work hard.

**heaps:** lots. "Give it heaps."

**hei toki:** pendant (Maori)

**holiday:** vacation

**honesty box:** a small stand put up just off the road with bags of fruit and vegetables and a cash box. Very common in New Zealand.

**hooker:** rugby position (forward)

**hooning around:** driving fast, wannabe tough-guy behavior (typically young men)

**hoovering:** vacuuming (after the brand of vacuum cleaner)

**ice block:** popsicle

**I'll see you right:** I'll help you out

**in form:** performing well (athletically)

**it's not on:** It's not all right

**iwi:** tribe (Maori)

**jabs:** immunizations, shots

**jandals:** flip-flops. (This word is only used in New Zealand. Jandals and gumboots are the iconic Kiwi footwear.)

**jersey:** a rugby shirt, or a pullover sweater

**joker:** a guy. "A good Kiwi joker": a regular guy; a good guy.

**journo:** journalist

**jumper:** a heavy pullover sweater

**ka pai:** going smoothly (Maori).

**kapa haka:** school singing group (Maori songs/performances. Any student can join, not just Maori.)

**karanga:** Maori song of welcome (done by a woman)

**keeping his/your head down:** working hard

**kia ora:** hello (Maori, but used commonly)

**kilojoules:** like calories—measure of food energy

**kindy:** kindergarten (this is 3- and 4-year-olds)

**kit, get your kit off:** clothes, take off your clothes

**Kiwi:** New Zealander OR the bird. If the person, it's capitalized. Not the fruit.

**kiwifruit:** the fruit. (Never called simply a "kiwi.")

**knackered:** exhausted

**knockout rounds:** playoff rounds (quarterfinals, semifinals, final)

**koru:** ubiquitous spiral Maori symbol of new beginnings, hope

**kumara:** Maori sweet potato.

**ladder:** standings (rugby)

**littlies:** young kids

**lock:** rugby position (forward)

**lollies:** candy

**lolly:** candy or money

**lounge:** living room

**mad as a meat axe:** crazy

**maintenance:** child support

**major:** "a major." A big deal, a big event

**mana:** prestige, earned respect, spiritual power

**Maori:** native people of NZ—though even they arrived relatively recently from elsewhere in Polynesia

**marae:** Maori meeting house

**Marmite:** Savory Kiwi yeast-based spread for toast. An acquired taste. (Kiwis swear it tastes different from Vegemite, the Aussie version.)

**mate:** friend. And yes, fathers call their sons "mate."

**metal road:** gravel road

**Milo:** cocoa substitute; hot drink mix

**mince:** ground beef

**mind:** take care of, babysit

**moa:** (extinct) Any of several species of huge flightless NZ birds. All eaten by the Maori before Europeans arrived.

**moko:** Maori tattoo

**mokopuna:** grandchildren

**motorway:** freeway

**mozzie:** mosquito; OR a Maori Australian (Maori + Aussie = Mozzie)

**muesli:** like granola, but unbaked

**munted:** broken

**naff:** stupid, unsuitable. "Did you get any naff Chrissy pressies this year?"

**nappy:** diaper

**narked, narky:** annoyed

**netball:** Down-Under version of basketball for women. Played like basketball, but the hoop is a bit narrower, the players wear skirts, and they don't dribble and can't contact each other. It can look fairly tame to an American eye. There are professional netball teams, and it's televised and taken quite seriously.

**new caps:** new All Blacks—those named to the side for the first time

**New World:** One of the two major NZ supermarket chains

**nibbles:** snacks

**nick, in good nick:** doing well

**niggle, niggly:** small injury, ache or soreness

**no worries:** no problem. The Kiwi mantra.

**No. 8:** rugby position. A forward

**not very flash:** not feeling well

**Nurofen:** brand of ibuprofen

**nutted out:** worked out

**OE:** Overseas Experience—young people taking a year or two overseas, before or after University.

**offload:** pass (rugby)

**oldies:** older people. (or for the elderly, "wrinklies!")

**on the front foot:** Having the advantage. Vs. on the back foot—at a disadvantage. From rugby.

**op shop:** charity shop, secondhand shop

**out on the razzle:** out drinking too much, getting crazy

**paddock:** field (often used for rugby—"out on the paddock")

**Pakeha:** European-ancestry people (as opposed to Polynesians)

**Panadol:** over-the-counter painkiller

**partner:** romantic partner, married or not

**patu:** Maori club

**paua, paua shell:** NZ abalone

**pavlova (pav):** Classic Kiwi Christmas (summer) dessert. Meringue, fresh fruit (often kiwifruit and strawberries) and whipped cream.

**pavement:** sidewalk (generally on wider city streets)

**pear-shaped, going pear-shaped:** messed up, when it all goes to Hell

**penny dropped:** light dawned (figured it out)

**people mover:** minivan

**perve:** stare sexually

**phone's engaged:** phone's busy

**piece of piss:** easy

**pike out:** give up, wimp out

**piss awful:** very bad

**piss up:** drinking (noun) a piss-up

**pissed:** drunk

**pissed as a fart:** very drunk. And yes, this is an actual expression.

**play up:** act up

**playing out of his skin:** playing very well

**plunger:** French Press coffeemaker

**PMT:** PMS

**pohutukawa:** native tree; called the "New Zealand Christmas Tree" for its beautiful red blossoms at Christmastime (high summer)

**poi:** balls of flax on strings that are swung around the head, often to the accompaniment of singing and/or dancing by women. They make rhythmic patterns in the air, and it's very beautiful.

**Pom, Pommie:** English person

**pong:** bad smell

**pop:** pop over, pop back, pop into the oven, pop out, pop in

**possie:** position (rugby)

**postie:** mail carrier

**pot plants:** potted plants (not what you thought, huh?)

**pounamu:** greenstone (jade)

**prang:** accident (with the car)

**pressie:** present

**puckaroo:** broken (from Maori)

**pudding:** dessert

**pull your head in:** calm down, quit being rowdy

**Pumas:** Argentina's national rugby team

**pushchair:** baby stroller

**put your hand up:** volunteer

**put your head down:** work hard

**rapt:** thrilled

**rattle your dags:** hurry up. From the sound that dried excrement on a sheep's backside makes, when the sheep is running!

**red card:** penalty for highly dangerous play. The player is sent off for the rest of the game, and the team plays with 14 men.

**rellies:** relatives

**riding the pine:** sitting on the bench (as a substitute in a match)

**rimu:** a New Zealand tree. The wood used to be used for building and flooring, but like all native NZ trees, it was over-logged. Older houses, though, often have rimu floors, and they're beautiful.

**Rippa:** junior rugby

**root:** have sex (you DON'T root for a team!)

**ropeable:** very angry

**ropey:** off, damaged ("a bit ropey")

**rort:** ripoff

**rough as guts:** uncouth

**rubbish bin:** garbage can

**rugby boots:** rugby shoes with spikes (sprigs)

**Rugby Championship:** Contest played each year in the Southern Hemisphere by the national teams of NZ, Australia, South Africa, and Argentina

**Rugby World Cup, RWC:** World championship, played every four years amongst the top 20 teams in the world

**rugged up:** dressed warmly

**ruru:** native owl

**Safa:** South Africa. Abbreviation only used in NZ.

**sammie:** sandwich

**scoff, scoffing:** eating, like "snarfing"

**selectors:** team of 3 (the head coach is one) who choose players for the All Blacks squad, for every series

**serviette:** napkin

**shag:** have sex with. A little rude, but not too bad.

**shattered:** exhausted

**sheds:** locker room (rugby)

**she'll be right:** See "no worries." Everything will work out. The other Kiwi mantra.

**shift house:** move (house)

**shonky:** shady (person). "a bit shonky"

**shout, your shout, my shout, shout somebody a coffee:** buy a round, treat somebody

**sickie, throw a sickie:** call in sick

**sin bin:** players sitting out 10-minute penalty in rugby (or, in the case of a red card, the rest of the game)

**sink the boot in:** kick you when you're down

**skint:** broke (poor)

**skipper:** (team) captain. Also called "the Skip."

**slag off:** speak disparagingly of; disrespect

**smack:** spank. Smacking kids is illegal in NZ.

**smoko:** coffee break

**snog:** kiss; make out with

**sorted:** taken care of

**spa, spa pool:** hot tub

**sparrow fart:** the crack of dawn

**speedo:** Not the swimsuit! Speedometer. (the swimsuit is called a budgie smuggler—a budgie is a parakeet, LOL.)

**spew:** vomit

**spit the dummy:** have a tantrum. (A dummy is a pacifier)

**sportsman:** athlete

**sporty:** liking sports

**spot on:** absolutely correct. "That's spot on. You're spot on."

**Springboks, Boks:** South African national rugby team

**squiz:** look. "I was just having a squiz round." "Giz a squiz": Give me a look at that.

**stickybeak:** nosy person, busybody

**stonkered:** drunk—a bit stonkered—or exhausted

**stoush:** bar fight, fight

**straight away:** right away

**strength of it:** the truth, the facts. "What's the strength of that?" = "What's the true story on that?"

**stroppy:** prickly, taking offense easily

**stuffed up:** messed up

**Super 15:** Top rugby competition: five teams each from NZ, Australia, South Africa. The New Zealand Super 15 teams are, from north to south: Blues (Auckland), Chiefs (Waikato/Hamilton), Hurricanes (Wellington), Crusaders (Canterbury/Christchurch), Highlanders (Otago/Dunedin).

**supporter:** fan (Do NOT say "root for." "To root" is to have (rude) sex!)

**suss out:** figure out

**sweet:** dessert

**sweet as:** great. (also: choice as, angry as, lame as … Meaning "very" whatever. "Mum was angry as that we ate up all the pudding before tea with Nana.")

**takahe:** ground-dwelling native bird. Like a giant parrot.

**takeaway:** takeout (food)

**tall poppy:** arrogant person who puts himself forward or sets himself above others. It is every Kiwi's duty to cut down tall poppies, a job they undertake enthusiastically.

**Tangata Whenua:** Maori (people of the land)

**tapu:** sacred (Maori)

**Te Papa:** the National Museum, in Wellington

**tea:** dinner (casual meal at home)

**tea towel:** dishtowel

**test match:** international rugby match (e.g., an All Blacks game)

**throw a wobbly:** have a tantrum

**tick off:** cross off (tick off a list)

**ticker:** heart. "The boys showed a lot of ticker out there today."

**togs:** swimsuit (male or female)

**torch:** flashlight

**touch wood:** knock on wood (for luck)

**track:** trail

**trainers:** athletic shoes

**tramping:** hiking

**transtasman:** Australia/New Zealand (the Bledisloe Cup is a transtasman rivalry)

**trolley:** shopping cart

**tucker:** food

**tui:** Native bird

**turn to custard:** go south, deteriorate

**turps, go on the turps:** get drunk

**Uni:** University—or school uniform

**up the duff:** pregnant. A bit vulgar (like "knocked up")

**ute:** pickup or SUV

**vet:** check out

**waiata:** Maori song

**wairua:** spirit, soul (Maori). Very important concept.

**waka:** canoe (Maori)

**Wallabies:** Australian national rugby team

**Warrant of Fitness:** certificate of a car's fitness to drive

**wedding tackle:** the family jewels; a man's genitals

**Weet-Bix:** ubiquitous breakfast cereal

**whaddarya?:** I am dubious about your masculinity (meaning "Whaddarya … pussy?")

**whakapapa:** genealogy (Maori). A critical concept.

**whanau:** family (Maori). Big whanau: extended family. Small whanau: nuclear family.

**wheelie bin:** rubbish bin (garbage can) with wheels.

**whinge:** whine. Contemptuous! Kiwis dislike whingeing. Harden up!

**White Ribbon:** campaign against domestic violence

**wind up:** upset (perhaps purposefully). "Their comments were bound to wind him up."

**wing:** rugby position (back)

**wobbly; threw a wobbly:** a tantrum; had a tantrum

**Yank:** American. Not pejorative.

**yellow card:** A penalty for dangerous play that sends a player off for 10 minutes to the sin bin. The team plays with 14 men during that time—or even 13, if two are sinbinned.

**yonks:** ages. "It's been going on for yonks."

# links

Never miss a new release or a sale—and receive a free book when you sign up for my **mailing list.**

Find out what's new at the **ROSALIND JAMES WEBSITE.**

Got a comment or a question? I'd love to hear! You can email me at **Rosalind@rosalindjames.com**

## BY ROSALIND JAMES

The *Escape to New Zealand* series
Reka & Hemi's story: JUST FOR YOU
Hannah & Drew's story: JUST THIS ONCE
Kate & Koti's story: JUST GOOD FRIENDS
Jenna & Finn's story: JUST FOR NOW
Emma & Nic's story: JUST FOR FUN
Ally & Nate's/Kristen & Liam's stories: JUST MY LUCK
Josie & Hugh's story: JUST NOT MINE
Hannah & Drew's story again/Reunion: JUST ONCE MORE
Faith & Will's story: JUST IN TIME
Nina & Iain's story: JUST STOP ME
Chloe & Kevin's story: JUST SAY YES
Nyree & Marko's story: JUST SAY (HELL) NO
Zora & Rhys's story: JUST COME OVER

The *Sinful, Montana,* series
Paige's & Jace's story: GUILTY AS SIN
Lily & Rafe's story: TEMPTING AS SIN
Willow & Brett's story: SEXY AS SIN

The *Portland Devils* series
Dakota & Blake's story: SILVER-TONGUED DEVIL
Beth & Evan's story: NO KIND OF HERO
The *Not Quite a Billionaire* series (Hope & Hemi's story)
FIERCE
FRACTURED
FOUND

The *Paradise, Idaho* series (Montlake Romance)
Zoe & Cal's story: CARRY ME HOME
Kayla & Luke's story: HOLD ME CLOSE
Rochelle & Travis's story: TURN ME LOOSE
Hallie & Jim's story: TAKE ME BACK

*The Kincaids* series
Mira and Gabe's story: WELCOME TO PARADISE
Desiree and Alec's story: NOTHING PERSONAL
Alyssa and Joe'sstory: ASKING FOR TROUBLE

# acknowledgments

Many people helped with the research for this story. Any errors or omissions, however, are my own.

A big thank-you to Lisa Avila for her expert help with pilot/flying details, and to Megan Story of Fabula Flowers for help coming up with beautiful floral designs for Zora to make. Many thanks to Kisha Jones, Cassie Register, Barbara Buchanan, and Kim Castle for their aid with the US legal/child and family services aspects of the story. So grateful to all of you for helping me to get the details right.

Thanks also to my alpha read duo, Kathy Harward and Mary Guidry, for their advice and inspiration as they read along with this book, and to Barbara Buchanan, Carol Chappell, and Bob Pryor for their feedback.

A thank you as always to my wonderful assistant, Mary Guidry.

Thanks to my husband, Rick Nolting, for reading along and always being willing to tell me what a man would really do, and to my sister, Erika Iiams, for talking out the book with me.

Thank you to New Zealand rugby for giving me something to write about, and such good models. Go the mighty All Blacks!

And finally, one big giant thank-you to my wonderful readers. I appreciate you.